HOUSE
of
CORRUPTION

ERIK TAVARES

Valour Designs Books

Valour Designs Books
www.ValourDesigns.com

Printed in the United States of America
by CreateSpace, an Amazon.com company
ISBN 978-0-615-60375-9

Cover Art by Aaron Sims
Used by permission
www.theaaronsimscompany.com

Cover and Interior Design
by Erik Tavares

All characters appearing in this work are fictitious.
Any resemblance to real persons, living or dead, is purely coincidental.

To Christopher and Peter.

Thanks.

Alea iacta est

PROLOGUE

The Monastery of Jerónimos
Lisbon, Portugal
October 1885

A house holds only what you bring inside, Artémius Savoy thought, remembering his father's voice. *So why would this house of God feel so...* He considered the right word and, strangely enough, could only think in Portuguese.

Unhallowed?

Midnight bells tolled outside the transept chapel as he shuffled up the aisle, feeling cold, wishing he could find satisfaction at the end of another busy Sabbath. His spirit ached for the comfort of prayer and the silent pondering of God's graces. A wraith of an idea lingered just beyond perception, a subtle intuition or whispering of the Spirit that something—

Something is coming.

The rough fabric of his woolen robe itched as he slumped into a pew near the chapel's head. He scratched at his collar, smoothing a callused hand over the cloth at his knees. By all accounts he looked the part of a monk; he could be easily mistaken for a member of the order. Yet his robe and sandals and sash felt more like a costume, as if he only pretended to serve God.

I serve Him, do I not?

It had been a productive four months among the Hieronymite friars, adapting their skills in herbs and potions and alchemistic folklore. The fact he was a foreign academic, a Jew by birth, and a secular priest of the Catholic Church did not diminish their hospitality. They patiently bore his verbal clumsiness until his Portuguese improved. It was a rare opportunity to commune with one of the last surviving religious communities within the Church even if, on paper, the order had long been dissolved. The adepts of St. Jerome enjoyed a keen interest in gaining knowledge, and the practical application had been, as an extracurricular activity, a welcome break from his frustrations at Cambridge.

A soft clinking caught his attention. A white-robed initiate snuffed those candles farthest from the altar, his motions practiced and quick from many such nights. He was no older than sixteen. He smiled a tired greeting at Savoy's glance. Twelve hours of masses and confessions took their toll.

"*Noite boa, abade,*" he said.

"Thank you, Jorge," Savoy replied in Portuguese.

"Will you be here long?"

"Go and get your rest. I can finish in here."

Jorge nodded in gratitude and disappeared down the aisle into the vastness of the darkened church. Savoy felt a fatherly sort of attachment. Though he did not regret his service in the Church, his place in academia, there was a part that wondered—*what might have been?* Was it worth spending his days seeking the unknowable, perusing old books, gaining knowledge in strange places...when he might be happier with a wife, children, a son like Jorge to call his own?

Then he considered his own father, and dismissed it.

With Jorge's leaving the chapel felt immense and vacuous. Those candles left burning cast distorted light over the paintings depicting the Passion, glinted off the altar's silver trappings, bled up into the high arches, and danced along the stones to Savoy's sandaled feet. Many shadows, ensconced in deeper corners, refused the light.

He glanced at the vaults along the wall, considering the innocuous tomb of Juan de Aleres of 1537, the lid bearing two different dates of death. Four days after Juan had been entombed, the monks heard his muffled, frantic screaming from inside his stone coffin. When they opened it, they found the poor wretch shivering and babbling, his fingertips rubbed to bony stumps. Ragged gouges marked the inside of the stone lid.

The second date marked his true death, nine days later.

To endure such darkness...

A chill seized Savoy's neck; tiny hairs stiffened.

Need some air.

Three candles upon the altar flickered and died.

—and a swig of brandy.

He left, leaving those few remaining candles to burn out. He had no interest in walking with no light behind him—with its vaulted ceilings and octagonal pillars, the Church of Santa Maria de Belém stretched like a vast cavern. The further he walked, the more he focused on the *clack-clack* of his sandals, drawing solace from the repetition of sound.

Earlier that day the Church teemed with the faithful and those seeking alms, but as he passed the abandoned confessionals and exited outside into the central courtyard, the silence was almost deafening. There the two-storied cloister, with its many arches and windows, coiled around the yard like a snake with candlelit scales. The night was cool, clear and inviting. Under different circumstances he would have snatched his spyglass and followed the movement of the planets.

Yet with each step his discomfort deepened. He mentally examined the day, those things to accomplish the upcoming week. He respected the voiceless whispering of Spirit, but he wished it a language he better understood.

Then it happened.

He knew it, felt it, a half-second before. The air cracked with the tolling of Santo Hélena, the monastery's largest bell. It rang six times. As its sonorous cry echoed, doors of the cloisters opened—*boom, boom, boom, boom*—and monks fled into the night. He expected the bobbing lantern before he saw it, gleaming ever closer from the far side of the courtyard.

"*Abade!*" Jorge ran toward him, breathless.

"What is it, boy?"

"The devil...it is here!"

"The dog?"

"It is no dog, *abade*. Three goats are torn apart. A horse is gone missing. The snares are sprung, empty, and the other animals are in a panic. The brothers have gathered what they could, and the House Guard have their rifles—"

"That will not help." Savoy placed a hand on the young man's shoulder. "Collect yourself, Jorge, and be brave. Tell Irmão Guadal I will attend to it. We have discussed this."

"Yes."

"Throw the bridge into the trench before you ignite the oil. Prevent the beast from crossing over. Remind the Guard! It is imperative they do not let it escape, not until I can deal with it directly."

"You will face it alone?"

"I am prepared. Can I trust you?"

"But—!"

"Can I trust you?"

Jorge frowned. "I will tell them," he said.

He left, running back the way he came. Savoy ran in the opposite direction toward the cloister. Those meeting him for the first time—well-aged, ample frame, iron-flecked beard—often suspected him better suited for antique books and a pipe in a comfortable chair, his passions confined to dead languages and politics. They would never have imagined him racing in robe and sandals, his elusive dread replaced with the knowing—

I was right!

He sped to his room at the corner of the cloister's ground floor. He lit an oil lantern and turned the wick up, the light revealing stacks of books and papers and arcane items strewn upon shelves and heaped in corners and scattered across his unmade bed. He plucked through bowls and packets, opened drawers under the table, tossed bottles and sheaves of papers aside as he dropped to hands and knees to search his collection.

He found a sheet with his long, looping handwriting and fingered at a column of dates. He focused on the last, checked his pocket watch, a calendar on the wall, then at his pocket watch again.

His hands trembled with euphoric rush.

It was true.

Six weeks and two days.

The beast's first assault, three months earlier, ended with mangled, half-eaten sheep strewn about the stables. The next attack–six weeks and four days later–claimed five goats, with only the bloody scraps of entrails to mark their passing. The monks and their House Guard tried snares, doubled sentry routines, intensified their prayers, and still the offending animal left its message: a gnawed foreleg from the groundskeeper's prized Arabian stallion.

In a drawer Savoy found the leather pouch. He tugged open the drawstring. Six bullets poured into the palm of his hand.

Damn Cambridge's narrow minds–

I was right!

⁊

"*Rapidamente!*" shouted a monk.

For many years the monks cultivated three acres of gardens to the north of the monastery, using the balance of the land to raise livestock. A high wall of stone surrounded the lot of it. Though the growing parish of Belém huddled just beyond, the gaslights of the town did not penetrate, leaving the pasture dark and shapeless.

In a swath of noise came three cows, five horses tugging at ropes, a mule-drawn wagon filled with crates of chickens and rabbits, a herd of sheep floundering before shepherds who slapped any who dared wander. Monks and acolytes drove the livestock through the pasture, forcing them to keep them moving. Those older men on the fringes carried bright lanterns like so many stars, while younger boys kept within their light in tight orbits.

A snap of bone echoed behind them, the bloody cry of a lamb that had wandered into the dark. Boys began to cry and men dared glance back, stricken, clutching at rosaries or crossing their chests.

"There!" someone cried. "It is there!"

They urged the animals faster toward the east gate. They crossed over a makeshift bridge of hewn beams where, beneath, ran a trench surrounding the pasture just inside the wall. The trench was deep, heaped with hewn logs and branches, husks of dead shrubs and grass and wicker, broken casks, shards of old tables and chairs, torn cloth, used paper, firewood—filled to the brim and soaked with oil. Every monk and acolyte, even some of the locals, had taken shovels and dug as they could, contributed whatever fuel they could, emboldened by Artémius Savoy's knowledge of such things.

It is real, he had told them. *Do not give this devil any advantage.*

Now, beyond the bridge, the monks and their livestock spilled through the east gate and onto the cobblestone street of Rua dos Jerónimos, the air rattling with hooves and sandals upon the stones. Shutters opened from tightly bunched flats lining the other side of the street. Heads peered outside, annoyed, but before anyone could complain a monk cried out:

"The devil! The devil! It is here!"

Shutters slammed closed. Bolts slid tight.

Four uniformed men, the monastery's House Guard, lifted themselves to sit on the top of the wall—two elderly men on either side of the gate—and pressed the butts of their Cadet rifles into their shoulders.

As the last man passed through the gate, Jorge and three other acolytes struggled to dismantle the bridge, tugging at the poles, heaving them into the trench. The heaviest pole refused to slide off the far bank, lodged in the stubborn earth. The boys dropped to their bellies and reached, straining, but the pole did not budge.

"Leave them," said Rogé, the oldest.

"He said they must all go in," Jorge said. "If it comes this way, we cannot let it—"

"It will not," said another, Daniel.

"It is enough," Rogé said.

"But he *said!*" Jorge said.

A heavy whuff of breath echoed from the heart of the pasture. The boys froze, staring into the dark with wide eyes. "That old man says many things," Rogé said, his voice quivering. "I'll not wait any longer."

The acolytes retreated through the south gate, to the safety of the monks crowded on the other side. *He said,* Jorge thought, his heart fluttering madly against his chest. He regarded the wooden poles still leaning half-in, half-out of the trench.

Do not give this devil any advantage.

He drew back four steps, ran, and leaped the trench.

"Fool!" a guard said.

"What are you doing?" Rogé cried.

Jorge landed on the far side, his feet thudding into the soft earth. He knelt, cupped the end of the pole in his hands and lifted it, gasping, straining at its weight. The pole resisted, caught against branches.

"Come back at once!" someone shouted.

"Almost—!" Jorge started.

"Come back," Rogé said. "They will throw the torches."

"Throw the torches?" a monk cried in panic.

"No, wait!"

"Torches?" many voices erupted, confused, the word spreading.

"Wait!"

"*Torches!*"

Monks threw dozens of flaming brands through the gate and over the wall. Many landed square into the trench. As fire touched oil, greasy flames burst into life. Fire raced down the trench in both directions, burning high and fast with tongues of dirty smoke. Jorge raised his sleeve against the acrid smoke and heat, coughing, but he did not stop. With a final effort he pushed the pole into the trench. When a lick of flame dropped he took three steps back to start his leap back over the trench.

"Jorge!" someone cried, distant.

He paused, confused. The other acolytes stood at the gate, horrified. Rogé stared first at him, then to the dark, then back to him in terror.

"I am fine," Jorge said.

"Run," Rogé said.

"I can leap it. Do not worry."

"*Run!*"

The dark exhaled a wild, heavy breath.

A massive portion of darkness separated itself from the night, its teeth reflecting the firelight like bloodied pearls. It came like an immense wolf but, as their eyes made contact, it rose up on its hind legs and extended its arms with long, spidery claws. Jorge stared at the monstrous beast, breathless, recalling inked images in old books of Lucifer and his bestial minions, wreathed and writhing in flame.

I shall be late, he thought, *for vespers.*

The creature fell upon him.

Rogé screamed and monks pulled him back through the gate; the two elderly guards discharged their rifles simultaneously with a crack of smoke. The creature's shoulder splashed with blood. It detached its mouth from Jorge's throat, dropped his remains and retreated along the trench. When flames burst in a cloud of sparks the animal recoiled, snarling. The guards fired again. Bullets grazed the animal's arm and rib. The thing did not seem to feel it, pacing angrily along the rim, snarling and spitting at the oily curtain of fire.

"You see?" a guard shouted. "*O Diabo!*"

The guards fired a third volley. The creature dropped to all fours and bayed a loud, feral cry. The echoing sound sent monks to shuddering, acolytes to crying and neighbors to toss in their beds and dream of monsters. For years those who witnessed such a scene would whisper of the *lobis-homem*: The wolf that stood like a man.

"*Deus,*" someone cried. "Protect us!"

☙❧

Savoy examined the six bullets, the silver and platinum alloy flecked with garlic and aconite and other rare herbs. From under the table he removed his Remington Army revolver and pressed the bullets into the chamber with a last, whispered prayer.

Pray always, an old priest once told him, *but keep a pistol handy.*

Good advice.

Stuffing the revolver in his robe he left his room and hurried across the courtyard. He felt the fool, his handmade bullets a madman's errand, but it was the right thing to do. It had to be. He had made it his life to study those things others refused to believe. Superstitions had their foundations in truth, and truth could be found in silver and wolfsbane and garlic.

He entered the Chapter House and slowed his pace, the vaulted chamber dense with silent midnight. He wished he had brought his lantern—someone had forgotten their duty to light the evening sconces. Faint light flickered through the narrow windows, illuminating rows of oak chairs that faced the dais at its head, the altar empty of cloth or candlestick or book. Dominating the center of the room crouched the rectangular tomb of Alexandre Herculano, each corner snarling with the head of a lion. Saint Bernard and Saint Jerome watched from their stone posts on either side of the main door.

Savoy had visited that room only once (the reading of the Rule came so infrequently) but he knew a doorway to the pasture waited along the far wall. His nostrils caught a whiff of smoky air. The outer door had been left open. By the acrid smell and growing light Jorge delivered his message—a curtain of fire now surrounded the pasture, keeping the animal at bay. Cornered, he could deal with it directly. He felt irritated at the clumsy act of whoever had left the door open; it was a dangerous omission, for then *anything* could—

He stopped short.

The door was not open. It lay in pieces, metal hinges squealing on broken boards. Massive, dirty prints spotted the floor at his feet. Its elongated toes reminded him of a timber wolf or mastiff, but such creatures did not roam the hills above Lisbon. This was an animal never classified, never catalogued, never displayed in museums to gather dust. This was a thing that should not exist.

Lycanthrope.

The musky fragrance of blood filled his nostrils. He froze.

"I can see you," he lied.

The dark behind Herculano's tomb took a breath.

"I have sworn to protect the brethren." Savoy motioned the cross with his left hand while he removed the revolver with his right. "If you are not of the order, I would request..." The dark behind the tomb moved. "These bullets are anathema." With his thumb he eased back the hammer. "They will harm you. Stand down."

A long-fingered claw emerged from the upper edge of the tomb's lid, then a shaggy, muscled shoulder and lupine head lifted up, a single eye glaring—

Dear God.

"Stand down!"

The animal bolted from its hiding place. Its gore-flecked muzzle drew back to reveal sharp, grinning teeth, its muscles expanding and contracting under bristled hair the color of bloodied ivory. It may have been a wolf but its sinewy limbs and throat were unnatural, horrifying. Its nails gripped the stone floor as its powerful legs launched it forward—first on four legs, then rising to charge on two.

Savoy pulled the trigger, the pistol cracked—

Missed.

He considered first the exit into the monastery's interior, then the open door to the pasture. He was a dead man on the open field, and he had no intention of leading such a demon deeper inside. He never, in his wildest imagination, expected such a powerful thing. What senile old fool would stand alone against such a creature and...do what? Kill it, stuff it, take a photograph?

He retreated—running down the aisle toward the pulpit, desperate, cursing himself for thinking he might confront this thing with empty threats and handmade bullets.

The Beast pursued. It ripped away chairs in its wake, growling, racing up the aisle after him. Savoy scrambled up the pulpit steps, leapt over the dais gate; he slipped and fell, crushing his shoulder against the edge of the altar. He felt no pain, his heart pounding panic as he scrambled backwards past chairs and footstools and hymnals until he was flat against the back wall. He could go no further.

The animal stopped beside the altar on its hind legs, quivering as neither wolf nor man but both. Savoy gaped. He could have faced a bear or rabid dog and knew, instinctively, they were but dumb animals following their nature.

Yet this?

This thing was deliberate, aware, regarding him with pale, human eyes. The two locked gazes. What sort of man, Savoy thought, would allow himself to become such an abomination?

"Do not do this," he whispered.

The creature crawled onto the altar.

Savoy lifted his revolver and squeezed the trigger.

VEXAMEN

*The wicked are wicked, no doubt, and they go astray
and they fall ... but who can tell the mischief
which the very virtuous do?*

– William Makepeace Thackeray

1

Chalmette, Louisiana
Four Years Later

La Taverne du Roi loitered under a balcony between a dank alley and Frederick's Funeral Emporium and, by all accounts, served as a perfect go-between. Without sign or lantern the place enjoyed anonymity, known by those familiar with its reputation and happened upon by those with nowhere else to go.

Mahonri Grant sat at a table in one of the darker corners of the commons. It served him well enough; no one bothered him. The waitress gave him a quizzical look when he refused alcohol (they served the best Gullah Rum in town, after all) but her complaint faded when he ordered a hearty dinner of chicken and fried potatoes.

Grant was a big man, over six foot three in his boots, broad in his shoulders with a shock of dark hair. A large black moustache sat under his straight Cornish nose, and had he cared he might have waxed it into a fashionable handlebar. Many days had passed since he last used a razor. The result left him scruffy, a bear of a man garbed in practical clothes, scuffed Calvary boots and a worn leather overcoat.

The waitress brought him bread and sarsaparilla. He could not help but notice the lewd conversations of other customers amid clouds of tobacco, the underdressed serving girls wriggling onto drunken men's laps. By the time his dinner arrived he had the waitress wrap it in waxed paper. This was the wrong place for much of anything. He started for the exit.

"Salut," said a drunk, a fleshy Frenchman with a face swollen with whiskey. "Who'd you serve with?"

"What?" Grant said.

"Your boots. Calvary. Where'd you serve?"

"Tenth." Grant continued walking.

"Apache country? Where you from?" the man asked, as Grant reached the door. "I *said*," the drunk shouted, "...where you from?"

"Salt Lake."

The man slapped down his mug. "Makes sense, *mes braves*," he said. "We've here a More-mon from the Promised Land. How many wives you have?" More laughter erupted and spread to other patrons.

Grant stiffened.

"I hear most th'women 're unsullied," the drunk said with a wink. "Get myself married to three virgins..." He grabbed the nearest serving girl around the waist, his beefy arm drifting down to her rump. She slapped his arm. "...Think of what I could teach them, ay?"

"You'd marry three versions of your wife," the serving girl drawled. "Th' Promised Land would be Certain Hell."

The commons burst into laughter. The drunk howled and raised his glass and spanked the girl off his lap. She wrapped her arms around his neck, planted a wet kiss on his cheek, and his fingers slid over the floppy curve of her breast. She slapped him again, this time across the face, and that only made everyone laugh louder.

Another fleshy drunk began a loud rendition of *Jonesy and His Molly* and the tavern band (two old men with concertinas) soon struck up the note:

> "–'Twith every Bird old Jonsey meets,
> He naught bu' coos them 'tween his sheets!"

Soon everyone was singing the chorus, bellowing each verse with drunken abandon. Customers stood on tables and added warbled voices, clapping for others to sing louder, and two men contested who could invent the bawdiest lyric. The bartender shouted a makeshift stanza in French and the room burst into raucous applause.

No one noticed Grant leave.

Colorful types still haunted the midnight streets of Chalmette: well-dressed patrons returning from 'Orleans and its more dignified delights; clusters of sailors looking for another groggery or a woman to rent; street musicians of various skill and diverse color; fading conversations in Creole and English and Spanish. Gaslights burned in globes of moist, foggy air and pedestrians wiped at their slippery faces. Rain was coming.

The riverbank avenues became a tangle as Grant walked, one corner leading into another. With each passing turn, he found himself abandoned. Streetwalkers disappeared, drunkards blended into shadows, and decent folk long since faded behind closed shutters. At one intersection, where the buildings sat low, he saw the oily surface of the Mississippi River. He turned toward it—better chance of getting a flophouse near the docks.

A huddled shape crouched on a tenement porch, a trail of steam pouring from a heap of blankets. There sat an old man with his arms wrapped around his chest, a filthy scarf tied over his etched and saggy head. He glanced at Grant with rheumy eyes.

"Here grandpa," Grant said. He pressed the packet of his supper into the old man's hands. "You've a place to sleep?"

The man gave a toothless smile and stuffed a wedge of potato into his mouth. In three soft bites, he crammed in some chicken and sucked the grease from his fingers.

"You take care of yourself, old timer," Grant said.

He left the man to his feast. He had seen too much human flotsam, too many old men begging for alms, too many Indians and Negroes and Chinese with their haunted children hawking rugs or trinkets or baubles. Utah had its problems just the same, and he did not relish the cold justice of a noose if he returned, but—

What am I?

He was as much a spinning bit of debris as that old man, albeit better fed; when things went bad—bad as anything, worse, the blood still dry on the memory of his hands—he fled Utah and joined the Arizona

Calvary. It lasted a year. The dirty name *murderer* found him, splashed across a wanted poster on the desk of his commanding officer, a man Grant called his friend. *I never knew you*, the officer said, releasing him from his commission with a horse and a head start.

Make sure no one else does either.

He took his advice. Grant fled to New Mexico and tried railroad work, blasting tunnels, hammering rails, baking under the dirty southwestern sun. When he moved to Washington State he froze while blasting tunnels in the bitter Cascades. When the word *murderer* caught up to him he moved again—Montana to Kansas to Illinois to St. Louis, pushed onward by circumstance or cowardice or guilt or a faint stirring of Spirit. What did he expect to find? Redemption?

No. There was no repentance for him. Emily was dead. No matter how many bullets Grant emptied into a wretched sot who had sullied her, choked her, *killed* her, the shame and despair only grew larger, consuming him, until all he could do was run and run and hope he might forget. It was a fool's hope. One did not forget such a crime. Some sins were so heavy that it crouched on a man's shoulders and gripped him so tight he could hardly breathe.

Now he was in Louisiana, poised to work on a merchant vessel in exchange for a one-way ticket to Jamaica. Maybe there, with warm beaches and simple living, he might lose himself in fresh opportunity.

You are a coward.

He rubbed at his forehead. Time to stop thinking about it.

At Butler Avenue a cold drop of rain found its way beneath his collar, slithering like ice down his back. Mist glazed the sidewalk as a carriage driver hurtled past, whipping at his horses. In minutes the drizzle strengthened into a downpour.

From across the street echoed the voices of two men singing, their drunken melody punctuated with the occasional belch.

"*Alors*, More-MON!"

Grant twitched and kept walking.

"You've an extra wife for us?" The drunk's familiar voice called. "*Abruti!* You gonna look at me?" His voice grew louder. "Hey, Apache killer! You look at me, *oui?*"

The two drunks crossed the street and followed half a block behind, accelerating when he did, slowing when he slowed, a trailing stream of obscene whispers. Grant's neck tightened, his hands clenching into fists. Maybe he could work out his frustration with a few choice blows to the souse's gut. He was tired and wet, and the last thing he needed was an idiot cat-calling in the rain.

An attractive young woman approached as he arrived at the corner of Butler and Jackson. She wore no coat or scarf, her candy-red hair swept up and pinned in a crow's nest as was the fashion. She wore too much perfume. Her frilly dress and laced bodice reminded him of the pub's serving-girls and their wandering hands. She flashed him a full-lipped smile. Her face was smooth and flawless, the ruddy complexion of a girl innocent to the world's advances. He wanted to ask her name.

He nodded a polite recognition but kept walking.

She passed by. "Bonsoir," she said to the two men following.

"Ah, sweet frenchie," one drunk said.

"Vous aiment une certaine compagnie ce soir?"

Grant's face flushed. A whore.

He kept walking, pushing the dull temptation from his mind. There had to be a place to flop for the night, somewhere to sleep and forget. If he had to hunker down in an alley, then so be it. It would not be the first time.

The sooner I've left this godforsaken—

A shriek echoed, high-pitched.

He turned around. The two drunks and the lady were gone. They were just behind him, weren't they? He chided himself, not caring for whores or drunks, but the sound was a terrible cry. He backtracked. Halfway up the block, he discovered an alley disappearing into the dark. He had heard no doors, saw no lights. If they had gone anywhere, this was the best option. The last thing he needed was to stumble upon a sordid scene, but he cast his doubt aside—he had heard a scream.

He knew what drunks could do to young women.

From under his overcoat he slid his Colt revolver from its holster and thumbed the hammer. He worked his way into the alley, past dripping waste bins and stacks of rotten crates. The alley opened into an uneven courtyard formed by three buildings wedged unevenly together.

Refuse crowded in corners. Black rain pissed from the gutters, splashing into potholes with filthy rainwater. The air reeked of rotten fruit. He winced at the idea of finding the woman's remains, discarded by two drunken bastards who deserved a bullet in the head for their work.

He pulled back the hammer, then stopped.

There lay the pestering drunk, a heap against the wall, his throat splayed open. Blood poured from the wound like water. The man struggled to breathe and gagged, his head lolling, his fish mouth agape and steaming. The second drunk, a man Grant did not recognize, lay sprawled nearby in unnatural directions. Over him the woman crouched, her body heaving with a deep gurgle. Vomiting, he guessed.

"Ma'am?" he asked.

She stood. With a click-click of heels the frilly-dressed belle emerged from the shadows, her skirt and bodice streaming with rivulets of bloodied rain. Some of her hair had loosened from the bun. Crimson beads gleamed across her right cheek, caught the vague light, and water sent them oozing into her collar.

"I'll fetch help," he said. "Get you dry and safe."

"Dry and safe," she wheezed.

His left hand extended to lead her out of the alley. Her skeletal hand slid into his own, clammy and cold and solid. As she emerged into the wan light he saw that the flesh of her face tightened against her skull, her eyes—her *eyes*—wide, lidless and unblinking, goring into his heart, rooting his feet. Blood boiled from her mouth and down her chin.

"Mahonri," she said.

Emily?

He felt her in his arms, his skin, alive, bright with summer and smiling. Grant felt nothing but to stand there and drink her in. He smelled the perfumed stench, saw her hideous face, and still he could not help but draw the woman closer. His discomfort became dread, the dread a panic yet he wanted—ached—to hold her, to press himself against her, to run away, to shout her name in pleasure and scream at the twisting fear in his gut.

"Let me have you," she said.

"No."

Her hand caressed his face, her skin cold as a fish and slippery with blood. "*Let me have you,*" she said. "Kiss your sweetheart."

Grant tore away. He sprinted from the courtyard, scattering crates as he crashed through. He launched out of the alley into driving rain and, as he landed upon the sidewalk, his feet gave way and he fell splashing into the street.

His Colt skidded into the gutter; he gained his feet and scrambled into a run. He did not look back.

Following, a gurgling laugh croaked from the alley—

"I am here to love you, Mahonri."

2

Cold. Foggy cold. Soaking through fabric, biting into skin, clutching bones. Black without moonlight, the night was lit with a dozen orange, smoky lanterns. The lights made the snow glitter and turned the shadows into blood.

Artémius Savoy walked the dirt path between the trees, joined by a silent procession of men and women in their heavy overcoats, expelling steam from their mouths, saying nothing. A coffin bobbed between six of the men in cadence to their footsteps. He expected weeping, tears on women's cheeks—a sign of grief from the poor girl's mother, for God's sake—but he heard naught but his own heartbeat.

The small crowd coalesced around a plot of earth covered with snow. He wanted to be necessary but felt extraneous as men chipped at the ground with the points of their shovels. Hardened earth gave way. Black soil became clay, then stones and sterile grit, and soon the grave stretched down deep and black. Ropes creaked as the coffin was lowered into the hole. Someone tossed a sprig of hawthorn inside.

The priest said his blessing in Hungarian, a mingling of religion and superstition—*where did one end and the other begin?*—ending with a prayer over the iron coin set upon the dead woman's tongue.

The other mourners left. He stood alone in that old place of oaks and shadows, of silent stones shrouded by dead grass and snow, memorials stretching in the wilderness in all directions. He huddled in his heavy longcoat and waited. He tried to remember why he watched over the dark slash of freshly turned earth.

Segítség, came the soft voice in his brain. *Help me.*

The wooden cross that served as the woman's marker leaned to the right, slightly, but he dared not set it straight. He dared not move.

Help me.

The gravesite shifted. Dirt boiled to the surface, forced up by pale things like spiders grasping. He felt the vibration beneath his feet. Scrabbling fingers became hands and the hands pulled free two willowy arms, and those arms pulled out of the ground until the dead woman's face appeared.

Help me.

She gibbered out of her unclean womb, weeping without tears, gasping without breath. Free of the earth she stood upon her dirty, bare feet in her filthy burial dress. She looked at him—*blazes, but her black, dead eyes*—and while her left hand played with the ribbon between her breasts, her right hand slid down the pale curve of her throat. Two puckered, pale scars shone at the curve of her shoulder.

So cold.

She approached him. He could not move. Her fingers, sticky with rancid blood, flittered out against his face, along his shoulders.

Hold me, Arté.

She clutched his right hand and slid off his glove. He could not move. He had loved this woman with all his heart. Now she touched him with dead hands. Those hands once fed his love for her; the memory of her private embraces died as her dry lips pressed against his palm. He felt no warmth.

She pressed her mouth against his wrist, tongue sliding over his frozen sweat. He watched her, transfixed, as she licked his wrist clean.

Make me warm again.

Then she bit his wrist.

Savoy shuddered, opened his eyes.

His head leaned against the window of the train, the glass foggy from his moist breath. The lush, swampy flats of Louisiana rolled just outside, capped with low, grey clouds threatening to spill over. At his feet lay the sprawl of his notebook, dropped from his lap. When had he fallen asleep?

It had been a long time since he had dreamed about that night. He lifted the cuff of his shirt to reveal six pale scars where that abomination had bit him. Over twenty years now, and still the tokens of that night glared from his skin. They served to remind him when his faith, his purpose, his very name would change forever.

At the time, he could not tell his father of that experience, could not disrupt the tenuous reputation he had developed amongst the academia of Cambridge—his father a professor and his son, Artémius, a promising student. It was bad enough they endured the subtle prejudice against those of Jewish heritage, the anti-Semitic ravings in the newspapers. There was no need to bring shame and suspicion. Yet he wanted, *needed* to tell someone.

The only person who might give him a decent hearing was his mentor, Professor Ernst Stronheim. He considered the memory of Stronheim's sitting room in Vienna, the fireplace banked and warm, the air thick with tobacco smoke and coffee and cinnamon. The two had talked much of the night as Savoy recounted his story—though he did not share his profound grief at Llona's death, a woman whose life had briefly, passionately, intertwined with his own. Ernst may have suspected the affair, but said nothing.

When Savoy finished, he expected the professor would scoff, raise an eyebrow, *something*. Yet Stronheim spoke in his usual measured tone:

I believe you.

How? Savoy asked. *How can the dead walk?*

There are powers under Earth and Heaven older than God Himself, Stronheim said with conviction. *When Mankind was granted dominion we were given free will, an intellect, and a curiosity.*

To deliver such horrors? Savoy countered.

We are allowed to wage war, to hurt, to defame, to be cruel. We are allowed to sacrifice and show compassion and serve others. We are allowed to open doors that should never be opened, to test the will of man. Some of these doors refuse to stay shut.

Why?

Perhaps God wants just men, like yourself, to manifest His power on Earth, to see if we have faith to overcome all things.

That last always surprised him. Ernst was never shy about his agnosticism. To a scholar like Savoy, at the crossroads of his religious and intellectual career, the idea made perfect sense. When the local priest had returned to Llona's gravesite, concerned at Savoy's absence, it had been his cross and prayer and splash of holy water that made the dead girl recoil in horror. Llona had been a gentle spirit, a Russian Orthodox, yet what crawled from the ground shrieked and profaned. Whatever had stolen her soul both hated and feared the symbols of Christ.

Some doors refuse to stay shut.

He paged through his leather-bound notebook, stuffed with handwritten notes, clipped newspaper articles, photographs, drawings—the collection of years of study. He removed a handwritten note from Stronheim's hand. It had arrived a month earlier, addressed to Savoy's apartment in Boston, stuffed in a weathered envelope with many foreign postmarks:

> *Parce ego non multatsed tibi*
>
> *Whited sepulchers! beautiful outward inside be dead men's bones. Then Simon Peter having a sword drew it. Then said Jesus unto Peter Put up thy sword into the sheath The Cup which my father hath given me. That ye may put difference between unclean and clean*
>
> *Alea iacta est*

Haec ego non multis, sed tibi.

Whited sepulchers beautiful outward, inside lie dead men's bones. Then Simon Peter having a sword drew it ... Then said Jesus unto Peter, Put up thy sword into the sheath: The Cup which my Father hath given me ... That ye may put difference between unclean and clean...

Alea iacta est.

He still had no idea what it meant. If it indeed came from Ernst—and the handwriting seemed to be his—it had been written with urgency. Perhaps it was a sick joke? It very well might have come from one of his detractors at Cambridge. Humiliate the Jew, he thought, imagining their condescending voices. The mad Catholic Jew who teaches lies.

He wished he could contact his old mentor for guidance. Here he was, en route for New Orleans with a stack of clippings and apprehension, dreading a visit that he had made a half-dozen times since that night in Lisbon. Four years had passed, and in that time his relationship with Reynard LaCroix was clinical, if not pleasant. That terrible night had been shelved away in an unspoken covenant: to never speak of it again.

Why not tell Reynard I am coming?

He paged through his notebook until he found the clipping from the New Orleans Advocate, dated five days earlier. He made a point to have New Orleans newspapers delivered to him both in London and in Boston, to keep vigil until he ever found such a headline:

GRUESOME DEATH
AT GRETNA RIVERSIDE

Gretna, October 12 — The mutilated body of an unidentified woman, found near Sutton's Warehouse yesterday evening, has authorities speculating if feral dogs roam the south quarter.

The grisly discovery was made by Able Seaman Edward Trellis, formally of Baton Rouge and on leave from the USS Brooklyn. He deposed that a strong stink and noise like water inside the warehouse attracted his attention. Upon investigating, he discovered the remains of a woman, decapitated, her limbs dismembered and strewn about the floor. The unknown victim's head has yet to be discovered.

Chief Constable Thornton of Jefferson Parish, in charge of the investigation, was heard to say that wild dogs may again be on the loose, alluding to the three ferals that attacked the Wesley child in June '87.

'Until capable servants can hunt them down,' he said, 'mothers are strongly advised to keep nursery windows securely shut.'

Savoy replaced the clipping and blindly watched the bayou slide past, its endless stagnant pools and drooping trees. The tension in his stomach grew tighter.

Please God, he thought. *I pray it is not him.*

3

Reynard LaCroix stared fascinated, disgusted, unable to comprehend the two bodies lying beneath their spoiled white sheets. The corpses sprawled in that backwater alley like discarded decorations, grotesque puppets left to sag in the rain. He was equally surprised at the burly police inspector, Legrasse by name, blandly crouched beside the closest body in his longcoat and cap as if a regular witness to such horror. The inspector pulled down the sheet.

Reynard pressed a silk cloth against his nose and mouth.

Blazes, but his throat!

Reynard could not look at the man's ruined face any longer; he focused on the tenement walls of pale brick and plaster, the grimy windows crawling higher and higher until he saw, clouded by wire and strung laundry, the pale gray of morning. He wished fresh air could find its way into that filthy place, but the rotten, greasy smell saturated everything. He wiped his face. Sweat beaded under his eyes, unclean.

"This your man?" Legrasse asked.

"Yes. Bill Tourney. Ran errands, but I did not—"

"Next of kin?"

"Wife and daughter. Do they know?"

Legrasse replaced the sheet. "He wasn't a real good runner then, sir. We knew to contact you because he held correspondence addressed to your business, though he stank of gin. Lucky break, that, or we'd've trouble identifying him. We're also lucky t've found him so soon...after, I mean. Th'rats can make things tough if they've got on too long."

Reynard tried not to retch. This was not the smell of death or sewage or decay, not anything rotting in that isolated hole, not quite. A random memory came, of fourth-year biology and the stuttering old professor who never remembered to set out the scalpels before class. His classroom reeked of formaldehyde and animal blood and lye and turpentine.

Unclean.

That was how the alley felt—unclean, stained with violence, stinking of booze and blood and putrefying fish and—

"Sir?"

Something else.

"Sir?"

"This is just..." Reynard exhaled. "Horrible."

"The pulpits'll 'ave fodder for a month," the inspector said, "more proof against public inebriation. You'll be good to write a statement? Include his address and all that? We prefer to notify the family ourselves."

"Of course. How did this happen?"

"That is the question, isn't it?"

"Have you a theory?"

"Not proper to spread rumors," Legrasse said. "Consider it your civic duty t'keep this out of the rags." He motioned toward the alley exit. "Not had a proper breakfast myself. Seems a good day for a stiff one, if you take my meaning."

"Yes," Reynard said. "I think I do."

Escorted out of the courtyard, Reynard pressed through a knot of policemen and onlookers at the alley entrance, the usual crowd who seemed to materialize from nowhere. A reporter from the *New Orleans Picayune* attempted an intrusive question, but Reynard pressed past him. He had always been sensitive to subtleties others did not, or chose not, notice—but it required selectivity. Most men could filter the mundane; Reynard heard every voice as he passed from the throng, smelled every scent, knew which among them were drunkards or wife-beaters or lied in their daily prayers. He could feel their emotions like oil over his skin.

Today he allowed himself to listen to the crowd, officers and gawkers alike. None could account for the brutal deaths of two ordinary men.

Billfolds remained in the dead men's pockets. Watches and keys, boots, wedding rings, pearl cufflinks on Bill, a gold tooth on the other—all untouched. He heard the whispered theories from those behind him:

Animal.

Dog.

Rabid dog.

Man-eaters!

He stopped listening. He buried his hands into the deep pockets of his wool ulster coat, crossed the street and strode down the block into pedestrian traffic. He walked three blocks up Butler until rain splattered his hair and down the nape of his neck. When the horse and driver of a covered hansom slowed against the banquette, he signalled it with a wave and climbed aboard.

"Parish constabulary," he said. "Be quick."

Images of dirty brick walls and slack mouths crowded his mind as the hansom raced him along. They fought to gain his attention as he gave his full account to an officer at the police station, and persisted when he continued along the river to New Orleans. He passed warehouses and smokestacks, sawtooth storehouses full of rice and cotton. The air tasted of refining sugar from the Filter House and the morning breath of thousands of chimneys. Perhaps no one would smell the alley on his clothes. Soon more hansoms and carriages and carts and coach-and-fours, the city's routine, swallowed him up.

It was familiar territory. In the four years since returning to America, he struggled to restore order to his shattered life. The first stage renewed his late father's business. Within two years he regained a measure of prosperity to LaCroix Brokerage. He expanded his influence as a commodities agent from river and Gulf shipping to the railroad, brokering trade with rail lines still months from completion. He soon bought out his partners and returned the business to complete family control. He did not consider himself the son of a carpetbagger; no, he was the promise of New Orleans made flesh, a French-born making good on the capitalist promise.

Locals recognized provincial stock with his slender gait, his long, straight nose and pointed jaw. His family line came from both eastern Europe and a rarely-mentioned strain from North Africa (that business with his great-great grandmother, quietly hushed up), producing a ruddy, olive complexion with hair like wheat. He was a handsome man by all accounts, if not aquiline in his symmetry as the season kept him hunched, bundled in his heavy ulster, his high collar perpetually raised over his neck. In warmer climates his skin would catch the light, the picture of health; in Louisiana's soggy autumn he was almost transparent.

He pulled his hands from his pockets and gazed at the cracks in his skin, his slender wrists, the long fingers ending in gnawed fingernails. He could only imagine the terrible voices that could condemn him from those hands.

Could it have been?

Rain pounded against the hansom's coverage. He looked into the sky and his eyes dilated as he took in more light, hoping to convince himself he was lucid. He was awake, was he not? Truly awake? Four years had passed since his last living nightmare and yet...

And yet.

He touched at his chest, pressing down against the upraised scar—the smooth, thumb-sized blotch set an inch above his heart. Through the thick fabric of his coat and waistcoat and shirt and undershirt and skin and muscle he felt the hard knot of tissue, the silver bullet worming its way a little deeper, a little closer, every day. It had given him what he wanted most: time, the prodigal's chance to regain a life he had lost.

Yet the bullet served its blessing on a shallow plate. One day it would complete its slow and dirty work as it burrowed ever deeper. How would it feel when it pierced his heart?

The Beast is gone, he thought. *It has to be.*

Four years had passed, and yet...

Could it have been me?

He arrived at a bland four-story brick building on New Orleans' Royal Street. The anonymity of LaCroix Brokerage's main office made men like Bill all the more necessary; he found the wheels of business moved easier when he was unburdened with unsolicited salesmen, unhappy clients, tax collectors and other such rubbish.

"Monsieur LaCroix?"

A man in a stiff frock coat stood beside the front steps. By his polished shoes, a high-collared suit, and an umbrella draped over his arm, he was as grim as a barrister attending a partner's funeral. He had the look of a bird with his hornbill nose and high forehead and long, mobile throat, his black hair slicked back save three, unruly hairs at attention behind his left ear.

"Edward Tukebote," he said with a thick accent Reynard could not identify. He extended his hand and a business card appeared. "I represent Miss Kiria Carlovec, daughter of Sir Wilhem Carlovec of Her Majesty's North Borneo Company."

"Are you from the constabulary?"

"No. Her message may have mentioned me?"

"I received no message."

"Ah yes, of course," Tukebote said. "Forgive my imposition. I supposed your man upstairs would have..." He cleared his throat. "I wonder if you might spare a moment to—"

"No."

Reynard did not take his card. He moved past him up the steps, entered the building and ascended the stairwell. The man did not follow. At the uppermost floor, Reynard went to the third door on the left, an inconsequential flat without sign or label. He glanced over his shoulder, expecting the solicitor at his heels. Thankfully, the man did not follow. They were like cockroaches, weren't they?

He went inside, and stopped short.

"Hello, Reynard."

Artémius Savoy sat in one of three chairs that made up the flat's waiting nook, a carpetbag at his feet, his familiar notebook resting on his lap, and a steaming pipe and cup of tea set on a sidetable. He smiled as if he had always been there. He was alone—which meant Mister Burlington, the office manager, was out on errands and Betty, the part-time secretary, made good to stay home with her so-called influenza.

"Just how did you get in?" Reynard asked.

"I have been here since ten o'clock," Savoy said. He was at least twenty pounds lighter, the grey in his hair and beard more pronounced than Reynard remembered. "Mister Burlington trusted me to mind the store. Your manifests make for fascinating reading. I was not aware you secured the Kansas line. When did you start brokering cotton into Texas?"

"It has been a long time."

"Too long, my boy, too long."

"And not a word you were coming?"

Savoy stood and drew him into his arms like a father reuniting with his long-lost son. Reynard allowed himself to be embraced, arms at his sides. When they separated, Reynard coughed into his fist, hung his coat in the hall closet, and continued down the short hallway to his office. Maybe if he stopped believing he was there, he considered, Savoy would vanish.

"How is your sister?" Savoy asked, following.

"Fine, thank you."

"And her health?"

Perfect as always, he wanted to say, *not like she is any of your business.*

Reynard's office was filled with overflowing bookshelves and cabinets, dominated by a massive oak desk. The closed windows left the room smelling like the radiator. He opened his liquor cabinet, removed a bottle of Svënets-brand vodka, and poured himself a splashy drink. He swallowed and poured himself another. On the third he caught Savoy standing in the doorway, watching him.

"Drink?" Reynard offered.

"What is wrong?" Savoy asked.

"Did you know Bill Tourney?"

"An employee, yes?"

"He has been murdered."

Reynard recounted the details of the dead men in that filthy alley, the words of the inspector and the theories germinating from spectators. He noted Savoy's attention, the quickening of one intrigued, how his methodical mind began turning over the story's minutia with alarming tenacity. Reynard took another drink, disgusted at the man's morbid interest.

Yes, he thought, *it has been a long time.* Here stood the one whose silver bullet staved off that which nothing else had power. Yet with each twinge under his scar he wondered how much thanks he really felt. *He's almost glad to hear my news.*

"A wild animal?" Savoy asked.

"It is not what you think."

"What would I think, Renny?"

Reynard pressed his glass to his lips. He remembered a clay mug pressed against his weakened lips, drinking water as greedily as he now took vodka. He remembered itchy, woolen blankets, the burnt-herb scent of dying candles, the distant sound of bells and boys singing hymns. He remembered the hollow pain in his chest that saturated into his tissues and veins and between his ears. When the burning of his wound eased, the subtle torture of silver in his blood lingered; it was nearly six months before he managed a full night's sleep.

Why did he save my life?

Savoy had shot him—and then he had saved him, for the monks of Jerónimos never suspected the wounded stranger under their care was the very creature who had slain one of their acolytes. He was a wretch, Savoy explained, a vagabond. They had accepted his explanation without suspicion—for Artémius Savoy had driven the *lobis-homem* away, and that was all that mattered.

"Do you have time to spare?" Savoy asked.

"I can make some."

"Then let us take a walk."

They took the back stairs and avoided the bustle of Royal Street, working their way toward St. Philip underneath terraced, terra cotta apartments with their many balconies and iron-lace galleries. The wind brought a southern breeze from the river, smelling of smoke and burnt leather. Savoy kept his umbrella under his arm and an eye on the darkening sky.

They walked until their pauses grew longer, their casual discussion less productive, keeping pace as if both expected the other to know their destination. Despite Savoy's subtle attempts to draw him out, to reveal the day-to-day goings on in his life, Reynard proved less than candid. Upon reaching Esplanade Avenue with its wide sidewalks and whitewashed trees, they headed north at a more leisurely pace. Rain began to fall; Savoy popped open his umbrella.

When the sidewalk emptied of pedestrians, Reynard finally asked:

"I want the truth. Why are you here?"

"I told you," Savoy said. "To check on your progress."

"There is more."

"Yes." Savoy removed the newspaper clipping from his bag. "Are you aware of the similar incident in Gretna, last Saturday, described in the *Advocate*?" He gave Reynard the clipping:

GRUESOME DEATH
AT GRETNA RIVERSIDE

Gretna, October 12 — The mutilated body of an unidentified woman, found near Sutton's Warehouse yesterday evening, has authorities speculating if feral dogs roam the south quarter.

The grisly discovery was made by Able Seaman Edward Trellis, formally of Baton Rouge and on leave from the USS Brooklyn. He deposed that a strong stink and noise like water inside the warehouse attracted his attention. Upon investigating, he discovered the remains of a woman, decapitated, her limbs dismembered and strewn about the floor. The unknown victim's head has yet to be discovered.

Chief Constable Thornton of Jefferson Parish, in charge of the investigation, was heard to say that wild dogs may again be on

Reynard stopped reading. "You're not serious."

"You know me better than that," Savoy said.

"You know of what I am capable. And not."

"No recent blackouts?"

"None."

Savoy took a deep breath. "By your description Bill's death is the ninth of its particularity this year—*ninth*—with very specific physical trauma. A headless woman was pulled from the Thames in February. I first thought it another in that horrid Ripper business...then a decapitated girl with nearly identical wounds washed up on shore near Boston, soon after my arrival for my summer sabbatical. Another appeared in Baltimore in July, a man that time. Pensacola in September, Gretna last week, and now Chalmette."

"All headless?" Reynard asked.

"Yes, though the male victims showed some considerable..." He cleared his throat. "Unusual damage. Their...personals...were also ravaged."

Reynard grimaced. "Their personals."

"Yes. Every report blamed a rabid dog, a lunatic, an accident, random events to random people with little to no social standing. None saw any connection."

"And you do."

"Of course," Savoy said. "A murderer's style is as unique as his fingerprints. By the time I saw a trail developing, I thought it prudent to investigate. That trail has led me here."

"I have visited neither of my offices in Baltimore nor Pensacola since May," Reynard said, "and I've not been to London since eighty-six. You may check with Mister Burlington if you do not believe me."

"I never said otherwise," Savoy said.

"Yet you doubt me."

"I see a trail. That is all."

"Not every death has its monster."

"And how is Lasha?"

"My sister..." Reynard stammered. "The curse must pass her by."

"LaCroix blood runs in her veins," Savoy said. "She may not be immune. I have an obligation to your family, Reynard. I must assume every possibility."

Reynard's anger grew hot, stronger than he anticipated. This was a sore subject since the Lisbon Incident, as Savoy liked to call it. Savoy had made it his duty to visit when he could to monitor Reynard's remission. The positive reaction to his silver bullet was unexpected, but they both suspected the lycanthropy had not been cured. Reynard sensed the ebb and flow of his internal cyclical habits as if the Beast waited deep inside, tethered, straining to break free.

So Savoy dedicated himself to his study. One visit became two, then many, and in time Reynard found he dreaded his comings. He saw his own late father's disapproving face, the judging drop of his eyebrows or turn of a lip, the subtle yet familiar message:

It does not matter what you want, boy.

"You promised me permanence," he said.

"I did not promise anything."

"Are you so sure?" Reynard's voice was hard. "You've promised with every examination, every bitter concoction, every poppycock you've thrown at me. I've to accept every flim-flam and now...now...you accuse me?"

"I—"

"Tell me Arté, why are you here?"

"I told you."

"To help me?"

"But of—"

"Or stop your Cambridge cronies from laughing behind your back? I'm not about to be your thesis. I'm bloody well sure you won't start on Lasha."

Savoy gaped, looking very old, the color drained from his cheeks, the muscles in his face gone slack as the accusation emptied its bitter poison. He considered the pavement then walked from the moment, uneven, drifting away as if the breeze caught his umbrella and whisked him lazily down the street.

"You can go to hell, sir," he muttered.

"The Beast is gone," Reynard called to him. "It is."

By that point, he doubted Savoy could hear him.

4

Savoy wandered off Esplanade Avenue and down an adjoining street, not looking back, wishing he could get more air into his lungs, wishing he could walk faster. No apology from Reynard followed, and he was not in a forgiving mood.

So be it.

When a hansom drew near he hailed it, climbed inside and commanded the cabby to drive. He felt numb, stunned by the crucifying of his service in Reynard's behalf.

Is that what he thinks of me?

He was no detective, true, neither empowered to pursue such matters nor authorized to do anything about them. He felt obligated as Reynard's friend—current or former, he no longer knew—to keep vigil against the Beast's return. Was this not the same as in Lisbon? Iszkáz? Santiago? Winnipeg? Unusual circumstances to the naked eye, with patterns only those with open minds might see? What would it take to convince Reynard—convince everyone—to see beyond their narrow vision?

For a werewolf in remission, he is a remarkable skeptic.

Why was he surprised? His hope for tenure at Cambridge was threatened by many who labeled him "neo-platoistic" despite his adherence to the scientific method. It was an ironic criticism, especially with London's growing interest in spiritualism. He had pursued an appointment with Cambridge, above and beyond his father's connections, due to its rich history of accepting new ideas; its Ghost Society and current incarnation, *The Society for Psychical Research*, included those who adhered to a study of the unknown while honoring their religious faith.

In time he realized the S.P.R. and other such groups had more to do with political connections, illicit practices and clubbish habits than a real interest in supernatural phenomenon. He neither believed nor enjoyed the mania of sitting-room séances, their moving planchettes, the ethereal knocking, the claims of otherworldly visitations. More often, such so-called gifts manifested only when there was a crown to be earned.

Academia is notorious, his father once said, *for punishing those who do not follow the mob.*

Savoy refused to take the oaths required in his colleagues' cabals and Masonic clubs, and his opinions were often in opposition to those with influence. Many academics sought to redeem a religious culture tainted by Darwinism, to uncover empirical evidence God did indeed exist, that faith was not the only method of divination. Their interest in spiritualism was a sign of their doubt...and *that* was why they hated him.

Because he could see right through them.

He had no agenda other than truth. Were not the scoffers the ones whose motives should be questioned? A darkened-room séance was all the rage, but declare that lycanthropy can alter a man's fundamental shape? That a man of Haiti, dead and buried, was seen by at least a dozen people as he walked in the night? That a South American woman drank the blood of her newborn daughter and, when discovered, transformed into mist? That a dead girl, one he once loved, could crawl out of her own grave?

Yes. I ought to be used to it by now.

Some time later he caught sight of a newspaper boy hawking a broadsheet with the title *Slaughter in Chalmette!* The rag had already typeset what they could glean and sold pages by the penny. He ordered his driver to stop, bought a sheet, and continued his random tour. He read laughable opinions from so-called "experts" to idiotic assumptions from onlookers.

Yet one section caught his eye:

...victims' remains were transported to Charity Hospital for further study.

Early in their investigation officers uncovered a Colt .45 pistol. It was soon traced to a Mister Mahonri Grant, 28, from Salt Lake City, Utah. The suspect was apprehended before he was to board a ship bound for Kingston, Jamaica. He is now held in Parish Prison awaiting a preliminary hearing.

Julia Blanchet, an employee of the King's Tavern where the victims were last seen, claimed that '...big man (Grant) and Paulie (Rabeaux, one of the victims) had words before they went out that night. The big man said he would kill Paulie the next time he saw him.'

Why assume this man a suspect? The victims were slit open like fish, not fired upon with a pistol. *Frontier justice*, he guessed, *snatch a likely suspect to pacify the mob.*

The Southern hobby of jumping to conclusions was clearly in full swing, and he prided himself as being above such notions. He was a part-time American with Victorian sensibilities; he preferred a spot of tea while thinking things through.

A telegraphed query to Salt Lake City's Deseret News confirmed what this reporter suspected: Mister Grant is no stranger to crime. The State of Utah may extradite the prisoner on unrelated murder charges if Mister Grant proves locally innocent.

Allegations of military desertion and attempts to avoid justice in both Arizona and Washington State may add to the man's already heavy crimes.

The suspect claims his innocence, but does not deny being at the crime scene. Investigators suspect, however, that he, if found guilty, is either a liar or a madman:

> 'He claimed the murders done by the hand of
> a lady,' Inspector Lagrasse stated, 'one who
> alone slaughtered both victims and drank
> their blood.'

"Unless you plan on paying my day's wage," the hansom driver said from his seat above, "you may want to give me a destination, sir."

"Yes," Savoy said. "Charity Hospital, please."

5

Lasha LaCroix sat in the dimly-lit dining room, picking at the buttery crust of quiche in front of her on the table. The gaslights were turned low, the candles dripping with wax upon the tablecloth. She pinched off a sizable piece and slipped it into her mouth.

I did a good job.

She sucked the flavor from her fingers and plucked another bite. Reynard would have chided her for eating without a fork. Not ladylike, he would say, behavior beneath a young woman of her character. Posh. What did *he* know of character? Her brother had promised, *promised*, to escort her to the vaudeville starring the incomparable Robert Neville. Not only had he not arrived, he did so on one of those rare nights when he knew, he *knew*, the caretakers had taken the horse-and-buggy and would not return until morning. She was stranded.

It did not help she was alone in that great house, enduring the kind of night that feels more closed and less free, the kind of night when life turns its attentions inward with a million eyes watching. She lit many of the gaslights throughout the house. Even when it positively glowed with light, their mansion, nestled against the liquid dark of Lake Pontchartrain, still felt too large and too empty.

The crumpled flyer in her hand—a woodcut of Mister Neville's face headlined with *One Night Only*—tightened in her grip.

She looked over the supper she had made: baked lamb quiche and asparagus with hollandaise sauce, homemade rye bread, and a lemon-balm cake with custard sauce cooling in the icebox. She had spent hours with flour-dusted apron and a proud smile on her face, proving her gratitude for a brother who normally avoided such events. She was *sure* he would come through this time. Why was she surprised?

Does he even know I exist?

She considered herself in the dining-room mirror, feeling sorry for herself. She had dressed to the nines in an embroidered vest and bustled skirt, her hair upturned with pale-gold ringlets falling down her neck. Reynard once said that, at seventeen, she had the look of a charging goose. Maybe he was right. Yet tonight, of all nights, this goose held tickets for fourth-row-center seats! Fashionable people would have been there. She would have sipped from crystal goblets and chatted in French with fetching young men and now...

And now.

There may be a very good reason, and I am a spoiled brat.

"Yes," she answered herself, "but it was Robert Neville."

She smoothed a bead of sweat from under her eye and looked into her reflection, considering the crook of her full mouth. She wished she had more color, more height, more courage against such nights.

A knock echoed from behind her.

The sound startled, which made her laugh, and she practiced her best scowl. Home already? The nerve. They could have made the curtain call! She marched to the foyer to throw the door open in indignation. Tomorrow the buggy would return and she could go to town all by herself, visit her best friend Elisabeth and see how the vaudeville went. Perhaps Mister Neville was simply *atrocious* and she had a miserable time? She could only hope.

"Forgot your key yet again," she said, entering the foyer.

She opened the front door. It was not Reynard. A tall gentleman stood on the porch, dressed in a black tweed suit and cravat and polished shoes. The lines at his eyes suggested he was twice as old as she, but his skin was taut with healthy color. With his slicked black hair and narrow, almond eyes he was an exotic reminder she had not seen a stranger on LaCroix Manor's porch in a very, very long time.

"Oh," she said. "Excuse me. I–?"

"LaCroix?" he asked with an accent.

"Yes."

"An urgent message for a..." He removed an envelope from his vest and glanced at the name. "A Monsieur LaCroix? Your...husband?"

"Dear me," she said, laughing. "He is my brother."

"Is that so?"

"He takes all mail at his office. Who sent this?"

"It is a private affair, *m'oiselle*."

"My brother is a private man."

"Indeed."

She stood, waiting, wondering if this courier would stand there all evening. Did he expect a gratuity? Behind him, outside at the edge of light at the rim of the front lawn, the shadows between the cypress lingered in drapes of Spanish moss. She hated those trees. They always seemed to be hiding something.

"It must be frustrating," the courier said.

"I beg your pardon?"

"I see we were meant for the same experience." He motioned to the flyer still clutched in her hand. "Sir Neville was to perform this evening."

"Oh. This?"

"A remarkable man. One who attracts only the finest of patrons. It is a privilege to be invited, all the more distressing to know another has missed out on such a rare occasion. I would have gone myself if my duties did not detain me otherwise."

"Yes," Lasha said. "I wish Reynard had come."

"He was to escort you?"

"Yes."

"He did not keep his word?"

"Yes."

He bowed stiffly and descended the porch, trailing a whiff of expensive cologne. Only when her senses registered the feel of rough, expensive paper against her fingers did she notice the envelope in her hands. When had he given it to her?

"I would not despair my dear," he said at the bottom of the porch steps, his accent thickening. "You might find him more interested in your welfare in the days to come." He bowed slightly, gathering the reins of his horse. "I am sure he—you both—will find this most exciting."

"What is it?"

"I guarantee."

ⅾↃ

Late into the night, the stagecoach stopped just long enough for Reynard to descend and pay his fare. The driver snapped his reins, the horses resumed their pace, and the coach clattered down the lonely road. No lamppost illuminated the gate leading to LaCroix Manor, no sign or marker. The driveway slithered so deeply into the trees that few knew a mansion lurked at its end.

He walked up the driveway, comfortable for the first time that day. The city and its unwashed masses could be endured for business, but he craved solitude and shadows and fresh air and an unobstructed view of the lake. He relished the frog songs and insects, the darting streaks of fireflies, how the drapes of Spanish moss caught the breeze like festival ribbons.

Two hundred yards further, the lights of LaCroix Manor gleamed into view, a former plantation house—modest by Louisiana standards—with Grecian columns flanking the front porch and whitewashed walls contrasting sharply against the night. Most of its outlying acreage had been sold to the parish to extinguish his father's debts, save seven acres along the lakeshore. It was a life with well-defined borders, money in the bank and insurance for his sister's future happiness.

Lasha had left on the porch-light—and every other light on the first floor—which irritated him. Ascending the steps, he unlocked the front door and smelled the lingering residue of her perfume, cooked eggs, asparagus, cheese, the smoke from snuffed candles, white wine left out to breathe too long...

Tonight, he realized. *I'd promised her.*

At his feet lay an envelope. The vellum envelope smelled of dead roses and vinegar, the flap sealed with red wax and pressed with a lion's emblem on a circle. He started to pocket it for the morning but something, perhaps the scent, prompted him to tear it open:

Dear Mr. LaCroix,

It is with much gladness I have found you.
Please accept my heartfelt wishes for your
continued health and happiness.

Please forgive my imposition, but I must be
direct. I am aware of your condition. I have
learned you found means to fend off your
terrible symptoms. It is of the utmost urgency
that we speak concerning this matter.

I have come to propose an offer that will prove
beneficial to us both. I respectfully request
an immediate appointment: south gate of City
Park, nine o'clock tomorrow evening. There,
with some measure of discretion, we might make
negotiations to our mutual satisfaction.

Please RSVP at the St. Charles Hotel. My valet
will assist you with whatever needs you might
require.

I look forward to meeting you in person.

Yours,

Miss Kiria Carlovec

Reynard read it three times.

He turned the paper over, expecting it to be a gag, a cruel prank. He did not recognize the signature. The name Kiria and the family name Carlovec felt vaguely familiar, but he had no thought as to where he had heard the name before.

He burst upstairs, bounding three steps at a time, racing down the hall to Lasha's bedroom. He knocked hard. From inside he could hear a startled sound of movement, the clatter of something striking the floor— books, a cup.

"Lasha?"

"Leave me alone," her voice came, irritated. "I was asleep."

"Who sent this letter?"

"Which?"

"The one on the floor."

"Which?"

"Do not play games with me," Reynard said. "Fancy envelope with a red seal. Was it here when you arrived? Did Eleanor give it to you?"

"Eleanor is gone," she said, "*remember?*"

"Who brought it?"

"Foreign gentleman. Far more manners than you seem to have. Now leave me alone. I shall chastise you in the morning."

He stood ready to fly another harsh word, but checked himself. She deserved no hard words. He had been a jackass; he promised her a pleasant evening and had forgotten in the midst of a terrible day. He had left her alone in that house, one she secretly hated for its memories, and now here he stood with his glowering tone as if their father had come back to life.

He moved to the staircase. Since their relocation from Montreal he could not remember a time when an unsolicited courier visited their doorstep. His officer manager Frederick Burlington had strict orders to direct all personal correspondence through the office. He knew well the fickle tides of social commerce, and he chose not to invite them into his own home.

Someone knows.

Halfway downstairs he felt the thrashing body of the acolyte he had killed in Lisbon, felt his soft flesh in his mouth, tasted the boy's coppery blood. All at once he tasted countless throats like filth boiling from a drain—the slick stones of back alleys and moist grass from nameless wilderness, the bells of old churches and the stink of immigrant ghettoes, gunshots and shouting, rushing scents and wet muck beneath his naked palms, the stink of peppermint blood screaming in his throat and the taste, the *taste*, between his teeth. Most fragments came so sudden, so bitterly, he nearly collapsed with shaking.

Not true not true not true.

They were real, and he was damned, dripping with darkness, the heavy weight of sin choking until he thought he might die. When he felt this way—more often than not—the pain came so palatable he thought he might scoop it from his belly and smear it across a wall.

He remembered the funeral for the Portuguese acolyte in Lisbon. Friends and members of the young man's family wept upon the coffin, each draped in various shades of grief. Some rubbed ashes on their faces, commanding damnation against the devil responsible for his death. He had sat in the back row, terrified, supplicating no God other than his fear. He was there only because Savoy, seated beside him, said it would serve to see the results of his behavior—as if it might convince his rational mind to command the beast to stay away. He doubted it. If the mourners understood who sat on the back row, he who was responsible for that day, they would hang him from a tree and burn his carcass. More likely, he feared, he would stand and announce himself and get exactly what he deserved.

One woman sat frail and shrouded on the front row. She placed a briar rose upon the coffin and drifted down the aisle toward them. She paused only once, staring at Reynard—not a random glance—and whispered:

Lobis-homems queimadura no inferno.

Man-wolf burn in hell.

She knew.

Then came Bill's smiling throat with his pink and bloated face, glazed, white eyes rolled back into his head.

Go away.

He remembered.

How can—?

He stumbled to the bottom of the stairs.

How can anyone know?

Last of all came the memory of his sister's face. She shrieked at the monster, at *him*—the terrible thing that leapt from the shadows. She shrieked as he sank its teeth into her nanny's face—

Lasha.

—If someone knows...

Not her. Not her. Never her.

He flung open the front door and leaned over the porch rail. He retched once, kept it down. He retched again and spewed vodka and acid in a great, choking cough.

6

Excerpt, Artémius Savoy's Journal:
Friday, October 10, 7:35 p.m.

Interview with the chief coroner at Charity Hospital. He accepted my credentials and permitted a brief, firsthand examination of the post-autopsied bodies. The old fellow was glad to have an ear listen to his adequate, if incomplete, findings.

Bill Tourney and Paul Rabeaux died as a result of massive trauma to the neck between the mandible and upper clavicle. On Bill, subcutaneous tissue shredded, jugulars and sternohyoid cut. Would account for the extreme loss of blood—curious not much found at scene.

Mister Rabeaux deliberately emasculated. Femoral severed on both legs. Spinal damage (intervertebral, between third and fourth cervical) consistent with a neck broken by sufficient force. Why the throat was also shredded is beyond my guess. Bill's personals spared, but spinal column nearly severed a half an inch above the larynx. I agree with coroner's theory there is similarity to that from an edged blade, but such a wound does not leave the surrounding tissue in such poor condition.

Bill's spinal incision incomplete. Was he to be decapitated?

Bill's remaining blood infested with extraordinary clotting beyond livor mortis. Squeezed out like jam from open vein. Examined sample under microscope. No explanation other than caused by a coagulant of unknown origin. Laboratory work pending.

Damaged tissue along Bill's upper left shoulder, akin to bite mark; unclear if by vermin, scavenger or damage during transit. Mister Rabeaux had no such wound.

Odiferous substance upon both men's clothing, stains along their shirts and skin below primary wounds. The coroner would not have mentioned it; he assumed it spilled formaldehyde. Doubtful, for the scent is sharp yet more natural, like rancid oil. No explanation as to the liquid's source or composition.

Unable to retain any evidence. When authorities arrived, the coroner concluded our conversation and bid me leave at once.

Addendum, 9:07 p.m.

En route to Parish Prison. Will conclude the day's findings after interview with primary suspect, Mahonri Grant.

∞CஃQ

Parish Prison leered over Orleans Street, ivy infesting its towering brick and plaster walls, crawling up and over the scrubby roof until the place seemed caught in some ghastly web. Sheets of rain washed down its neglected façade before draining into the gutter. It was an old place, a sad place, one few dared consider with their full attention, known more for its reputation than its reality. The weather only added to its grim appearance as if, once inside, there would be no leaving.

I suppose, Savoy thought, *that is the point.*

The hansom abandoned him before the prison's leering front gate, the iron bars slick with rust and oil. A rat-faced old guard, sequestered in a booth with only a lantern as company, glared at his approach.

"I am here to see Mahonri Grant," Savoy said.

"No visitors," the guard said.

"I am Mister Grant's counsel."

"You know what bloody time it is?"

"And do you," Savoy said with a firm but quiet voice, "know the illegality of detaining a man beyond twenty-four hours without retaining adequate counsel? I dare say Phineas would be most displeased you—"

"Who?"

"Mister Phineas Mealey signs your pay voucher, correct? I wonder how he would react knowing you...what does your badge say? Officer Sills? Well, Mister Sills, I wonder what he would say you turned out his chum from the Chess and—"

The guard's face soured. "Damnation."

The front gate opened on screaming hinges. Another rifle-slung guard, looking just as cold and miserable, ushered Savoy into the gatehouse. He searched his person and his bag and, assured he carried no contraband, led him through another barbwired gate to a muddy courtyard. Lines of concrete and plaster cells stretched into the rainy black like cages from a forgotten zoo; the prison had not seen a coat of paint since it housed Union prisoners over twenty years earlier.

Savoy was glad the doorman did not make confirmations. Few would bother a warden as notoriously temperamental as Police Administrator Mealey, but he dared risk that temper for a first-hand account from the only witness. This Mister Grant was a man who, if guilty, was capable of unspeakable violence—quite possibly against old men who hadn't the good sense to conduct their interviews during the day.

The guard escorted him to a cell stinking of urine, empty save for three chairs and a rickety table. He waited a long time. When he thought to demand an update, the door opened and the guard shoved a tall man inside.

"Ten minutes," the guard said.

Mahonri Grant blinked with dark eyes as the door locked behind him. He examined his surroundings, focusing on Savoy. He stank.

"Mister Grant?" Savoy asked.

"Who's asking?"

"Doctor Artémius Savoy." He held out his hand. Grant did not take it. "Travelling lecturer from Cambridge University, Trinity College, professor of biology and secular member of the Order of St. Eustachius."

"I'm not Catholic."

"I gathered that."

"You know what time it is?"

"I am here to inquire on your extraordinary case." Savoy took his seat and opened his notebook on his lap. "I am curious, as you claim, when you first saw the—"

"Oh hell. Another rag-writer." Grant moved toward the exit.

"There is no proof you were capable of such a crime."

"You sure?"

"I would like to be."

"You a priest or something?"

"Something like that," Savoy said. "My place as a secular tertiary is confirmed, but it has been ages since I performed any useful service. I doubt my membership is still valid. I took an oath to dedicate myself to Christ and yet..." He took a breath. "I would like to think I can hear your case with...shall we say, an open mind?"

"Even what I've seen?" Grant asked.

"What exactly did you see?"

Savoy considered this bear of a man, his smell, his unkempt appearance. He had interviewed plenty of maniacs, and unless his intuition was wrong—which was rare—it seemed this man was not the type. Every lunatic he had known, in any capacity, always betrayed their disconnection. Grant's eyes held more depth than his look would suggest. *He could be a very convincing actor,* he thought. *He could have torn those men open in that alley and you, the idiot, sit alone with him?*

Yes, he could be guilty, but who else would have suspected Reynard LaCroix to be a penitent man, an honest businessman, a loyal brother...a friend?

"You're not really my counsel," Grant said.

"No."

"Read the newspaper. You won't believe me anyway. I don't need you to attract any more attention than I've already got. You understand?"

"No," Savoy said.

"I don't need her finishing what she started."

"Who?"

"*Her.*"

7

Darkness, then spots of creamy light came, like faint stars in the fog. Croaking frogs, the rotten stink of decomposing soil.

–Drink–

His clawed hands grasped at the muck to pull him forward, clawed feet and muscular legs propelling him like heavy springs. He darted around the murky water to thicker tuffs of grass, around cypress trees with their tentacle roots. He kept to higher hills, blending with the night—there, a blur—gone in a breath.

–Drink–

Globes of bright light appeared, stinking of rotten eggs, white in the center and blue-green at the edges. He paused where the bayou ended and the manicured lawn began, in view of the great house with its many windows. Voices echoed with a scattering of broken moments, memories: a flash of gunpowder, the stink of sewage, the dark, dripping recesses beneath streets and daylight, the ever-present raging hunger. He tasted the night air—the scurry of a lizard, the scum on a stagnant pool. The bayou breathed through him; every fleck and pebble and beating heart held its own glamour.

He considered the big house with its gaslights, his ears twitching at the faint, scratchy sound of music. He breathed in, deep, silent, pressing his nostrils to the ground, inhaling the scent of footsteps rolling over his tongue.

–Drink–

Too close. He flattened against the moist earth, did not flinch when a firefly lighted on his back. A part ached for the trees, but the deeper part, the wild part—

—Drink—

Sound. Wood on stone—*click, click, clack, click.*

Along a cobbled path walked two shapes: A taller female in a long, black dress and an old fashioned bonnet of black lace. She smelled of fish and lavender and hair oil. Beside her walked a small girl in a yellow dress and floppy round hat. She chatted with a constant noise like an excited bird.

—Drink—

—No—

—Drink—

He moved, his breath quickening, despite him. The craving raged from his gut, down into his groin and up his spine into his teeth.

—no—

—*DrinkDrinkDrinkDrinkDrink*—

He exploded from the darkness.

—Drink—

He leaped upon the woman and brought her down, clamping his teeth onto her face, inhaling the thrashing of her body and the sound of her voice in his throat. He gripped her tighter by the shoulders and breathed in her taste, her screaming vibrating the marrow of his teeth and he did not hear her, did not feel her fingers tearing at his fur, did not see the bawling lump of a girl shrieking nearby—

—*Yes YES drink yes DRINK drink DRINK*—

Reynard seized in a violent fit and bolted from his bed with a horrified cry. He reached for a bottle of brandy on the end table, drank, gulped, until threads of crimson liquid poured down his neck.

The wolf is dead it's dead it's dead and I know I know I cannot not another, not another terrible—

The bottle emptied. He tossed it aside.

—*terrible.*

Nightmare. He reached for another bottle. It too was empty. He found a half-filled decanter of vodka and flipped off the lid with a finger.

In great gulps he drained the alcohol down his throat. Disgust washed over him and he tossed the decanter, smashing it against the wall. Since Lisbon he could never get drunk, no matter how hard he tried—and he wanted, really *wanted*, to try.

That bloody presumptive, intrusive, miserable letter!

His rage intensified as he thought of Miss Kiria Carlovec and her pleasant vagaries. He imagined every lurid reason such a woman would flaunt his secret. The more he examined her false concern, the pretentious sweep of her signature—as if he would rush to her side!

No one was supposed to know.

The First Time came at age nineteen, sitting in the last row of the Western Civilization lectures at The University of Montreal. The professor was droning on about Cortez and his rout of the Aztecs when the pressure in Reynard's gut came so immediate, so demanding, that he spilled the contents of his stomach all over his desk. He panicked, his instincts warning him not to run to the nurse's station but to isolate himself, far away.

He knew, somehow. Something terrible was going to happen.

He scurried into a concrete maw of a drainage pipe outside the school grounds, huddling in wet sewage, wailing like a child. The bones in his face cracked and skin ripped like cloth and every joint pulled from its place, forcing him to his belly as if prostrating before an unclean god. When he was himself again, five days later, he was naked, alone, sheathed in dead skin and more than twenty miles from school. When he tried to remember where he had been, what he had done, his memories were but fragments: running through darkness between the lights, his ragged breath and heartbeat, a cascade of earthy scents, the dull satisfaction of filling his belly. Whatever he had eaten, he dared not speculate.

Over the months that followed, he read books. He asked questions. He raised his hand in his biology and psychology and anthropology classes, surprising those professors who marked him sullen and uncommunicative. He drew ire from those more conservative students with his keen interest in Darwinism, especially the science of mutation. Could this be, he speculated, some product of evolution?

He soon concluded his condition was beyond scientific understanding. He turned inward, to every myth he could gather matching his condition. He discovered the word *werewolf*, but he found his affliction had many differences from common folklore: his change had nothing to do with the moon, though his body kept to a rough six-week cycle. He carried no demonic sign, no magic belt, no animal skin. He offered no oath to God or Satan. As far as he knew, his parents were not inclined to dabble in anything supernatural other than their pointless social circles.

So it was, that after having tried to bind himself, drown himself, drink himself into oblivion and slit his wrists, he decided he was mad, alone, and there was nothing that could be done until God, or the Devil, or Fate, had finished with his sad and sorry life.

Until his great-uncle Lanquin.

At age twenty-two, Reynard and his family spent a summer family reunion in his father's ancestral village of Aix-en-Provence. It proved to be their last, a bittersweet gathering of those stubborn few, those remaining members of a line near to extinction. Reynard enjoyed the nostalgia of the old villa, the wild gardens, wandering through the dying vineyards. There the ancient, wrinkled shape of Marienne LaCroix, widow of great-uncle Lanquin, found Reynard alone in the conservatory. She had pressed a book into his hands. A strap and brass lock bound tight a leather cover with many yellowed pages. With it, she gave him a tarnished key.

"I see it," she said. "In your eyes."

"What?" he asked her.

"May God have mercy on your soul."

He did not understand until he opened the lock and began to read the scrawled handwriting:

I am Lanquin LaCroix. I bear a terrible burden.

Reynard sequestered himself in the garden near the old family tombstones, refusing sleep and food as he read the tale of another who had suffered the same condition. Lanquin wrote with clarity, an almost clinical detachment at first—he too had tried to determine the cause. It struck at random, never skipping more than two or three generations. He traced the unholy line back to their ancestor Giorgio Basta, he who called upon darkness to command the Habsburgs in some old war. The devil betrayed him, the legend said, but from there the trail turned cold. The chief players had long turned to dust.

Reynard read page after page, grimly noting the mind of his grand-uncle deteriorating with each passing entry. Clinical curiosity became ravings until the handwriting leaned heavy with a rush of crowded, half-formed letters. Dry blotches of ink flecked the yellowed pages. Reynard pressed his finger under the last sentence, looked hard at every word, read it over and over again to be sure—

If God saw fit to impart this impossible puzzle, the last sentence went, *then I must consider the final solution.*

A soft knock echoed at his door.

"Renny?"

He pushed the memory away. Ancient history. He slid off the bed, dressed in his robe, and opened the door. Lasha held a candle in one hand and kept her own frilly robe closed with the other, her pale hair loose and tangled over her shoulders.

I did not mean to do it, he wanted to say. *I did not hurt you, you see? You are my sister—I would never hurt you.* He imagined little Lasha, laughing, the halls of LaCroix echoing with her delight, and his heart felt it might burst with the heaviness of both love and regret.

"I heard a noise," she said.

"My apologies."

"Is everything—?"

"Nothing. Insomnia, bad dreams, that sort of thing."

"Well. I am glad it was nothing worse." She started to turn away.

"Lasha."

She stopped.

"About this evening," he said. "My reasons for not keeping my word were legitimate. But I could have contacted you sooner, provided a carriage, something. I had forgotten Eleanor and Gordon were away. I treated you poorly."

"Yes, you did," she said.

"Please forgive me."

Her eyes softened. "I...I thought I heard glass break."

"Good night, Lasha."

He shut the door. Her voice was sad and faint behind it.

"Good night, Renny."

8

Lasha slept, fitfully, feeling the outline of her bed and room every hour that passed, wondering if she only dreamed of sleeping.

In the morning, she awoke to discover sunlight in her window, the dying smell of sausage and an empty house; Reynard had breakfasted without her, having returned to the city without even a farewell—*of course*—and the caretakers were still away. As she bathed and dressed, she wondered if she had done something wrong, committed some crime to be exiled in that old and dreary house.

So it was that, still early, a heavy knock resounded against the front door. She rushed down the stairs and crossed the foyer, uncertain if she felt afraid or exhilarated at someone at her doorstep.

Twice in two days. Extraordinary.

"Why hello Freddie," she said, as she opened the door. "What a surprise, to come all this way."

Frederick J. Burlington, Reynard's office manager and financial clerk, managed a slight, if uncomfortable smile. He never liked anyone to call him "Freddie" and Lasha knew it, seeing he was incredibly shy around women. In finance Mister Burlington served LaCroix Brokerage with a maniacal attention to the bottom-line, but as an office manager he had the candor of a fence-post and (as Reynard once remarked, with no irony) the social skill of a block of ice. With his pinstripe suit and worn leather shoes and gold chain draped from lapel to breast pocket he tried as hard as he could to promote the clerkly image, as if his dullery might discourage conversation. It usually worked. His soft shape and rosy cheeks, however, encouraged the occasional girl to remark that, with some work, he might prove a plain but adequate catch.

"Forgive me, but I bring a message," he said. "Please accept your brother's apologies on yesterday's cancellation."

"Oh." She frowned. "Yes."

"*Monsieur* finds a messenger service too expensive. So here I am...all this way, as you said. He wishes you to join him for dinner this evening. A carriage will retrieve you at seven thirty."

"He sent you to tell me this?" she asked.

"He did."

"When he could have left a note?"

"He only just decided this morning, *m'oiselle*."

"That does sound like him."

"Pardon?"

"Inefficient."

"So it would seem. Seven thirty."

"Yes," she said. "Seven thirty. Thank you."

"Thank you, my dear."

He descended the porch stair to his horse, to the reins lashed loosely to the hitching rail. She did not know Freddie could ride, expecting him the kind of man who only used a cab, and was surprised he allowed a smattering of French into his conversation. She chided herself; he was a man, after all, and had to know something more than ledgers and inkwells. Perhaps that block of ice was beginning to thaw?

So Reynard does care.

She closed the door and leaned her back against it. This must have something to do with that letter, the fancy one addressed to him. A thrill of relief went through her chest. This was an uncommon gesture from an older brother who considered her as a cipher, someone to be tolerated while he shouldered father's burdens. This, from a brother who abandoned his family and fled to Europe, only to return years later with no explanation, inexorably changed as if a doppelganger had taken his place.

It may have been the timbre of Reynard's voice the previous evening, but she was reminded of the young man in her warmer memories, the one before their family knew such sorrow, he who laughed and chased her down hallways and taught her to swim and made her feel there was no brother in the world as fine as he.

"Robert Neville or no," she said as she raced down the hall to bathe, "Elisabeth will eat shepherd's pie tonight, while I enjoy veal."

&)03

That day in New Orleans came electric with the tang of impending thunderstorm. Pedestrians paced a little faster, and horses and their coaches clip-clopped as if to arrive sooner than usual. Savoy regarded the charcoal tint to the clouds as his coach stopped for the omnibus to amble past. The weather was taking a turn for the worst. When the coach kept on so did he, dictating his thoughts into his notebook as fast as his pen would allow.

Stretched out on the opposite bench, Mahonri Grant stared out the back window as Parish Prison shrank behind them. Even from that distance he considered the watchtower guards with their rifles slung at their backs.

"How did you manage this?" he asked.

"Barrister of a friend," Savoy said. "Warden Mealey is enslaved to his pocketbook, and miracles are often accomplished with the stroke of a pen. Besides—the police broke two or three laws regarding your capture. Irresponsible all around. The authorities were far too eager to pin those murders on someone, an outsider especially, and the Warden knows it. I've been granted authority to watch over you, Mister Grant, until your hearing. I do hope you'll mind yourself."

"What happens now?" Grant asked.

"That is a very good question," Savoy said. "Our first stop is to visit a colleague of mine. Some particular details of this crime have bothered me from the outset." He paused, stoic. "He may be of help."

"So why me?"

"You are the only lead I have and, frankly, I have no evidence to either confirm or dispute your story. If you are to be believed, then I would think there is a purpose in what this woman did, and to whom. I will need your help to identify what you saw."

"I'm sharp with a rifle."

"With all due respect, I'm no fool."

Grant reached across the coach, quick as a cat, and slipped his hand under Savoy's coat. He grasped the handle of the revolver holstered against his chest—a weapon Savoy thought unknown to his companion—and snapped it free from its strap. He pointed the barrel at Savoy's astonished face.

"You saw what that girl did," Grant said. "She'd would'of done the same to me. With all due respect yourself, you don't seem the type to face someone who killed two men without fuss. If you plan t'introduce us again, you'd better be sure you can handle her."

"Of course I can," Savoy said. "Do not doubt about that."

Grant slapped the pistol's grip into Savoy's palm. "I could've slit open those drunks and made up a crazy story to go to the looner. By the time they find your body I'd have your revolver, your thick wallet, and a head start."

"You could have shot me just now," Savoy said.

"Sure."

"I believe you innocent."

"Why?"

"Because." With trembling fingers, Savoy replaced the pistol into his holster. "I consider myself an excellent judge of character."

The coach deposited them before LaCroix Brokerage, where they ascended to Reynard's office.

Grant remained in the little nook of a lobby while Savoy continued down the hall. The window blinds in Reynard's office were all open—a rarity—providing a view of the Merchant Exchange. Sidewalks swarmed with suit-and-ties with their briefcases and derbies and coats and confident strides. Reynard sat at his desk with his back to it, his collar loosed, the sleeves of his white shirt rolled up to his elbows. A walnut pipe steamed from his mouth, a tin of Hignett's tobacco on his desk.

"I let myself in," Savoy said.

"I gathered," Reynard said, taking a puff.

"I did not know you smoked."

"I don't."

"And that thing in your mouth?"

"It is what men of business do, is it not?" Reynard said. "Starch my collar and join the Rotary Club and talk politics over cigars? Add to the ranks of those rail-steppers on the street..." He thumbed toward the window. "What do you think?"

"Where is your staff?"

"Excellent question. Betty is home with a sniffle, my manager's decided to take an unscheduled holiday, and my runner's been murdered. If you could solve my inability to retain reliable employees, I would grant you an immediate position." Reynard dipped his hand into his vest, removed a folded sheet of paper and tossed it across the room. Savoy snatched it. "You ought to find that amusing."

Savoy silently read Kiria Carlovec's letter. The vellum was thick and expensive. He guessed she used a Remington typewriter, based on the shape of each letter. The woman's signature proved she was Spenserian trained, and his understanding of graphology revealed an emotional susceptibility—the fluctuating middle zone size and baseline of her handwriting revealed she was under some emotional strain. He turned the paper over and brought it close to his face, sniffing, examining the envelope's many stamps.

"Delivered to my doorstep," Reynard said. "By a foreign chap."

"Where did this courier obtain your home address?" Savoy fished in his pocket and removed a business card. "I may have met this courier yesterday. He came by the office just before you arrived. I assumed him an associate and did not think to—"

"What of it?"

"That lion watermark is the same on both his card and her envelope. You see?" Savoy gave him Edward Tukebote's business card and Reynard acknowledged it with a cursory glance. "That is the crest of Britain's North Borneo Company, if I am not mistaken, a financial extension of Her Majesty's expansions. This Miss Carlovec came a long way to find you."

Reynard laughed. "She cannot prove anything. I will hear her accusations, laugh in her face and that will be that. If she came all this way from...where did you say?"

"Borneo."

"Yes, well. I shan't just ignore her."

"It is curious, the very morning after Bill's death, this woman's valet is at your place of business. When you proved unavailable, she had him personally deliver the letter to your doorstep. How would she know where to find you?"

"I am not invisible," Reynard said.

"Bill was one of a select few who knew your lakeside address. Mister Burlington would not have divulged it. Neither would I. I doubt Lasha or your caretakers would be so careless. You have made a point to keep your estate anonymous. Utility records are private. You maintain no significant patterns in your travel. You avoid most social calls. Your post is delivered here. For all anyone knows, you live in this office. All legal dealings are kept confidential."

"I could have been followed."

"You said the letter arrived last night," Savoy said, "and since Lasha received it, that means he arrived *before* you did. Do you recall anyone taking an interest? Asking too many questions?"

"Is this why you are here?" Reynard asked. "More conspiracies?"

"There is more," Savoy said, with some emotion. He sat down and, methodically, told him everything—the previous night's findings from the hospital morgue, his interview at Parish Prison and Grant's story of the so-called Lady of Chalmette. Reynard listened with grave interest. "I have gone so far as to secure Mister Grant into my personal care, seeing he is the only eyewitness."

"You believe him?" Reynard asked, incredulous.

"I do."

"Is he...here?"

"In the hall."

Reynard's voice dropped to a whisper. "Are you *insane?*"

"I trust him."

"What would you say to escape the gallows?"

"Last month," Savoy said. " I received this." He opened his bag and slid free a folded sheet of thick paper. "From Professor Ernst Stronheim. Know of him?"

"I have heard the name. Occultist?"

"A former professor of mine. Our careers have followed similar circles. His studies greatly influenced my own work. For years we maintained a correspondence, but I had not heard from him for over a year...until I received this. It was neither signed nor dated, but his handwriting is unmistakable."

"What does it say?"

"Read it."

Haec ego non multis, sed tibi.

Whited sepulchers beautiful outward, inside lie dead men's bones. Then Simon Peter having a sword drew it ... Then said Jesus unto Peter, Put up thy sword into the sheath: The Cup which my Father hath given me ... That ye may put difference between unclean and clean...

Alea iacta est.

"The first," Savoy said, "is a maxim from Epicurus: 'I write this not to the many but to you only.' The scripture is an altered portion of Saint Matthew, King James edition, chapter twenty three, verse twenty seven, combined with a conglomeration of verses from the Book of Saint John and Leviticus, respectively."

"And the last?" Reynard asked.

"Another maxim, *Alea iacta est*: 'The die is cast.'"

"Ominous."

Savoy nodded. "Indeed. It was posted from the city of Sandakan, North Borneo. Look at Mister Tukebote's credentials again. You see his city of origin?"

Reynard's face grew serious. "Coincidence?"

"I do not believe in coincidence. Ernst knew of you."

"And?"

"No. He knew of...*you*."

"Ah. I must make quite the dissertation."

"It is not like that."

"No?"

"No it is *not*," Savoy said firmly. "Ernst is a trusted confidant." He took the letter back from Reynard. "I cannot expect you to appreciate or even understand my feelings, Reynard. You may see me as an old fool—"

"Spare me—"

"*Regardless*," Savoy said tightly. "It has been my experience that when circumstances begin to weave together, there is an almost certainty of conscious design. This cannot be mere chance. Until we know more of this Miss Carlovec's intentions, I beg you not to keep her appointment."

Reynard stood and gazed out the window. He watched for some time. "Come to the house this evening," he said. "Feel free to bring that man Grant. Lasha ought to find perverse delight in having a murderer at our table. Afterwards we can meet this Miss Carlovec together."

"You'd have me?"

"You can ask her all the questions you wish."

Savoy considered it, his expression muted. "That seems...acceptable. Developing an opinion may simply depend on confirming her itinerary; if it matches these cases I have followed, there may be a connection. If not, then my claims are invalid."

"Fair enough."

The office door opened and closed followed by a brief interlude of voices, then Frederick Burlington appeared in the doorway. He glanced at Savoy—confused or concerned, it was not clear.

"Mister Burlington," Reynard said. "Punctuality was traditionally your strong point."

"My apologies. Errands, sir," Frederick said. "You asked for legal-sized folders, and a reply from the Levee Board on delivery of concrete from Atlanta."

"I did?"

"I have been in town all morning."

"Ah." He turned his focus back to Savoy. "Seven o'clock this evening?"

Savoy nodded. "Seven o'clock." He turned to Frederick. "Your arrival is most fortuitous, Mister Burlington. I wonder if you could be of assistance. Will you secure back issues of the *New Orleans Advocate* and

Picayune from the last ten days? The society sections would be paramount, anything that might announce the arrival of any notable visitors from abroad."

Frederick looked to Reynard. "Sir?"

"It's fine," Reynard said. "Indulge him."

"Thank you," Savoy said. "If you can also secure back issues of the *Boston Herald*, say, from mid-August to mid-September, that would be most appreciated." Frederick removed a small notebook and pencil from his jacket, writing down the request as quickly as he could. "I will inquire as to her route," Savoy said to Reynard. "Perhaps she has no bearing on my investigation. Perhaps this is just a dreadful misunderstanding."

"If it isn't?" Reynard asked.

"I shall be ready for her."

Savoy gathered Grant and left the office. Reynard returned to his desk, paging through papers as if the previous conversation had never occurred. Frederick Burlington remained in the doorway. "In the future," Reynard said to him, not looking up, "a note regarding your morning activities is appreciated."

Frederick continued to watch the front door. "Why do you associate with that man?"

"Arté?"

"I do not like the look of him," Frederick said.

"He is harmless."

"That other one—I saw his likeness in yesterday's paper. He is the very murderer accused of poor Bill's death."

"So it would seem," Reynard said.

"You telephoned the police, I assume?"

"Allow me manage this, Mister Burlington."

Frederick stiffened. "I do not wish to be disrespectful, but Mister Savoy barks orders as if..." He squared his shoulders. "...as if to replace your late father, God rest his soul."

That made Reynard laugh. "You *are* cheeky, Freddie."

"Forgive me, but I—"

"I appreciate your concern, however you—"

"Of course," Frederick said. "*You do not need his help.*"

This last came almost whispered, solid. Of course, Reynard thought, Freddie was right. An appointment with Miss Carlovec would be more successful without Arté's meddling. Why did he have to be there? Why did he agree that he *should* be there? He could ask Kiria Carlovec all the questions he wanted, anything to dispel that old man's presumptions of conspiracy—insane accusations from an eccentric who spent more time meddling than keeping to his duties at Cambridge. This woman was harmless. How would Savoy's presence make any difference?

"Shall I send word," Frederick said, "to cancel your appointment?"

Reynard stared blindly outside, over the sidewalks and dark-suited pedestrians. Why did he not have the courage to stand up against Savoy? To think that criminal who had just been sitting in his foyer, the very man accused of Bill's death invited by Savoy himself—

Damn you!

Frederick was right. Savoy wasn't his father. He did not have to cower whenever that old man spoke his mind. It did not give him license to bark whenever he felt like it.

"Sir?"

"Yes," Reynard said. "Thank you, Freddie."

"Shall I confirm tonight's original appointment with Miss Carlovec?"

"Yes."

"Thank you, sir."

Frederick left, returning down the hall to his office.

He considered the manager's desk, the piles of stacked papers and contracts, bundled receipts and promissories, page after yellowed page stuffed in folders and filed and stacked along every inch of the walls. A waste of meaningless economy, all of it. He expelled a breath, smoothing a hand over the back of his neck.

Absolute waste.

He tore the paper from his notebook, scribbled with incomprehensible writing as if he had ever meant to do *anything* for Professor Savoy. He crumpled the paper tight and tossed it into the wastebasket.

9

In a rented two-horse cart, Savoy and Grant followed the riverside road to Chalmette. When they arrived at that familiar dead-end alley, the crowds were long gone and rain had erased the examiner's paint. They found burnt-out flashbulbs and discarded cigarettes and a spoiled sheet balled up and thrown in a corner. Traces of blood flecked the far wall. Rats scattered at their arrival.

Savoy proceeded to ask Grant questions as he recounted his story. Grant neither changed nor embellished his previous claims. They examined the places where the dead men had lain and searched every trail where the Lady might have walked. Savoy gathered what scraps of evidence others might have missed: flecks of blood into a vial, strands of long, white hair, and other items that might have had no connection.

They took a late lunch then returned to the city, bound for the opulent St. Charles Hotel. The concierge there confirmed the arrival of a Miss Kiria Carlovec of Sandakan, North Borneo, someone so wealthy and exotic that she, rumors said, had hired her own train-car on a personal tour of America. She rode in opulence, a black Concord Stagecoach that seated ten passengers. With a few dollars from Savoy, the concierge added that Miss Carlovec secured three rooms on the upper floor for herself and her retinue: five native servants of cinnamon skin and black-dot tattoos, arrayed in silk robes and turbans like a Raja's House Guard. They were commanded with skill by her personal valet—the very model, the concierge added, of an old-world gentleman. Their arrival had made quite the scene, even among the jaded *glitterati* that frequented the hotel and fashionable cafés along the adjoining street.

Savoy and Grant spent the remainder of the afternoon keeping surveillance in the foyer, idling through the hotel stables, asking questions, and doing all they could to glean information without attraction attention. None of it mattered. Neither Miss Carlovec, nor any of her servants, arrived or departed the hotel.

"This woman," Grant asked. "You think she—?"

"I do not know," Savoy said. "I do hope tonight proves more productive."

When they arrived at LaCroix Manor later that evening, they were intercepted by Mrs. Eleanor Quibb, the house's caretaker. She was a mature woman with a gray dress and gray hair pulled back in a bun, wielding the mansion's needs with an uncompromising grip and just a touch of Southern grace. Her husband Gordon served as the groundskeeper and groom, a man as meek as Eleanor was flinty, spending his time in the stables or puttering among the shrubs.

She watched as the men climbed the porch steps. She regarded first Savoy, then Grant's tall, imposing shoulders, her expression less than ecstatic. It was downright put out.

"Mister Savoy," she said.

"Eleanor," Savoy said. "Always a pleasure. Did Reynard mention our coming?"

"Neither hide nor hair of that boy today," she said. "And *no*, you were not expected. I have not done a thing with the guesthouse in months. There is not enough supper prepared." She looked up at Grant again. "Especially if you've come with an appetite. If you wish to call another day—"

"Arté!"

Lasha glided through the open front door and tugged at Eleanor's apron; the gray-haired matron puffed a breath of discontent and moved out of the way. Lasha was dressed in an ivory frock and embroidered vest with just the slightest hint of a bustle, emulating the current fashion down to the overturned cuffs of her puffed sleeves. Eleanor took a look at her, frowned, and left her to handle the guests.

"I did not know you were in town," Lasha said, leading Savoy inside to the foyer. Grant followed. "It is a delight to see you again. I challenged my geography professor on the Columbus issue as you suggested, and I must tell you what he—" She stopped, noticing Grant, and regarded him from boots to the top of his head. "My, sir, but you are tall."

"*Miss*," Savoy chided. "Mister Mahonri Grant, I introduce Mademoiselle Lasha Rosemarie LaCroix."

"Pleasure," Grant said.

Lasha's cheeks bloomed red, a blank smile on her face. She led them to the study, a cozy den of many bookshelves and cushioned nooks with plenty of lamps. "Have you seen Reynard yet?" she asked. "Does he know you are here? He sent Freddie, er, Mister Burlington this morning to invite me to dinner. In town, even." She laughed with a wag of her head. "Very impulsive. Renny *must* be ill."

"This morning?" Savoy asked, confused. "He told you this morning?"

"Are you joining us? Please say yes."

"Where is he taking you?"

"He means to surprise me," Lasha said, "seeing he owes me for last night, but I assume things have been very bad at work. He will not mind if I bring you along." She looked at Grant. "Though I dare say dining with strangers can be *such* a bore."

"I'd like to think I make good company, miss," Grant said.

"Oh my," she said, covering her mouth. "What I meant is...with strangers *you* might be..." More red blushed her cheeks. "You seem a man of the west. Am I right?"

"Rocky Mountains."

"I almost thought you Wyatt Earp."

"I've met him. He's much shorter."

"I can imagine." She sighed. "I envy you. I *so* look forward to visiting San Francisco one day." She led the men to the library's cushioned couches in the corner. "We can catch up," she said to Savoy, "and I will sneak you some scones and you'll tell me all about London."

She left.

"Like a whirlwind," Grant said, smiling as Lasha's happy voice echoed from the kitchen. "I thought your friend invited us here for supper."

"As did I."

"Do we wait?"

"Reynard will keep his word," Savoy said. "I imagine he has a perfectly good explanation for this confusion."

☙☙

Time had drawn short. Reynard was surprised at how quickly the day had flown. He thought about all he had done, the memory muted, foggy. What all had he accomplished that day? It had been productive, hadn't it?

It's that woman.

His anxiety had grown in proportion to the reduction of time toward his appointment with Miss Recently Arrived from North Borneo. He poured himself a glass of vodka and hoped to clear the cobwebs with a late supper and fresh air. Mr. Burlington had been gone on errands much of the day, but now sat at his desk filing papers with no discernable purpose. Reynard gathered his overcoat and started for the door.

"End of day, sir?" Frederick asked.

"Yes," Reynard said. "You'll lock up, please?"

"Certainly." Frederick managed a curt smile. "Good luck, sir."

"Thank you."

Outside, Reynard headed north as he considered his options. The restaurants along Royal Street were full of pompous types and inflated prices. The French Quarter was eight or nine streets away, but in the last few years it had become less the city's jewel and more a haven for those who preferred shadows and cheap rent. Around him came the exhaust and gutter-muck and smells of fish, the shouts of a costermonger, the rattle of the omnibus on its rails, the clatter of hooves on chert and gravel. The strings of telegraph and electric and telephone wire stretched above him as if the city quivered beneath the black webs of some industrial spider.

His path followed busier lanes where late afternoon traffic spilled along the avenue, ruffle-necked ladies clutching gentleman's arms to attend another blathering opera or cocktail party where photographs would be taken. New Orleans had unearthed itself from the Southern

Rebellion with a desire to be noticed, its wealthier citizens building their monuments and acting the part as if they strolled the banquettes of Paris. Lasha preferred that they mingled among those peacocks, but her delight was naïve. How could he convince her of their duplicities?

Within an hour he arrived at *Le Restaurant de la Louisiane* nestled on a quiet side street, took a seat in the outdoor café and ordered a late supper of *Onglet à l'Echalotte* with the meat especially rare. As shadows lengthened, a gaslighter fired a streetlamp's jets with white-blue haze.

He should have contacted Savoy personally. Arté meant well; he had done so much, sought his welfare. Yet he imagined exchanging awkward pleasantries with him and his companion Grant—quite possibly the man responsible for Bill Tourney's death, a hulkish murderer glaring at Lasha with lurid glances, invited into his private circle solely on unsubstantiated presumptions.

What the hell was I thinking?

Thank God for Freddie.

ഇരു

Savoy checked his pocket watch. *Where is he?*

He, Lasha and Grant spent the last hour visiting, sharing stories in the study while they enjoyed fresh scones lathered in butter and honey. He told what he felt to share about his previous year's events, any stories of gossip and scandal—a visit to the inauguration of the Eiffel Tower in Paris, a large dock workers strike, various aristocrats caught in compromising situations—all to Lasha's delight.

The conversation turned to Grant, who kept his topic squarely on his time in Arizona, of Apaches and cowboys and towns where everyone—*even the ladies*, he said with a wink—wore a pistol on their belt. He proved a friendly conversationalist. Lasha sat spellbound even if, Savoy suspected, details were dipped in a thick sauce of exaggeration.

"Mister Burlington's come to fetch you," Eleanor said, appearing in the study doorway. She motioned for Lasha to stand and examined her dress, tucking a strand of hair into her crow's nest. "You mind yourself, miss, and be sure your brother returns you at a decent hour. When is the last time that boy had a good night's sleep?"

"Yes," Lasha said. "I will tell him." She looked to Savoy. "Will you join us?"

"Thank you," Savoy said, "but we were not invited."

"Then I am inviting you."

"Reynard made it seem he would meet us here for supper, but I..." He wagged his head. "I must have misunderstood." He took Lasha's hands in both his own. "Have a pleasant time."

"Good bye, Arté," she said. "I hope you will stay with us. The guest house is always open, despite what Eleanor might say." She extended her hand and Grant took it. "Goodbye, Mister Grant. I will ask Renny to invite you too. I *do* want to hear more about Indians."

"Yes," he replied with a wide smile. "Goodbye, miss."

Out in the driveway Frederick Burlington waited beside the coach in his usual suit and tie. When Savoy raised a hand of greeting he did not acknowledge it, focused only on Lasha as she descended the porch steps. Could he blame him? Grant himself had a difficult time taking his eyes off her—she was luminous, delighted at the anticipation of a pleasant evening. She turned and waved vigorously with a bright smile. Savoy waved back as the coach bore her away.

Savoy worried he might be the victim of a sophomoric prank. Why would Reynard treat him so shamefully? Why not just tell him he was not invited?

Grant, beside him, watched the coach leave with an expression equally grim. "Perhaps we should follow," he said.

"Unwise," Savoy replied. "Monsieur LaCroix has enough grievances against me already."

෫෬

Lasha's coach rattled down the driveway, met the lonely road and continued east toward New Orleans, the way lit by two candlelamps on either side of the driver's seat. Faint, diffused light managed into the coach through the thick muslin curtains. The dark might have been oppressive, uncomfortable, yet Lasha was too busy smiling as she huddled in her wrap.

Where were they going? She had mentioned her desire to dine at the Commander's Palace in the Garden District—were they going there? She imagined chilled oysters on the half shell, rich crawfish bisque, and spicy barbecued shrimp. She focused on the images of reds and whites and browns from such delicacies, the nutty smells, the aromas of garlic steam, the miasma of high-class conversations.

"Where are we meeting him?" she asked.

Frederick Burlington did not hear, apparently, seated on the opposite bench, but she had never been so close to him before. When the coach leaned into a rut, her knee brushed ever-so-slightly against his own. He twitched. She would have laughed at his discomfort, but that would only embarrass him. What could she say? Did he secretly fancy her?

Lasha doubted her brother would take to her making a match with a clerk; the gift of her inheritance needed—according to everything she had been taught—to be passed on to those of standing and strong lineage. Those young men who fit that description often bored her. She would gladly give it all away for someone who loved her, someone who made her laugh.

Like that man Grant, she mused, smiling.

The estate lay far behind when she registered how dark it was, the depth of the profound silence. She pulled the beaver fur wrap around her neck, smoothing a hand over its glossy surface. When she inhaled she noticed the faint residue of perfume and bathing powder—her mother's smell—and she closed her eyes and wished she sat there in Freddie's place. She wanted smiles and light conversation, not an icy wall of silence.

"I am sorry for the imposition Freddie," she said, still gazing out the window, "having to make this trip so often lately. I suppose Renny will have to employ a service, or something, and give you a night off." She laughed, slightly.

He did not speak. When she turned to look at him, really *look*, he was staring at her. It was like looking into a mirror and seeing no reflection, empty and hard and shiny, and then she noticed another man seated on the other side of the coach. Why had she not noticed him before? This one blended into the dark has if he was made of it, his head wrapped in a dark turban, his dark skin barely visible in the gloom. Black dot tattoos crawled like a serpent from his left eye, down his face, and disappeared below his collar.

"Freddie?"

"Be quiet, my dear," he said, his voice wrong. "You were promised something exciting, were you not?"

She stiffened. "What?"

"You shall never be left alone again."

10

The night hung cold and thick by the time Savoy and Grant returned to LaCroix Brokerage, fog creeping along the sidewalk in a cottony tide. No note of explanation was posted on the door of *LaCroix Brokerage*. No light shone through the frosted glass.

"This is unlike him," Savoy said.

"Why not wait at City Park?" Grant asked.

"Eventually." Savoy rubbed his hands together. "I did not intend to blunder into the appointment, especially before she arrived. Perhaps we were expected to dine with them tonight. I am not the most fastidious in my scheduling." He pressed his hands and face against the glass to see inside. "His clerk *is*, however. There must be a calendar."

Savoy knocked and, to their surprise, the door opened on oiled hinges. The office was dark. "Reynard?" Savoy called. "Mister Burlington?"

No answer. They moved inside.

Savoy pulled the cord for the electric light and the ceiling fan clucked into life. He glanced over Mister Burlington's desk; with the stacks of papers and pens and bottles of ink, piles of packets and envelopes and folders, he found any search for Reynard's schedule problematic. He examined the pathways of the mess, wondering how a man with such a desk could manage much of anything. Grant drifted down the hall while Savoy looked for an appointment book. Mister Burlington may not have been the most organized of clerks, but—

—He sent Freddie first thing this morning, Lasha had said, *to invite me to dinner.*

Now that he stood in that office again, the memory of his visit that morning came more clearly. He imagined the smell of stale tobacco and the irritation in Reynard's voice, the stiff manner of Mister Burlington and his subtle, spicy scent of cologne. He remembered the flat disinterest of a civil servant who did his very best to remain innocuous.

Errands, he had said. *I have been in town all morning.*

Reynard did not know where Mister Burlington was that morning—a man who had traveled to LaCroix Manor personally to invite Lasha to dinner. Frederick knew Lasha was invited to dine with her brother. He had announced the invitation! He had known and yet stood there in that office, listening as Savoy made his appointment with Reynard. They thought him a fool, knowing full well Reynard would not attend—a ploy to keep him out of the way.

What bloody gall!

He rubbed just above his right eye, a bloody headache cramping his sinuses, and he wished Reynard would open his bloody windows more often. He felt a bloody mind to air out the whole bloody excuse for an office that reeked with a bloody—

He stopped and looked down the hall to meet Grant's gaze.

"You smell that?" Grant asked.

Savoy inhaled, walked into the hall, sniffed again.

"Yes," he said, "like the—"

"Alley."

"Morgue."

He followed the scent to a utility closet. He had passed that very spot earlier in the day, smelling nothing, but now as he approached Reynard's office the pungent stink caused his stomach to clench. He clasped the doorknob and turned it, slowly, hoping to find a cluster of mops and a spilled bottle of cleaning fluid.

He pulled the door open.

A headless body fell from the closet.

A sound gurgled from Savoy's throat, a cry of alarm, as he caught the thing under its arms as it bore him down under its weight. Grant grabbed it by the lapel before it could smother Savoy to the floor. Both eased the body down and rolled it onto its back. It was a man's ample frame in a pinstriped suit and worn leather shoes with a gold watch-and-chain stretching from breast to hip pocket. Pearl buttons latched all the way up from his belt to his open collar—the raw circle of flesh lay exposed, yet no blood stained his clothes, their hands, or upon the floor where he had been cached.

"Remarkable," Savoy said. "This wound is as clean as if by an edged blade. Look at his neck. Do you see?" Grant leaned in, his face puckering with disgust. "A cut such as this should reveal his spine, just above the larynx. But it is gone, Mister Grant. It is *gone*. His spine is missing."

"Who is this?"

"You saw him," Savoy said. "This is Frederick Burlington, Reynard's office manager. He was just at the—"

His voice caught in his throat.

"Dear God," he said. "*Miss Lasha.*"

⊱⊰

Reynard looked both ways at the empty intersection of Anthony and North Metairie Road, found it empty, and crossed the street. There waited City Park, ringed by a large iron-wrought gate and fence nearly ten feet tall. He had employed no driver; he wanted no witness. Alone, with the dark wilderness at his back, a single streetlamp threw vague, uncomforting light. He was grateful no one shared that portion of sidewalk, glad no one could see. He clasped his hands together, tight.

At the top of the hour, a black stagecoach with crimson trim, pulled by four black geldings, materialized from down the street. The driver was a native man with cinnamon skin, a blue turban and robe fitted with silver buttons, fir-trimmed muffler, feet shod with black boots, and his waist swathed with a wide leather belt. As he drew the coach to the curb and descended the bench, Reynard noticed small, black dots punctuated his skin from his cheeks and down his neck to disappear under his collar, swirling tattoos of pagan ritual, but he handled the coach door with all the solemnity of a London driver.

The door opened and a woman emerged to step upon the walk, assisted by her driver who kept watch beside the door. Her square jaw and full mouth and olive complexion contrasted against her lace-trimmed dress with its mother-of-pearl buttons and puffed sleeves. She wore a long, crimson cloak with hood, her black hair free on her shoulders. She smoothed a few strands behind her ear as if waiting to be noticed.

"Miss Carlovec?" he asked.

"Monsieur LaCroix," she said. "I have traveled for so long, over such a distance. I have waited to meet you for a very long time."

"Do I know you?"

"Not yet," she said. "I have confidential matters to discuss. It may not be entirely proper, but I request we hold our discussion in my coach— it allows privacy..." She motioned toward the driver at attention. "...albeit chaperoned."

"I see." Reynard did not smile. "If I refuse?"

"We share a common history, *monsieur*, one that needs closure. Am I being clear?"

"How did you—?"

"If you have indeed found the means to fend off your condition..."

"Who told you this?"

"Please."

"Who?"

"*Please*," she said. "My father suffers the same, and it is killing him."

₮₯℟

Savoy and Grant sat in their cart across the street, a half-block from City Park's south entrance, hidden under the dark recess of a balcony. The horses nickered at mosquitoes clouding above their ears. City Park's wrought iron gate stood locked, the gaslight nearby muted and grey, transforming the drooping oaks beyond the fence into foggy silhouettes. The yellow fog stank of wet soot.

Mister Grant was right, Savoy thought. *I am an unprepared fool.*

Involving the authorities with Mister Burlington's corpse would embroil them in such legal mire that their efforts would be delayed. They grimly decided to leave the body at the office, and prayed no cleaning staff would stumble upon it until a report could be filed...but what would he say? What *could* he say? What could sever a man's head so cleanly, and leave no bloody trace? Why remove the head at all?

Tell the police!

No, he countered himself. Not yet. I want to see.

It was exactly nine o'clock—Savoy checked his pocket watch to confirm—when a clattering of oiled wheels interrupted the silence. From an adjoining street came a black stagecoach with crimson trim, its driver wrapped in a robe and turban and heavy fur muffler. Four black geldings pulled with their mouths puffing steam, their iron-clad hooves cracking against the brick of the street. The coach rolled to a stop beside the park gate, and the driver descended.

"Is he here?" Savoy whispered. "I do not see him."

"There." Grant motioned ahead and to the left. "Someone."

Savoy strained to see, and saw only muddled shapes. Soon the driver returned to his perch, flicked the reins, and the massive coach rolled away. Before Savoy could urge his horses forward they saw another shape: a shrouded hansom, materializing from the fog, following the coach as it rolled down North Metairie Road. The driver was a typical New Orleans cabby in his longcoat and top hat and whip, but there was no indication as to the identity of the passenger. When the black coach turned south, the hansom did also.

Savoy snapped the reins and the horses lurched forward. He kept pace with both vehicles, keeping well enough back. They left the park, down twisting streets where lamps flickered like sickly stars, the street checkered with light from tenement windows. Wherever the stagecoach turned, the hansom followed.

Savoy did his best to keep sight of them both.

ഇൽൽ

"I know what plagues your family," Kiria said, Reynard seated across from her, "because we are distant kin, *monsieur*. Our common curse began nearly three hundred years ago with Giorgio Basta."

"I know of him," Reynard said with distaste.

"Then you must know of his unholy pact to serve the Church, or thwart it, whatever tale you might have been told, and the price his children have since paid for his blasphemy. He was a prolific man, easy with his mistresses, and his blood spread. Two hundred years ago one branch, the Family Carlofé, returned to the Balkans and became Carlovec, and there we remained until great-grandfather relocated to South Africa seventy years ago. My grandfather joined the Dutch in their expansion to Kalimantan...then relocated to North Borneo once the British made their claim. We have been there ever since." She knitted her fingers together. "We thought Basta's blood all but spent."

"You say your father is dying."

"He is afflicted."

"How can you know?"

"I know," she said, looking away. "My grandfather was also burdened. It was thought such a curse had no cure, having come from Hell, but we Carlovecs are stubborn people. We defy the devil himself."

"The Beast has no master," Reynard said.

"Indeed," she said. "Father maintained a stellar career despite his burden, but Basta's Curse is destroying his health, his mind, his will to live. He has spent his life and fortune to find a cure; my grandfather spent his life in the same pursuit. Only recently did my father see progress. He is on the brink. When he learned there was someone else like him, another so afflicted, someone who had found the means to hold off his own curse—"

"Just *how* did you learn this information?"

"—He sent me to plead for your help."

"I do not think it can be replicated," Reynard said.

"Then come with me. Teach us. I would front all expenses."

"You could afford me?"

"Father has done well for himself," she said.

"Do you bear this burden?"

"No," she said.

"Then why not wait until his death?" Reynard asked. "If we are all that remains of Basta's blood..." He picked at his teeth with a fingernail.

"Seems a waste to have devoted his life when celibacy would have done the trick."

"You are wrong," she said. "The affliction stains our blood, regardless. It is arbitrary. My father cares for his family line. He thinks of those not yet born. I do not think your sister wishes such a burden."

Reynard stiffened. *How does she know about her?*

"Does she wish to forgo love and family?" Kiria asked.

"She is none of your concern," Reynard breathed.

"Then I do not want such a life," Kiria said. "If my blood can be purified then we Carlovecs can flourish again..." She looked to her hands, her face all but hidden in the shadow of her crimson hood. "Instead of ending with me."

Reynard lifted the drapes of his window, catching the vague shapes of apartment buildings with their closed shutters, the night ripe with cold and moisture. Despite his doubt and the coiled anxiety in his chest, her could not help but look at her. The shadows played across her throat and face inside her hood until her complexion seemed to radiate. There was something oriental in the shape of her eyes. He liked that. He liked that she wore her hair down off her shoulders. He fancied the turn of her lower lip, that she did not wear too much—or too little—color.

Perhaps that was her game. To intrigue him.

With a turn of her head and a renewed whiff from her perfume, he realized it had been a long time since he enjoyed a private moment with a beautiful woman. He would never admit it, but he found her audacity charming. He watched her lips as she spoke, catching the breathy sound of an accent not quite British, not quite anything he recognized. When she glanced in his direction and locked gazes she turned away, never to look at him for long.

She is shy, he considered, *or coy, or polite.*

Ask about her route.

He shook off Savoy's presumptions. What did the old man know? He assumed everything involved a ghost or goblin or whatnot. He spent far too much time lurking in alleys and digging through people's rubbish and sticking his nose in news articles not worth the paper it was printed on. How could such a woman be any threat?

Her valet arrived mere hours after Bill's death. On my doorstep.

Savoy's accusations percolated. Blazes, but that man could be tiresome! Perhaps it was best if he asked her a few questions. Settle the matter once and for all, then see if the coach might take them someplace warmer with fine wine and candles.

"It was an effort," he asked, "to find me?"

"An understatement," she said.

Just a dreadful misunderstanding.

"How was the Gulf this time of year?" he asked.

"We arrived by train. My ship is docked up north."

"New York?"

"Boston. We had little information as to your current whereabouts, but we followed a lead and learned you lived in Montreal. When we discovered you had moved, we were soon directed to LaCroix Brokerage. I traveled from rail office to rail office for two months. None of your employees were helpful. You do a superb job keeping inconsequential."

"I do what I can," Reynard said. "How did you find Baltimore this time of year?"

"Charming."

"You must have visited Pensacola's waterfront."

"We only spent a day there." She smiled suspiciously. "Were you aware of my inquiries?"

Reynard expelled a long breath. Boston to Baltimore. Baltimore to Pensacola and now to his doorstep—the very route Savoy had predicted, littered with brutalized victims too horrible to contemplate.

Coincidence.

You don't believe that, do you?

He felt sick, cursing his interest in her, reviling the growing duplicity that now seemed so obvious. He hated duplicities, hated them all. Beyond the curtains he saw, beyond another tall, iron fence, numerous burial vaults stretching into the dark. Cypress Grove? Perhaps he could find a hansom in that more isolated corner of the parish that time of night; he could not breathe. Perhaps he misunderstood everything, and Savoy's ideas had tainted what was, in reality, innocuous.

He needed to go home. He needed a tall brandy. Time to think.

The stagecoach rolled to a stop against the sidewalk. Kiria pulled aside the curtain and slid down the window. "Driver," she said. "Why have we stopped?"

"It grows late," Reynard said. "I wish I could be of service—"

"Driver, *why* have we stopped?"

"Miss," Reynard insisted. "My responsibilities preclude being away for so long. If your father could attend personally to complete his research, I am inclined to—"

"No," she said. "You cannot dismiss me."

"Your terms are impossible," he said. "I cannot—you cannot—afford to compensate my losses." His hand settled against the door. The driver had not descended. "I think it is best we close these negotiations and leave it at that."

"Have I offended you?" she asked. "This is not a trifling. We are prepared to pay any price. Anything. I will do...whatever you ask."

"*Madame*, please."

"I have no pride in this. You cannot condemn our families with your indifference. How could this offer be any disadvantage to you?"

Reynard faced her squarely. "You choose not to reveal how you learned about my curse," he said, "so how can I trust anything you have to tell me?" He opened the door and stepped onto the sidewalk. "Do you want to know how it's done? This..." He tapped at his left breast. "A silver bullet, lodged on my chest, inexorably boring toward my heart."

"I..." She paused. "I did not—"

"Do not lecture me on suffering," he said. "You have no idea."

"Please."

He shut the door, motioned to the driver and the man cracked his whip. The stagecoach pulled forward into the dark. Reynard watched it leave, noting the fading scent of Miss Carlovec's perfume, how it mingled with the fetid smell of the gutter. He tried to forget her last, incredulous look.

Arté has to be right.

He rubbed his hands together and took his bearings. By the dual arches and gatehouse he realized this was not Cypress Grove but Metairie Cemetery. That meant New Basin Canal was at his back, and that meant New Orleans proper lay east and south from his current location. The soonest chance to hail a cab, at that time of night, was at least a mile or more down Metairie Road. No matter. A long, cold walk would clear his senses, clear the scent of that perfume, clear away the realization that he had been a fool.

He managed four steps before a hansom emerged from the fog and stopped beside him. A gentleman descended the stair, paid the driver, and the hansom clipped away with a snap of a whip.

"Monsieur LaCroix?" the thin man asked with an accent, removing his top hat. "I am Edward Tukebote, Miss Carlovec's valet. You may recall my attempt to speak with you the other day."

"I could have used that hansom," Reynard said.

"I doubt you wish to be here, alone?" The valet gestured toward the graveyard. "The dead do not make good company."

"Audacious, don't you think?"

"Pardon?"

"I have spoken with Miss Carlovec," Reynard said. "I have given her my reply. It is not your place to convince me otherwise."

"Oh, I see," Tukebote said with a hard grin. "You take me for a mere valet. Allow me to clarify. I have been granted a measure of trust, *monsieur*. I must ensure that those whom I represent are satisfied in this regard. I am sure you can understand."

Reynard smelled the musky odors of men emerging from Metairie Gate, heard their footsteps as they plunged at him from the fog. He tried to turn but strong arms wrapped around his back. Another man buried his heavy fist into Reynard's gut, doubling him over.

When he struggled, another emerged from the dark and cracked a heavy blow across his head—something heavy but pliable, throwing his senses into a spin. The thug struck again, planting a knuckled blow across Reynard's chin. That sent him to his knees.

"I regret," Tukebote said, "to employ more persuasive methods."

11

"Here."

Grant pointed to the sidewalk and Savoy pulled the reins tight, drawing the horses and cart to a stop before Metairie Cemetery's main gate. Grant lighted off the bench. With his finger he called attention to two steaming piles of horse manure near the gutter.

"Four horses yoked together," he said. "They stopped then kept on. Not long ago."

"How can you tell?"

"The droppings would have trailed off, like so." He motioned down the street, then to muddy tracks along the sidewalk. "At least two men crossed here, maybe three. If—and I say *if*—your friend was one of them, and *if* he was aboard that coach, they *might* have gone inside."

"It does not make any sense," Savoy said.

Grant's eyes examined the walk before the gate, then to the gutter, kneeling to touch at droplets upon the flagstone. He sniffed his fingers, wiped them on his trousers.

"Blood."

Savoy descended the bench. Metairie's front gate consisted of two iron-barred arches with an empty gatehouse in the center. Beyond the gate rose a tall obelisk to the left and a grassy hill to the right—the Tomb of the Army of Tennessee. Beyond them both stretched countless funereal vaults until the dark and fog swallowed them up. Savoy pulled open the left gate, the metal squealing, his finger sliding under the lock.

"It has been forced open," he said.

"Why here?" Grant asked.

"It's private."

Savoy reached behind the cart's bench and removed a satchel, slinging it over his shoulder and off his hip. He lifted a tarpaulin and revealed a new Winchester lever-action rifle; he slid open the chamber, confirmed it was loaded, and cocked it with some effort.

Grant watched him. "Know how to use that?"

"Well enough."

Lantern in one hand and rifle in the other, Savoy led them through the gate and down an avenue into the cemetery. Soon they were surrounded by row upon row of whitewashed vaults decorated with bundles of flowers or nameplates or crosses, an endless depository of memorials. Metairie Cemetery, once a horse track and since converted to housing the dead, stretched with such vaults as far as they could see. The moist earth unsuitable for traditional graves, the vaults preserved the remains but made the cemetery, in the dark and mist, a misleading maze of granite and marble blocks.

Grant watched the ground, turned right and followed a smaller path. They wove through the vaults until their way ended in a thick grove of trees. These were the gardens where more elaborate tombs sat under oaks and cypress, adorned with rose-blossom wreaths and braided flower-fences. With the trees tangling the way, fog erasing the finer details, the two examined the dark; first here, then there, turning this way and that, raising the lantern to cast more light.

"This is a wild goose chase," Grant said. "I have no idea where they went, even if they were here, and there's no proof that ever happened."

"You said you were a scout," Savoy said.

"Arizona Tenth, sir, but there are countless prints and none too fresh, and I ain't an Indian besides. There was a set that ran heavy a while back, but I could be making more of it than it warrants."

Savoy sighed. He was right. They had lost the stagecoach's trail a few blocks beyond City Park, regained it, and had lost it again. Grant's skill had led them here, but Savoy found he was following his gut rather than logic. There was no real proof Reynard was here. His parents' remains were buried elsewhere. Bill Tourney still lay in Charity Hospital. It was an odd place to speak with a lady, much less visit after hours.

Dramatic, he thought. *Am I being dramatic?*

Mister Burlington's strange death made his inner voice an unfamiliar companion. He now mistrusted his instincts. He envisioned Reynard again—dining and laughing, raising his cup in silent victory, Lasha laughing beside him at the thought of a stupid old man wandering aimlessly in a boneyard. He outstretched the lantern above his head. With his other hand he tightened his grip on the rifle. He had some practice firing a Winchester, but he was beginning to feel idiotic. What would he say to a constable who caught him hunting in a cemetery?

"Your light," Grant said, "douse it."

"What—?"

"*Now.*"

ℰℴℭℛ

There was a marked difference, Reynard noted, between waking from sleep and the muddled return from unconsciousness. The emergence from his throttling came like being dropped naked in freezing water. One moment there was nothing. Then came confusion and dizziness and the groggy, staggering pain of nerves competing for his attention.

The broken memories of his assault returned in distorted segments. He remembered a heavy feeling like wet sand crashing against his skull. The stinging pain in his left jaw and along his swollen ear, he guessed, was where his face connected with the sidewalk.

He could barely move. A thick knotted rope, tied at his back, bound his wrists to his ankles. When he shifted his weight, the rough hemp scraped against his flesh. It sent spasms of burning down his arms and legs, like tiny ants burrowing under his skin, into his blood. He tried to stop moving, to shallow his breath. The pressure of the knots at his wrists and ankles dominated his senses, hammering into his brain, the rope scratching as if it rubbed open his skin, ground his muscles raw, and now scraped coarsely along his bones.

Aconite.

Wolfsbane had been soaked into the rope; he could smell it, feel it bleed into his veins. The burning worked into his joints, becoming pain, blossoming into an agonizing spasm down his back. He closed his eyes, opened them, straining to see.

Where?

He was in a windowless chamber of stone. Granite. Walls notched with horizontal alcoves. In the alcoves lay the moldering remains of corpses—at least six of them—in various stages of decay. A mausoleum. Its solid slab of a door hung ajar to the night, and outside laid the viscous outlines of cypress trees behind rows of whitewashed vaults. A lantern hung from an iron hook in the ceiling, but its vague light could not dispel the uneasy glamour of death.

Reynard strained against his bonds, pulling, heaving, until blood oozed where rope ate into his skin. With open wounds, the wolfsbane soaked faster into his bloodstream; a heavy shudder clenched his muscles into his neck and forced him to stop.

"Do not hurt yourself."

Mister Tukebote eased into the mausoleum, the light carving shadows into his sallow face. Just outside the doorway stood three cinnamon-skinned servants dressed akin to Kiria's exotic driver—robes and turbans and black-dot tattoos—the same three men who had pounced upon him at Metairie's front gate. Each wore a leather belt with a wide-bodied dagger sheathed at the hip. Reynard smelled the electric tang as soon as they arrived; the daggers were made of silver. One man led a woman by her shoulders, face shrouded by a cloak and oversized hood. Reynard glowered. So Miss Carlovec came to gloat. That venomous shrew had been the very best of actresses; he cursed his lack of discernment.

"Renny!"

Lasha. She wrenched from the man's grip and the hood fell to her shoulders—ringlets of white gold hair in her eyes, her powdered cheeks streaked with tears. She rushed for her brother's side, only to be caught and held fast by the servant at her back.

"Let me go!" she cried.

"Have they hurt you?" Reynard asked.

"No," she said. "Freddie came to get me, like you said, then—?"

"I never sent anyone to—"

"He *told* me—"

"Be still, child," Tukebote said. "Contrary to rumor, *monsieur*, I see your reaction to *aconitum napellus* proves you are still very much afflicted."

"Why is she here?" Reynard shouted. He strained again and the ropes caused more clenching. "Damn you, man! Get these ropes off me!"

"Renny," Lasha said. "Why are they doing this?"

"I have no idea."

Tukebote knelt, removed the glove of his right hand and slapped him across the face. "Tell her the truth."

"I—" Reynard shuddered. "I did."

Tukebote slapped him again. "Liar."

"Please!" Lasha cried. "Stop!"

"You should have taken your sister to her vaudeville," Tukebote said. "You left her alone and afraid in that obscene, soulless house that stinks of dead women." He slapped a third time and split Reynard's lip. "Is that what makes you a man? Making women afraid?" He slapped a fourth time. "*Is it?*"

Lasha began to cry. "*Stop!*"

Tukebote spoke sharp words in a strange language. The man holding Lasha smothered his hand over her mouth and pulled her outside.

The valet clutched Reynard's throat, squeezing, his long fingernails sharpened with the polished edges of a surgeon's scalpel. His fingers were long, too long, the joints and knuckles fluid as they rolled against fibrous tendons under almost translucent skin. Reynard attempted to inhale and gasped, wheezing, all his strength gone as if it had bled into the stones of the floor.

With a deft flick of a fingernail, Tukebote sliced open Reynard's shirt. He flicked again and the cloth tore away like tissue paper, revealing the puffy white scar above his heart. The edges of his nails brushed like knives over Reynard's flesh, settling over the scar like a pale spider.

"So it is true," Tukebote said. "*Be still.*"

Reynard thrashed, near bursting with terror.

Breathe.

"*Be still.*"

Can't—

The words slithered into Reynard's brain. They crawled into his neck and down his spine, echoing faintly, until he could no longer move. He wanted to, really *wanted*, but his body found no will in it. He could only lie there as Tukebote swept his hand across Reynard's chest, the nails scratching like dull razors, and his fear became panic as Tukebote lifted his hand and brought it down.

Nails sliced through Reynard's skin and opened his left breast. Scarlet blood erupted. He quivered, gasping, locked in a lingering seizure, as the valet's fingers dipped inside the wound. He fished about and pulled free the misshapen silver bullet.

"Was this your solution?" he said as Reynard's blood pumped across his hand. "The leeching from amateur metalwork?" He wiped it clean on his trousers and stuffed it into his pocket. "Extraordinary."

He wiped his bloody hands with a nearby burial shroud. Reynard writhed at his feet and, when the smothering voice left his brain, he sucked in a deep draught of air and coughed blood. He inhaled another breath and the pain gripped his senses, forced him to scream. The rope binding his wrists to his ankles snapped in two. He rolled to his belly, pressing his chest against the floor as if to quench his gaping wound. Slithering toward the mausoleum entrance, his wrists and ankles still lashed, he left a trail of dark blood in his wake.

He crawled outside. Lasha sobbed in the dark, the imposing shape of the native man pressed against her.

A heavy sensation, a tremor, seized his spine.

–No–

Pressure pushed behind his eyes. He squeezed them closed and he coughed, retching. He rolled to his back and fresh blood burst from his wound.

–Not–

Muscle mass increased in his limbs. Bones and skin strained to compensate but they were sluggish, agonizing against a body reorganizing itself. The knuckles in his hands and feet spread wide. Muscles thickened in his shoulders and joints, forcing him to arch forward as bones slid from their sockets. The pressure snapped the remaining ropes from off his wrists and ankles. Bruises splotched the flesh where the ropes had been, around his throat and under his eyes. Seams at his shirt and trousers split open. Toenails plunged through both stocking and shoe-leather as bones cracked under translucent flesh. His breath deepened into ragged, feral gasps full of fluid.

"I'd thought a man of your reputation..." Tukebote said, emerging from the mausoleum. The crushed bullet moved between his fingers. "...Would have cultivated some discipline. The finality of your cure was greatly exaggerated."

"What is wrong with him?" Lasha asked. She sobbed, held in place by the strong hands of the man behind her. "What have you *done?*"

"Prepare yourself, child. It is a terrible thing to keep secrets. Best you see the truth whilst under my protection."

Ivory hair thrust from Reynard's hands and up into his arms, blooming along the curvature of his spine and beaded with blood. Muscles rippled under ruined clothing as the last vestige of Reynard LaCroix fell headlong into darkness. He wept, shuddering, as his face cracked into a lupine muzzle. Screams of a little girl fired into his head, the cries of men and women and children bleeding in his mouth.

He bellowed a deep, agonizing cry. It was no longer was the cry of a man. The Beast, chained and lashed and denied for years, came raging to the surface.

Lasha started to scream, her horror—

She knows she KNOWS oh god she knows don't look DON'T LOOK!

Tukebote spat upon him. "Pathetic."

Lasha gasped a breath and started to scream again. Tukebote slapped her hard across the face.

"Quiet, child."

"Leave me alone!" Lasha cried.

Tukebote raised his hand, higher.

The air burst with sound—a loud *crack*—and the valet's shoulder exploded with a splash of blood. He thrust backward upon the grass. Racing into the clearing, Grant held the Winchester and cocked another bullet into its chamber, Savoy following alongside with his bag slapping at his hip.

"*Arté!*" Lasha screamed.

The servant holding her cuffed a hand against her neck. She collapsed limp into his arms. He hefted her over his shoulder and bore her into the trees. Grant altered his course in pursuit. Another servant raised a pistol but Grant fired the rifle first; the bullet tore through the man's forearm and sent his pistol spinning into the brush. He shouted a fell oath and raced after his fellow into the dark.

"Maligang will devour you," said another voice. The third servant stood at the edge of the clearing. "Eat you both."

"Best keep your mouth shut," Grant said.

"Cast your souls to the River of Death."

The man slid his silver dagger from his belt. With deft hands he separated the blade's handle to reveal a smaller blade attached by a strong cord. In a blur, he spun both blades in a fan-like motion—spinning at his waist, to his shoulder, raising to throw.

Before the knives could fly, a violent shape leaped from the lawn. It caught the man by the shoulders, bore him down, and sank its fangs into his throat. The man screamed. The creature bore down again, biting, thrashing him like a rabbit until his voice died with a wet gurgle. The beast was neither wolf nor man but both, immense and heaving. Flesh peeled from its wrists and ankles where hemp had rubbed raw; bruises strung from muscle to muscle like cancerous pearls; a pink, fleshy wound in its chest throbbing with heartbeat.

The beast released its grip, swallowed, and tore the man so violently his head split off his shoulders.

Grant cocked the lever and lifted the rifle.

"No!" Savoy cried.

Grant hesitated. The creature roared at them, teeth snapping with flecks of blood. It dropped to its hands and feet and ran with leaping strides, shouldering through the surrounding trees where Lasha had been taken, snapping branches in its wake. Savoy started to speak. He expected Grant to say, do something, but instead saw him watching—

Edward Tukebote.

Gone were his formal posture and barrister manner—replaced by a rotten scarecrow, his suit a mockery upon his ghastly frame. As if unearthed from a dry grave his head was now a mummified shroud, grinning with drawn-back lips and eyelids, oblivious to the green fluid bubbling from the wound in his shoulder.

"*Put down the rifle,*" he whispered.

Grant hesitated, bent toward the grass.

"*Put down the rifle.*"

Tukebote began walking toward them, grinning his death's mask.

"Mister Grant!" Savoy cried.

Grant lifted the rifle and fired. The bullet buried into the valet's stomach, but he did not slow, lurching first into a swift walk then faster, faster, reaching with hands like ten little knives black with blood. Grant fired again. The second bullet blossomed near the first and still Tukebote grinned, unmoved, nearly upon them.

"By the power of Father, Son, and Holy Spirit...!" Savoy cried.

He removed a vial of clear liquid from his satchel and squeezed off the cork. With a sweep of his arm he splashed the liquid in the sign of the cross; as the droplets struck Tukebote's face they turned to steam, dancing across his pallid flash. Savoy dropped the vial, reached into his satchel, and raised up a brass crucifix.

"I adjure you, evil spirit," he cried, "and stand fast!"

Blisters erupted across Tukebote's face, breaking open with moist pops. He fell to the ground, shrieking. His body writhed until his throaty noise became awful, a breathy, choking heave. He stiffened, tight, and with a sickening crack his head wrenched upwards from his shoulders. It tore away from his body, slithering, the head trailing its dripping spine like a grotesque worm. The headless body collapsed inward with a stink of rancid vinegar.

The skeletal head and spine lifted into the air. It hung liked some ghastly balloon, glared at them with dead eyes—then came at them like a snake. The men dropped to their knees. The death's head snapped with sharp teeth, sailed over them, and disappeared high into the dark with a high-pitched wail—

—then it was gone.

For a moment, both men could only breathe.

"What in the hell," Grant said, "just happened?"

12

Savoy cracked the reins, sent the horses into a gallop, and the cart's wheels clattered along the cobblestone. When tongues lolled and sweat foamed on the animals' backs he snapped even harder. The horses turned a tight corner and the cart skidded, the wheels slipping, throwing the cart hard against the curb with a resounding thud. The horses thrashed their heads. Both men strained at the reins.

"That's enough," Grant said. He tore the reins from Savoy's grip.

"The alarm has been sounded," Savoy said. "Lasha's abductors are revealed and we are still alive—and that means they must leave town. Miss Carlovec is a woman of wealth. The concierge at her hotel said something about a private Pullman. The only place engines leave this time of night is from Louisville & Nashville Station." He looked up and down the street. "And Reynard is—*Dear God*—he is..."

"You're saying that animal was Lasha's brother."

"Yes," Savoy replied.

"You're insane."

"You may be right," Savoy said, with no irony. "I cannot adequately explain what we saw, but you have seen it. You have *seen* it! If poor Lasha is alive, I am confident they will smuggle her out of the city by train."

"Tell the police."

"And say *what?*" Savoy said. "I also cannot stand idly by while that poor creature runs wild in the streets. There is no telling what it might do in his condition." His voice shook. "How could things have gone so terribly wrong?"

"Tell them any damn story you want," Grant said, giving the reins back and stepping down from the cart. "Tell them *something*." He unhitched one of the horses from the cart, pulling its leather harness off its back. The other animal sensed the change and tried to move, but Savoy urged it back with a tight pull. "I can try that station, see if I can head them off. Give me the rifle and—"

"You're still a wanted man," Savoy said.

"I'll take that chance."

From his bag, Savoy removed a brochure from the St. Charles Hotel, and upon it he wrote directions to the train station. Grant took his blanket from the cart, threw it over the horse's back and climbed on, soothing the animal with steady strokes down its neck. Savoy pressed the directions, the rifle, a tie-string satchel of extra bullets and a pocket watch into Grant's hands.

"Can you hitch that cart with just one?" Grant asked.

"I'll manage," Savoy said. "Find Miss Lasha and bring her home."

"If I cannot find her?" Grant asked.

"You must."

In twenty minutes Grant arrived at the Louisville and Nashville Station. He pressed the bullets Savoy gave him into the Winchester's chamber and loaded the first with a swift snap of the lever. The depot was little more than a coal-and-oil stained crossroads for every freight train passing through town. At that time of night it was quiet, a nest of sleeping iron serpents.

He urged his horse alongside the passenger platform, a gaslight oasis where a few men gathered in common attire, some lounging on benches, others waddling with luggage. A train steamed on the far side of the platform. Grant dismounted the horse at a hitching rail—two other horses stood hitched there—and hurried to the train, peering into windows, calling Lasha's name, giving her description to anyone who cared to listen.

No one had seen her. He approached a man in a blue uniform, someone he guessed was a conductor. "Anything else leave here recently?" he asked.

"Freight to Nashville," the man said.

"Any foreigners?"

"Don't recall."

"How about a fancy car? A Pullman?"

The conductor looked at Grant's rifle, then at Grant's face. "Now that you mention it, there was a Pullman at the end of a freight line, bound for Houston, maybe. Or Atlanta." He motioned to the east. "Just missed it."

"Anything else?"

"Another freight headed west, 'bout an hour ago."

Grant raced across the platform. He slid upon the horse's back, kicked it into a gallop, and raced from the station. When the hooves touched clear road he kicked again and the animal burst into lightning.

He followed the rail line heading east, crossing from street to street, behind tenements and rickety warehouses, weaving along rough trails as he rejoined the tracks. Two miles further, where the tracks curved away from the road, he caught sight of a head of steam.

There.

In the distance, cutting a leisurely path through New Orleans' outskirts, a train puffed a column of smoke as it clacked out of town. The engine indeed pulled a long line of freight and lumber with a private Pullman weaving at the back, complete with an iron-wrought balcony and woodwork trim as if for a presidential candidate. Its speed was subdued, sluggish, but Grant knew it would throttle to full steam by the time it left the city proper.

Grant raced down Lafayette Street and closed the gap. When the track curved north he followed, urging the horse off the road and along a grassy ridge. He gained ground until he rode alongside the car, catching slim silhouettes behind curtained windows. Was Miss Lasha one of them? He barely knew the girl and here he was, riding like a madman. The thought came to hightail it south and catch the first steamer into the Gulf, yet that temptation died at the sick knowing he had not been there, *not been there* when Emily needed him—

"Miss Lasha!" he cried.

The night air cracked like a whip. Crouching upon the balcony, a wiry man lifted a rifle and squeezed off another shot. Grant felt the bullet's wake as it screamed over his head.

Right train.

The man fired again. The bullet whistled near Grant's ear. He urged his horse to slow and cross the tracks. Legs tight against the flanks he raised the Winchester to his face, daring to pause and aim before he pulled the trigger. With a squeal and a spark his shot ricocheted off the balcony railing. Grant cocked another bullet into the chamber and fired again—

The bullet splintered the sniper's rifle stock. The man fell back with a cry, tossed the ruined weapon off the train and disappeared into the car.

Grant urged the horse with one, final sprint, pulling beside the balcony. He reached, clutching the iron post, until the horse jerked to the right and Grant did not think, did not consider his options as he slid off its back. One foot caught the balcony while the other dangled in space, just a moment, before he pulled himself onto and over the railing. The horse tossed its head, slowed, and disappeared into the dark.

He had never jumped onto a moving train before, and his pounding heart felt no thrill in it, but now he was in familiar territory. His time in the Calvary returned to his muscles like memory—*keep low, breathe slow, here you go.*

He cocked the lever as he crouched against the door frame.

Here you go.

He kicked open the door, expecting a volley of gunshot as he waited five, ten seconds. The rifle comfortable in his hands, finger on the trigger, he swung around and inside. This portion of the car contained a half-dozen padded benches on burgundy carpet, three on either side of the center aisle, the varnished mahogany trimmed with velvet drapes and rose-tinted lanterns. End tables jingled with tea services and potted plants. To the left and right hung mirrors with French gilded trim.

Lasha LaCroix sat on a rear-facing bench at the far end, eyes open, hands in her lap. She did not look at him. She did not move. She did not smile. She did not seem afraid.

"Miss Lasha?" he asked.

The door swung violently against his right shoulder, forcing him back. From behind leaped a brown, wiry man garbed in a blue robe and turban, his hands and face pocked with black-dot tattoos. He gripped Grant's rifle and pulled, hard. The weapon fired its loaded shot into the ceiling and dropped to the floor. The sniper backed up, quick as a snake, and slid his silver dagger from his belt.

"Miss Lasha!" Grant shouted.

The sniper slashed. Grant rotated, let the man lunge too far, and cocked him across the jaw with his fist. Grant struck again—an uppercut—and the man staggered back. He raised his silver dagger; Grant caught the man's wrist, twisted, and the dagger fell to the floor. He rebounded, took Grant by his lapel, and hurled him against the wall. The impact of Grant's back cracked a mirror and sent a sidetable tumbling. With a heavy shove, he pushed the man away and reclaimed his rifle.

The man lashed, hands extended as if to tackle; Grant thrust up with the butt of the Winchester, connected against the man's throat, and dropped him with a moist wheeze.

Grant spun to grab Lasha and run.

"*Mahonri.*"

The Lady of Chalmette stood in the aisle.

She was as he remembered her: porcelain skin and ruddy cheek and red hair and comely shape. She wore a dress of deep green and rounded cap with a gauzy veil that hid the details of her face, but he could see her smiling her white teeth. There was something different about her; her face was as lovely as he remembered, but then he saw red blotches pocked along her forehead and cheekbone and throat.

"*Kiss me,*" she whispered.

He envisioned that smile splattered in blood, the ghoulish face glaring in that back alley, yet he still wanted to hold her close and breathe in her sour scent until he trembled at his revulsion. He could not move, could not breathe. Her voice slithered into his brain.

"*Let me have you.*"

"No," he started, craving her skin against his own. "I don't, I—"

Metal clicked and he saw—too late—the Lady raise a four-barreled derringer. She smiled. The gun fired in a burst of smoke. Grant watched, indifferent, as pain like a white-hot hammer nailed into his shoulder and flung him around on his heels. The Lady smiled wider. Behind her, Lasha watched as placidly as a manikin.

Don't you care I'm dead?

The Lady aimed at Grant's head. Grant squeezed the trigger of the Winchester. It discharged in a thunderclap and the Lady's shot went wild; the bullet slashed hot fire across Grant's left side—flinging him through a window, breaking through glass and fabric, toppling into the black air until the world became an emptiness of cold, spinning dark and he landed, hard.

His shoulder slid with a wet pop from its socket. He rolled, tossed down a grassy slope. Heartbeat pounded as the train clack-clacked faded away—away—

—his beating heart—

Dead.

Nothing.

∞Ↄᴈ

thiswaythisway—

The beast slid through dark streets, from one shadow to another.

whereamIamILashawherethiswaywayway—

Barking caught its attention. A hound bounded from a dark place, snapping and howling. The creature tore into it. It ripped the animal's belly open, pulled its entrails away with its teeth, and left its steaming remains in the gutter. It licked the blood from its claws, only to drop to all fours when voices and electric torchlight headed its way.

awayawaykillmeaway—

It raced from alley to street to alley again beneath a waning moon, the night so dark that those few who heard the scratching of nails, or saw its passing, dismissed it as another dog. Soon the streets ended. Stone became muck and brush, and then the thing plunged between trees. Lights disappeared and the ground softened under its feet. Its claws gripped the pliant earth, found traction. It accelerated out of the city and into the bayou.

runawaynrunthiswayLasharunLashaRun—

Every splash and cry and bubble, every scent and movement of air, all filled the thing with thoughts so contrary it relied on instinct. It ran for an hour. Two. It reached the shore of the lake and followed it. Sometime it raced over manicured lawns, through gardens. Once another dog pursued, gnashing and barking at the intruder, and the werewolf dispatched it as violently as the first.

The creature slowed. Ahead lay a large house with many windows. The backyard was cut, a stony path weaving around decorative ponds, a trellis wrapped in ivy, a fallow patch of garden waiting for spring.

–homehomehomehomehomehome.

It thought of that path, the dead garden. It remembered crying, and blood, a tiny little girl crying. It remembered angry faces and glaring eyes drowned with hatred, the sick guilt of murder and shame and loneliness so bitter it hurt to breathe, a mother's and father's hatred–the unspoken secret. That house with its dark windows was empty now, a tomb, its soul torn free because of him, him, him–

whatIwhatImememememeLashadontlookdontlookletmediediedie–

The creature howled, screamed, and fled into the forest.

Screaming again, distant.

The sound grew louder until he realized it was his own. He snapped his mouth shut. Nerves registered cold, gripping and wet. Naked. He was naked, filthy, sprawled in the brush in some wilderness. Moss hung above him, brushing his face. He inhaled a deep breath, dispelling the sticky fog, his heart slowing to a gentler pace.

His fingers lingered at the round, silvery scar above his heart.

So it was true. The bullet was gone.

Metairie.

She knew.

He inhaled a deep breath, then he saw her face.

Her horror. Her disgust.

Oh God.

Broken thoughts came scattered–the smell of herbs, sepia photograph of a stern woman with eyes like flint–*Mother*–beside a fairy-eyed, ten-year-old girl with a big, floppy hat–*Lasha*; Striped wallpaper with cedar trim; Anaglypta peeling around gaslamp fittings; Four-drawer walnut cabinet with lace cloth and a cracked, alabaster vase full of combs; Books stacked on an endtable; The *tip tip tip* of stocking feet. Was that her room? His own? He tried to see his sister's face, all smiles and patience and love for a brother who gave back little but distance.

It was the right thing to do, wasn't it? To protect her?

Now she was gone. She had seen him.

If God saw fit to impart this impossible puzzle, great-uncle Lanquin had written. *I must consider the final solution.*

Why hadn't Arté aimed for my head?

He pressed his palms against his eyes, his body shuddering as sobbing grief consumed him.

13

Grant awoke, his shoulder and ribs feeling broken, tearing, the stiffness in his neck like iron hands twisting. He perceived pale light. He lay in bed, draped in white cloth, the air illuminated by dusty sunlight through heavy curtains. He tried to move and regretted it.

"Take it slow."

"Mister Savoy?" Grant saw him seated nearby. "Where?"

"St. Catherine's."

Savoy looked ten years older as he sat beside Grant's hospital bed. His brown tweed suit was clean and his carpetbag sat at his feet, but exhaustion lay heavy in his eyes. A surrounding curtain provided some privacy in the recovery ward, but voices and footsteps milled just beyond as nurses pursued their duties, the air redolent with alcohol and blood and sweat. Savoy kept his voice down.

"They found you half-dead in a ditch," he said. "You had a dislocated shoulder, a cracked rib, and a bullet to the shoulder and your side. The wounds are superficial and stitched up tight. You'll be on your feet very soon."

"I lost your rifle," Grant said.

Savoy smiled. "I wouldn't worry yourself."

"She's gone."

"I know."

Grant recalled what he could remember.

"You are certain it was the same woman?" Savoy asked. Grant nodded. "Extraordinary. Your healthy constitution's the only excuse for you being here. You have survived this creature—twice now, it seems, though I doubt you feel any success. It is a strange affair we've stumbled upon."

"A nightmare," Grant said.

"A very real one, I am sorry to say. I have spent hours in research while you recovered. A creature such as what we saw, something so horrific—I focused my attention upon those legends of the East where the Carlovecs reside. Folklore always has its origins in truth. There is a legend among the Malay and the native tribes of upper Borneo, a thing known as a *penanggalen*."

"What?"

"A vampire," Savoy said, to Grant's incredulous expression. "Do not allow popular definitions sway your perception. I describe a creature that sustains its life by taking it from another. What we witnessed defies all logic, but we saw it, Mister Grant. We *saw* it. The stories say penanggalen remove their head and entrails and float about, feeding on human blood."

"You're joking."

"I never joke, Mister Grant," Savoy said. "I do not fully understand the relationship between the Lady of Chalmette and Mister Tukebote, but clearly there is collusion in this affair. You said the woman read your thoughts?"

"She...she knew things."

"Such a skill might subdue prey. I doubt they could keep Miss Lasha docile without resorting to mesmerism or drugs or similar coercion." Savoy sat back in his chair, solemn, his expression darkened. "I saw to poor Mister Burlington," he continued. "Thankfully, we have a timeline of alibis. The authorities are convinced you were shot trying to apprehend Lasha's kidnappers. It took some convincing, but they now believe Mister LaCroix was targeted for some inexplicable purpose. They believe these same men responsible for Bill Tourney's death."

"How?"

"In their zeal to find a suspect, the police broke two or three laws arresting you. How much better to sweep that little scandal under the rug then to blame foreigners?" That gave Savoy a vague smile. "Yet here is the puzzler: Miss Kiria Carlovec, the author of our troubles, continues to reside at the St. Charles Hotel. She is still here. I confirmed it this morning."

"But the Lady. Wasn't she—?"

"I thought the same. The deeper we become embroiled in this affair, the less I understand it. She is bound to know something."

"So what shall you do?"

"The question is what shall *we* do, Mister Grant?"

"I don't follow."

"I hope you can be persuaded to see things through," Savoy said. "You've proven your skill, your honesty." He shifted in his seat, clearing his throat. "I cannot do this alone."

Grant closed his eyes.

"Consider it repayment," Savoy continued, "from sparing you the gallows. That should be worth something."

Grant opened his eyes again, a strange look on his face. When he spoke, his voice came measured and soft, the sound of consignation. "Fair enough," he said. "So what shall *we* do?"

"A bit of turnabout would serve, I would think."

∽∾ℭ℞

Miss Carlovec:

I must see you regarding our recent appointment.
A messenger with more specific instructions will
arrive at your residence, no later than eight
o'clock this evening. Please dress for supper.

Discretion is essential, as I am sure you will
agree. My urgent wish is that we can come to a
decision to our mutual benefit.

Regards,

R. LaCroix

80CR

The next evening, five minutes to eight o'clock, Savoy and Grant entered the foyer of the St. Charles Hotel. The hotel held the glamour of the rich: plants and portraits and French wallpaper, slim columns wrapped with roses, the air filled with perfume and cigar smoke. Unlike more northern accommodations, black men and women served as porters and maids and servants. Savoy regarded the division with distaste. Despite the Southern Rebellion losing its cause, they still maintained a caste system based on color, as if to stubbornly resist the notion they had lost anything.

The men entered as confidently as other guests. They did not stop at the counter, and no servant questioned them. None regarded Grant's arm in a sling, tucked away beneath the fold of his coat. The hotel was one of the few with an elevator; they ascended to the top floor dedicated to the executive suites. Miss Carlovec occupied the largest, with two suites on either side housing her retinue. They did not know who, or what, they would encounter. The thought of more turbaned thugs lay heavily on both men's minds.

Savoy knocked on her door, waited, and knocked again.

"Yes?" came a soft voice.

"Miss Carlovec?" Savoy said. Grant stood beside him in his longcoat, his arm in a sling. "May I speak with you?"

She opened the door, regarding them with a cautious expression. She had dressed as if expecting to go to dinner: a supper gown of olive velvet and satin stripe, trimmed with lace and tied with an embroidered yoke. Her dark hair had been lifted into a pleasant style, fitted with pins shaped with roses. She wore a touch of rouge on her cheeks, and smelled of expensive perfume.

A lovely young woman, Savoy thought. *Quite a lure for a young man.*

"You have a message?" she asked.

"I wonder if we might speak inside," Savoy said.

"That would be improper."

"This matter requires discretion," he said, "as you may be well aware. We are happy to entertain a chaperone. You must have a guardian, a valet, someone?"

"He is not available."

"I must insist."

"Call again in the morning," she said.

She began to close the door. With his free hand, Grant slid a new Colt revolver from beneath his coat. She recoiled. The men moved forward, forced her to retreat, the motion so sudden, so unexpected she did not protest until they had driven her inside.

When she appeared she might scream, Grant extended the pistol and she fell silent. Savoy closed and locked the door. They were in a lavish sitting room with windows facing the river; a dining room branched off to the right with a table set with silver and laced cloth, while a bedroom lay behind double doors to the left. From the ottomans and lamps and decorative wainscoting, the apartment seemed more fitting for royalty.

"Sit," Savoy said firmly.

"How dare you!"

"Best keep your voice down," Grant added.

"Where is Miss Lasha?" Savoy said.

"Miss–?" Kiria started.

"Reynard LaCroix's sister."

"She was taken on a north-bound train," Grant said, "a fancy Pullman. With a redheaded woman and some brown men with knives." He motioned toward the hole in the shoulder of his coat. "Made sure I didn't stay aboard."

"You met with Monsieur LaCroix," Savoy said.

"How did you–?" She stopped and took a deep breath. "You have me at a disadvantage. Saturday morning I awoke to find my valet and my servants gone, my private car taken. I contacted the authorities, but they have done nothing. If my retinue did head north on a Pullman, then they probably make for Boston."

"Why?"

"My steamship is docked there."

"Why would they leave you?"

Her eyes narrowed. "You are Professor Savoy."

"Yes."

"My valet mentioned your name."

"He did, did he?" Savoy asked, glancing at Grant. "It is concerning your valet we meet in these circumstances. If you know who I am, then you know I am a close friend to the LaCroix family and fully aware of Reynard's...shall we say, *gifts*. I must know the nature of your appointment."

"That was between he and I."

"No longer."

"Ask Monsieur LaCroix," she said.

"I cannot," Savoy said. "Your valet nearly killed him."

Her expression changed. "Edward?"

"Allow me to be frank," Savoy said. "Miss Lasha has been abducted by your retinue. Two of Reynard's employees are murdered. Would you like to explain this to the police? The constabulary is close." A telephone hung on the adjoining wall—a luxury—and Savoy moved as if to use it.

"Wait."

She took a deep breath, eyes glancing at Grant's pistol, and proceeded to rehearse her offer and Reynard's refusal. She spoke of her father, how he both suffered the same curse and sought a cure. Savoy, in turn, told all he cared to reveal of their showdown in Metairie Cemetery. He spoke with assurance as to the more extraordinary details, especially the astounding nature of her valet. She listened, rigid, the color in her face nearly spent.

"You are lying," she said.

"If only that were true," Savoy said.

"This is absurd. Impossible. *Ridiculous*." She glanced at Grant again. "My men are natives of my homeland, dedicated to my care and security. I trusted them with my life. Edward Tukebote has served my family for years."

"There must have been something odd about him," Savoy said.

"Nothing."

"And Friday evening?"

"He fulfilled his duties, then pursued personal matters."

"He would have given you his itinerary."

"I trusted that he could manage his own life without my meddling," she said curtly. "Saturday morning, I discovered him gone, my retinue with him. I spoke with the desk, with the police, nothing. He has disappeared."

"What of his effects?" Savoy asked.

"Nothing," she replied. "He took everything." She hesitated. "He may have more in storage, but there is no guarantee. We cart a good deal of luggage."

Savoy stood. "Take us there."

"Why should I do anything for you?" she said. She focused her anger on Grant. "And stop waving that thing in my face! Call the police if you wish. What would they say to the Butcher of Chalmette? I've seen the newspaper. There was a very good likeness of you on the front page. If you mean to kill me, then do it now and be done with it."

Grant hesitated. "No, ma'am."

"Threatening a woman...you should be ashamed of yourself."

"We're not going to hurt you."

"There is a pistol at my heart!"

"Look." Grant popped open the cylinder. "See? It isn't loaded."

Her eyes narrowed into angry slits. She slapped Grant across the face with a resounding *crack*. He took the blow, saying nothing, as red spread across his cheek. She considered them both with a tight jaw.

"Your storage," Savoy said.

Kiria led them downstairs. Savoy thought certain she would reveal them at many points along the way, especially when she collected the storage keys from the concierge. To her credit, she said nothing.

She led them outside behind the hotel, past the stables, and down the back alley to a line of large sheds. Unlatching the padlock of the largest, she opened the gate to reveal a mountain of wooden crates, casks, locked trunks, and at least three traveling wardrobes. They walked inside; Savoy lit an oil lantern from the wall, illuminating numerous unmarked crates with no visible manifest. Kiria's cursory glance revealed she knew little what she might find.

"Edward kept the inventory," she said. "He is fastidious."

Savoy gave her the lantern and removed a crowbar from the wall.

"What are you doing?" she asked.

"If your valet is so organized," Savoy said, "why are those crates in the center so *disorganized?*" Indeed, crates had been sloppily moved aside as if some, deep in the center, had been removed. The surrounding stacks had not been replaced. "We forced your valet's hand, so he left town very quickly. There must be something here that might provide insight."

"There is nothing."

"Let me be the judge of that."

He pried off the lid of the closest crate. She started to protest then relented, biting at a fingernail, as the men rifled through her supplies, regarded every stamped name and opened box. Most contained clothes upon clothes upon clothes, bedding, canned food, furniture, tools and other provisions. Savoy's face beaded with sweat as he pulled free another crate full of fancy dresses.

"I did say there was nothing," she said.

"Interesting choice of words." Savoy smoothed a hand over the small of his back. "There is nothing here that belongs to Mister Tukebote?"

"You smell that?" Grant asked.

Savoy inhaled. He caught the dull stink of manure in the alley, the smoky breeze, the smell of cedar and sawdust and mothballs. As he walked toward the back of the shed where Grant stood, he inhaled—now he too smelled the faint miasma of rancid oil, the same where poor Mr. Burlington's body had been cached. The men moved a stack of banded trunks to reveal a long, unmarked crate. It was the heaviest of the lot, and he and Grant strained to push it to one side.

"What is this?" Savoy asked.

"I do not know," Kiria said.

With the crowbar they pried open the lid. Inside lay a rectangular glass tank, at least six feet long and three feet tall, fitted with riveted iron strips. Pale green liquid moved inside, like seawater in an escape artist's bizarre aquarium. A pale, blubbery shape bobbed to the top and sloshed against the glass.

Kiria gasped.

"I'm beginning to understand our Mister Tukebote," Savoy said. He removed a handkerchief from his pocket and covered his mouth. With the lid open, the stink redoubled. "It all makes sense in a perverse sort of way. This creature, this *penanggal*, described as a vampiric head and entrail, has been described as using multiple husks to walk among the living. A body-stealer. Have you heard such stories amongst the locals of Borneo?"

Kiria nodded. "Horrible."

"I submit Edward Tukebote and the Lady of Chalmette are, in fact, the very same creature. Our poor Mister Burlington's body also seems to have been used for a time, if only to manipulate events in its favor. I would not be surprised it has access to even more hosts at his, her—*its*—disposal."

Savoy reclaimed the lantern from Kiria's hand and drew the light closer. Inside, the pale body of a nude woman floated in the glass tank, bobbing like a pickled curiosity in a back-alley sideshow.

A body missing its head and spine.

14

The Next Day

"Has there been any word?" Savoy asked.

Eleanor Quibb regarded him as he stood before the front door of LaCroix Manor, his notebook tucked under his arm, his carpetbag at his feet. His buggy and horses waited in the driveway, while Kiria stood at the base of the stairs as if trying not to be noticed. At this she failed; she wore a pearl-ivory dress with high collar, her hair hidden beneath a wide brimmed hat. Grant was spared the housekeeper's wrath, having remained at the City Hotel to mend.

"He is not here," she said curtly. She had been crying. "The police have come twice already. I know about poor Lasha, so don't bother asking." She started to close the door. "Now good day, sir."

He placed a foot just inside. "Do you know where he might be?"

"No," she said. "Now remove your boot."

"Any friends or places he might frequent?"

"I would have told the police," she said. "Now turn right 'round and go home, Mister Savoy. This dreadful business started with your arrival, so your leaving may improve things. Poor Renny's never glad to see you as it is, and you addle poor Lasha's head with your ramblings. I'll be damned why you come along at all."

Savoy frowned. "He told you this?"

"He did not have to," she said. "I know that boy like my own."

"Even so," he said, "I hope you can..."

"We'll manage this ourselves."

"But if I could just—"

"Gordon," she shouted in the direction of the stables along the west side of the manor. "*Gordon!*" She focused on Savoy. "You are done here. Kindly step off this porch right this instant, or my husband will see you personally off. He was a prizefighter in his day, so don't be thinking he can't handle your lot. If I'd my way, I'd never see you around here again with your bloody—!"

"Now, now, Eleanor," came a voice.

She froze.

"There's no reason to be rude."

Reynard stepped down the stairs to the foyer, dressed in clean clothes and shoes, hair washed and smelling of cologne. He wiped his face from a towel around his neck, removing traces of shaving foam, his skin ruddy and smooth. He smiled as if nothing unusual had happened; indeed, Savoy noted, he appeared almost manic in his energetic gait and cherubic skin.

Reynard rose up behind Eleanor and wrapped an arm around her stunned shoulders. She looked at him as if upon a ghost, so dumbfounded was her expression that he laughed. She burst into tears. He squeezed her affectionately like a father humored at the gentle emotions of a child,

"Where have been, you thoughtless boy?" she asked.

"Did not mean to frighten you," he said. "I've only just arrived."

"But poor Lasha," she said, sniffing.

"I know all about it," he said. "We'll get it all sorted out." He glanced at Savoy. "Just a terrible misunderstanding, am I right?"

Savoy nodded, no voice in his throat.

"But that dreadful business with Mister Burlington," she continued. "Horrible. The police have been asking about you, where you were, about poor Mister Tourney and..."

"Would you do me a favor?"

"Anything."

"Kindly whip up a spot of tea and your famous scrambled eggs."

Eleanor pulled away. "Eggs?"

"I've quite an appetite."

"You wander in like a cold breeze," she started, her voice like flint, "with nary a word...and now you want *eggs?*"

"With jalapeños, if we have any left."

She huffed. "Would his majesty prefer toast, or scones?"

"Surprise me."

She started to say more, huffed again, and embraced him in her arms like a grandmother. He squeezed her back and, wordlessly, encouraged her toward the kitchen. She left, sniffling. When she was gone, Reynard's smile faded. Clearly his lighthearted façade was intended for his housekeeper's benefit. The two men considered one another for a long and awkward moment. He did not invite Savoy in, and Savoy did not request it.

"Are you...are you well?" Savoy finally asked.

"Fine enough," Reynard said.

"But how did you...?"

"Where is my sister?"

"On a train. Bound north."

"Where?"

Kiria Carlovec walked up the steps to join them on the porch. She came quietly, her voice conciliatory, but when Reynard recognized her he gazed as incredulously as Savoy gazed upon him. She offered a wan smile. "My steamship is docked in Boston," she said. "We can assume they have taken your sister there."

"What the *blazes* is she doing here?" he demanded.

"Reynard," Savoy said.

"Please, *monsieur,*" she started, "if I can but—"

"Get out."

"Allow her to explain," Savoy said.

"She is the cause of this," Reynard said.

"I can assure you I had nothing to do with this," she said quickly. "I had no intention to harm anyone. I am as helpless as you, sir, abandoned by my—"

"Leave my property at once," Reynard said.

"Please, just listen—"

"—Or I will toss you out myself!"

Many things happened all at once. Reynard's cries brought Eleanor back into the foyer and her husband Gordon racing from around the side of the house; Reynard commanded *escort this bloody woman off my property* as Kiria stormed off the porch, hot tears in her eyes as she fled to the buggy. Savoy turned to stop her and dropped his notebook, spilling papers and clippings across the doormat. Then came the eye of the storm, the silence that falls after feelings are hot, filled with the *ding ding* of the foyer clock as it chimed the hour.

Reynard wordlessly encouraged Eleanor and Gordon back to their duties. Gordon led his wife back inside. When they had left, Reynard knelt to catch some of Savoy's papers threatening to blow away in the breeze, taking care to organize what he gathered: photographs, clippings, letters, envelopes. Savoy took them with silent appreciation. He did not know what to think, what to say. As far as he knew, a manifestation of lycanthropy lasted for days. To suffer such a violent transformation, only to be restored within a day?

Unprecedented.

He glanced at Reynard's wrists, hoping to see the scarring, the raw flesh where his bonds had left such terrible marks. Reynard caught him looking. He buried his hands in his pockets.

"Why is Lasha going to Boston?" he asked.

"What Miss Carlovec says is true," Savoy replied. "We are dealing with forces, believe it or not, far worse than your current predicament."

"Is she alive?"

"Yes."

"Have they harmed her?"

"I do not know."

"Then tell me everything," Reynard said, "on our way to the train station. You can start by explaining this business about Freddie Burlington."

15

"We have missed you, Lasha."

"Where have I been?"

"You are with friends, those who love you. You are returning home, the place you missed so terribly."

"I...I do miss it."

"Where the water is warm and the air is fresh?"

"Yes."

"You will sit still and dream?"

She strains to push the whispers aside and focus on another voice from her memories. How can she feel the cold air on her face and smell the coal smoke past her window? How can she read books the woman gives her to read, of jungles and tall mountains and primitive men and women who walk as brazen as if among the fruit-bedecked halls of Eden?

"I do not want to go," she says.

"You will go," the voice replies. *"You will sit still and dream."*

"No."

"Be still."

"Yes."

A hand caresses Lasha's shoulder, lingering, and she stares into the face of the woman sitting by her side. It seems she is always by her side. Why can she not see her reflection in her eyes? Why does she speak of trees when her eyes are ripe with rage and bleached bones?

"You are a good girl."

She leaves Lasha alone—blind, examining the drapes and buttoned leather benches and the gentle sway of the train as the world drains away. She considers the broken window, sad, not knowing why. She remembers a tall man with a handsome moustache and she wants to cry. There is a man with a sad face and she wants him near, to tell her she is safe. Does he even know she is gone?

Then she remembers an animal, snarling, spitting, crying. She wants to scream. She wants to scream and hold him and beg him to tell her it isn't true.

"I want to go home."

"*Be still.*"

She obeys. She is a good girl.

So why do tears drain down her cheeks?

VENATIO

...More bitter than death the woman, whose heart is snares and nets, and her hands as bands: whoso pleaseth God shall escape from her; but the sinner shall be taken by her.

- Ecclesiastes

16

Reynard LaCroix's Journal –
Tuesday, October 14, Mississippi

I sit in the Southern-Atlantic meal car with dinnerware jingling, the horizon blurring past my window. Normalcy during abnormal times.

I am accompanied by Artémius, a Mister Mahonri Grant (gunslinger from the Salt Lake of Utah) and—against all better judgment—Miss Kiria Carlovec. Who would have thought the man accused of the very crimes Arté first attributed to me now rides in our custody, courtesy of a delay of extradition? My lawyer could haggle Judas out of Hell.

As for Miss Carlovec, she travels in the first-class car and rarely makes an appearance. I am not convinced of her innocence. Savoy has taken her at her word, but that old man is apt to believe first and disprove later. Such a philosophy will never be mine.

We will apprehend my sister's abductor and Miss Carlovec's valet, Edward Tukebote, before they reach Boston—or are we dealing with a woman, the one Mister Grant encountered in Chalmette? Both Arté and Mister Grant claim he (or she) is a supernatural creature manifested as a vampiric head that employs multiple bodies as hosts. I, for one, cannot fathom such an outlandish bit of hogwash.

Of course, who am I to judge?

In Lasha's abduction I feel less a participant and more an observer, drawn close by grief. I am not a man of distant feeling (on the contrary, I fear I care too much), but in my self-centeredness I hardly noticed my brotherly attachment. I cannot adequately express my torment.

Thursday, October 16 – Kentucky

Traced Miss Carlovec's Pullman to Louisville. We are at least four days behind. Kiria claims contractual obligations will keep her steamship, the Kalabakang, in Boston Harbor until the thirtieth of this month. Having wired Boston authorities of Lasha's abduction, that ship will be barred from leaving the country. Once Lasha is safe, perhaps I can convince her she did not see what she saw in Metairie.

I have not been good company. I am a different man. My metabolism is extraordinary during my transitions, leading to both advanced healing and ravenous appetite, but I cannot explain the speed in which I found myself again. I do not understand it. I do not know how I feel about it.

The remains of the bullet once in my chest, fished from Mister Tukebote's discarded pocket, now lies in my own. It pains me to touch it, its sting of memory rather than chemistry, yet I cannot set it aside. Sometimes I want to stare at it, move it between my fingers, memorize every detail.

Addendum

It is waiting.

Saturday, October 18 – Boston Harbor

The Kalabakang is gone!

There is no official record of the ship's departure. There is no record of anyone having received our wire. No one seems to know that the ship even existed. After railing on the harbormaster and whoever else would listen, I could not get a straight answer. How did a large steamer slip away undetected? Especially when we wired local police to have the ship detained? Where is the copy of the manifest? Custom papers? Did it even exist?

Miss Carlovec insists it was there, that she has a copy of the contract to prove it, and she pleaded her case nearly to the point of tears. Her dramatics are impressive. She almost makes me believe she had no knowledge of this plot.

Addendum (3:07 a.m.)

Private courier delivered letter, addressed to me, to Arté's Boston residence. Postmarked from New York City:

Dearest Reynard:

I am safe and in good spirits. Once I learned of Sir Wilhem Carlovec's urgent need, I agreed to spare both his (and our) descendants from future contagion. Why did you refuse such a cause?

Please do not be angry, darling brother. I have come to terms with this decision. Please respect my wishes.

I would have expressed my complicity to Mister Grant had he been of sound mind. As a lunatic he was ushered off our train before he could do me harm. I hope you do not associate with that troubled man.

I am on a swift ship, and I will send word when I arrive at my final destination.

God bless you,

Lasha

Her letter is a forgery. She would never write "God bless you" or "darling brother" or some other insipid phrase. She would have written "damn well your fault I am in this mess" or something in that vein. What sort of lies or threats might our adversary used to coerce her?

This is a clever creature that means to lure, or dissuade me, for reasons I cannot fathom. I sense arrogance, a personal message directed at me alone:

"I have her...and you cannot catch me!"

Sunday, October 19 – Boston

Arté maintains his spacious residence in the North End, his American base of operations when England does not hold him. I still wonder how he manages on an adjunct's salary, but I suspect he employs his intellectual talents toward a broad base of investments. We are spared the expense of a hotel, though Miss Carlovec lodges in an opulent monstrosity of an apartment along the bayside. My opinion of her degrades every day.

We have little to go on, other than her word that the Kalabakang does exist, that it left, and that it held a scheduled itinerary. With this in mind I chartered passage on the steam turbine Kaiser Friedrich, due to debark Boston for New York, and then Liverpool, in two days.

Miss Carlovec claims the Kalabakang must make mandatory stops in Marseille, Port Said, and Singapore, though most everything she has claimed in the last week has proven false. Arté tells me passage on the 'Friedrich is a sign of providence and, from its description, I am inclined to agree. This steamer's built by the same company that won last year's Blue Riband. Perhaps it can overtake them?

Savoy's examination of Lasha's letter revealed a trace of the acrid liquid we associate with Mister Tukebote, a substance found both on Bill Tourney's remains and in that glass coffin in Miss Kiria's storage. It is vinegar derived from the thatch palm, apparently designed to preserve flesh, but it leaves a telling scent. I always thought Mister Tukebote wore too much cologne.

Addendum (4:35 a.m.)

Cannot rest. Could lose mind this way.

Thursday, October 23 – Atlantic Crossing

Aboard the Kaiser Friedrich. Two days out from New York. Spoke with a yeoman about this ship and its pace across the Atlantic; he said the firm of Harland & Wolff boasted building an even larger fleet in the near future. I may look into transatlantic opportunities when I return home. Might be a lucrative venture.

Arté provided a silver crucifix to wear around my neck for reasons that are his own. I agreed to placate him. I barely notice its presence. The silver no longer vexes when it touches my skin. I wonder why?

Friday, October 24

Arté and I had time to ourselves this evening on the port deck. Awkward at first, considering. Our conversation soon focused on the subject at hand.

"I've spent many days," he said, "pondering why (Mister) Tukebote would make such a long and expensive journey. I can only deduce Miss Carlovec's claim of her father is an honest one. You said he too is cursed, and he is dying?" I told him that was her claim. "Then this penanggalen must have a vested interest in seeing him well again. What sort of hold would her father have on such a creature?"

It was a good question. I do not know if there could be anything Miss Carlovec would say that could satisfy me, but I must try. We have not spoken much since leaving New Orleans, much less concerning these issues at any length. We continue to spend very little time in each other's company. I will broach the subject tonight.

Addendum (9:15 p.m.)

As the poet once said, "All schemes of love and war end at a woman's locked door." Such was the case when I arrived at her cabin. She would not respond to my inquiry. I admit to a bit of intrusion as I pressed my ear and heard her distressed sounds in the throes of nightmare.

I shall ask her tomorrow.

Saturday, October 25 – Atlantic Crossing

Spoke with Miss Carlovec at breakfast. This was our first full conversation since New Orleans. It provided no insight. I treated her poorly last week, and I doubt she's forgiven it.

Her valet, she said, was a loyal addition to her father's retinue. London-born, raised in Singapore and served a number of influential citizens during his eighteen-year career. She continues to assert his integrity. She fully believes it was his shell, powered by Arté's vampire, rather than the man himself.

I would like to consider myself a man of some insight, empathetic to a degree, and I was very careful in watching Miss Carlovec's behavior. Either the thought of this vampire is incredulous to her, or she is a very fine actress.

Perhaps she is what she claims—an innocent, fooled by devilish machinations. If so, then I have been unduly hard on her.

Addendum (12:37 a.m.)

Cannot lower my guard. Not for her.

Addendum (4:13 a.m.)

Closer still.

17

Reynard, Savoy and Grant stretched out upon plush leather chairs, the gentlemen's lounge empty of other guests that late hour. Stewards left them cold canapés and aspic, an array of bottles in ice, glasses within reach, and the privacy they demanded. Wide windows allowed an excellent view past the deck and over the moon-glazed ocean, but their conversation commanded their full attention.

"Our quarry is a chameleon," Savoy said, "as long as hosts are at its disposal. I can suppose that this creature has used plenty of bodies in its quest to find the source of your remission. It would explain the attempt to use poor Bill Tourney—aborted, I would guess, when our friend Mister Grant stumbled upon the scene."

"So it used Freddie Burlington instead," Reynard said, with distaste. Freddie's funeral had been three days earlier, and he had missed it. "You saw him with your own eyes. You saw no difference?"

"We both saw him," Savoy said. "Miss Carlovec was in her valet's presence for many months without suspicion. A man's blood, his cells and membranes—the penanggalen must be subject to the chemical and physical forces the body once enjoyed. It must have some conscious or unconscious control over its muscles to resemble the original."

"But I saw her—his—face change," Grant said.

"It may require effort to maintain the host's features, but upon feeding or transfer to another host that illusion is discarded. Folklore recalls many a maiden who has fallen prey to vampiric advances, only to see upon the swooning moment of her death, the horrible creature in its reality."

Reynard laughed. "Honestly, Arté. How can you say that with a straight face?"

"It does no harm to offer conjecture."

Reynard raised his eyebrows and craned his head to include Grant in his incredulity. Grant would have none of it. He was convinced. Reynard felt the odd man out as he drained a tall glass of sherry with a hearty gulp, poured more of the red liquid into another glass, and lifted it in Grant's direction.

"Thanks, but no," Grant said.

"A teetotaler. Wonderful. I do not trust a man who does not drink."

"Don't trust a man who does."

Reynard shrugged, draining the glass with a loud swallow. "This excursion ought to keep you from the noose a good while longer."

"That's not why I'm here."

"So, it's my sister," Reynard said. "She is a pretty thing, aye?"

Savoy coughed.

Reynard poured himself another sherry. "Artémius pays your expenses. You've proven yourself a fine lackey, and you've the bruises to prove it, but every mile is another further from your fate. I figure you're with us until we find a port where you can...how might you cowboys say it? Mosey off?"

"You're free to think what you want." Grant replied.

"You'd stay among our damned fellowship for...what?" He gave a terse smile. "You've seen what I am."

"I have."

"And that doesn't shake your faith and doubt your God."

"*Reynard*," Savoy whispered.

"I know what you are," Grant said.

"You know what I am capable of doing."

"I've seen it."

"And that doesn't bother a man of honor like yourself."

Grant paused, the color draining from the knuckles of his fingers knit tightly together in his lap. "You're right; Mister Savoy has treated me fair, and I mean to help. My reasons are m'own."

"Not for me, surely."

"Not particularly." Grant took a breath. "I could've easily put a bullet in your brain and left a long time ago. From everything I seen, as you say, you might deserve it. Hopefully you'll behave yourself."

Reynard opened his mouth. Savoy's teacup suddenly fell off the table, struck the floor and broke into three pieces. It was followed by his dish and spoon, the lot clattering loudly to the floor. "My apologies," he said, crouching to dab at the growing spots of brown liquid on the carpet. He spoke quickly as he scrubbed. "I have spent a good deal of time studying the mythologies of Miss Carlovec's homeland, the various indigenous beliefs, whatever information I could find in Boston. I have spoken with her at length."

"And?" Reynard asked.

Savoy returned to his seat. "*And* I have found striking similarities to tales found all around the world. Faith and vampirism are closely linked. Most supernatural manifestations are fueled by one's faith that he is, in fact, a monster, that he wants or deserves his condition."

"I did not ask for this," Reynard said, managing a hard look at Grant.

"True," Savoy said. "Your condition reorganizes your body until your resources are inexorably depleted—one cannot help but be a ravening creature. Yet it is still you, Renny. It is your hair, your blood, your bones. If it is still you, then your reason and ethics must also remain...albeit pushed aside in some darker place."

"I am a murderer," Reynard said, his voice low, glancing at Grant. "I deserve a bullet, correct? Are those my ethics?"

"That was the animal, acting against you."

"It is a disease."

"Of a kind, yes."

"I cannot command influenza to step aside."

"The origins are demonic," Savoy said, "and must conform to certain spiritual laws. Mankind must be free to choose; none, no matter their actions, have ever fully lost that right. Your disease may be crippling, pervasive, but you have been changed." He paused. "Either by my bullet or its violent removal, you are different now."

"I did not choose this," Reynard said. "I did not choose it for my sister. There was no free will. God saw fit to—"

"God had nothing to do with this," Savoy said. "Yes, you are burdened by the sins of another man, but such demonic conditions are as much of the mind as the physical body. A man afflicted by lycanthropy is subject to law, such as the penanggalen must be. Ordinary things such as silver or wolfsbane, once benign, now have great power because the folktales, or one's sworn religion, say they *should*. This creature used silver and aconite against you. It knows the folklore. It traveled for months in the guise of Mister Tukebote. It expelled so much effort, so much time and money and risk to find you, to take the bullet from your chest."

"It should have gone after *you*," Reynard said. "You made the bloody thing."

Savoy offered a sardonic grin. "Indeed. I can only deduce she did not know about the bullet until very late in the game. All it knew is that *you* had it. And *you* still have it."

"Why?"

"Because it *believes*. It accepts the limitations of its condition, and the condition of Master Carlovec. It must have been a creature of faith once...a Christian, I suspect, devout. I never told you what I threw in Mister Tukebote's face at Metairie. The liquid that seemed to burn his skin?"

"Acid," Grant said.

"Water. Not even blessed. In my secular role I doubt my authority to consecrate is still valid. Yet when I cast it into its face with all the confidence of a priest...*it* believed it was blessed—and you saw the effect."

"So what else might it believe?" Grant asked.

"Exactly."

18

From Liverpool they used coach and train and boat, working their way across the Channel southward to Calais, train to Paris, Lyon. In three days they entered the arid, rocky hills of France's Provence region.

Reynard spent much of the journey alone, sequestering himself in whatever empty compartment he could find. He watched for hours out the window as the train passed through little towns, through rolling hills carved with orchards and vineyards. He recalled fragments of memories of no real significance: running along dirt roads, the smell of olive oil and cinnamon, dusty summer afternoons, the white-washed planks of a tall fence, aged faces of relatives long since buried.

He remembered the day Father announced their move to Montreal; Reynard had run off and cried that day—alone, so father would not see. Now, back home for the first time in many years, the familiar landscape offered no comfort. The simple pleasures he once knew felt shrouded, as if his old happiness had been a lie, as fallow as the dead fields that blurred past the train's window.

The further south they travelled, his growing anxiety became a dread. He feared what they might find once they intercepted the *Kalabakang*, what he might say to Lasha when they found her. Would she slap him? Scream? Would she refuse to come close? His tension became nearly unbearable as the train eased past white, rocky hillocks, the earth rich and red, the air pungent with the smell of the sea. He read the same newspaper articles over and over again. He found scratch paper and a pencil and scribbled—circle upon circle upon circle—to ignore the fluttering madness as he imagined all possible futures.

Hurry, he wanted to tell the conductor. *My sister is waiting.*

When the train lurched into Marseille's Gare St. Charles late in the afternoon, Reynard was one of the first to descend upon the platform. He was the first of his party to discover the broadsheet, to read the awful headline:

LE BATEAU DE LA MORT
ARRIVE AU VIEUX PORT!

"'The steamer *Kalabakang,* registered out of Singapore, was found adrift three miles south-southwest from Château d'If,'" Savoy translated as he, Reynard, Grant and Kiria rode together in a brougham down Canebíere Avenue. "'Towed into shore by a Corsican trawler, authorities have since moored the doomed ship near Le Quai de la Tourette for examination.'"

"It cannot be true," Kiria said. "It cannot."

Reynard glanced past the curtains and watched the flow of pedestrians, forcing himself to ignore the smell of her growing emotion.

As France's largest port, Marseille held a French flavor with a North African spirit, a city growing steadily against the Mediterranean. At one turn one might see half-timber and plaster apartments like in Dijon, or tall, narrow brick-and-stone *maisons* with their iron-lace railings like in Paris, or fountains of Grecian figures spouting water like many in Lyon. Yet one might also hear the drums and shrill whistles of Moroccan musicians, see women in black shawls and tinkling jewelry, or pass a cluster of buildings the color of sandstone, the shops sporting wicker baskets filled with peanuts or figs or brassware like so many markets in Cairo.

The city was alive and breathing, the mongers and beggars and well-dressed debutantes, a silent truce among the disparate cultures. Reynard hated the disinterest of the city streets, all those thousands who lived casually this day—for everyone aboard the *Kalabakang,* including his sister, might be dead. Newsboys still hawked their broadsheets and earned money at the expense of others, those suffering grief for their dead—

"'At least twenty bodies have been recovered,'" Savoy continued. "'The remains of seventeen men and three women were confirmed by Inspector Jean Pourry earlier today. Victims were discovered from the bridge to the...'" He showed the page to Reynard. "What is *cargaison?*"

"Hold," Reynard said.

"Ah, yes. Obviously. 'Victims were discovered from the bridge to the hold, where one victim apparently attempted to hide.'"

"Horrible," Kiria said.

"How many were in the *Kalabakang's* compliment?" Savoy asked.

"Twenty-one, at least on the journey to Boston," she said, "which included myself, Mister Tukebote, my secretary Miss Lourdes—" Her hands clutched at her mouth. "Oh God, *no.* She'd remained in Boston to visit a cousin in Philadelphia. I do hope." She pressed both hands to her cheeks. "Oh *please*, let her still be in America."

They said no more after that.

The brougham sidled off the avenue, crossed Le Quai des Belges and continued along the north end of Vieux Port. It soon deposited them at the quay, the driver ordered to transport their luggage to the *Hotel Vauban* across the harbor, and with a crack of the whip the horses and coach pulled away.

The four walked down the quay without a word. On a typical day fishmongers hawked fresh-caught crab and lobster, eel, mackerel, and pageot, the air ripe with the scents of garlicky rouille and fennel and pungent sardine pastes. Today it was hosed down, empty. The air stank of bleach and seawater. To their left, the grey water of the harbor sloshed against the docks, many boats of all sizes, both steam and sail, bobbing in the tide. To their right stood a line of elderly buildings. Straight ahead, the grey horizon of the Mediterranean lay sterile and cold.

The white-hulled shape of the *Kalabakang* leaned against the far end of the dock. Numerous police wagons huddled in conference, their horses twitching against their tack. The four eased through a crowd of curious onlookers, stopping before three uniformed officers of *La Sûreté Nationale* who kept vigil at the head of the plank. The tallest of the three, in his blue uniform and cap, wore the most stripes on his shoulder.

"I wish to speak to *l'inspecteur principal*," Reynard said to him, his French sharp and full of authority. "This woman, Miss Kiria Carlovec of Sandakan, chartered this very steamer. It left her behind in Boston."

"Did it now?" the officer replied.

"My sister was an unwilling passenger. I believe we can identify..." His voice thickened. "We may be able to identify many of the victims." He motioned to Savoy. "This man is a doctor. He will also be of service."

The officer looked over their papers, regarding each of them in turn. He waved Reynard and Kiria to board, but stopped Savoy and Grant. "We have plenty of doctors," he said. "Speak with Inspector Pourry and tell him Janoux gave you permission."

"Thank you."

Reynard took Kiria's hand, assisted her onto the plank, and the two crossed over to the *Kalabakang*. It was an aged four-deck steamer with twin smokestacks towering above whitewashed planking and rails, decorated with oriental symbols Reynard did not recognize. His stomach twisted as they stepped onto the deck.

I can smell it already.

"Are you certain you can do this?" he asked.

"Despite their behavior," Kiria said, "my retinue treated me with the utmost respect. Miss Lourdes, my secretary...she was a dear friend. I must do this." Her composure faltered. "I must."

He nodded, and led her on. After haggling with various lower-ranked officers and showing and re-showing their papers, the two were finally ushered downstairs to the Crew's Galley.

They entered.

Kiria stiffened, closed her eyes.

Tables and chairs had been pushed aside, the linoleum floor lined with three rows of bodies shrouded with vulcanized tarps. Five of the remains retained no recognizable shape, and beside these sat buckets swarming with flies. Though every door and window was open to invite fresh air, the room reeked with gore—a makeshift abattoir. Reynard removed his white handkerchief and pressed it against his nose, overwhelmed by the stink, wondering why he did not anticipate such an awful scene.

"You can identify this crew?" came Inspector Pourry. He stood off to the side in his smart blue uniform and square cap, stout of build with a swarthy complexion. He spoke with the subtle drawl of Provencial stock. "You are not spies for *Le Provence?*"

"No, not journalists," Reynard said.

"No," Kiria said in serviceable French. She explained her relationship with the *Kalabakang*. "I can identify the passengers, if I must."

Sergeant Pourry hesitated but, at her silent approval, he crouched near the closest body and lifted the sheet. This first victim was a man with a shock of black hair, his fleshy neck splayed open to the spine, his cheeks and what remained of his throat punctuated with the dotted curves of his tribal tattoo. It was the native man who had taken Lasha from Metairie Cemetery.

Kiria closed her eyes. "So it is true."

Pourry lifted another sheet to reveal the mangled remains of Marion Loudres, a young woman of twenty. She may have been pretty once, if not plain, yet now there was nothing but glazed eyes and drooping jaw above the ruin of her shredded clothing and mangled body. Silent tears poured down Kiria's cheeks. Her hands shook. As Pourry revealed each victim, she relayed names and ages and whatever details she could provide as another officer transcribed into a notebook.

Nausea clutched Reynard's stomach at the mangled flesh and muscle, the horrified expressions on those few faces still retaining shape. Yet deeper, lingering below his revulsion, he felt the same, terrible need— he could not describe it. It took all his strength to not rush to the outer deck, spewing the contents of his stomach into the sea.

"*Monsieur*," Sergeant Pourry said. "You look pale."

Reynard wanted to tell him that *of course* he was pale and *yes*, he was going to vomit, that any reasonable man *should* vomit, but he constrained himself. This craving was unnatural, abominable, a damnable stain of the Beast and its unwanted appetites. He refused to accept it. Reynard LaCroix— anyone of sound mind—was incapable of such feeling.

No.

By the fifth victim the bodies became unrecognizable. In the midst of these another sheet was lifted, the body mangled like the rest, but this one still retained its complete skeleton. Reynard shuddered. The body wore the shredded remains of an ivory frock and embroidered dress, the same worn by Lasha at Metairie.

Reynard began to shake.

Not her.

He looked at his knuckles, his fingers and nails, turning his palms upward. The muscles beneath his skin shifted. They tensed against his slender bones, tightened down his forearms and into his shoulders. He tightened his hands into fists and opened them again, watching the ruddy imprints of his fingertips bleach into white. When his muscles tightened again he shook his hands vigorously. He plunged his hand into his pocket and fingered the silver bullet. He squeezed it, pressing it into his palm.

"*Monsieur?*" Pourry asked.

"When did this happen?" Reynard asked.

"As best we can tell, a day. It will take time to confirm if this ship saw harbor since leaving Boston, for there is no manifest, no itinerary. Nothing."

"This steamer was bound for North Borneo," Reynard said. He turned to Kiria. "Miss Carlovec." Kiria did not seem to hear, her gaze connected by an invisible thread to the shrouded remains of her secretary. "Miss Carlovec."

She looked up, dazed. "Yes."

"This ship was bound for North Borneo. Marseille was part of its itinerary."

"Yes."

"Were there any other stops planned?"

"Marseille, Port Said, Bombay, possibly; Singapore, Sandakan. It held a strict manifest, for it carried additional cargo aside from my contract."

"If we assume," Reynard said, "she was in complete control of the crew, then one might wonder if..."

"*Pardon moi,*" Pourry said, "but is there more you might share?"

"I told you everything I know," Kiria said.

"And you, *monsieur?*"

"A woman," Reynard said.

"A woman?"

"She is responsible. Upper twenties to early thirties, milky white skin, red hair, shapely, fond of saucy dresses. That is the description I have been given. She would have been in the presence of my sister, Lasha LaCroix, who was taken against her will upon this steamer back in Boston—and whose description I wired in detail to your headquarters not one day ago. This woman, and my sister, are headed for North Borneo."

"You mean they *were* headed."

"No. My sister and this woman are still alive. They must be. It would not surprise me if two of the female victims are women of similar size and shape, slain in their places." He considered the ivory dress and vest. "My sister is not here."

Pourry pondered this information as he glanced over the shrouded corpses. "I know nothing of a kidnapping, *monsieur*. You say a woman did all this?"

"Yes."

"On her own?"

"She is responsible for two deaths in New Orleans," Reynard said, "including a host of others from Boston down the eastern seaboard. She is extremely dangerous." He noted the incredulity on Pourry's face. "I suggest you write that down."

"Again, my pardon," Pourry said, "but this terrible scene is the work of...pirates or strife among the crew. The hold especially held a dangerous concentration of foul vapors, and such unhealthy air has been known to make men do all sorts of unnatural things." He motioned toward the exit. "Your description of the victims is most appreciated. If we have further need, I hope you can avail yourself to—"

"Write it down," Reynard said.

"—Assist us, as necessary. Please furnish Officer Janoux, the one who saw you aboard, the name of your hotel and your—"

"Write it down."

"I shall."

"Do it now."

"You may need some fresh air, *monsieur*," Pourry said. "You do look a little pale. Do you prefer to leave on your own?" He looked to two junior officers on the other side of the galley. "Or may I provide an escort?"

"Monsieur LaCroix," Kiria said, squeezing his arm. "I think I have seen quite enough today."

"Write it down," Reynard said firmly.

Pourry snapped his fingers and the two officers responded, moving around the galley. Reynard took Kiria's hand and led her toward the exit. The officers followed casually but steadily.

"Red hair," Reynard said, his voice rising. "My sister's name is spelled—"

Pourry's voice followed. "*Oui, monsieur.*"

හබ

Shadows lengthened along the quay as lamplighters began their duties. Kiria materialized into view of Savoy and Grant, who waited at the table of an outdoor café overlooking the sea. Her expression offered no relief.

"Where is Reynard?" Savoy asked.

"He will join us at the hotel," she said.

"Lasha. Is she...?"

"Three women are dead. One is my secretary. The other two are so badly..." She choked on her words. "Horrible."

Grant helped her take a seat, while Savoy ordered a round of hot cocoa and a platter heaped with warm rolls of *pain au chocolat*. They sat in silence for a time, drinking their cocoa and eating warm pastries.

"It is the crew of the *Kalabakang*," she started, "and my retinue. It was as if a deliberate...malice was manifested upon them. Such savagery. All the lifeboats are gone. The inspector presumes there was a riot, or mutiny."

"They cannot be serious," Savoy said.

"They suspect nothing, and everything," she said, sipping her cocoa. "This is delicious. You are very kind."

"It always lifts my spirits," he said, giving her a fatherly smile. He folded his arms and took a deep breath of thought. "The crew and passengers are slain and the ship set at full steam toward Marseille," he continued. "She knew we would attempt an interception here. Customs would have noted any change in the *Kalabakang's* itinerary."

"There is no itinerary. There is no record of anything."

"Of course," he said. "This way her road is erased."

"Miss Lasha—?" Grant asked.

"Is alive," Savoy said. "I am certain of it. I admit to some perverse admiration at this creature's audacity, her sheer lack of morality. I wonder if learning Reynard's whereabouts was the sole reason for visiting Marseille?" He leaned back in his chair, reaching down remove his leather notebook from his bag. "Have you ever met Professor Ernst Stronheim?"

"The name is not familiar," Kiria said.

"A mentor. He teaches in Vienna but enjoys a summer cottage in Cassis, not far from here. He is a trusted confidant in my work with Monsieur LaCroix. Some time ago I received a strange note." He removed Stronheim's letter from his notebook, allowing her to read:

Whited sepulchers beautiful outward, inside lie dead men's bones. Then Simon Peter having a sword drew it ... Then said Jesus unto Peter, Put up thy sword into the sheath: The Cup which my Father hath given me ... That ye may put difference between unclean and clean...

"I see," she said. "It is unusual."

He held up the letter's envelope. "It was posted from Sandakan. You see the stamp?"

"Curious."

"Is that where Lasha is going? To your father?"

"I do not understand," she said. "Father has always been a pillar of strength, an essential part of Her Majesty's success there. I cannot see how..."

"And yet you say he is dying."

"His curse has ruined him."

"Until he would go to any length?"

"I did not say that."

"And your valet?"

"Edward was not...obsessed, if that is what you mean."

"We may not be dealing with Edward Tukebote," Savoy said. "Who else might be obsessed for your father's well being, as you say?"

"I...I do not know," she said. "Not like this."

Beyond the docks and the high-masted ships, lamps glittered along the limestone hills rising on the other side of the harbor. At the highest point shone the Catholic basilica *Notre-Dame de la Garde*. It stood like a lighted beacon against the heavy darkness spreading inland from the sea. In the distance, a pleasant sound of provincial music wafted from another café. Grant had listened quietly during the exchange, drinking deeply from his mug.

"I've never left America," he said. "Now here I am, eating fancy bread and chocolate."

"We will return on a better occasion, my boy." Savoy gave him a pat on his arm. "Yet Miss Lasha still requires our help."

"I'll trust in that."

"This creature is a blasphemy. I mean to see it pay for its crimes."

೮つ೧೪

A petite blond woman seated at the next table stood, smoothed wrinkles from her white dress, and left the remains of her half-eaten supper without a gratuity. She pulled long strands of her golden hair behind her ears, tucking her parasol under her arm, as she worked her way around the tables to exit the café.

She noticed men turning their heads—subtle, trying not to be noticed, but she saw them looking. She could feel their eyes on her, drifting across her pretty face, imaginations leering past her dress and petticoat and garters to the smooth curve of her stomach and breasts and thighs.

You bastards and your lusts, she thought with disgust, *undressing women with your minds*. She wanted to tear open their throats and lap the liquor from their veins.

Animals they were, all of them. Animals wearing men's skin.

Blasphemy, professor? You have no idea.

19

When Reynard descended the gangplank off the *Kalabakang*, he had bid Kiria Carlovec good evening and walked in the opposite direction. He did not look back.

He dissolved into the randomness of the city, down narrow brick alleys, across wide avenues where carts and coaches shared the road with the autobus, slipping again into less traveled lanes to avoid the glare of lamps. He reconnected with Rue Canebière and continued inland, making distance between himself and the stinking quay. He ignored beggars who cried out to him. He passed the occasional uniformed *gendarmes* out patrolling their beat, resisting the urge to bury his fist between their eyes.

He turned south along Rue Saint-Ferréol where the crowds faded into the sound of his own footsteps. The further he walked, the more the buildings began to change; whitewashed plaster buildings and framed European tenements gave way to older shops with rounded archways, the grays and eggshell blues fading into browns and adobe. He passed cafés selling shaved pork and couscous, the dimly-lit streets redolent with urine and spices. Without a coat he plunged his hands into his pockets and tightened his arms against his body, his thoughts so pervasive he barely noticed the darkness coming on.

He considered what he might accomplish, what a few hundred francs might buy. Records could be procured. Men could be bought. In seventy-two hours he could learn every unscheduled stop of the

Kalabakang, who descended and who boarded, the exact nature of its cargo. For another hundred francs he might even learn what every member of its crew had for breakfast.

She could be anywhere.

Lasha and her captor could already be slumming on a low-cost steamer through the Suez, riding ponies on one of the Napoleonic roads through Italy, on a rickety train to Istanbul or headed over the Juras for Germany. She could be lying under a tarpaulin in a filthy galley, wearing her favorite evening dress, festering in a—

No, he commanded himself. *No.*

She is alive.

He forced himself to think of Kiria Carlovec, the gentle curve of her throat and the straight line of her jaw, the black eyebrows she meticulously plucked until they arched like thin lines of ink. He imagined her smell, like coffee and roses, the way she walked by placing each foot *just so*. She was a careful, calculated thing, someone whose composure made him suspect duplicity. But why? Promote an image that was not her own? Or manage a life fraught with more horror than she cared to admit?

He could not deny her courage aboard the *Kalabakang*. A lesser woman would have fainted at the sight of such violence. A lesser man would have emptied his stomach all over the floor, but he managed to stay strong because...

Because?

Because she was there beside him?

It was on Rue Paradis when he realized he was being followed.

He caught the rhythm early, the same *clack, clack, clack* of footsteps for three, perhaps four blocks. By the gait he knew it was a woman, matching his pace some ten yards behind. She had slowed when he slowed, accelerated when he did. He did not pause to look. He continued straight but focused on the sounds of her movement—stockings sliding against a petticoat, the swish of a hem as it brushed against the sidewalk. He tilted his head and inhaled, hoping to catch a scent of perfume. The stink of horse manure permeated the street.

At a fruit stand he feigned an interest, pausing to admire a stack of mandarins, stealing a glance as she passed: a petite blond woman in a white dress and heeled boots with a closed parasol at her shoulder, her hair wrapped in a psyche knot and tied with a white bow. She passed, continued a half block further, and Reynard followed. Downwind, he could now smell her—like lavender and soap, a scent like—

Lasha?

He accelerated as pedestrians filled the gap. She crossed the street. He stepped off the curb only to stop, retreat, as an omnibus clacked between them. When it finally moved aside, she was gone.

He dashed across the street. Beyond waited the sprawling outdoor Immigrant's Market: clustered tents and canopies squatted around a large public square beside carts filled with fruits and vegetables, antiques, old books, kitchenware, pots, clothing, spices, furniture, rugs, baskets, and rolls upon rolls of multi-colored fabric. Voices came from customers and vendors alike—French, Arabic, German, Italian. Amid many lanterns, they haggled and wandered and reveled in the lovely chaos of commerce.

Reynard plunged into the midst. He passed old men crying for his attention, women displaying bottles and beads as if they hawked treasures along the dusty streets of Egypt. A bonfire burned in the center of the square where men with fez hats danced to wooden *dumbeks* and an out-of-tune, guitar-like *oud*.

There he saw her, illuminated by the bonfire's flickering light.

She was looking at him.

What am I doing?

Reynard retreated into the crowd, heart hammering against his chest, his face burning with shame. She was not following him—he had been following *her*. All evening he had been looking, *hunting* for any girl who bore the least resemblance to his sister. What would he have said if he caught her? Ask her name? Grab her shoulders and embrace her, frighten her, demand she forgive him, assure him—

Would you terribly mind if I called you Lasha?

He pulled himself from the market and regained the street. With a quick touch at his belly he was glad his money belt was still there; perhaps he could find a pub. Perhaps they served vodka.

He left, and did not look back. Had he done so, he would have seen her looking with a smile. Watching.

20

Kiria ran down many steps carved from rock, deep into a cold, heavy darkness. Her footing failed. She reached to steady herself against the side of the stone wall and gritty slime oozed over her fingers. She recoiled, impulsively popping her fingers into her mouth. The taste of slime—rancid, heavy with vinegar—made her retch.

Ahead, the air rattled with angry words, climaxing with a bloodcurdling scream.

Go back, she thought. *Go back. Why is she screaming?*

Shadows spilled away and orange light stabbed her eyes, the air was saturated with smoke and the sickly-sweet nectar of death. Here was her dream-place, a gaping maw of a cavern rising high above her head and falling below her feet like some cavernous pocket of Hell.

Human bones piled at her feet. A thousand skulls leered, mandibles gaping, ribcages, vertebrae and spines, countless little bones, heaps like piles of discarded ivory, the lot slippery with slime. The stairs were gone, the firelight gone, the dark heavy with the same graveyard stink. She touched at her face, reminding herself she was alive.

Alive!

Rotten hands slid up her legs. Bony fingers grabbed like spiders and pulled, tugged, until she fell into the nest of skeletal bodies. She kicked and screamed. Bony hands crawled into her mouth. Brittle fingers pressed against her eyelids, forced them open. In the midst of that squirming pile of dead she saw the woman's face, the same charcoal flesh and muscle stretched over blackened bone, eyes melted from their sockets, her long hair black like burnt glass and stinking of lye.

At first Kiria thought this horrible apparition was her mother, long dead. Then it became Miss Lourdes, then a native Dayak woman with charred tattoos splattered across her face, then another woman and another and another and another, a thousand women screaming until there was nothing but a skull wreathed in dead hair.

The apparition smiled her lipless smile, and drew her in.

My little girl.

She awoke.

She wept bitterly at that last, horrible image, willing herself to breathe, pressing her hands against her face as she sobbed at her poisonous terror. The sight of that terrible woman with her ruined face dominated the reality of the silk sheets, the ordinary ticking of a clock, the smells of cool air and candles and canna lilies.

She reached for a match with trembling hands, lighting four candles set in a candelabra on her bedstand. Each successive light revealed broad curtains of ruffled taffeta, a stuffed embroidered chair and sofa, a sitting desk with its requisite writing set, and more vases of cannas that, as she considered it, felt more appropriate for a funeral parlor. They had chosen the *Hotel Vauban* because it stubbornly refused the encroachment of modern thinking; it carried no electricity, no telephone. No one could bother them. The dusty smell, coupled with the chill, meant the coal in the furnace had long died.

The memories of the *Kalabakang*'s galley returned and she willed them away. She commanded herself to keep breathing, to think of her friend Marion's happy face, her laughter, the delicate way she ate, the fine curves of her handwriting, how she blushed when a gentleman spoke to her. Kiria tried to think of beaches and hot cocoa and palm trees, the colors of her garden, the smells of begonias, the morning church bells from the hilltop—

My little girl.

"Go away," she whispered.

At first her dreams were came inanimate and bodiless, but in recent weeks they clarified until she feared she was going mad. Some days the residue lasted for hours; more than once she spent a large portion of a day on the ship's deck during the Atlantic crossing, hoping the air and spray might make her feel clean.

She lifted her hands to wipe her tears and recoiled, expecting slime.

A dream, a dream, a dream.

She examined her chewed fingernails, the cracks in her knuckles.

Marion. She began to cry.

I'm so sorry.

She rolled to her side and clutched her pillow between her breasts. Her body felt too small and too frail as if the sadness, the loneliness, might tear open her skin.

How can anyone bear such pain?

A faint knocking rapped at her door. She sat up, startled.

"Miss Carlovec?"

Reynard.

They had not seen him, had not heard a word since he left the quay. She looked to the clock on the mantle: seventeen minutes past midnight. She felt equally embarrassed and irritated, surprised at his audacity, at the softness of his voice.

"Miss Carlovec," he said. "Do you need assistance?"

"I am fine," she said.

"Pardon?"

"Just a moment."

She climbed out of bed, pulled a shawl over her shoulders and shuffled to the door, feeling a disaster, wishing Reynard would just go away. He had heard her sobbing. She took a deep breath.

"It is after midnight," she said through the door.

"May I speak with you?" he asked.

"No."

"Please."

"You forget your manners," she said. She envisioned him standing there, his gaze boring into the wood. She pulled the shawl tighter. "We can all meet for breakfast."

"I shan't manage a minute's rest," he said.

"That is not my concern."

"I shall sleep out here in the hall."

"Do not make a fool of yourself."

"Too late for that."

"Blazes," she said with a sigh. "You must wait."

She took her time. She washed her face, combed her hair, and slid a heavy cotton robe over her cambric nightgown and silk undergarments. She pulled her dark tresses behind her shoulders and tied them with ribbon, sliding errant strands out of her face. She slid her bare feet into a pair of slippers, making sure the hem of her nightgown hung low enough to hide the olive tease of her calves. The last thing she needed was to enflame the man's base instincts, especially this time of night.

Just go away.

She opened the door a crack, hoping he had left. He was still there, pacing, wearing his open-collared white shirt, brown vest and slacks, his black leather shoes. At first he did not notice her, too engrossed picking at a fingernail with his teeth.

"Yes," she said.

He stopped, red-faced. "My apologies, but I could not help—"

"Are you eavesdropping?"

"No. I...I've only just arrived. Passing by I thought I heard, well, I was concerned that—"

"I cannot imagine what you think you heard."

"Oh." He looked at her, confused. "I—"

"Good night."

"I suppose you do not want to admit it," he said. "One cannot see such horrors and not be affected. May I come in?"

"Excuse me?"

"I must speak with you."

"Are you drunk?"

"No." That sent him pacing again, like a caged animal. "Well *yes*, perhaps, I don't know. Not particularly. I have gone over everything. I see those people in that horrible ship, imagine Lasha lying there. I hear you weeping, and then I—"

She flushed. "It was unexpected."

"But appropriate."

She looked up and down the hallway, her hand clutching the collar of her robe. She had allowed this conversation to go on far too long.

Someone might be wandering the halls. They might see her in her nightgown with a man just outside her door. What would people say?

"Good night, *monsieur*," she said.

"I still have questions."

"Tomorrow."

He approached the door and she closed it, softly, listening to his breath and restless movement on the carpet. He was not a man to be ordered about, especially from her. Would he scream and tear at the latch? Would he rail at the servants and smash bottles against the fireplace? She had seen what Basta's Legacy had done to her father—was Reynard LaCroix just as tormented? Would he rise up like a wild animal?

"Miss Carlovec," he said through the door.

Go away.

"You have not been honest with me."

"I told you the truth," she said.

"I find that hard to believe."

"Leave me alone."

"This is my sister we are—!" He caught himself, lowering his voice. "There is a private balcony at the end of this hall. Meet me there in five minutes."

"That is not—"

"Five minutes."

"I will not be ordered about," Kiria said, throwing open the door. It startled him. "There is nothing I can say that will satisfy you. I am as much a victim as—"

"We are here because of you."

"We are here because you refused me."

"I refused you," Reynard said, his voice rising, "because your journey was marked by murder. Two men are dead. My sister is captive. You have seen what this creature is capable. How could you have traveled so long, so far with your valet and not suspect something?"

"I told you."

"You've told me nothing, Miss—"

"I do not approve of your tone," she said. "Since you continue to refuse my requests, let me be frank. You have treated me with disdain from the very first. You have offered me naught but doubt and suspicion.

Mister Savoy and Mister Grant have accepted my story, but you speak to me only when you wish to order me about, or rail on me for offences I did not commit. There is nothing I can say that will satisfy you."

"How did you learn about me?" he asked. "About my condition?"

"My father," she said.

"How did he know?"

"Leave me alone."

She shut the door hard, latched it.

"Tell me!" he cried on the other side.

Her heart hammered so hard against her chest she could feel it in her throat. She heard him move. She reached for an iron-wrought chair, forcing it up against the doorknob, expecting the door to thud, the hinges to squeal as he forced his body against it. She waited like a taut wire, expecting the doorjamb to break and the chair to spin away.

Nothing happened. She sat on the edge of her bed. She felt Reynard's anger and frustration as bitterly as her own. She wanted to scream at his rudeness, his brazen indifference and lack of manners. She wanted to beg his forgiveness. She wanted to tell him he was a fool, a cruel, heartless fool at his the presumption that she was responsible for all his troubles.

But he was right. He was *right*!

What could she tell him? Nameless fears? Nightmares of dark stairs and a cavernous hell full of bones? She had agreed to her father's mandate, her eyes wide shut, because it was her family—the very survival of the Carlovec line—that mattered. It was not her father she was trying to save, but herself, forever safe from Basta's dreadful curse. How could she admit that every moment in Reynard's presence—every *moment*—filled her with a choking dread, as she waited for his passions to consume him?

What could she say to him?

She removed her slippers and robe and crawled back into bed, pulling the covers up tight to her chin. She listened to Reynard pacing in the hallway.

Let him rail. Let him pout!

She envisioned him grabbing the knob and leaning his shoulder into the door, shoving until the latch broke. She imagined his body standing in the doorway. She thought what she might say, how she might scream.

Perhaps he would cross that invisible barrier, put his hands upon her shoulders and throw her onto the mattress. She considered the musky smell of his neck, the faint aroma of vodka and cologne, and wondered if his hands were soft.

What if he did, she thought.

What if he did?

She clutched her pillow tight and willed him to leave.

Just leave.

Reynard would have pounded his fists into the wall if it did not mean waking half the floor. The tension in his neck and arms had no release. Why did she refuse to speak with him?

He suddenly realized what she must have thought.

It's not what I meant.

The damage was done. She must have thought him a drunken lout, red-faced with lust, a genuine bastard. Here he was, standing alone in the hotel hallway, confused and stupid and angry. He considered how things had gone so badly. When it came to speaking with the female sex, it did not matter what was said. He always managed to offend them.

He placed his hand into his pocket, his fingers brushing against the misshapen remains of the silver bullet. Of *course* she thought he was drunk; he smelled like the floor of a gin parlor. Would she believe him if he said he spent most of his time just sitting, nursing drinks he never finished, preoccupied with his thoughts?

He went to his room, adjacent to hers. His luggage sat at the foot of his bed, a peppermint and card of welcome resting on his pillow. One of the windows had been pulled up halfway, allowing in cool air. He poured water into a china basin, washed his face, pushing his head into the water until his nose pressed against the bottom. To bury himself in water and never surface—it was a comforting thought.

With his towel around his neck he collapsed upon the bed and kicked his shoes to the floor. He did not bother to undress. He crunched on the peppermint and tossed the welcome card aside.

Sleep caught him without his knowing. Dreams came as a dull, heavy fog of shapeless colors. He saw a forest of tall stones, misshapen tombs rising from the mist, sepulchers carved with granite faces of cherubs staring with dead eyes. Stone angels wept, faces half-hidden by their hands, their wide, pale eyes staring at him through their fingers.

His dream-hands found the metal chain around his neck, the one holding the silver cross Savoy had given him; his skin felt warm where it rested against his flesh. Or was it the bullet, burning its hot-poker fire in his heart? Or was it the scratching, the incessant raking of claws in the back of his brain?

Renny.

Half-formed pictures came and went: shapes of women in white dresses, hands on his face and neck and chest, and the outlines of dead faces under black sheets—a nebulous chain of incomprehensible phantasms.

Renny.

He dreamed of a little girl, or the idea of a little girl, for he could not see her face. At times she stood as tall as he, then she became a tiny shadow on a very wide wall. He focused on her voice, concentrated on it, so he might see her clearly.

Renny.

He opened his eyes.

He recognized his hotel room, the fireplace and sitting chairs to his right, the window to his left. Outside he heard the clopping of hooves and the rattle of a coach, fading, the cracking of a crop, the *clack clack clack* of shoes. Then it grew silent as if the city held its breath.

He looked again.

A woman stood at the foot of his bed.

The lights of the street refused to play across her, but he knew it was his sister. This did not surprise him; she often visited his dreams. At first he thought she was ten years old again, but when he blinked he she wore her long, frilly nightdress with its high collar and long sleeves, her golden hair loose behind her shoulders. He could not see her feet, but he suspected she wore her favorite pair of white-and-pink striped stockings.

"Lasha?" he asked.

Help me.

"Where are you?"

Pray for me, Renny.

At the feet of Our Lady.

There was much he wanted to say, to beg forgiveness, to convince her what she thought she saw in Metairie was not true. He wanted to declare that *yes*, the curse had him, but he was not a monster. He would cross the world to bring her home. He was not a monster. He would never hurt her. He had hurt others, yes, but never her.

Pray, Renny. Pray beneath Our Good Mother's feet.

Blood surged from the crook of her neck, down her white nightdress, fingering in long tendrils across her bodice, dripping until blood pooled at her feet. When she inhaled she gasped, the color in her skin so pale it was translucent, the bones of her skull gaping.

"Lasha!"

It hurts.

Reynard sat up. "Lasha!"

Please.

The skin of her face melted, nose and lips and eyebrows sliding off her head like hot wax to expose a mummified mask—lipless, ancient, skin pulled taut against her skull like a thin veil of silk. Her neck arched backwards with a crack, her muscles tightening. She lifted from the floor, a twisted mannequin on invisible strings.

On the shore of the River of Death—

"Lasha! Where are you?"

—Pray for me.

"Lasha!"

Reynard slid off the bed. She was gone. He stood dumbfounded, yet absolutely certain he had seen his sister. He touched his sweaty face and felt tears on his cheeks, and when he inhaled he smelled Lasha's scent. It had felt so real. It had to be.

Pray.

He knew exactly where she wanted him to go. Our Lady. A little more than a mile from their hotel stood the tallest hill of the city where, at its crest, waited the basilica *Notre Dame de la Garde*. It had been build upon a great spike of limestone, its foundations set into much older fortifications. Upon its highest tower stood the gilded statue of Mother Mary with the Christ Child in her arms. Our Lady kept guard over the sea and, for reasons yet unknown, Lasha wanted him there.

You are mad.

Perhaps, he considered as he slipped on his shoes, but it was something. Something. Even if the horror aboard the *Kalabakang* had fractured his mind into pieces, he would rather follow the bidding of a hallucination than lie there helpless, grief-stricken, wondering every day if his sister—the last hope for the LaCroix Family—might be gone forever.

He left his room, closed the door quietly.

"I'm coming."

21

He ran along Marseille's dark streets, aiming for the tall hill where the basilica shone at its peak. He crossed an empty avenue and plunged into the scrubby pines of the hillside, the *Bois Sacré*, following a trail hundreds of years old. He knew the way well enough, having climbed it many times in his youth. He trusted his instincts as he raced up the broken path, back and forth up steep grades.

At the top of the hill he continued up the white steps of the stone fort—the foundation upon which the basilica had been built—and crossed the broad esplanade. He avoided the glow of electric lanterns, splashed across the basilica's outer walls. With its alternating bands of light- and dark-colored stone, its large dome, the tall belltower capped with the golden statue of Mary holding Her Child, the church stood as a symbol of Marseille's disparate personality: a blend of Roman Catholic and Byzantine, old world and new.

At the front entrance Reynard gazed at the familiar statues of the prophet Isaiah and Saint John the Apostle. They watched as he dared cross the threshold beneath the tympanum. He felt like a criminal.

I do not belong here.

He *was* a criminal, invading this sacred place.

Yet he *had* been invited, hadn't he?

He pushed against the bronze doors. They were unlocked. That should have worried him, but as they opened soundlessly, drawn forward with a strange feeling of inevitability, he moved inside. Diffused light illuminated the chapel proper, but the inverted dome and the many mosaics above his head were completely invisible. The basilica chapel felt vast in its darkness. Along the walls hung small wooden boats, photos of sailors, scraps of sails or ribbons or trinkets or old paintings, offerings of those who prayed for safe passage on the sea.

He found the tower stairwell and climbed the steps. It was a long walk, over a hundred feet past the belfry and its silent bells to emerge outside again—the Angel's Terrace, where an angelic statue blew a trumpet at each corner. Reynard paused to catch his breath, his lungs burning. The lights of Marseille, far below, surrounded him like so many pale stars. Beyond the coastline lay a scattering of bare, rugged islands where the Mediterranean black stretched away and disappeared.

Rising in the center of the terrace lay a giant pedestal surrounded by columns, forty feet tall or more. At its top stood the massive golden statues of Mary holding the infant Christ. They gazed over the sea, indifferent to his presence.

Pray at Her feet.

Reynard skirted the pedestal and found another unlocked door; he passed inside and climbed a short stair to a tall, cylindrical chamber. Cold air slid from between the columns. He had expected a lighthouse, a large bell, an altar, *something*—not a bare room exposed to the wind. A good leap between a pair of columns, he considered, and he could sail over the terrace rail and recite the alphabet before his head splattered across the esplanade.

He looked up, imagining the soles of Mary's gilded feet.

Here I am.

Fool. He was a fool! He had come all this way, only to stir from some waking dream. He considered his hands, at the city lights beyond the columns, the wind biting against his face. A nightmare. He thought certain it was Lasha, thought sure he had seen her, heard her voice. It had felt so real.

She's dead, came the despair. *She's dead.*

Emptiness filled the hole where his heart should have been. He put his hand into his pocket and gripped the silver bullet, squeezing it tight as if to leech the silver into his skin.

Dead.

A faint light caught his attention. It was a lantern, flickering fitfully against the breeze, set on the floor some distance to his right. Had it always been there? He approached and picked it up, its light pushing away the thick shadows.

A slender white shape crouched on the far side of the chamber, moving rhythmically as if lapping at water. Beneath this laid a smaller shape outstretched upon the stone floor, pale and small and moaning a piteous cry. Reynard raised the lantern higher. A woman in a white dress suckled at a bloody wound from the crook of a little girl's shoulder. The girl was no older than eight or nine years old. When she started to cry the woman smothered her mouth with her hand and continued drinking, slurping with a dull sound of pleasure.

"What the hell is this?" he said.

The woman stood. She wiped her mouth with her sleeve, blood staining the white fabric. Terror seized him—it was *her*, the woman from the Immigrant's Market. She no longer looked like Lasha; the turn of a head, the wide look in her eyes, the thin-lipped, oversized mouth. There was something familiar about her now, like a fell bird crouching over its prey, much like—

"Where is Lasha?" he demanded.

"You took something of mine," she said.

"I have nothing."

She laughed. "That bullet was an infestation. I saved you by removing it."

"Who do you think you are? I do not know you."

"Of course you do," she said. "Now give it back."

"I have nothing to give."

She clapped her hands together. "Oh good, *good*. You continue to lie to me. It makes things so much easier when I must hurt you. I *want* to hurt you, Renny." She extended her hand. "Give it to me."

His fingers slid back into his pocket. "You lured me here," he said, "for a bit of silver? Your Master Carlovec needn't have bothered."

Her smile disappeared. "He is not my master."

"You are his bitch."

She slapped him across the face, hard, the chamber echoing with a resounding *crack*. His head recoiled against the blow but he did not move, did not cry out, glaring at her as the ruddy imprints of her fingers materialized upon his cheek. The blow cleared his head. There was a girl— a real little girl—lying on the floor with her blood pouring from her throat. He tried to move toward her, to help her, and found no will in it. When he considered moving his legs he heard only the woman's voice in the back of his head.

The little girl started to cry again. She coughed and her blood pumped faster from the crook of her neck, draining along the stone floor. Reynard inhaled and caught the scent. He thought of the galley of the *Kalabakang*, the filthy square with Bill Tourney's body, the taste of a man's throat where granite vaults watched.

Down deep, a dull thirst grew inside his belly.

"You feel it," the woman said.

"No."

"You beg for the animal, crave it, *ache* for it. You want it to slide over your skin and cover you." She brushed her finger along his shoulder. "I could sing to you, and the animal would come. All I need to say is *come out, my darling, come out* and your body would release into my hands." Her fingers caressed his neck. "*Come out.* Doesn't that sound exciting?"

"Not particularly."

"We know what it means to suffer. We have given up everything, lost everything, and yet we keep living." She pressed her body against him. "You suffer, Renny."

"Leave me alone."

The little girl moaned, her breath rapid and shallow, inexorably getting slower with each exhale. Reynard felt her life slip away long before he saw her chest stop moving, long before the last of her color drained from her face. He wanted to scream, to rail, to beg this woman to release him so he might *do* something! Yet he could not move. The woman's lips brushed his cheek as she whispered, her mouth getting closer, her words steaming like smoke into his head.

"*Come out,*" she said.

"Stop."

"*Come out.*"

"Stop."

"Help me," she said, "and save us both."

Reynard strained against the desire raging deep inside himself—*out, out, out*—and then she was wrapped upon him as a lover. The curves of her shape pressed against his own.

Come out.

She kissed him. First along his neck and edge of his jaw, then she drew his lip into her mouth and bit through the rind of his flesh. He winced. She suckled his lip, drinking, pulling him tight against her body with every swallow. Pain ached down his neck to his scar, mingled with dull lust, and he forced himself to burrow through those memories he desperately kept away:

—Burning ropes burning wrists and ankles—

—cutting oozing—

—high heady laughter—

—his laughing, sallow face—

—fingers cutting into his chest, clawing bloody—

—Lasha screaming screaming screaming—

"*I said stop!*" he shouted.

He shoved her away. She grinned with hateful eyes and started for him again, her lips smeared with his blood. In a wide sweep, he raised the oil lantern and smashed it across her head.

The woman's head ignited as flames burst down her neck and shoulders. She fell back, shrieking. The skin of her face tightened against her skull with shades of another woman, and another, and another, then a man with high cheekbones and forehead, then a shade of Frederick Burlington in a gaping mask of horror. At the last came the reflection of Edward Tukebote. It lasted only a moment before her face simply became death—the head of a lidless corpse.

"I will drink her," she hissed, as the flames died. "I will drink Lasha dry and tell her you are a monster, that you gave her to me."

Reynard removed the silver cross from around his neck and raised it up. She grabbed the cross with both hands and crushed the token like brittle paper, throwing the useless metal to the floor. She slashed her fingernails across his stomach, the sharp edges tearing through cloth from his navel to his throat. Blood splashed. He doubled over and stumbled back, gasping.

"*Ici,*" a man's voice cried outside. "*Viens!*"

From the stairwell outside came the rattle of many footsteps, the slam of a door being forcibly opened. The woman laughed—first a subtle sound, deep in her abdomen, then a shrill cackling. She extended her hand. The remains of the silver bullet gleamed in the center of her open palm. She slid it into her grinning mouth, her tongue drawing it into the hollow of her right cheek. Reynard's bloodied hands became frantic as he searched every pocket along his trousers and shirt.

The bullet was gone.

She pressed a finger to her withered lips with a naughty smile. "Get off!" she cried loudly in French. "Get your hands off me, *salaud!*" She gasped with a throaty moan. "*Get your filthy body off me!*"

She turned and ran across the room. Reynard started after her, to catch her, dully realizing the ramifications of this final game she played—and could only watch as she slipped between two of the columns. She leaped and hurled herself into the air. She flew over the terrace railing and fell, fell, screaming with a horrible grin on her face. She stared at him as she plummeted off the high spire of Notre Dame, *watched* him, until the shadows swallowed her up.

The door to the chamber flew open. Four *gendarmes* spilled inside, police officers garbed in dark blue cloaks and caps, bringing chaos as wild lights and shouting as someone commanded *see who fell outside!* Two men turned back. The remaining two thundered up the steps, their lantern lights blazing over Reynard. He stood with blood soaking his shirt and hands, a dead girl on the floor behind him.

"No," he started, shaking. "It's not what you—"

The officers slid batons from their belts. Reynard lunged at them. He plowed between them and knocked them aside. He fled down the steps out the open door. He ran across the Angel's Terrace, plunged into the belfry, and started down the stairwell.

"He is up here!" a voice echoed at his back.

"Hurry," Reynard shouted down the stairwell, "a man's crossing the esplanade, heading south for the steps! He's not alone!"

"—Up here!"

"—Faster, before he reaches the *Bois Sacré!*—"

"—Don't listen—!"

"—Right below you!" Reynard added.

Every man shouted up and down the stairwell, those both ahead of him and following behind. Some gave contradictory orders. Others shouted for everyone to keep quiet. Reynard kept his pace as he descended, gripped with rage at having been played, at having lost the bullet, at his naïveté. He raged at the dull, heavy sensation prickling at his spine, commanding his weak and faithless body to ignore that horrible woman's voice as it encouraged the Beast to emerge.

Out, out, out—

"Turn around, you fools!" someone shouted from above. Below, footsteps stopped, paused, started back up the steps. "He's up here!"

Reynard froze. He had about thirty seconds before he was pinned between two groups of policemen who would pummel him with their batons—if he was lucky. To his right, a shallow balcony overlooked the spine of the chapel's roof. He did not think. He crawled over the balcony's rim and dropped ten feet onto the iron ridge flashing. The roof led straight to the Byzantine dome where, he hoped, he could skirt its perimeter to another balcony on the far side. His impact was loud but he ran, knowing they would hear him, desperate to get distance.

Behind him came a loud *crack* and a metallic squeal off to his right— a bullet ricochet—as two officers dropped off the balcony in pursuit. A third in the window raised his pistol for another shot. It fired.

A heavy burning exploded in Reynard's left shoulder, flinging him hard to his stomach, sending him tumbling down the steep flashing. He scrambled to catch himself as he slid off the roof and into open air.

He dropped.

Twelve feet below lay a stone veranda. He landed hard, knocking the wind from his lungs, firing pain through his ribs and into his throat. Somehow he got to his feet. He burst through a wooden door into the basilica and sprinted down a twisting stairwell, gasping, the muscles in his thighs and forearms tightening like leather straps. The edges of his vision began to darken.

Keep moving!

He descended lower and lower down the steps, expecting to emerge into the nave or one of the transepts, and then he reached the bottom and shouldered his way through another door into a flickering dark. Polychrome mosaics at his feet dazzled his senses, the sweeping curves of the ceiling and the iron-wrought bars surrounding the basilica's lower crypt. Dozens of votive candles burned in black sconces, bathing the crypt in deep, orange light.

He dropped to his knees. He could not breathe. Pain fired from the base of his spine into his lower gut. His teeth clenched so tightly his jaw shifted from its place in his skull, sending racking pain through his head and into his neck.

Come out.

The Beast was his, not a dog to come at that whore's beck and call. His!

"It's not time," he whispered, shaking.

It's mine!

Save me—

Mine!

—Slide over your skin.

Lasha's voice shrieked, *What have you done to him?*

—Slide over my skin.

It is still you, Renny. Your hair, your blood, your bones.

Save me—

If it is still you, then—

—Save—

—Your reason and ethics must also remain.

—Animal—

—Pushed aside in some darker place.

He fell to his face, tremors cascading up his legs and down his arms, his body drawn taut until his head touched his knees. Pale, prickly hairs, beaded with blood, stiffened on his arms and legs. The stitching on his shirt and vest began to give.

Pushed aside—aside—push it aside—

"It's not time!" he screamed.

Footsteps pounded on the ceiling. Another involuntary spasm sent him groaning, joints cracking as bones shifted in his wrists and ankles. The taste of coppery blood filled his mouth.

—Not—

A door slammed open. Footsteps thundered down steps. His eyes caught the bars of a wide grate set in the floor. He crawled to it. He looked through and saw a shaft dropping into the dark. He pulled the grate free and discovered a strange thing: an iron ladder dropping down the side of the shaft. He guessed it was part of the ancient sewer system, the old bones of a foundation that the basilica had been built upon, and that meant he might—

A latch quivered. Muffled voices.

Metal jingled—keys—a latch squealed.

Reynard looked at his long and crooked hands, his fingernails bleeding, and when he closed his mouth his teeth cut through his upper lip. He sucked at his own blood, voracious, wondering if Savoy would notice he was missing, if Lasha—

—Lasha?

Who? He tried to remember.

A pale girl bleeding on the floor?

"Inside," came a muffled cry.

He crawled into the shaft, replaced the grate, and descended.

22

Upon disembarking at Cassis Station, Savoy headed east on a rented one-horse cariole, following a winding road with an excellent view. The sea swelled against the shoreline cliffs. He thought about what he might say if Ernst Stronheim was lodging at his winter retreat, what questions he might ask. There was scant guarantee he would be there.

It cannot be coincidence, he decided. *Of all the ports along the Mediterranean coast, why would the Kalabakang stop here?*

Yet the further he traveled, the worse he felt.

I do not believe in coincidence.

He had first encountered Doctor Stronheim at the University of Vienna, a prominent biology and philosophy instructor at the time, back in the day when Savoy's family lived in Berne and still bore the ancestral name *Soloveichik*. Ernst proved a man of keen intellect and reason, but maintained enough of a rebellious curiosity to expand his thinking beyond the narrow-mindedness of academia. From the very start, the two men got along famously. In time, Stronheim guided and supported him, encouraged him to follow any path he wished to take.

Savoy saw no such support from his own father. *You betray your name and your people and your history,* his father had said, soon after the family's arrival in London. Artémius Soloveichik had announced he would become Artémius Savoy and, even worse, baptized in the Catholic Church. *You betray God himself, clamoring after their false messiah.*

Years later, Savoy wondered if guilt and fear contributed to his decision. Jews were objects of derision, even in progressive London, when many men and women changed their names to avoid the anti-Semitism boiling beneath the surface. Following his father's angry claims there came more words, raised voices, his mother weeping. It ended when Savoy left his family's house vowing never to return.

He did not see his father again until he watched his coffin lowered into the ground. Even then, he watched from a distance.

Blazes, but he missed the old man.

Why think of his father now?

Within an hour he arrived upon a high ridge overlooking the sea; at the end of a long driveway stood a gabled cottage. Weeds choked the front lawn, the worn fence leaning too far, the front steps strewn with drifts of sand. He had never seen the place looking so shabby. Ernst usually employed a housekeeper to maintain the house when he was away. When Savoy knocked, the front door pushed inward.

"Ernst?"

He walked inside, cautiously. It was the smell that struck him—bitter, like spilled milk. Dust frosted the chairs and sofas of the parlor, cobwebs stretching between the bedposts in the master bedroom. Flies flitted about in the kitchen above a tin of rotten herring, the floor scattered with rat pellets and tiny bones.

He entered Ernst's study. Books and papers, textbooks and tomes and first-edition books—dumped from the many bookshelves, shredded, torn apart, the floor ankle-deep in ruined papers and broken artifacts. A statue of the Egyptian god Horus, dated from the fifth dynasty, had been bludgeoned against the wall and beheaded. Savoy rushed to the hearth in horror, discovering in the ashes the charred remains of a 500-year old hand-lettered Latin page from the Book of Psalms.

He sat down in Ernst's great leather chair, overwhelmed. If this was the work of thieves, then why the vandalism? Professor Stronheim had the dubious habit of examining—and often discrediting—many religious artifacts around the world. His stern rebuttal against a piece of the true cross, found at the Santo Toribio de Liébana monastery, led to many critics accusing him of blasphemy. Could one of them have done this?

You don't believe that, do you?

Savoy left the study and descended into the basement, down where Ernst kept more fragile manuscripts in the cool, consistent dark. Lighting a lantern he discovered even more bookshelves broken, cast down, their contents as ruined as the rest. A larger shape, heaped against one bookshelf, caught his attention.

A rotten corpse lay on the floor.

It was the remains of an old woman, long dead. He guessed it was the housekeeper. Her neck had been snapped rudely to one side, her mouth agape with a surprised expression. Savoy pressed his sleeve against his nose—he had discovered the source of the stink—feeling as if a lending room of the Library of Alexandria had been torn apart and the librarian found dead.

For what purpose? Why destroy Ernst's prized collection, kill an innocent old woman and leave her to rot? To discover Reynard's whereabouts?

No, he reasoned. It was more than that.

"What did she say?" he said to himself. He considered the previous night, of Kiria's testimony of the horrors aboard the *Kalabakang*. "'...As if a deliberate malice had been manifested upon them.'"

It was late afternoon when Savoy arrived back at Cassis Station, only to find a telegram waiting at the ticket office:

NOTRE DAME DE LA GARDE
MEET THERE NOW GRANT

He went immediately to the basilica the moment his train arrived in Marseille. By the time he arrived, the church grounds were already swarming with uniformed officers. Police carts littered the drive. An ambulance with four horses waited on the far side of the yard, and beside it a man in a white coat conversed with two policemen. Another officer guided two mastiffs on taut ropes; the dogs sniffed and barked and tugged at their leashes as they made a slow and careful search along the grounds.

Savoy found Grant at the outer rim of the organized chaos, away from a modest crowd of people trying to catch a glimpse, sitting on a stone bench. Grant handed him a rolled up newspaper, the evening edition of *La Provence*:

Expatriate sought in brutal slaying of woman and child.

Savoy read the article, then read it again. He read it a third time. Police had arrived at the high tower, led by a tip from a confidential source. They discovered Reynard with a dead girl at his feet, blood on his clothing, and the remains of a headless woman splattered near the basilica's foundation. Police had heard the woman scream as she fell. Reynard allegedly assaulted two officers and had been shot trying to escape across the roof. He had fled into the church's lower cellars, where investigators were scouring the scene.

Even worse, as Savoy's stomach turned to ice, Reynard had been named as the likely suspect—his description confirmed by Sergeant Etienne Pourry.

Savoy rubbed between his eyes. "Have the police spoken to you?"

"Yes," Grant said. "Miss Carlovec and I both."

"Where is she now?"

"Having supper." He lowered his voice. "She didn't tell them everything. She and Mister LaCroix had a quarrel, 'round midnight. Soon after he left the hotel."

"Did she tell the police?"

"Not that I know."

Savoy stood watching, not seeing much of anything. Every fiber wanted to see the crime scene for himself, to examine every bit of evidence that might exonerate Reynard. He knew the author of this scandal. Thinking about her, or him—*what shroud might it wear today?*—filled him with dread. He would never forget that bodiless head and spine float through the Metairie darkness. Horrible.

First the *Kalabakang*, Stronheim's ruined home and dead housekeeper, and now this tragedy. He felt the chess pieces as they moved inexorably around him.

23

Kiria sat eating supper, alone.

She tried to look and act older, more important, than she felt. She wore a khaki-colored dress with a puffy bodice and ankle-length skirt, her shoulders draped with a lacy shawl more appropriate for her grandmother, and for once her hair was tied up in a tight bun. She felt dowdy and unattractive, and maybe that was the point. She had nearly finished her humble repast—tea, cantaloupe, a croissant—at one of the outdoor tables in front of the *Café Jardin*.

Perhaps she was being foolish. Did the threat of another nightmare warrant such girlish behavior? Wasting time, eating slowly, burning away the hours? Sitting alone in a darkening city was no option. Returning to her hotel room, she told herself, did not mean she had to sleep. She could read a book or write a letter—something productive, instead of sitting at a lonely café feeling sorry for herself.

She had not seen Monsieur LaCroix all day. Mister Savoy had gone to visit a friend and Mister Grant...well, Mister Grant did whatever Mister Grant did. They all seemed focused on their own agendas so she decided to do the same, taking in a few sights, doing a little shopping, acting as if she had a purpose and that she had never, ever, seen those sights aboard the *Kalabakang*. She refused to look at a newspaper or even look at a *gendarme* so long as she was in Marseille, so disgusted she was at the experience the day before.

She paid her bill and left, walking slowly along the sidewalk. She liked the cold wind biting on her face, how it made her earlobes numb and cheeks tingle. The sensation made her feel more alive, if only to keep awake, to keep from dreaming.

A young woman approached from the opposite direction. She was no older than nineteen, dressed in plain clothes and a ragged overcoat. She held a baby against her chest, a thin cotton blanket draped over its little body. When the wind came stronger the mother leaned in and held the baby closer. Kiria felt a sudden urge to hold the child, smell it, to feel its skin against her neck. The woman glanced but did not meet her eye. Poor women never looked her in the eye.

"Excuse me," Kiria said in French. "It is very cold."

The woman slowed. "*Oui, madame.*"

Kiria removed her lacy shawl. "Take this."

"Oh no, *madame*. I've nothing t'pay you."

"A gift," Kiria lifted the shawl. It smelled like her perfume.

"I'm not a beggar," she said.

Kiria smiled. "Your baby is so precious, I imagine he could use it."

"She."

"Even better."

The young mother's expression softened. She took the shawl from Kiria's hands, draping it over her baby and off her shoulder, smoothing her hand around the contour of the baby's back.

"God bless you," she said.

∞∞

Savoy and Grant waited until dark.

It took twenty minutes of skirting walls and skulking up stairs, but in time they managed to slip undetected across the esplanade. The basilica's front doors were, for the moment, left unlocked for those watchmen on patrol; Savoy led Grant inside and they passed through the dark chapel. Twice they ducked as heavy footsteps approached and the beam of a flashlight flew past.

They found steps descending into the lower crypt. A scattering of votive candles still burned here now, flickering, their meager light leaving the arched chamber heavily shrouded. Savoy took the largest candle and examined the room. They saw chalk markings where investigators had made notes along the floor: blood droplets here, torn fabric there, traces of hair and dead skin.

Savoy's heart felt like an iron stone.

It was too soon. It had to be.

"He came here on his own volition," he said, "or he was compelled. He had an urgent reason to ascend the tower. He encountered the Lady, the police arrived, and Reynard fled to this point. Here, the trail goes cold."

He stopped beside a large metal grate. "This grate's been moved."

"Down there?"

"Possibly."

"They would have found him."

Savoy set down the candle and, with effort, pulled the grate from its place. "I doubt they would assume anyone foolish enough to do so...but then, they have never met Reynard."

At his silent request, Grant removed a small, flickering votive and tossed it into the shaft. It fell ten feet to land on a hard-packed, rocky floor.

"As I suspected," Savoy said. "The foundation of this church is much older than the building. Ancient sewers crisscross beneath the old city, linking three of the oldest churches and down to the sea. It stands to reason the only exit, save traipsing out the front doors, was down here." He knelt and sat at the shaft's edge, dangling his feet into the hole.

"Seems a stretch," Grant said.

"Shall we see for ourselves?"

"You must be joking."

Savoy gave him a blank stare. "You keep saying that."

They dropped into a musty passage of fitted stone, black as pitch, leading straight and deep below the church.

The tunnel to their left, Savoy guessed, led north. Reynard knew the city's general plan; the best course would to go right and head seaward.

The way was gentle but sloped gradually lower with each step. Occasionally another passage emerged but Savoy kept them straight. Once he paused, cupping the light, and examined the floor. The stone floor revealed no footprints. A trickle of fetid water flowed in the same direction they walked, so they were indeed heading toward the sea. At this rate, Reynard would have his choice of at least two of the churches' basements and multiple exits to the Mediterranean shore.

The passageway turned and wove in no discernable direction, sometimes becoming so narrow they had to walk single file. Above their heads stretched many cobwebs and pale, spidery roots, the air thick and dry, but when Savoy inhaled a faint, coppery aftertaste coated his tongue.

A noise echoed—they stopped.

"I don't think this is a good idea," Grant whispered.

Another sound came, closer, like breaking sticks.

They emerged into a chamber of fitted stone, the walls dripping with moisture. Three exits led straight, left and right. Savoy lowered the candle; dozens of oily rats scattered at their feet, carpeting the floor, and dozens more squirmed from countless nests piled along the walls. Heaps of earth and straw lay in unclean hillocks, carpeted with pellets and little bones, the air stinking of urine and sewage and the dusty stink of vermin.

Rats coalesced into a wave, rushing toward them. One rat became three, and three became a dozen, and the dozen became a hundred. The men moved aside, disgusted, as the host of vermin passed over their feet, scrambling and pushing into the tunnel where they had come. One large rat crawled on Grant's boot and started up his leg. He kicked and retreated into the center of the chamber.

Savoy coughed, impulsively brought his arm to his mouth to ward aside the revulsion. The candle dropped, bounced, and died.

Darkness overwhelmed them. Grant sucked in a breath.

Savoy bent down and reached around his feet, recoiling when oily shapes slid past his hands. He commanded himself to stay calm. He reached into the pocket of his coat and rummaged, finding his matchbook, his quivering hands flexing to strike another match, another match—just strike another match and, *yes, that's it*, relight the candle and—

The candle's wick caught the flame.

Something large breathed above them.

A ledge surrounded the stone chamber ten feet up, pocked with ancient metal grates where smaller shafts diverted fluids from other chambers. Huddled there, crouched, two bright blue eyes appeared. Beneath them opened a lupine muzzle smeared with blood, lips stretched back to expose red, rubbery gums above crowded fangs. Muscles tensed in its heavy back, rippled down its powerful forearms.

Grant scrambled at the buttons of his longcoat, to his belt, sliding his Colt from its holster. The werewolf leaped from the ledge, swatting at Grant with a claw, and the pistol discharged with a tremendous *crack*. Rats scattered in all directions.

The beast went wild at the lightbulb-flash of gunpowder—it stumbled back against the tunnel wall, claws scraping stone. It scratched at its head and arms, drawing blood, thrashing, howling, tearing at the air and its head and the stones at its feet. There lay countless dead rats, bitten, tore into pieces, blood flicked along the walls in tiny sprays. Their blood congealed all along the thing's fur. The beast redoubled its anger and struck the walls and floor like a gorilla, screaming with its deep, wild bass rising into a furious echo.

The men did not move.

The beast screamed again, scratching at the ground, looking to Grant, then Savoy, and back to Grant. It snap-snapped its teeth, shook its shaggy head and, with a cry, raced down the left tunnel. In five steps it dropped to all fours and loped into the dark. A minute passed before the men reminded their bodies to move, to think.

Grant expelled a heavy breath. "It's true."

"You see him now," Savoy said.

"Can't mistake those eyes," Grant said, nodding. He bent, hands on his knees, face drawn as if to vomit. "How the hell do these things happen?"

Savoy following the beast, hurrying down the left tunnel. Grant started to protest and resisted, keeping his pistol in hand. Ahead they heard the thing running, growling, then an angry cry and a grating sound of crashing and squealing metal. They ran a long way down a straight corridor, until the tunnel turned sharply into faint, rising light. At its end lay the ruin of an old and rusted gate. The beast had torn through it like paper.

They entered a basement of fitted stone with a curved ceiling, filled with boxes of powdered mortar and paint buckets and wooden scaffolding, the tools of extensive restoration. They hurried up a staircase into a chamber of yellow stone. Fading frescos of ancient saints adorned the walls, while alcoves held statues worn away into smooth nubs.

"St. Victor's," Savoy said. "I knew it."

Screams led them to the left. Savoy and Grant ran into another chamber to find an old woman on the floor in a heap, crying out in German. More voices of alarm erupted ahead, as men and women scattered in panic from the creature that ran through the church like a rabid dog. The two followed the cries through a foyer and emerged outside into fresh air. The inky water of Vieux Harbor stretched ahead, the city glowing around it with hazy streetlamps. They had emerged onto the front porch of St. Victor's Abbey, an austere church with high crenellated walls overlooking the harbor.

A woman's shriek pealed up the street to their right. They managed half a block before Savoy's pace slowed to a trot, then a walk. He doubled over, wheezing.

"Call the police," Grant said.

"They'll...shoot him down...like an animal."

"He *is* an animal."

"Please," Savoy gasped. "This wasn't...not *now*. Not...yet." He coughed. "Please. Please do something."

"What could I possibly do?"

"I do not know," Savoy said. "Do *something*."

The animal ran with an air of confused defiance; on the one hand it loped confidently along the dark city streets on its hands and feet, the muscles of its back shifting like cords under its taut hide. Yet as it passed from shadow to shadow its angry muzzle caught the air, its ears stiffened. When a carriage rambled in the distance or a horn bellowed from the harbor it twitched, its attention taken first here, then there.

It accelerated, using its long forearms to pull it forward. It paused at a street corner, its head considering both directions.

Behind it, Grant pursued. He hissed out breath with each stride, ignoring the pain in his arches as he ran after the thing.

He followed the beast onto the street *Rue Sainte*, as it crossed the road and turned, he noted with irony, onto another street named *Rue de la Croix*. The beast ran quick but erratic, snapping its jaw at anything that caught its attention: the rush of a crowd of pigeons, the panicked flight of a pedestrian, the snap of a flag in the stiff wind.

The beast turned right when Grant hoped it might turn left, running straight into the glare of streetlights and the noise of the wide *Boulevard de la Corderie*. It emerged into a knot of men and women in their coats and umbrellas and mufflers; the women shrieked as the creature sailed over the sidewalk and into the busy street.

An immense coach-and-four materialized; the driver grasped the reins as the creature leaped across its path. The horses' hooves clattered and scraped against the bricks. The coach swerved. It struck the beast against the shoulder, sent him sprawling with an audible howl, and slammed against the curb. The right wheels jumped up and the coach leaned straight into a streetlamp. Glass popped with a spurt of gas-fueled flame. The horses jerked the coach across the opposite flow of traffic. Carts and coaches and hansoms became chaos, voices shouting and cursing, women crying, whistles blowing.

Grant wove his way across the street. The beast had regained its feet and reached the far side of the boulevard. It skirted a tree-lined promenade and fled down the smaller *Rue d'Endoume*, beneath shopkeeper signs and iron-wrought balconies, past plastered tenements and tightly-packed shops. Here the streetlights were gone and the dark came in great swaths, hiding doors and alleys and details.

Grant kept the thing in sight—barely.

More than once he considered letting the thing go. He thought of that drafty cell at Parish Prison and he knew that *yes*, Mister LaCroix had been right, he felt an obligation to help because he'd been spared the hangman's handshake, and *yes*, he had been tempted to slip away in the night and never look back.

Now here he ran, following this abomination for no other reason than he said he would. This was not the wild running of a frightened, mindless animal. He had hunted enough predators to know—

It's caught a scent.

The beast snuffed, rose to its hind legs, and made a hard left. It ran along the tenements for half a block then, with a sudden leap, caught the bottom rung of a fire escape and scrambled up the ladder. From stair to landing the beast worked its way toward the top floor. Grant came to a stop at the ladder's base, incredulous.

That's it, he thought. *I'm done.*

The beast reached the uppermost window, smashed through the glass, and crawled inside. There came a shriek—a woman—a crash, and the sudden wail of a baby.

Dang it.

Grant gripped the rung of the fire escape and pulled himself up, running step after step up the spiraling iron framework. Gasping, legs burning, he reached the top and sucked in a breath. From beyond the broken window came heavy breath, the wake of foul musk, and a wild scuffling. Crashing and snarling erupted. The baby cried louder, followed by a sound like tearing cloth.

Grant slipped through the broken window. He entered a kitchen. There was no icebox, but a coal stove sat next to a sink piled with dirty dishes. He removed his pistol with his right hand and grabbed a serrated knife with his left. He would shoot the thing between the eyes if he had to, kill any damned man or beast that would harm—

—Emily?

He entered a parlor with a patched sofa and ottoman and dirty lampshade. The werewolf hulked in the middle of it, tearing apart a white, lacy shawl. A trembling young woman, clutching a baby, cringed on the sofa. When she moved, the beast snapped it teeth and she shrieked, clutching her crying child tight against her chest.

She saw Grant, and screamed.

The beast struck at Grant like a wild dog. Grant plunged the knife into its shoulder, burying the blade down to the bone. With his other hand he raised the pistol; the beast caught him by his face and wrist, shoving both hard against the wall, keeping the weapon away. Grant struggled. The werewolf lifted him off the floor. Grant did the only thing his mind suggested—kicking the beast between the legs—and the animal shuddered. It tossed him across the room.

He struck the wall hard, and collapsed. He did not get up.

The beast jerked the knife free with a spurt of dark fluid, licked it, and tossed it aside. It considered the woman and child. It snarled at Grant with another loud *clack* of wet teeth.

"Mon *bébé!*" the mother cried. "*Ne nous faites pas mal!*"

The beast looked at her, at the pieces of torn shawl at its feet—then it shuffled into the kitchen, through the broken window and back into the night.

ഇരു

Kiria passed beneath shopkeeper signs and balconies, past plastered tenements squeezed tightly together. Her heeled boots clucked along the deserted street. Why did she walk this far? Was it her anger, her need to walk free her feelings, the fear of being alone in a vast city, the need to lose herself so someone might take pity on her?

You're acting like an insolent child.

She hoped to hail a cab, something, not exactly sure where the road might lead but knowing she was heading in the wrong direction. She would backtrack and return to the wider street she had crossed earlier. Using the shining shape of *Notre Dame de la Garde* as her landmark, she guessed the hotel lay on the far side, and that meant she should have turned left a while back instead of straight. There were busier lanes in that direction, and many large fountains and shops still open, and there *had* to be a telephone somewhere, though it occurred to her the *Hotel Vauban* did *not* have a telephone, so why in the bloody *hell* did they—

She stopped short.

A misshapen, shadowy figure appeared in the distance. Its appearance sent electric charges into her legs, sent her heart to racing. She could see its cloudy breath with each exhale. The shape turned toward her. *Stray dog*, she told herself. *That's all, that's all it is, and you're all worked up you silly, prattling thing, and what a tongue lashing I'll give those thoughtless men when I—*

The animal stood on its hind legs.

Oh God.

Long, sinewy arms ended in claws, the glow of its wide eyes watching her. She remembered the stink of the jungle and the smell of whisky, the scream of her father's voice. She remembered, hidden in the greenhouse, watching her father, watching when she was supposed to be upstairs, watching as his eyes held the same reflection like an animal skulking the night.

Father?

She ran, blindly. She did not look back. She could not breathe, could not scream. She heard the thing's nails as it scraped on the pavement closer, getting closer, accelerating into a run. It would leap upon her. It would tear out her throat and, when she fell, claw open her breast and eat her heart. Lap up her blood. Bite out her eyes. She would still be breathing as it tore her skin into ribbons, feasting upon her with the last seconds of her life. She had seen such things, seen them, *seen* them, *felt* them when she saw her father, knew it was only a matter of time before it would be *her* throat—

The heel of her boot snapped.

She fell, hands flailing, as she struck the curb with an audible cry. She rolled to her back, ignoring the tears in her eyes as she saw the beast running at her there, *there*, its mouth open to tear her. She scrambled backwards across the sidewalk, pressed against a tenement wall. No one could help; no one would see her die. Her composure, her false bravery— gone in a swelling of panic as she shrieked before she realized:

"*Reynard!*"

It flinched. The beast stumbled backwards, struck a pile of rotten crates and sent the lot crashing into the street. It thrashed at the wood, barking, its claws raking along the dirty flagstones. It scratched at its head and pulled out tuffs of filthy white hair. Copious amounts of blood splattered its shoulder. It shook with a tremor and great drops of mud and sweat and blood fell like raindrops.

She forced herself to stand. Blood stained her palms, registered at her knees and ankles and elbows, inside her mouth. As she regained her feet the beast lunged, snapping with a furious growl, retreated, pushed forward again like a mastiff at the end of a chain. She pressed against the wall. She had seen such things from hiding places, from distances, from the confines of her dreams, but this—

Reynard's blue eyes met hers.

She saw him reflected there, recognized his gait and swagger. She saw the man like a flimsy veil draped over a bestial frame and, for a moment, felt no fear but pity. Her heart swelled with emotion; unlike her father and his raging passions, Reynard LaCroix was little more than wind and bluster. Friends dead, sister stolen, dragged across the world only to suffer such a thing?

"Reynard," she said.

She realized she was crying.

I'm sorry.

The beast wagged its head and fell back to the far side of the street. Claws scraped brick, left gouges across the wall in jagged strips.

"Please do not hurt me," she said.

It stopped shouting. It stood there, mouth and nostrils steaming with bellowed breath. It regarded her for the longest second of her life. With a snap of its jaw, it huffed a heavy exhale and fled, racing down the street into the dark.

Kiria watched it go. She registered how tightly her corset squeezed against her ribcage, how hard it was to breathe, how brightly the spots around her eyes began to glimmer. She had about three seconds, she guessed, before she would faint.

24

Reynard's nerves registered cold mud oozing into his right nostril and ear and mouth. He did not move. He could not feel his body. Where were his feet? He could not feel them. Numbness ached with a dull, prickling sensation.

He opened his mouth to breathe and rank, oily water poured over his tongue. He retched, spewing the fermented water. He coughed bile in sticky threads from his lips.

It was dark. To his right stretched the sea. To his left lay a stout, rocky cliff topped with a line of dark, dilapidated buildings. He pulled himself from the shore, along the posts of a wooden dock, his bare feet sucking through thick mud. He regarded his hands as they brushed over wood and sharp bumps of barnacles, fingers black with filth, over his naked belly and up his neck to his face. He touched his nose and mouth and behind his ears, reminding himself the details of his own shape.

Alive?

His soles and palms hurt, the flesh rubbed raw. He swallowed and his throat constricted, his ragged breathing leaving thin, vaporous trails in his wake. From a metal pipe along the shore came a trickle of water; he scrubbed his hands and face and neck, the water stinking of offal, the sharp coldness forcing feeling back into his limbs.

He considered the tenements huddled against the shore. Many shoreline villages held families who relied upon the ocean, men from North Africa or the East who fished in the early hours. There were no gaslights here. The only light came from pinprick glimmers in the far distance, ships set upon the black horizon.

Naked he slipped up onto the dock and into the crooked streets, skulking from corner to corner, huddling and shivering. He tried to reconnect the fragmented memories of the last...hour? Day? Week? How long had it been? With every bare step upon the cold flagstones his heart shrank at the realization—

What have I done?

He leaned against a wall, heaving, spewing water and bile. He knew he had changed again but could scarcely believe it. He was naked, slipping among the slums like vermin. *He* was vermin. He stank of slime and fish and excrement and blood. His fingers felt up his arm and over his shoulder, finding an ugly pink gash the length of his thumb.

How did I get these?

Dead skin freckled his arms and shoulders like dried blisters, caused by the expansion and deflation of his physical body. He crouched against an alley wall and picked at some of the larger pockets, peeling them away, scrubbing the dead sheath of flesh with his broken fingernails until he bled.

He broke down and wept, bitterly. He pulled his knees to his chest and clutched them, rocking slightly, and with each upswing he cracked the back of his head against the brick wall at his back. After three blows a sharp, piercing headache shot above his left eye.

What have I done?

She did this to me.

Miserable whore!

You did this to yourself, he thought, as if another's voice spoke from a distance. *She tempted you, lured you—but you, you, you YOU YOU YOU—*

No, came another part. *It was that woman.*

Woman.

He remembered the smell of roses, the feel of lace on his—

—Kiria?

He fled down the alley, along dark and quiet streets, keeping sight of the coastline, hoping the buildings would end and he could disappear into the wilderness and die in some hole. Let the beasts eat his flesh. It would serve him right to be consumed by them.

A metallic jingle caught him short.

He slid behind a rotting rain barrel as a door opened on the far side of the street, one of many single-level flats visible in both directions. A plain man in a threadbare overcoat and wool hat started down the sidewalk. Reynard walked him leave. When he was out of sight, Reynard rushed across the street and tried the doorknob. Locked. With a fist he punched a hole though the adjoining window.

He slipped inside. The flat was like many for the poor: a small kitchen and a single room for everything else. Entire families would squeeze into hundreds of such flats in Marseille, a mother and father and six children all sleeping and eating and living in the same ten-by-twenty foot space with only a rickety radiator and a coal stove for cooking. This man, a fisherman perhaps, had it lucky. By the looks of things he lived alone.

Reynard washed up from the kitchen sink. He scrubbed the blood and filth off his body as best he could, working quickly, fearing the front door might open. He searched the man's bedroom, finding a woolen shirt and pants and socks, two sizes too big but adequate. He slid his feet into a large pair of worn leather shoes. In the kitchen he found cheese and stale bread and a half-eaten tin of sardines, stuffing the lot into his mouth, chewing as fast as he could. He drank water until he was filled, splashing the wet coldness over his face again and again and again. He could not feel clean.

A noise echoed from outside, the clip-clop of hooves. He slipped to the door and flattened himself against it. If the police tried to open the door he would open it first. He would push past them. He might knock their guns aside and give himself enough time to—

To do what?

He could never return to Marseille. The woman had not only violated him in the deepest sense, taken everything of worth—his dignity, his self-control. As he considered it—*I can never return home*—made the hate rise hot in his body. When he thought of Marseille he would forever think of a dying girl in that desecrated tower, the filth and mud of the coastline slums, the woman's awful laugh as she fell.

I will kill her.

The hooves faded. Reynard released his breath and stuffed his pockets with anything of use he could find. He grabbed a scrap of paper and a stub of a pencil. He scribbled a note and, just before disappearing back into the dark streets, left it on the kitchen table:

Forgive me.

෩൦ൠ

Night turned to day, to night, to day again.

A rapping came at Savoy's room at the *Hotel Vauban*—a postal carrier, delivering an envelope with no return address. The envelope was badly creased and dirty, and the postal carrier expected a few centimes due to insufficient postage. Inside was a single sheet of paper written with scrawled handwriting:

Home.

Savoy closed the door, drew the shades closed, and removed a match. He burned both the paper and envelope—this was something the police did not need to see—and buried the ashes in the wastebin. He gathered up his luggage, left a note with instructions for Grant, and went downstairs to catch a hansom. He headed for the train station.

Three miles outside of the village of Aix-en-Provence waited the remains of a once sizeable estate—a two-storied whitewashed house with a covered porch and many windows. Here and there stood palm trees and Roman statues and fountains where water once poured into stony pools. Today the fountains were dry, the statues chipped and weathered and crusted with moss. Ivy choked the house's ruined face, the windows either broken or boarded over.

Savoy lashed his horse and cart at the hitching rail and ascended the weedy steps, taking a long look at Reynard's ancestral home. He walked through the front doorway—the door was long gone—and padded through empty rooms with floors littered with pebbles and broken plaster and animal droppings. Much of the wallpaper had fallen, but here and there the walls held impressions where a painting or bookcase or chair might once have been.

He returned outside and skirted the house's perimeter, passing through overgrown bushes into a fallow garden where plants and fruit trees and berries now grew wild. He followed a little stone path that curved around dead flower beds to a grove of olive trees. There, nearly lost in the grass, a dozen tombstones stood in an uneven line, the names and dates moving further back in time.

"All dead."

Savoy twitched. In the shadows beneath the trees, Reynard knelt beside one of the more recent markers, brushing off moss and grit from the stone. He wore ragged, plain clothing and oversized shoes. Pale stubble marked his jawline and upper lip. To Savoy he seemed empty, transparent, the haggard look of a man who had lost too much weight, too much light.

"Don't look at me that way," Reynard said.

"I'm sorry. It's just..."

"We are all dead," Reynard continued. "Seven generations are buried here, my grandfather being the latest. He had his body shipped back so it might lie with the others. There was never a desire to build a crypt. They all wanted to become part of the earth. It had given them so many good things. The grapes that used to grow here, the olives. I remember the smell of olive oil and vinegar and wine in that house. It smelled like that every day, Arté. Roses, and azaleas, and mint." He shook his head. "But we are dead."

"The soil is still good," Savoy said. "A little work and it can be itself again."

"Words."

"Is it not true?"

"It is too far gone," Reynard said. "It is too late."

"It is never too late, Renny." Savoy smiled. *Are we still talking about the house?* "Will you tell me what happened?"

"Is Kiria—I mean, is Miss Carlovec...is she safe?"

"Yes."

"And Mister Grant?"

"He is fine," Savoy said. "Though the poor boy does seem to get the worst of it."

Reynard brushed away the dirt from his knees, emerging from the shade as he vigorously rubbed his hands together. "I could do with a hot bath and a change of clothing. I trust you brought my luggage." He inhaled deeply, waving nonchalantly at the remains of his old home. "It was better to imagine what this place used to look like, rather than see it like this. No point in coming back, really. I never much liked Marseille. The more I think about it, the more I want to leave New Orleans. Move my base of operations further inland, like Chicago or Saint Louis..."

"Reynard, I—"

"Farther away from the sea." Reynard started toward the empty house. "We may find better luck sailing from Genoa, or taking a train to Rome for the Suez this time of year."

"Lasha?" Savoy asked.

"She is alive."

"Do you know where she is?"

"No. So we best get to it, shall we?" Reynard's hands padded at his chest and hips, digging into empty pockets. "I seem to have misplaced my matches. Do you have any tobacco?"

Savoy paused. "I've my pipe."

"May I?"

"Have you started smoking again?"

Reynard smiled with hard eyes and Savoy acquiesced, giving Reynard his matchbook and packet of Colonial Fields tobacco. Reynard took both. Savoy offered his pipe but Reynard waved it away, removing a slip of rolling paper from his pocket. He filled it with a pinch, sealed it up, and with a match lit the end of the makeshift cigarette.

Savoy led the way, Reynard lingering. Reynard did not look in the house's direction, did not seem to notice his own smell, the ragged state of his clothes. He did not seem to notice much of anything as Savoy turned the corner of the house and Reynard disappeared from sight behind him. He reappeared after a few moments, smiling with an empty expression like a ghost.

Savoy did not know what to say. He supposed nothing could be said. There was no precedent. For all he knew, Reynard's curse had returned in full force—like a man sworn off opium, overdoses, and poisons himself.

Are you poisoned, Renny?

The two men ascended the cart. They did not speak. Savoy did not think again about the makeshift cigarette. He did not see Reynard take two puffs to encourage the tobacco to burn, did not see him flick the burning paper into the house.

He did not see the cigarette land on a pile of dry weeds and branches heaped against the wall, did not watch the cinder smolder and burst into flame. He was not there when the fire grew like a hungry animal, spreading, licking at dry peelings of wallpaper to crawl up into the plastered ceiling. He did not see the smoke as it filled every ruined chamber, up steps to lonely hallways where Reynard once played. Fire spread from room to room and, when they were miles away, the old villa became a maelstrom of fire.

Only the tombstones watched the old house burn.

25

Time passed, lost its way, and disappeared.

Lasha awoke to the sound of her own tears, her pillow soaked with moisture. Had her dreams been less potent she would have pulled the sheets to her chin and dismissed them; yet she dreaded sleeping, hated even more the thought of waking. She rolled to her back and stared at the folds of the netting above her bed, the room pitch-dark and heavy with the stink of rotten fruit and dust and mold.

"It is time," came a voice.

Had she the strength to scream, she would have. The woman stood in the dark beside the open door with her hand upon the latch. She was a wraith, her red hair loose down her back, her hollow face both pale and ruddy like a painted cadaver. The fabric of her nightdress fell off her shoulders and spilled like cobwebs over the full shape of her breasts and hips.

"Come, child," she said.

"Leave me alone," Lasha whispered.

"Do not make this harder on yourself."

Lasha clutched her wrist and the skin throbbed underneath the bandage. She was thirsty. She gazed over her four-poster with its mosquito netting, the rosewood sidetable, armoire and washstand, objects as oppressive as if stone and iron surrounded her.

"I feel sick."

"That will pass," the woman said.

"Why not kill me now, instead of a little bit each day?" Lasha said. "Why..." She outstretched her arm to flash the offending bandage. "...do *this?*"

"You are young. You will understand one day."

"You know nothing about me."

"I know you better than you know yourself. Stand."

"No."

"*Stand up.*"

Lasha closed her eyes as the woman's voice bled into her ears. She could not help but sit against the edge of the bed, but damn her if she can make her stand!

"*Stand up.*"

To her shame, Lasha's legs lifted her to her feet.

"What a good girl," the woman said.

"Go to hell."

The woman grinned bright teeth. It was only recently that Lasha even had a mind to resist; since Metairie Cemetery she traveled in dreams—by train to Boston, up the gangplank to the *Kalabakang*, through one exotic port after another, day after day strolling the deck and playing cards and drinking tea and speaking with the woman...

The woman.

She had been there from the beginning: whispering, comforting, chatting and giggling as if they were life-long sisters pledged to the most intimate of secrets. They had laughed together, read together, spoke of jungles and pirates and wild peoples living free. Lasha had spoken of her life, her memories, her voice a rushing stream. During her entire journey—train or boat or carriage—she considered this woman her mother, sister, friend, privy to all her secrets yet as mysterious and unreachable as a stranger. She did not understand why she unloaded her thoughts when this woman returned little of herself.

Yet during the last few days the fog dissipated from her mind and she knew, truly understood, that she was awake. She did not like what she saw. The house. Though she had not been allowed outside since entering that vast place, she had a window, she could hear the jungle outside, and the moisture on her face told her she far, farther from home than she ever dared imagine—

I am alone. No one can help me.

The house.

She feared the sounds in the night. Creeping whispers along the old corridors when no one was there, voices flittering outside her door. Daytime was tolerable but night—

"I will protect you," the woman said.

She left and Lasha followed, furious, wishing her body would listen. Garbed in their white nightdresses the two women floated down the unlit corridor like ghosts. The hallways of that obscene mansion were always longer than anticipated. The walk to ground level felt like endless wandering through curtained hallways and down countless steps, drapes billowing with unfelt breezes, rooms smelling of velvet, rotten anaglypta and mildew, ticking with the pattering of clocks. Their bare feet padded on dusty carpets.

Around them, lingering, lurking, voices whispered as they went. At first Lasha found herself turning to look, expecting someone beside her. After two days she suspected they were voices inside her own head. In five, she was sure she was mad. She felt those voices seething from beneath the floorboards at night, evaporating with morning, the house saturated with them.

They walked down to the laboratory on the ground floor. To the left, the room served as a sitting room with Savonerie rugs and mahogany furniture and a great, leather couch near the fireplace. On the right, a long metal table lay covered in rolls of gauze, bottles of carbolic acid and ether and chlorine and a dozen other chemicals, empty flasks and rubber tubes, Bunsen burners and vials filled with blood and other liquids, and a handful of steel medical implements in a tray. Beside the table stood a wheeled gurney, fitted with leather straps and brass buckles.

Lasha's stomach tightened.

Wilhem Carlovec stretched out upon the couch, reading a leather-bound book. He was a tall, gray man, his body a wiry reflection of past youth with short, iron-white hair. He sported both a prominent chin and a sharp, Grecian nose, and he moved with deliberation and focus. His haggard complexion contrasted against his fine silk vest, shirt and cravat that smelled of musky cologne. He shut his book with a slap and stood.

"My dear," he said.

The woman swept into his arms and kissed him full on the lips. Lasha looked away. If she had not been so disgusted by Master Carlovec's passion for that horrible woman, she would have been offended by his lack of tact. A look of love, a sweet word, the touch of a hand were appropriate tokens. Their public affections were far from chaste.

"So prompt," he said, "so prompt. My apologies for waking you, but I have come across the most extraordinary bit of insight. I hope you understand."

"Please do not cut me again," Lasha said.

"I know this must be a terrible thing..." His hand swept toward the table. "Had I any other choice I would have taken it. I am nearly there, my child, nearly there, and then this horror will be forgotten."

"Please."

The woman gripped Lasha's arm and pulled her to the table, squeezing, her free hand unwrapping the bandages to expose a raw, blotched wrist. Lasha jerked back. The woman forced her arm above a metal bowl, twisting, until Lasha cried out.

"Please hold still," Wilhem said.

"Don't cut me again," Lasha said. She squirmed. "You shall burn in hell next to this horrible creature...you miserable, filthy old man!"

The woman slapped her across the face.

"Lucinda," Wilhem said. "Your temper."

"Why do you allow her to say such things?"

"Do you blame her?"

Lucinda drew the nail of her index finger across Lasha's wrist. Flesh split, blood erupted and, with a squeeze, the fluid dribbled into the bowl. Tears poured off Lasha's cheeks, her pain replaced by the sickening cold like poison under her skin. They would squeeze her, then force sour wine down her throat and send her back to her room with nightmares that raped her dreams.

"It hurts," she said.

"It is for the best," Wilhem said. "I promise."

MALEFICUS

"Whoever fights monsters should see to it he does not become a monster ... if you gaze long enough into an abyss, the abyss will gaze back into you."

- Friedrich Nietzsche

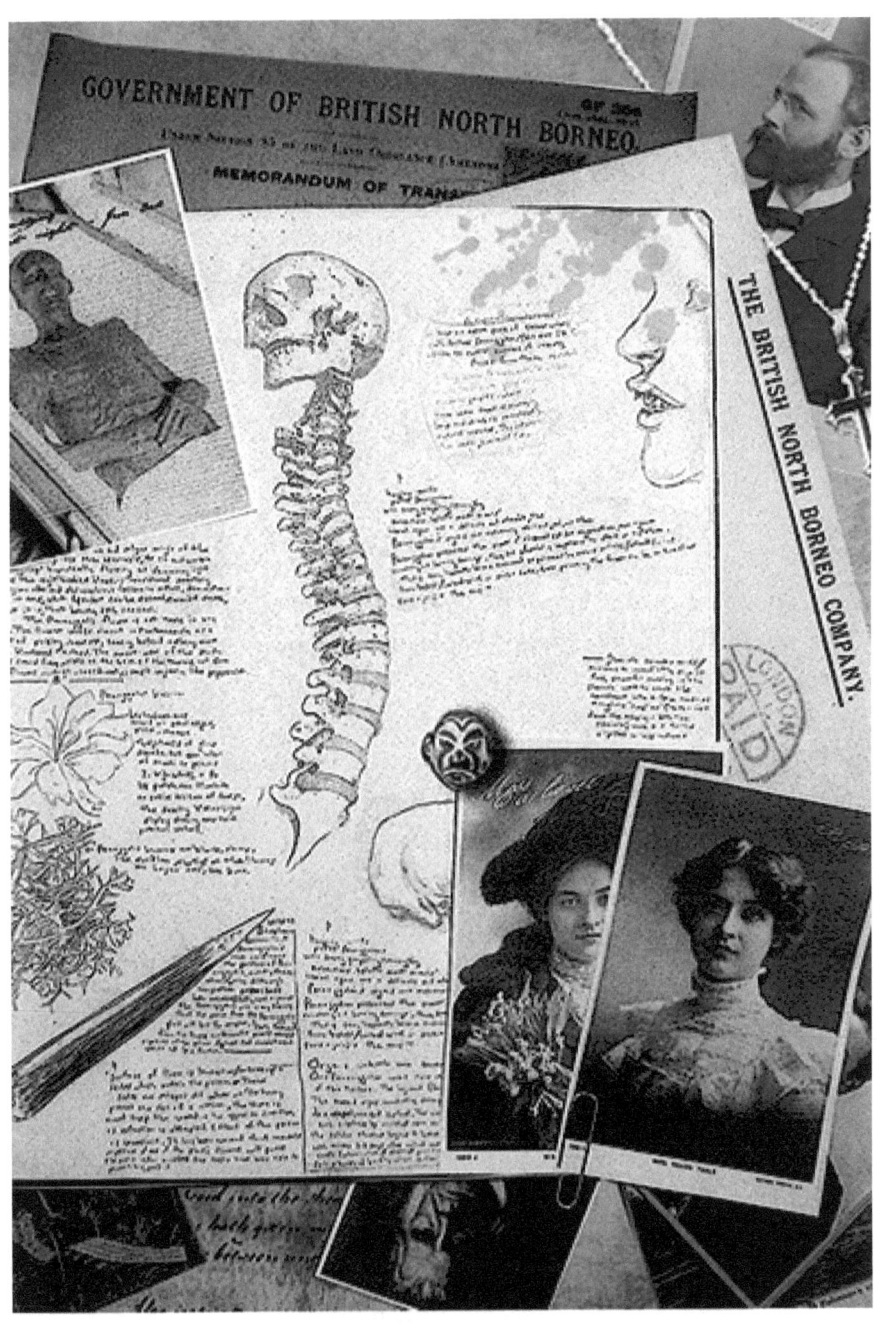

26

Sandakan, British North Borneo
December 1889

As soon as the steam-fueled clipper *Tatakan Ruy* nestled against the dock, workhands tied it into place. Ramps fell. Retainers began their ant-like precision unloading cargo, swarming to tasks, blending into the heartbeat of the wharf.

Sandakan stretched along the shoreline with tin-shingled houses and tenements belching smoke, punctuated with warehouses and mills and canneries where the spoils of harvest were processed for export. Muddy roads dissected most of the city into misassembled blocks. Further east, the city ended and jungle stretched along the coast over a line of rolling, primal mountains. Though much smaller than Singapore, Sandakan retained the air of British rule; Her Majesty's flag caught the breeze above the wharf and declared confidently that yes, Victoria's Own were in charge.

Reynard inhaled the thick air as he stood on the forward deck. Borneo beaded on his skin, stinking of rotten vegetation and brine. He did not care for it. The heat and humidity made him perpetually moist in all the wrong places.

He had both longed for, and dreaded, this day. The four had reunited in Rome where they secured a sailing ship through the Suez to India, around Siam to Singapore and finally to Sandakan. It was a long voyage. At first Reynard spent much of the time avoiding the others, keeping to himself, wallowing in the memories of recent events. He did not look Grant in the eye for over two weeks, though nothing had been said, nothing confirmed. Denial and time served their purpose, easing his conscience, with each passing day. He grew more animated, more social. He spent more time with Savoy, the two meeting daily for bridge or gin or chess. Artémius always tried to draw him out during their games, but Reynard proved unwilling.

Why, he thought, *should I revisit ancient history?*

Kiria emerged from a stairwell. A porter followed close behind, his arms weighed down with her luggage. She was garbed in her white dress and hat and parasol, and the climate agreed with her—the sun highlighted the olive in her skin and drew a healthy blush in her cheeks. The curls of her black hair had been pulled back to reveal a long and ruddy neck after many afternoons gazing over the sea. She was not a woman to seclude herself indoors. She had spent much of their journey keeping to herself or—when she did associate with them—keeping with the group, never allowing herself to be alone.

At least, Reynard noted, when he was around.

Many times he had tried to talk to her, to explain himself, to learn exactly what she had seen in Marseille. It was no use. She spoke to him only in the most formal of terms. She did not mention their argument, the horrific sights aboard the *Kalabakang.* Nothing had been said about *anything,* but he knew. He knew how she would avoid his gaze, how her scent changed when he was nearby.

"Miss Carlovec," Reynard said, nodding a greeting.

"It is good to be home," she replied.

She continued down the gangplank. Reynard followed her, hating the heaviness of his heart; Savoy and Grant soon joined them on the dock, trailed by the porter who pulled a cart with their immediate belongings. She led them from the water to Pryer Street, a rutted and muddy road that curled along the shore. Horse and wagon traffic flowed in both directions. At her suggestion they waited for a prearranged transport, and the longer they waited the more they were conspicuous strangers amid coffee-and-cream faces.

"I thought this was a British colony," Reynard said.

"The North Borneo Company is in control," Kiria said. "The Great Financial Experiment. We export a good deal from here alone, so by and by it has proven profitable. Father's fortune is in tobacco." She looked at Savoy. "His *Colonial Fields* is quite popular."

"Your father's?" Savoy asked, impressed.

"Miss Carlovec?"

An open carriage, pulled by four horses, slowed to a stop. A tall Englishman descended, clad in a khaki helmet, uniform and shorts, knee-high leech socks and round glasses perched on his hawkish nose, an Army-caliber pistol slung at his waist. His wide smile revealed a fellow more than pleased to be shaking Kiria's gloved hand. She grinned broadly.

"Duncan," she said. "You received my message."

"Only just. I am afraid your more extensive letter arrived just five days ago."

"I sent it late November."

"Pirates," he said. "Despite our best efforts. Both mail and wire from Sarawak is delayed—the Iban are upset at the Chinese, who are upset at the Bujan, and the governor's too busy expanding the railway, it seems. Most off-island mail's not arrived this month. I'm surprised I received your wire at all."

Reynard coughed to gain attention. Kiria introduced her three companions in turn. "May I present Duncan Barnett, Sandakan's Chief Inspector."

"Just a humble member of the constabulary," Duncan said as he shook their hands with a firm, British formality. "Miss Carlovec informed me of your plight. May I offer my warmest wishes that Miss...LaCroix, is it?...be found safe."

"She is my sister," Reynard said. "Any news?"

"Nothing, I am afraid. The only ship from your direction docked at Tambisan over a week ago, but no word as to its passengers or cargo."

"There must have been a record."

"There should have been, but local bureaucracies are not as efficient as Our Majesty's. The opium trade's booming and still they feel the need to sneak under our noses. We have circulated your sister's description to every regional office. It is the best we can do."

"And Master Carlovec?" Reynard asked. "You have questioned him?"

Duncan looked to Kiria. "Miss?"

"Yes," she said quietly. "My father may be of service."

"You never told him?" Reynard asked.

"I did not think—"

"Obviously," Reynard said. He focused on Duncan. "Miss Carlovec's father is directly involved in my sister's abduction, if not the author of it."

"Sir?"

"I urge an immediate investigation."

Duncan paused at that. "Unfortunately I cannot be much help there either," he said. "It is one thing to implicate one of the governor's trusted associates. It is quite another when I cannot question him, even if I felt it necessary. He left for Saint Dismas...months ago. I've not seen him since August."

"Where?" Savoy asked.

"My grandfather's old estate," Kiria said. "Carlovec Manor is a hundred miles inland. It is so isolated now...we've all but abandoned it. I cannot fathom why he would travel there, much less this time of year. Not in his condition."

"Convenient," Grant said.

"Nonsense," Duncan said, his smile gone. "Cannot fault a man for traveling to his own property. I refer you to the Office of Indigenous Affairs, which can direct you to whomever handles that region." He offered his hand to Kiria and helped her step up into the carriage as the porter stored her luggage. "I did not expect so large a group, so you will understand if you secure your own transport. I recommend the Victoria's Lion Hotel on Harris Street. If we learn anything more, someone will contact you."

"You are leaving us?" Savoy asked.

"Another conveyance ought to arrive shortly, "Duncan said. "Again, Victoria's Lion. Good day, gentlemen."

With that he ascended the carriage and sat beside Kiria. With a word, the driver flicked the reins and the carriage pulled forward, leaving the three men standing in the mud with their luggage slowly sinking in the road. Kiria did not look back, engaged in animated conversation, her open parasol spinning as she laughed.

"What a pompous ass," said Reynard.

"At least where it concerns Miss Carlovec," Savoy added.

The next morning Reynard awoke to hard rain outside his hotel window, rushing off gutters and into the sidewalks. With a heavy thunder, the downpour delivered a month's worth of Louisiana. He stared past the bed's mosquito netting and over the bare furnishings of his room, brushing his fingers against his slippery face. The *Victoria's Lion* did indeed have as many amenities as any hotel in London, but the furnishings and smells and feel of the air made it clear London was in a distant country.

He listened to the rain. He thought of Kiria, her olive skin, the play of her hair over her shoulders. Regardless of her many faults, he closed his eyes and imagined her smiling at him with pursed lips—

A knock rapped at his door. He rose from bed, touched his toes and stretched. He looked at his right hand, the muscle between his thumb and index finger rippling with an almost imperceptible tremor. He squeezed his hand into a fist.

Stay away.

Out in the hall waited Grant with his overcoat dripping, his Calvary hat spilling rainwater as he tipped his greeting. "Wet morning," he said. "Seems Miss Carlovec wants us to join her to go to her family's mansion, wherever her father's holed up."

"She did?" Reynard asked.

"You figure she wouldn't?"

"I don't know what to think about that woman. So when do we leave? A week? A month?"

"Three hours," Grant said. "We've a train to catch, and she's sent along a shopping list. We're to plan for the jungle, and that means leeches, snakes, crocodiles and mosquitoes plum full of the malaria."

"Wonderful."

"Care for some breakfast?"

The three men spent their morning in a supply store buying mosquito nets and creams and long socks and powders and dry-pack matches and hammocks and tents and an ammunition belt for Grant's

Winchester rifle, each item revealing its own peculiar story. Though Reynard and Grant ordered their malaria pills with less than enthusiastic faces, Savoy slapped down a wad of bills before the cashier like an enthusiastic schoolboy.

They organized their supplies into packs then waved down a cab—a Chinese in a surrey—who drove them through the outer streets of Sandakan. Outside the British quarter the city sprawled with ramshackle dwellings and tenements; warehouses filled with drying tobacco and pre-processed rubber; smelting plants stinking of tin; rows of groggeries and brothels. They saw too many native children—dirty, barely dressed—lingering in doorways with empty expressions.

"They say the jungle will rot your clothes," Grant said. "We're to sleep in hammocks 'cause of the ants. Men have died 'cause of the ants."

"Couldn't be much worse than the bayou," Reynard said.

"The locals there don't cut off your head."

"There are headhunters here?"

Grant nodded.

"As soon as we find Lasha," Savoy said, "I hope to document an *orang utan* in the wild. The boys in Biology would pull their beards off knowing I was here." He watched the city's outskirts roll past. "I made inquiries concerning my colleague Professor Stronheim. He was indeed here, having arrived last year—but none seem to know why or where he's gone off to."

"A dead end?" Reynard asked.

"He was involved," Savoy said.

"He told them about me, didn't he?"

"If so, not voluntarily. I assure you."

They rode until the city transformed into lush rows of palm and bamboo and fig trees with long, crawling roots. They wondered if their cabby had taken them in the wrong direction, but soon the trees moved aside as they arrived at Sungai Station. Native Dayaks and Chinese and Indians and Europeans clamored onto the single train hissing against the platform. British soldiers with bayonet-tipped rifles tried to keep the crowd in check, with little success. In the midst of the din, the surrey stopped and the cabby, without a word, unloaded the men's luggage.

"Gentlemen. You are late."

Kiria appeared in a long-sleeved shirt and trousers and knee-high boots, her hair pulled back in a knot and scarf. Beside her, Duncan Barnett stood with not a speck of mud on his trousers. He nodded curtly.

"I hope my list was satisfactory," Kiria said.

"Now you dress like a man," Reynard said.

"Would you wear a frock out here?"

"Why would your grandfather build so far outside the city?" Savoy asked.

"Carlovec Manor was built along the Kinabatangan River in hopes of founding a strong port further inland," she said. "A town was started. Monks built a monastery nearby as a sign of good faith. It would have flourished if the governor hadn't moved the railway to Jesselton..."

"It was the proper choice," Duncan said.

"So he says—but the house is now stranded, an oddity."

"The road to the monastery of Saint Dismas is flooded ten miles west of Kinda Lu," Duncan said. "The only remaining route is downriver, and the Kinabatangan is out of the question. The docks are burned at Lamag and there are reports the insurgent Mat Selleh is to blame. I doubt he would take kindly to whites attempting the interior. You might try the Jebata River out of Takala, but you will need a guide. So far, no one is willing."

The skies cracked with thunder and dropped more rain. They gathered their belongings and hurried up the ramp onto the covered platform as locals crowded in around them. The air stank with unwashed bodies. The air shuddered and rain fell in heavy sheets until the mud boiled.

"We press on, with or without you," Reynard said to Kiria. "Point us in the right direction and we should find our way."

"You would be dead in two days," she said.

"Abandoning us would be tantamount to murder then," Reynard said. "Am I right?"

Twenty minutes after eleven o'clock they bid farewell to Duncan Barnett. He watched as their train pulled away, a stiff, khaki island lost in a sea of clamoring natives. Passengers filled the train to capacity, spilling onto the roof, crouched on the stairs or leaning out open windows. Kiria craned out of their window (having managed to secure a compartment to themselves), returned Duncan's enthusiastic wave, and settled back into her seat.

"He is fond of you," Reynard said, seated across from her.

"He is a dear friend," she said.

"I see."

"Not that it is any of your business."

"Just an observation."

"Full of innuendo."

"Therefore *true*, based on that reaction."

"Our families have known each other for many years," Kiria said. "He is a gentleman, willing to serve without compulsion."

"Ah," Reynard said. "Unlike myself."

"That is not what I said."

"You are still angry with me."

"Whatever gave you that idea?"

"You two feel free to discuss this elsewhere," Grant said with his legs outstretched, his face covered with his hat. "I reckon we could use some rest?"

His gentle rebuke served its purpose. The two focused their attention out the window, avoiding each other's gaze, as the train burst another cloud of steam. It lurched on the track and accelerated. Soon the jungle raced past in a nutty blur, the air ripe with frond and branch and flower. Reynard nodded his head against the window and soon both he and Grant were snoring.

The train bore them west then curved to the southeast, passing through *kampong* villages and makeshift camps of seasonal farmhands and tin miners. Plantations hewn from the mangrove swamps stretched with rubber trees or pepper or coconut. The land simmered in leafy swamps or towered with cliffs pocked with vegetation; the train wove through one nest of ochre bluffs like a snake slithering through an anthill. Savoy lifted his gaze from the *British North Borneo Herald*, a newspaper devoted more to the glories of Her Majesty's influences than accurate news coverage.

"I imagine this is an odd homecoming," he said.

"Pardon?" said Kiria.

"Returning to your ancestral home...in these circumstances."

"Yes."

"You are convinced we cannot find a guide?" he asked.

"I tried wiring Takala," she said. "There is always someone looking to earn money. Now I cannot convince anyone."

"Why?"

"I can only guess. Carlovec Manor was built near what many believed to be...what is the word? Taboo? Superstition is ignored when money is involved. Yet when the railroad moved and the town died, the money stopped coming. Too many promises were broken." She paused, still gazing out the window. "It was better when my mother was alive. I see that now. She respected the legends, treated the people fairly, so they were patient. The time we spent in Carlovec Manor were safe, so long as she was there."

"Then it stopped?"

"Two years ago there was a fire in the outlying villages," she said. "Terrible. No one knows the cause. Many longhouses were destroyed. Mother left to help the women...and she never came back." She opened her mouth as if to say more, wagging her head. "When she died...we lost that trust. They blamed my father, blamed the monks at Saint Dismas, blamed the town my grandfather started and never finished. Their threats grew more serious, so we left with no intention of returning. We did not know when an overzealous warrior would take our heads."

That lifted Savoy's eyebrows. "And us?" he asked.

"Let us hope we can find a guide."

Two hours later the train pulled into Takala Station. The four descended onto the empty platform, the depot half the size of Sungai and without the tin roof. With the storm moving swiftly to the south, the bright sun broiled the afternoon and made them earn every breath. No others descended with them. There were freshly-painted signs in English and Chinese, and a ticket booth still attached with a telegraph wire, but the platform was deserted. The conductor watched them leave from his perch between two cars.

"Locals say the train shouldn't stop," he said with a Dutch accent. "Bloody jungle talk, ma'am, but I've not seen this place so empty. You sure you don't want to go on to Lahad Datu? No extra charge."

"No," Kiria said. "Thank you."

"Good luck then."

The conductor gave a whistle and the train lurched, puffing a loud column of smoke. A head peered from one of the open windows: an old Dayak woman with fleshy jowls and bone jewelry dangling from her neck and ears, her long hair streaked with iron gray. She cried out in a strange tongue:

"*Eng Banka! Ma'tu paa Eng Banka!*"

A girl drew the old woman back inside her window, but it was too late—her words spread to other passengers, whispers traveling from compartment to compartment, moving to those seated atop the train or standing in the open vestibules. Even the caboose man, a tattooed Dayak in a smart trainman's suit, made a tribal sign with his hand.

"What did she say?" Savoy asked, as the train faded away.

"'There walk dogs who drink blood,'" Kiria said.

"We are not as bad as all that, are we?"

"That was not about us," she said. "Foolish old ghost stories."

"When is the next train?" Grant asked.

"Three days."

The village of Takala was little more than a single dirt road stretching from the platform to the shore of the Jebata River. They passed a church with a tall cross and whitewashed planking, two pubs fully stocked with liquor, a bunkhouse with so much bright paint they suspected it served as a brothel, a blacksmithy and a dozen other buildings reminiscent of a gold mining town. They peered through windows and knocked on doors. One pub's door swung open against the wind, the commons empty, tables strewn with plates and dinnerware, platters and supper dishes filled with rotten food and crawling with cockroaches.

"This is a one-horse town," Grant said, "without the horse."

"There were two hundred people last I was here," Kiria said.

They arrived at a two-storied boarding house, the *Takala Hutch*. Grant peered through windows webbed with cracks and punctured holes. He pushed at the door and it opened, casually, the jamb unbroken. "There's empty casings all over the floor," he said. "Two different rifles. Someone held their ground inside here."

"Natives?" Savoy asked.

"I could not imagine," Kiria said. "The Dayaks in general are peaceful people. They only attack when provoked, and they have always been friendly here. There's been local trouble; a man named Mat Salleh's been known to attack British holdings, but...he would have looted the whiskey and burned the church to the ground."

"I've not seen any livestock," Grant said. "The tack shed we passed is plum full, but all the horses are gone. This place's been empty a while."

"Wonderful," Reynard said. "There will be no guide. We should have kept on for the Kinabatangan."

"I could guide us," Kiria said.

"I've never known a woman to guide much of anything."

"Then you've not met the right one," she said.

"Aren't you all the same?"

"Only if all men are as asinine as yourself."

Whatever further retort Reynard cocked in his chamber proved to be a blank. The obscenities boiling on his tongue would not be appropriate for a lady, a Mormon, and a former Catholic priest. Best to write them down in his journal and underline them twice and add plenty of exclamation marks.

Kiria led them west through a line of trees to the Jebata River, its dock empty. With the butt of his rifle Grant broke the padlock off a supply shed—inside were stacked six long-necked *prahu* canoes. The Jebata, by nature of its flow off the highland, worked its way south-westward until it connected with the Kinabatangan and returned in a wide and meandering course back toward the sea. Where the two rivers met, Kiria explained, the monastery and Carlovec Manor stood waiting.

"I see no other alternative," she said. "We can canoe for Saint Dismas in the morning. Or we wait three days for the train back to Sandakan, or continue to Lamag and hope we can charter something along the Kinabatangan, but there is no guarantee if what Duncan says is true. We can hike over twenty miles back along the tracks to Kinda Lu and hope the road is open, but we would need horses, and it is forty miles through the hills."

"I vote we try this river," Grant said.

"I wasn't aware this was a democracy," Reynard said.

"Wasn't aware you were elected to anything."

"It is my *sister* they have out there!"

"I can do it," Kiria said.

Reynard started back toward the village. "I am beginning to think you did this on purpose."

Nightfall brought warm rain and swarms of black flies. They slept in the boarding house, keeping doors locked and windows shuttered. The men took shifts sitting in the front parlor with the rifle in hand. None of them slept well.

At dawn they packed two of the prahu canoes. Grant offered to steer with Savoy on one and Reynard, offering no objection, with Kiria steering on the other. They shoved off the shore and, paddles in hand, began their trek downriver.

The Jebata began at a leisurely pace, weaving off the highland as granite cliffs rose on either side. The silt-brown water soon quickened between stacks of boulders down a long chute. Mangrove trees hugged the bank and dropped spidery roots as if gathering to drink; where the trees offered purchase, brush and creeping vines slapped at the canoes. Kiria kept the pace with her paddle and the men matched her rhythm.

"Keep as dry as you can," she said. "Do not splash to cool off, though you will want to. Infection kills more men than anything else. If we must camp, staying dry will keep you alive." The water rolled up and they crested a foamy hill. "I have been down this river a good dozen times."

"And the last?" Reynard asked.

"Some time back."

"Meaning?"

"A few years," she said.

"A few being?"

"Six."

"I see." Reynard said. "Gentlemen, we are all going to die."

27

In the hours that followed, Reynard's prophecy proved false.

Kiria led them skillfully as the Jebata grew difficult, dropping down long corridors of granite as the mountains fell away and the river rushed between the foothills. Grant proved an able handler of his own paddle as he fired his boat through the churning spray, Savoy clutching for dear life and paddling when commanded. They followed her directions to the letter.

It was late afternoon when the water fell glassy and sluggish, and there they rested and drank from their canteens and allowed the current to carry them along. A host of long-tailed monkeys bounded in the trees above their heads, squawking, pausing to consider the visitors. Savoy watched with a fascinated smile. From his satchel he removed a Kodak Brownie, extended its lens, slid in a plate of film and snapped a photo.

"Where did you get that?" Reynard asked.

"Sandakan."

"We row through the bloody jungle to face a demon from hell...and you bring a camera?"

"Have you *seen* these monkeys?"

"Shush," Kiria said. "We have reached Bukit Garam."

The prahus drifted into a lagoon, and Kiria led them closer to shore. Twenty yards from the river's edge stood a long, wooden building supported high off the ground by many poles. A veranda stretched along the length of the longhouse, separated into a half-dozen segments like tenement balconies. What sunlight that managed through the jungle caught and reflected off tin cups and cobbled plates of metal shingles, throwing beams of light through eaves and crossbeams where hung sheaves of dry herbs and bundles of gray lumps dangling in *rattan* nets.

"Heads?" Savoy asked.

"Those are very old," Kiria said. "A man's head holds power forever. Those in this village have long since given up headhunting. Someone here might be able to tell us about Takala." She cupped her hands to her mouth and cried: "*Muah! Muah! Nombu no raja tu'no?*"

They saw no one along the veranda, no smoke from the longhouse or from the commons yard where two other longhouses crouched further inland. Kiria called again, louder, guiding her canoe closer to shore. As she started a third time, a voice emerged, tentative, in a language the men did not know:

"*Who are you?*"

"*Daughter of Wadian Lucy,*" Kiria replied in the language, "*child of she who perished in the Great Fire. We are on the river without a guide. We are bound for Saint Dismas. Is Raja Tuah still here?*"

A loud, sorrowful cry echoed from the longhouse. An elderly woman with dark, nutty skin emerged onto the veranda, dressed in a simple cotton sarong. Swirling patterns of black-dot tattoos covered her skin from feet to her neck. She raised her palms high above her head, covered her eyes, then raised her palms again.

"*He is gone,*" the woman cried, wailing with a low voice. "*She has taken him. She takes all of them. We have none to hunt for us.*"

"*Who is She?*"

"*Maligang.*"

"*Who?*"

"*She from Lehan Antu, She and her Eng Banka. Oh, Tuah! Why has She taken you?*"

"*Who is She?*" Kiria asked, louder.

"*Deceiver. She who casts us into River of Death. She who is always hungry...*" The old woman raised her arms again, her cry echoing. "*Dark light made flesh.*" She disappeared inside, her dirge joined by other voices in mournful supplication.

Kiria motioned for the men to ease their boats against the shore, stowing them further up the bank in tuffs of thick brush and out of sight from the river. With a resolute heft of her pack, she started for the longhouse. The men followed. The palatable concern in her voice convinced them now was not the time for argument; even Reynard kept silent, following silently at the rear of the line.

Supported over ten feet off the ground by stout, ironwood poles, the open space beneath the longhouse stank of dung and offal and fish, pocked with muddy holes simmering with insects. Around the far side waited the front door. A notched log had been lowered, serving as a ladder, and the four crawled up like awkward spiders. With some effort Reynard and Grant hefted the pole back up to the porch, making the longhouse an island for the night. Clusters of dry thorns coiled around the entrance and at every window like barbed wire, some as long as the palms of their hands.

"*Jeruju* thorns," Kiria said. "A defense against evil spirits."

"Against a penanggalen?" Savoy asked.

"Most especially."

They stepped across the threshold into the commons-room, a wide, open space with an arched ceiling of reed and timbers, the floor scattered with rat pellets and old woven mats and husks of dried reeds. Surrounding the commons, five apartments shared the surrounding veranda. In happier times the house served many extended families, but no children ran here. No dogs barked, no women ground rice, no men sat smoking or gossiping. Kiria stood dumbfounded at the silence, the rotten scent of neglect.

The old woman emerged from one of the larger rooms. Behind her, three more elderly women huddled around a cold fire pit.

"*Where are the children?*" Kiria asked.

"*Gone. All gone,*" the old woman said, Kiria translating. "*I am Lingood. I have no riak to share. You do not have to remove your shoes. Maligang has taken our men.*"

"What does she mean?" Savoy asked.

"Superstitions," Kiria said. "She speaks of Maligang, a demon who denies spirits the afterworld. If you are not careful she catches your *beruwa*, or spirit, and casts it into the River of Death."

"That being—?"

"A spirit's death. Forever death. She speaks of Eng Banka, like that woman on the train, and *Lehan Antu*, 'Longhouse of Spirits,' a term that is new to me. Before my mother was converted to Christianity she was considered *wadian*, a wise-woman. She taught me all the stories. Now..."

"Do you believe them?"

"They seem to be coming true."

As night fell, they cooked a supper of fish and roots and bitter herbs. The old women made sure the men ate first, a strange charity when they, so alone, had next to nothing.

Kiria asked many questions. It began, Lingood said, when men did not return from hunting. Women too began to fade as they gathered rice, or went to herd goats, or to wash clothing in the river. Fires erupted in those villages that sent warriors to scour the forest. Bukit Garam was spared, Lingood said, only because there was no one of interest left to torment. She was not surprised to hear of Takala. Those evil spirits originating from Lehan Antu, she said, were widening their influence.

There were darker stories, the tales of men and women who had been taken by Maligang herself—male, female, white or black or brown or yellow, she did not care. These poor souls did not lose their heads. They lost their bodies, snatched away, never to return. The demons who served her, those called Eng Banka, took them and never gave them back.

"Surely the government would have made a fuss," Savoy said.

"*They blame the Tree Children,*" Lingood said, once Kiria translated. "*They think we take heads when it is she who takes them, and wears them, and sucks the marrow from their spirits.*" She grinned a toothless smile. "*Your ghost-face men, with their shiny...they mean nothing to Maligang.*"

"Nothing?" Savoy asked.

"*She is coming.*"

Reynard rose from the floor and slipped out of the apartment. He wandered the dark commons, his footsteps hollow on the planking. Birds shifted in the rafters above his head. The jungle was far more invasive here than at Takala, and he could not help but wonder how Lasha must be feeling in the midst of such an alien landscape. She had to be at the end of their road. She had to be. This place *was* alien, overflowing with shivery life in every blade of grass and frond and dangling root as if each step outside disturbed microcosms of uncleanliness.

He rummaged in his pockets and found four wooden matches—he had tried to reacquaint himself with the pipe at Takala, coughed himself blue, and vowed never to touch tobacco again. With a fingernail he scratched one alight, the flame tiny and useless against the encroaching night. This place was meant to be inhabited. What could make an entire village disappear?

He entered an abandoned apartment and stepped onto the veranda. The match died and he tossed it away. His fingers brushed along the teakwood railing, festooned with the carvings of animals like tribal gargoyles. The balcony faced the river, illuminated by a faint slash of moonlight on the lagoon. His arms shook and he folded them, and when the tremor crawled into his hands he pressed them against his face.

"What do you smell?" came a voice.

Lingood stood behind him, a wrinkled cinnamon-stick in her faded sarong.

"You..." he said. "You speak English?"

"Your God-men speaking," she said. "When they not grow yellow-snap they come and talk much." She pointed at his chest. "You men with poor Ki-Ki. You go Lehan Antu? What do you smell?"

"What do I smell?"

"You smell like dog."

He inhaled the sweaty tang of his odor. She smelled a good deal worse. She offered a grin, brushing toward him with her sinewy hands as if to sweep him off the porch.

"Dog," she said. "You wild dog?"

"What?"

"Hear her voice? Do not listen? Maligang fat with blood and hungry. Your God not here. Not here, and not there. *Aiso tuhun do obitua doid pomogunan.*" She motioned toward the river. "You not come here, wild dog. You not go *there.*" She tapped at his chest. "Sad." She laughed, and patted his arm like a grandmother. "You no cry. You no *laat.* You good boy."

"Why do you say this?"

"I see him from Lehan Antu. *Ka'a'ai mati' do mugad doid hamin diho'*. You listen to Lingood, boy. That old dog there. He not sad. Angry. That great *sandung nauang*, and no *kuangkai* for poor girls Maligang takes. She get Eng Banka every day, every day, foolish boys who listen only to Maligang. She make them love her. Kill for her. She sing and—"

She looked past him, distracted. The subtle change in her scent prompted him to follow her gaze, past the balcony toward the river. A dull, orange light appeared from between the trees, following the current as it moved into the lagoon.

"Here," she whispered.

Reynard led her back to the others. The cooking fire was already doused, the lanterns snuffed, Grant crouched on one knee with his Winchester poised upon the railing. Savoy pressed a finger against his lips. The others acknowledged with their eyes that yes, they too had seen the light.

"Eng Banka," Lingood whispered. "They come."

Savoy's eyebrows peaked. "You speak English?"

"She speaks English," Reynard said.

With a sweep of his arm Grant encouraged everyone to stay quiet. Reynard knelt beside him. The bobbing light passed through the lagoon: a lantern or a torch they could not tell, drifting from the water onto the shore. Its glow did not reveal who, or what, might have brought it. By the look on the old women's faces, it might as well have been a bodiless apparition. They huddled and wept silently and upturned their palms, pressing their hands against their eyes and lifting them again in silent supplication.

The light lifted, twice. From beneath the longhouse many shapes moved with deliberate, cautious steps. Grant drew in the rifle, pressed his finger against his lips, dropped his head below the railing, and tried not to breathe. Reynard followed his lead.

Beneath the floor came a snuffling, a scattering of movement in the muck, then a deep, loud, unearthly cry. It was followed by more cries at the river and others in the village proper, like wolves howling in the night, joined, then cut short.

The old women closed their eyes, shivering. Reynard glanced at Kiria. She returned his look, grim, clutching one of the women as if she held her own mother.

The light near the river moved up and down, twice, then died. They heard nothing leave. They saw no more lights, no boats. They heard no more. Those in the longhouse waited a long time, not daring to move, to speak, until long after they were sure they were gone.

The next morning Grant examined the grass beneath the longhouse, but the soft mud had erased any sign of what—human or animal or something else—had passed by.

They left what extra food and blankets they could spare. The men brought up firewood, many days worth, and still the old women did not see them off. The prahus were undisturbed in the brush where they had left them. As they repacked the boats Reynard watched the veranda, considering the nets filled with old skulls. He hoped he had misunderstood the old woman, that he had merely read meaning when none had been implied. When one was filled to the brim with shame, he reasoned, he often heard condemnation when none was given.

No, he thought. She knew what she knew.

How could that old woman know?

"Lingood seems fond of you," Kiria said. She reached into her pocket. "She told me to give you this." She gave him a small stone like a rough-hewn marble, etched with the curling head of a wide-eyed beast. "This is *petahu*. I have never heard of a woman giving this to a man, much less a foreigner."

"What is it?"

"A ward against evil," she said, "and some would pay a good deal of money to get one. Keep it close."

He placed it into his pocket, the same where he had once kept the silver bullet. His fingers felt along the rough scratches of the petahu stone, exploring its shape and density. Across the Atlantic his hand remained in that pocket most days, fingering and clutching the bullet. Now that the silver was gone, the emptiness still lingering, he now touched the stone as if this new talisman might make him feel better.

No. It did not feel the same. Yet it felt like *something*, something he could not place, so he would keep it close and remember.

You good boy.

If only that were true, he thought.

"What did you say to her?" Kiria asked.

Reynard did not answer. They climbed into the boat and cast off. They each took a final glance at Bukit Garam: the dilapidated longhouse, the empty, muddy flats and discarded reed baskets along the shore, the morning fog like hands finding naught but impotent teakwood spirits and the smell of old women's tears. The four drifted into the lagoon, dipping their paddles into the water.

"You think they'll get on?" Grant asked.

"The monks will lend aid," Kiria said. "They must."

Reynard thought he saw, peering from the veranda, an old face watching him—until the river's current caught their boats and the trees shrouded the longhouse from view.

For the rest of the day they fought the river, beaten by the relentless sun, the air so thick it hurt to breathe. When they thought to stop Reynard urged them one more mile, one more curve so that they might reach Saint Dismas before dark. Yet as the sun descended below the trees the shadows made each curve and rapid more difficult to navigate.

Then Kiria said, "There it is."

The river deposited them into a valley of thick jungle; a high, granite cliff wound its way to their right along the northern border, and the trees between it and the river fought to grow higher and wilder as if to blot out the sky. The Jebata ended at a watery crossroads where the slow Kinabatangan slithered southeastward in long, wavy curves back toward the sea.

In the last traces of sunset Kiria led them to a wooden dock where waited a tin-roofed shed and the head of a path disappearing into the trees. No signpost or light welcomed them. They eased their boats against the dock and crawled out, shouldered their packs and followed Kiria down the dark path. Savoy lit a lantern, the light casting strange shadows, as Kiria led them fifty yards to a grassy field. There she paused, looking about.

"Shine it," she said, "there."

Savoy raised the lantern high. Light splashed across blackened beams, piles of rubble and the ghostly shape of half-wrought bricked walls. The monastery of Saint Dismas hunched like a ruined castle, vines creeping through its broken teeth, burnt and broken and lightless. Twisted in the grass lay a bleached pile of ivory sticks; a skull grinned from the pile with leathery tissue. Insects scrambled into the dark recesses of the corpse's eyesockets.

Reynard's nostrils flared.

"We are not alone," he said.

He started back towards the dock and the others followed, feeling his urgency, and when they reached the river Savoy lifted his lantern, examining the dock and the shore.

"Good Lord," Savoy said. "The boats are gone."

28

Grant slid the Winchester rifle from its holster at his back and cocked it, adding bullets from his belt. Savoy and Reynard removed their field pistols and confirmed they were loaded.

"Where are the boats?" Kiria asked.

"They were waiting for us," Grant said.

"Evidently," Reynard said. "Is there higher ground?"

Kiria continued looking at the water. "They were just—"

"Higher ground!"

"This way."

She led them back up the trail, pressing past wide fronds and dripping overgrowth. Branches snapped from all directions. Wood clacked upon wood in a loud, harsh rhythm, followed by a long, terrible howl—surrounding them, from all sides, coming closer.

The four burst into a run.

Kiria led them into the ruins of Saint Dismas, through fallen chambers, over rubble and under blackened beams. The monastery had once been twenty rooms surrounding a central garden and well, the Gothic brickwork sporting fluted trim and deep, crenellated edging with arched windows like a medieval castle. Now it lay scattered like tumbled-down children's blocks. They passed through the ruins of the cloister. They hurried up a wide staircase to a plateau where waited the eerie silhouette of the ruined chapel.

Grant lowered his rifle, and they slowed to a halt. "There."

Shapes materialized—six men appeared from the trees behind them at the foot of the stair, six more arriving from behind the chapel. Savoy raised his lantern. Light reflected off oiled limbs, bodies sheathed with grass tunics and necklaces of bone, heads garbed with tall, wooden masks carved into the exaggerated muzzles of snarling dogs. Some carried palmwood spears lashed with steel blades, while others held machete-like iron *mandaus* slung in their woven belts. They barked and shouted and paced, acting more beast than human.

From the chapel's corner one of the men stretched back, barked a strange cry, and hurled his spear with a sinuous arm. It thudded between the opposing groups.

"I assume that's a challenge," Reynard said.

"Shall we give a response?" Savoy asked.

Grant fired the Winchester. The bullet splintered the spear in half; the natives howled and advanced, and those down below started up the steps. Reynard planted a boot into the chapel door and cracked it open like charcoal.

The large chapel retained most of its brick walls and half of a ribbed ceiling, dripping with rot and creeping growth. They raced around blackened pews and scattered rubble, the floorboards groaning beneath their feet. The building had been desecrated intentionally: altar and cross broken, statues decapitated, stained glass shattered. Dirt and stones and moss covered the wooden floor, the jungle creeping into the holes and broken windows.

A glance through the ruined ceiling revealed a stone belltower, fifty yards northwest from the rear of the chapel.

The four raced for the back door, Grant and Savoy ahead with their weapons extended. To their right, a cluster of the masked men slipped inside from a break in the wall. They shoved their shoulders against a massive beam propped against the wall, thirty feet long and as wide as a man's outstretched arms. The beam pivoted and, with another shove, spun away and fell into the center of the chapel.

It connected with the rotten floor and crashed through with an explosion of broken wood. The rest of the floor sighed and, with a great, snapping death-knell, sank into itself. Detritus slid into a black maw that swallowed the chapel's contents.

Kiria screamed and disappeared.

A hand snapped at the fabric of Reynard's shirt—he thought it was Savoy—before he too dropped into emptiness. Grant grabbed Savoy's coat and yanked him from the edge. They ran as boards disappeared at their heels, the sinkhole widening. They launched out the back door and onto moist earth, the floor of the chapel behind them a black, gaping mouth.

"Reynard," Savoy whispered.

Grant jerked him to his feet—natives swarmed from both sides of the chapel, clattering with bone and wood. Grant and Savoy sprinted across the yard to the belltower. A spear cracked above Savoy's head as they passed through the tower entrance and up a curling stairwell. The steps ended halfway up to a bare, stone room with a trapdoor in the ceiling and a ladder on the wall. Grant faced the head of the stairs, rifle loaded, while Savoy went for the ladder. He leaned it against the rim of the trapdoor and scrambled up.

Gibbering natives flooded up the steps. Grant fired as the first man emerged from the stairwell. He took the bullet in the stomach and dropped to his face. Grant cocked the lever and fired again, the impact throwing the man back down the steps. When a third came, Grant pulled the trigger with a *clack* as the chamber snapped, frozen. He tried again and the rifle groaned with metal against metal.

"Savoy!"

The native slid a bone-handled knife from his belt and charged. Grant thrust the rifle barrel into the man's gut, doubled him over, and cracked him across his mask to send him spinning. Grant used the rifle to throttle one, two, three more men. One attacked from the side, crouching, and stabbed up with his spear. Its point plunged in and out of Grant's left arm. The native slid his long *mandau* from its sheath and, with a shout, plunged forward—a *crack* of sound—

He fell to his back, dead.

On the ladder above, Savoy clutched his smoking pistol.

Two more natives emerged from the stairwell.

"Open that door!" Grant said.

Savoy heaved his back against the trapdoor—grunting, his breath hissing—until the door groaned free. He crawled up into the belfry. Grant started up the ladder as two more natives reached; he kicked the nearest dog-mask with a solid blow, scrambled up, and launched through the trapdoor. The belfry was a twenty-foot square stone chamber with little more than a floor, two open windows and a vaulted ceiling. An obese iron bell hung in the center.

They heaved to raise the ladder. Natives pulled from below and all strained at their tug-of-war. One native pulled a blowpipe to his mouth, fitted a dart, and inhaled; Savoy fired his pistol. The bullet struck the man in the throat, dropping him to the floor with a wet cry.

His fall loosened the natives' collective grip—Grant and Savoy pulled up the ladder, slammed the trapdoor shut, and slid closed the iron bolt.

ഇൽൟ

Reynard did not know how long he lay there.

High above, past the torn ceiling of the chapel, stars peered with hazy indifference. His shoulder blades and spine registered the sharp bumps of stones. Dust caked his mouth and eyes and ears, and a faint echo throbbed in his head as if his skull had been crushed and sloppily reassembled. It hurt to breathe.

I fell.

He forced himself to sit. Pain fired in his legs as he straightened his knees but he needed to move, now, move and gain his bearings. Nothing seemed to be broken, but then perhaps his brain had yet to register it.

How the hell did this happen?

He lay in rubble: broken pews and rotten books and soil and grass and moss and broken boards, the entire contents of the dead chapel poured into the basement. He recalled the loud cracking as the floor disintegrated, gunshots, the sensation of his stomach leaping into his throat, Miss Carlovec's screaming...

Kiria.

He found her, sprawled nearby. He crawled to her side and, with a gentle shake, tried to rouse her. He touched her neck and felt her heartbeat—the pulse under his fingertips stirred his blood—so he carefully lifted her head and brushed grass and dirt from her hair. She coughed.

"Can you move?" he asked.

"What—?"

"The floor collapsed, and we fell. Anything broken?"

"I do not know," she said.

Voices in a strange tongue drifted from above, getting closer. With effort he pushed himself to his feet, took a step, and helped Kiria to rise. She clenched her teeth, expelling heavy breath, but she did not cry out and refused when he offered to carry her. They saw no stair to the main floor, and the detritus offered no safe climb; their only recourse lay in a shallow stair that dropped to an even lower basement.

The voices entered the chapel.

Reynard helped her down the steps. At the bottom they found another door—this one of bolted iron—and he shoved his shoulder into it, pushing as quietly as he could through a thick, resisting layer. *Perhaps they think we are buried,* he thought, *think us dead.*

Kiria's hands clutch tight onto his arm.

We are trapped down here.

"I cannot see," she whispered.

Reynard's eyes adjusted to what vague, diffused light might possibly manage in such a dark place. Debris lay at his feet—bits of burned cloth and wood, crumbled stones, shattered glass bent into grotesque shapes. A shaft of broken board, a strip of charred cloth, his kerchief and a match provided a simple torch. They stood in a large cellar of brick, the walls and ceiling blackened like the innards of an enormous kiln. By the scattering of glass and ashen wood, he guessed it had once been a wine cellar.

Scattered along the floor lay clumps of heavier ash with fragments of burnt cloth and blackened bone. Kiria nudged one pile with her boot and a burnt skull rolled free. She shuddered and fell back.

Dead.

The charred remains of at least twenty or more bodies lay scattered, burnt like so much kindling. Some lay huddled in fetal positions. Others lay twisted, their skin ashes upon charred bones. Some were nothing but stains upon the floor. Reynard imagined the monks' screaming, as if their emotions splashed and dried upon the walls. He smelled their burnt skin, their fingernails, left behind in gouged scratches at the back of the blistered door.

"The monks..." Kiria started, stricken. "Who would *do* this?"

Reynard inhaled. "Do you smell it?"

"I do not want to go further."

The torch's feeble light revealed the far wall—crude brick-and-mortar, a rushed job by the sloppy set of the bricks, stained like the inside of a fireplace. The torch revealed a deeper blackness at the wall's base; he knelt, tossed aside a few blackened stones, and discovered a shallow hole. The fire flickered with a faint rush of air.

"It opens to another chamber."

"Reynard."

"I think I can—"

"*Reynard.*"

He followed her gaze. Twenty men stood in the room. Where before there was darkness and silence and evil memory, now the cellar was crowded with dead monks, each draped in their burnt stoles and cassocks. They stood silent with empty sockets and scarecrow limbs. Some retained scraps of charcoal flesh upon their broken bones, while others kept aloft as if by invisible threads. They gaped with broken jawbones and scorched teeth. Reynard tasted old death, far more ancient and vast than those remains glaring in the dark.

Kiria clutched her mouth as if to scream. The nearest corpse raised its skeletal arm toward her, then to the hole.

"*Persecutus,*" it said. A chorus of dead voices rose in unison: "*Persecutus.*"

"Let us do as they say." Reynard dropped to his belly.

"*Persecutus!*"

Kiria dropped to her stomach and crawled into the hole after him.

29

"Mister Savoy."

Savoy opened his eyes. It was still dark. He found himself stretched out on his back beneath the bell, his head resting on his arms. When had he fallen asleep? He sat up and rubbed his eyes.

"My apologies," he said.

Grant kept midnight vigil beside the open window overlooking the ruin of Saint Dismas, rifle stretched across his lap. He wore his overcoat draped over his shoulders, his left arm bandaged from shoulder to elbow. The Dayak's spear left a clean incision, and though tended with Savoy's antiseptic and field dressing, neither discussed the possibility of infection in that unhealthy climate.

He motioned for Savoy to approach the window. The belfry provided a clear view across the entire compound, high enough that they could see over the trees all the way to the river. Through the dark they saw a glimmer of lights—a paddle-wheel steamboat slid against the shore off the Kinabatangan, puffing a white column of smoke. Its windows were aglow, its deck patrolled by men with rifles. Its whistle blew three, distinct blasts as deckhands leaped onto Saint Dismas' dock and lashed the boat into place.

Savoy poked his head outside. He opened his mouth to shout for help before a stone cracked against the wall; fell voices gibbered in the dark beneath him.

"I wouldn't do that," Grant said.

"But that ship—?"

"Funny those natives don't seem to care."

Soon a horse and wagon emerged from the jungle to the west, rattling along a dirt road, the reins clutched by a single driver. It arrived as the deckhands finished unloading a fair stack of crates and barrels. The driver descended and engaged in brief conversation with a man—the captain, they guessed—as the deckhands loaded the cargo into the wagon. When they parted company, the steamboat did not linger. It puffed a head of steam and continued downriver. The driver and his wagon, still without lantern, returned back up the road and into the jungle.

"Who could that be?" Savoy said.

"Someone," Grant said, "who does their business, at night, with all those natives about." He leaned back against the wall, tucked up his knees and closed his eyes. "If you've any idea what to do when the sun comes up, you let me know."

Grant's breathing deepened, slowed, his head nodding. Savoy returned to his nest beneath the bell. Every sound in the night made him twitch. The first hour in the belfry, the natives outside had taunted them with cries like maddened animals. Stones came clattering next—first pebbles, then larger rocks cracking against the tower wall. Grant did not seem to notice. He had cleared his rifle's jam and cleaned the chamber. When their unearthly cries started again, he had removed his harmonica and began an enthusiastic rendition of *Oh Susanna*. The natives redoubled their assault.

Used to drive th'Apaches crazy, he had said.

It was quiet now, but Savoy knew those depraved men lingered, prowling, waiting like jackals. He rummaged in his pack, removed a candle and lit it with a match. Cupping the light he lifted it over his head, illuminating the vaulted ceiling. Wooden shelves lay stashed above the crossbeam, filled with earthen bowls and casks and burlap sacks, provisions long since spoiled by moisture and vermin. The north window facing the cliffs provided an unremarkable view but, unlike the south window, sported a shallow ledge. When he dared poke his head out he found a rusted iron bracket and a few links of chain bolted to the outer wall, the breeze tugging at the remains of a broken rope.

Saint Dismas was more than a monastery: stored provisions and a place to descend the tower, if necessary; the crenels and slim windows and castle-like arrangement of the cloister; the watchtower positioning of the belfry (a room, he noted, with its bolt on the *inside* of the door). It had been a fortress, a bulwark now utterly destroyed.

How long can we hold them off?

His thoughts turned to Reynard and Kiria, crushed beneath the chapel, telling himself to smother his grief. Reynard had survived worse scrapes. He begged God would protect them, somehow. He begged God Lasha was still alive, but he feared what terrors she might have endured. He feared worse that she was not there, lost or dead or worse. In his experience, there were worse things than death.

From his notebook he removed Dr. Stronheim's letter, though he had long since memorized the words:

Whited sepulchers beautiful outward, inside lie dead men's bones. Then Simon Peter having a sword drew it ... Then said Jesus unto Peter, Put up thy sword into the sheath: The Cup which my Father hath given me, shall I not drink it ...

What did it mean now, here, after all that he learned in the last few months? What had Ernst tried to tell him?

That ye may put difference between unclean and clean ...

Unclean.

He considered the ash and the cracks in his palms stained with dirt and blood. He rubbed his hands together, hoping to scrub them clean, wondering if the men he had killed down below had women, children— now abandoned in some isolated longhouse, crying for husbands and fathers who would never return.

He glanced at Grant, still asleep. The apostle Peter was also willing to endure such odds, to defend his Lord without question, even if he did not fully understand what was to come. He wished he had half of Grant's courage, his willingness to shoulder a cause that ultimately served others.

"Why did you stay with us?" he asked.

Grant's eyes snapped open. "What?"

"Forgive me. I just..." Savoy looked at his pistol. "I did not expect such a reception tonight. Not like this. I do not understand why you stayed with us." He shook his head. "Yet if you hadn't, I would probably be dead by now."

Grant smiled. "Probably."

"I never," Savoy said, "never thought I would have to..."

"You were defending yourself."

"Is it that obvious?"

"It never feels right."

"Is that why you are wanted in Utah?"

Grant fell silent, long enough that Savoy regretted the question. "He was a drunk," he finally said. "He deserved it. Some people do."

"Why?"

"My wife."

"Surely your feelings are justified," Savoy said.

"I should've seen justice done, Mister Savoy. He should've stood before a judge and been hung. Instead, I tracked him down. Shot him six times. I reloaded and shot him six times more. If I go back to Utah, I'll be the one to hang, and rightly so." He lifted his canteen and took a drink. "Sometimes you have no other choice. Sometimes you do. I came to see Miss Lasha gets home safe. It won't fix what I've done, but it's something."

"Yes," Savoy said. "I know how you feel."

Mahonri.

Grant opened his eyes. When had he fallen asleep? It felt only seconds since they had been talking, and now Savoy lay snoring in a heap beneath the bell, a crumpled letter in one hand and his pistol in the other.

Irritation twisted his stomach. How long had they slept without keeping watch? Wasn't the old man supposed to...

Here.

He rubbed at his head to dispel the hangover of sleep. He had not dreamed or spoken about Emily for years and yet, now, felt her lingering at the edges. Even his brief mention to Savoy felt like another man's story. She was still a palatable memory, but sometimes he wondered if she existed at all. Once, a year ago, he had forgotten her name, and it frightened him so badly he was tempted to cut the letters of her name into the palms of his hands.

He considered Lasha LaCroix with her smiling eyes and raucous laughter, of Kiria Carlovec and her distant, exotic beauty like a statue in a fancy museum. He thought of that poor, hysterical mother with her squalling baby in Marseille.

Did Emily look or sound like any of them?

He strained to focus on her face. She would take his calloused hand when they walked or knelt in prayer; he always felt so tall and raw and leathery next to her. She would smile and hold his hands and look up at his face and love him forever. She would hold him close in those private and tender moments, and he would look at her and wish he loved her as much. He wished he had done more, said more, felt more.

Bones ached in his arm and shoulder and ribs, the tokens of a hard road that had made him think that *yes*, Mister LaCroix was right, his journey to Borneo was just another way to escape from himself. Or was it Emily's memory, manifested as Lasha LaCroix, tempting him to catch it before it disappeared? Perhaps getting killed by a headhunter was preferable to the noose? Or, if he was lucky, saving Lasha might atone for that which had no repentance?

God had no use for murderers, did he?

I am here.

Grant set his rifle to the floor and looked out the window. He searched the dawn, hoping to find that voice. It was a dream, or the faint residue of one, but it was something, something to drive away the painful realization he would probably be dead in twenty-four hours.

I am here.

A woman stood at the base of the tower—young and petite with ruddy cheeks and smooth hair. There was something about her eyes, deep and black. When her lips parted he envisioned his wedding night and his wife's timid, awkward embraces, how masculine he felt, how soft she felt in his arms.

"Mahonri," she said.

"Emily?"

"Why did you leave me?"

"I didn't..."

"Why did you let him hurt me?"

"Emily?"

"Let me in."

"I don't—"

"*Let me in.*"

His muscles shuddered. Didn't she know her danger? Didn't she fear those murderers outside? Terror boiled up in his throat, the familiar knowing she would be hurt, abused, unless he could protect her.

"*Let me in.*"

Emily was dead.

Rufus. The man's name was Rufus.

He lingered around Bountiful from time to time—everyone in town knew him, a sot who begged for odd jobs or prospected or tried to raise chickens or goats without much success. Though alcohol was as hard to find as gold in those parts, somehow he reeked of the stuff. The locals kept a loose eye but saw no real threat; indeed, they more worried about what it would take to get Poor Old Rufus baptized.

Brother Grant should have been home that fateful evening. He promised to be home by dark, to be there with a wife and unborn child who labored in their simple home. Yet that summer had proved a restless one. It may have been the everyday tedium, the plainness in Emily's face and her growing belly, the fading memory of their courtship. Perhaps it was the feeling he was becoming an ordinary man living a mundane life.

Perhaps it was the arrival of Molly Crane. He and Molly had been friends as children, kindred spirits, until her family went south to Saint George and she had married and disappeared from his life. Now she had returned, husband dead from cholera, rebuilding her life as she cared for her aged aunt. When they had seen each other again, their reunion unexpected and pleasant, Grant felt different around her—virile, more masculine, younger. He had never told Emily about his friendship. He had known Molly for years. They were friends. What did it matter if he wanted to talk to her?

What did it matter to anyone if—on that terrible night—he took a long and private road to Molly Crane's house? What did it matter if he waited until after dark to do so?

"I never touched her," he whispered.

"*You opened your heart to her,*" she said.

"No."

"*You were with her...*"

"Go away."

"*...when you should have been with me.*"

Grant felt the pounding of the horse's rhythm, the hot baking glare of the sun and the dust in his mouth as he rode far and fast and angry. He imagined Poor Old Rufus in the distance. He felt the satisfaction as he caught him in some backwater town in the middle of the desert, the relief as he slid his Colt from its holster, the kick of the pistol as the first bullet caught the old sot in the leg. Rufus had crawled on his belly, crying for his mama, trails of spit and snot and blood running down his face. Grant pulled the trigger a second time, a third. Each shot smothered the pain yet made it larger, spread the poison until he was numb with it, numb with hot bullets and acrid smoke and Rufus bawling like a baby.

You see what you did to her?

By the fifth bullet Rufus had stopped crying. By the sixth Grant could no longer see him, his eyes filled with sweat and tears and smoke, for he knew he was dead—dead to God, dead to Emily, dead to the world, dead to himself.

You see what you did to me?

Dead.

He heard Emily's screams, imagined her broken body in that dry creek bed with blood splashed across her skirts. He smelled the stink of booze and blood.

"*Let me in.*"

She could not survive outside. He knelt beside the trap door, his fingers upon the latch.

"*Let me in.*"

He wanted to stop. He could not stop. He pulled at the heavy bolt.

"*Let me in.*"

He jerked the bolt free. A hand clasped his wrist.

"Stop," Savoy said, aghast. "What are you doing?"

"*Let me in.*"

"She has you, Mister Grant!"

The trapdoor shuddered and, with a heavy blow, flew open with a crash. In the room below, many Eng Banka held a notched log as a battering ram, stabbing up. Savoy threw the door closed, struggled to secure the heavy bolt. The log thudded against the door—once, twice—and the heavy impact knocked Savoy aside. They stabbed up a third time and the log ripped the trapdoor from its hinges.

Four gallon bottles, filled with liquid, launched up into the room, their necks stuffed with oily rags spitting licks of flame.

The first bottle shattered against the rim of the bell. Yellow kerosene splashed, caught the fire, and exploded in a ball of flame. The other three bottles dropped—*pop, pop, pop*—and each exploded, fire washing over the floor. Savoy and Grant retreated. Backpacks kindled, their provisions igniting. Fire consumed Savoy's notebook, his journal, his camera. He threw his coat off and batted at the rising inferno.

"What have I done?" Grant wailed.

"Your canteen," Savoy shouted back.

"*What have I done?*"

The top of the notched log emerged through the opening in the floor. A masked native, limber as a monkey, crawled up into the belfry. Savoy pulled his pistol and fired. The bullet caught the native's leg; he dropped, struck the edge of the opening and fell to the floor below.

Three more masked natives scrambled up the log on hands and feet, quick as oily spiders. Grant moved toward his Winchester—too late—before they piled upon him. When Savoy raised his pistol, a native slid a knife against Grant's neck.

Savoy dropped his pistol and kicked it away.

30

Reynard and Kiria followed a low tunnel. Behind them trailed fell voices, dry and ragged and angry—then silent, as if they had never been there. With Reynard's torch illuminating the way, they raced as quickly as they dared. Only once did they look back, as if expecting to see the phantoms standing behind them.

"We are dead," Kiria said. "In hell."

Reynard was tempted to agree. He did not tell her that this place, the very air he breathed, felt saturated with such feeling that stirred up the curse beneath his skin. Seeing dead men talk made some kind of perverse sense. What could he say? That his eyes absorbed more light, that he could hear the nuances of underground echoes and dripping water? That he could smell her blood beneath her skin?

He had heard of men sworn off opium for years, suddenly taken with cold sweats and trembling. Such were not committed to recovery, he believed, their hearts had not fully given it up. How *could* they give it up? A man so entrenched could never again be clean.

Unclean.

That is what he felt: a growing contamination beneath the earth, getting stronger with every step.

They discovered the corpse of another monk sprawled on the floor, swathed in rotten scraps of cloth, the flesh on his bones like dried jelly. His skull was missing. Reynard knelt and examined the dirt, discovering faint traces of footprints leading down the tunnel. He stood and, without a word, continued down the tunnel.

"Any idea where this tunnel might lead?" he asked.

"I knew the monks had the wine cellar," she said, following, "but this does not seem part of the complex. My grandfather mined in the cliffs behind the house, years ago, but I never thought near the monastery."

"Those..." He paused, unsure. "My Latin is wanting, but it was clear they...well, *they* wanted us to go this way. They knew and used this tunnel. The brick we crawled under was relatively new; I suspect that wall was added to seal them inside."

"Please, no more," she said with disgust.

She pressed her palms against her cheeks, regarding the dark tunnel as it continued down a long and gentle slope, the walls growing narrower as they went. She bit at her fingernail. She looked at Reynard, at the torch crackling in his hand, then back where the whispers lingered in their wake. She considered him with a troubled expression. He caught her look and stopped walking.

"What would you have us do?" he asked. "I do not know where else to go."

"No," she said. "I just..."

"Then it's me," he said. "You are afraid of me."

"No," she said.

"You saw me in Marseille."

"I..."

"Did I hurt you?"

"This is not—"

"Did I *hurt* you?"

"No." Kiria crossed her arms. "I had given a poor woman one of my shawls. You found her. Found my shawl."

"Following a scent," he said glibly.

"You tore it apart."

Reynard's mouth dried up. He wanted to curse, to command her to stop being such a prattling fool and making up hurtful stories. He wanted to fall to his knees and beg her forgiveness. *I did not hurt her*, he told himself, *did not hurt her, did not hurt her,* and all his feelings came in such a torrent he was sure she could see them on his face.

"I wish I could give you comfort," he said, trying to sound as casual as he could, "but I cannot. I could say violence and unearthly persuasion forced me to manifest, and that may be true. I could tell you the Beast is still with me. I feel it every day. I strive to keep it away. I cannot say what will happen if we continue forward. All I know is that I feel *something.*"

"What?"

"I do not know, but it waits at the end of this tunnel."

"I do not enjoy the prospect of traveling alone in the dark with you," she said. "For more reasons I care to give."

"Fair enough."

"Can you guarantee my safety?"

"I can only do my best."

"That does not make me feel any better. I am forced to trust you, Reynard. This from the man certain I would drown him in the Jebata. My old literature professor would call this a bit of dramatic irony."

"I wouldn't concern yourself," he said. "My life has proven less literature, and more penny dreadful."

For a long time they walked beneath the earth, silent.

This subterranean realm was a honeycomb of caves, narrow channels of rock they squeezed through, only to open wide into black expanses bristling with stalagmites. The torch caught every nuance of distorted shape and revealed a faint yet visible path. Within an hour they lost all sense of direction. In two they doubted they were still mortal, but empty spirits wandering the underworld.

To stave off their fear and hunger and fatigue, Reynard spoke, telling stories, sharing more personal details than he had with anyone. He did his best to add color to his tales, did he best to make her smile—especially the one about stealing his father's horse and getting thrown into the neighbor's rose garden. Kiria laughed until she wiped tears from her eyes.

"Incorrigible," she said.

"And you," he said. "You must have been a hellion, roaming the jungles like an ape. I imagine clothes were optional as a child?"

She laughed again. "There's not much to tell."

"There must be something."

"It is true that Borneo is wild and full of danger."

"Yet your grandfather came here."

"His reasons were his own," she said. "I spent most of my childhood in Carlovec Manor. Those days saw many guests and much commerce, but when the railroad moved and the township died, we were alone. Though we found comfort at the monastery, it was Mother's heritage that kept me feeling safe. She understood the wild...how best to survive it."

"You said she was Catholic."

"Devout, converted shortly before she met my father. The monks' rituals brought order, but it was never enough. The local legends are more alive...but then, Borneo is alive. There are spirits everywhere. We enjoyed friendship among those longhouses upriver, but soon they would have nothing more to do with us."

"Why?"

"My father's mood, his very spirit...it degenerated over time. It soured everything."

"The curse is demanding," he said.

"An understatement. Before I knew of his condition, I thought he was addicted to drink or opium, as was the case with many fathers of well-to-do families." She laughed a sad, hollow sound. "If only we were so fortunate."

Reynard felt a sudden rush of feeling, a tenderness he had denied himself from the very moment they met in New Orleans. Occasionally he gave himself permission to feel it, standing beside her in the abattoir aboard the *Kalabakang*, hearing her weep through a door, the sight of her alone on a steamer's deck. There were times he found her so beautiful he could not look at her. More often, he could not help but look.

He had been so critical of her, so demanding. He had, as she once said, given her little but distrust and blame. Of course she mistrusted him. She had every reason to fear him.

I do not want to hurt you.

You are what you do, his father once said. *Boys have all sorts of inklings; doesn't mean they should follow them all.*

"It was clear he suffered," she continued, unaware. "I heard the servants whispering. I knew the Dayaks regarded us with suspicion. I heard the monks' prayers." She breathed in deep. "Father's passions became more desperate, his rages more severe, until that night..."

She stopped, touched at her face.

"Tell me," he said.

"I..." Their eyes met. "I have such nightmares, Reynard."

Her hand slid onto his arm. He noted a change in her composure, softer and more frightened, but not of him. He smelled her impending tears, but she refused to let them fall. He admired her composure. What he had mistaken as complicity he had come to know as her strength of spirit; he wished he could be as strong.

"After mother died, father was never the same," she continued. "The curse used him up. He intensified his search for a cure, considered every option. He corresponded with great minds from around the world. After mother died I accompanied him to Europe in this pursuit: Vienna, Prague, Berlin, Geneva. Father discovered your existence somewhere along the way. We sought you in Provence."

"How did you know?"

"I honestly do not know," she said. "In London, we learned your family relocated to Canada. Edward suggested we continue the search while father returned to make the necessary arrangements."

"You obeyed the counsel of your...valet?"

"Edward Tukebote became my father's closest confidant. At least the Edward I remember."

"But you knew."

"The Edward whom I knew as a child and the Edward who accompanied me to America were two very different people. I could not see it at the time, but I knew it, somehow. Yet I never feared him." Her eyes grew distant. "He was more than a valet. He supported me after mother's death, helped me comprehend the full extent of father's nature. I refused to believe what seems now very plain. I thought him an extraordinary man in the most tragic of times. He knew exactly what to say. He knew how much I needed—"

She stopped, suddenly.

"What is it?" he asked.

She inhaled a quick breath, tears forming around her eyes.

"Please tell me," he said.

"I am weary," she said. "Weary of secrets."

She said no more after that.

The torch was nearly spent, a nest of stubborn coals. The two fingered along the tunnel walls to guide them, suppressing their terror, pressing onward until exhaustion forced them to stop. When they set themselves to the floor, Kiria fell asleep in moments. The dark came so complete Reynard could not see her, but smelled her sweat, hear the slow cadence of her breathing. He thought sure he could feel the beating of her heart in his throat. She moved, whispering a sad, childlike sound, and he reached out tenderly to touch her arm. She relaxed and returned breathing normally.

Still there.

She trusted him here, of all places. He felt comfort at her presence, even if he could not see her. How could he harm such a lovely thing?

I'm so hungry.

He bit down, cracking through the rind of his lip. Blood oozed and he sucked, reveling with the taste—

Then he spat it from his mouth.

Bloody weakling!

He opened he eyes. How long had he slept? The torch was dead. He blinked, surprised that he could see the curved wall of the tunnel—faint, monochrome—and the sleeping body of Kiria breathing upon the floor, her black hair in tangled ringlets.

"Miss Carlovec," he said.

"Yes." She sat up, startled. "What is it?"

"Light."

"I cannot see anything."

He helped her to her feet. "This way."

"How can you—?" She stopped. "Yes. I see. The dark never confounded my father. Are you—?"

"Not yet."

"Close?"

He led her along with urgency. Fifty yards further she pulled from his hand as the tunnel brightened and details began to emerge. Soon she led the way. The tunnel turned a corner and ended at a gaping slash of a hole with rubble strewn about in haphazard piles. They passed through and descended a stair into a stone gallery with high, pointed arches every twenty feet. The walls had once been smeared with plaster, but time had flaked much of it into dust, the stone behind it exposed like old bones.

Frescos illuminated those few portions of plaster still intact, and Reynard knew neither the symbols nor the mythology painted there: rotund faces with large eyes and drooping earlobes; multi-armed figures with animal heads and sharp teeth. Suns, moons, and rivers flowed from one patch of plaster to another, only to be replaced with animals standing on two legs with curving swords in their claws. The clearest figure was a four-armed man wearing the toothy mask of a monkey, and in each claw he gripped a curved blade. Each blade ran with red paint.

Long, rectangular niches pocked the walls down the length of the gallery, and upon every stone bed lay a skeleton. Grave upon grave of ancient dead lay on either side. Other corridors branched off into darkness.

"Your grandfather mined the cliffs," Reynard said. "Does this—?"

"Look familiar?" she said. "No. I never knew."

They descended another flight of steps to stop at a metal gate. It was locked. Light blazed from the other side.

"And this?" he whispered.

Beyond the gate stretched an immense grotto, the largest cave either of them had ever seen. Oil sconces, set into the wall, burned with orange light. The gate was one of many such entrances along the uppermost tier; a dozen shallow, circular levels descended like an ancient amphitheater. At the bottom, three misshapen monoliths of stone, each at least twenty feet tall, surrounded a round pool of black water. Countless niches pocked the tiers at each descending level, some filled with dusty cobweb, others empty, but most contained more corpses.

Those on the highest level held little but chalky bone, yet with each tier downward the bodies told a history of decomposition in reverse: flecks of bone at the outer ring took skeletal shape two tiers down, then into bodies clotted with mummified tissue and ragged clothing two tiers lower. Those lying upon the bottommost ring, nearest to the pool and standing stones, were freshly dead native men and women. Their bodies lay bloated and rotten with moist decay.

"It was a dream," she said, quaking.

Reynard too found his emotions sharpening, his chest heavy with despair. Into his mind came the drab colors of that alley in Chalmette, the sight of Bill Tourney's shredded throat and that sickly fruit smell—

—*Blazes, but the smell!*—

The unclean sensation of death since the monks' cellar, the dull, prickly feel that teased the Beast inside him—it came from beyond the gate, from the black pool between the standing stones.

"Where are we?" he asked.

"Directly," Kiria said, "beneath Carlovec Manor."

31

Six natives forced Savoy and Grant out of the tower, prodded by spears. They led them through the ruins of Saint Dismas, the early morning already hot and glutinous with the muddy smell of the river. Those few items spared the fire—Grant's rifle and the remains of their packs—were left behind.

They reached a dirt road that led west through the jungle. The natives had long removed their snarling wooden masks and slung them at their backs, their dark faces painted with swirling black-dot tattoos that contoured the lines creasing their skin. They did not smile, did not speak. When Savoy's pace slackened, a man nudged him between the shoulder blades with the butt of his spear.

Two hundred yards along they came upon the shell of a half-built village: storefronts and stables and half-planked, corrugated shelters, the skeletal remains of a town long abandoned. What was not shrouded with vine or moss was rust-brown and rotten and squealing. They passed through without stopping.

A half-mile further the jungle cast aside to reveal a broad, grassy hill surrounded by an ironwork fence. At its crest crouched an immense mansion—Carlovec Manor leered with shadow and climbing vine over brick walls and stone foundation like some hulking beast, its central tower branching into two wings with many windows. An even taller granite cliff rose behind the house, and from its lofty edge a waterfall cascaded into a pool or river they could not see. The manor seemed both new and ancient, European and indigenous, a monstrosity in the midst of the wilderness.

The natives nudged their captives through the gate and, as they ascended the hill, the building added windows, chimneys and tiled roofs, its arches craning to gawk. Savoy did not like it. It reeked of colonial pretension and old money, as if this aberration might alone conquer the jungle. The dirt road gave way to weedy flagstone, and they followed the driveway underneath the porte-cochere, up the front steps, and onto the porch. A native rapped heavily upon the massive oak door. He and the others took four paces back, leaving their prisoners alone upon the porch. Grant looked to Savoy, who looked to him—two unlucky salesmen forced to this imposing doormat.

The door opened. There stood a man in a smart black suit, regarding them with an air of stuffy indifference. He was thin and quiet and empty, like so many underappreciated servants in well-to-do homes. He did not seem to notice the natives.

"Ah," he said with an accent. "You are expected."

"If we refuse?" Savoy asked.

"Breakfast is served. If you please?"

The men took one last look at the natives at their back, and followed the butler inside. He led them down a short corridor into a foyer where a wide staircase climbed up more flights than they could guess. Mahogany walls and ornate wallpaper reminded Savoy of similar mansions found all throughout England, but he noted a Dutch influence in the linear angles of the paneling and a more Eastern touch by the rounded archways. The ceilings were high and crystal lamps were set into the walls every five feet; he did not see any pipes for gas, and the lamps did not appear to hold oil or candlewicks.

Savoy had to admit the house was impressive. Gaudy, pretentious as the Devil himself, but impressive. A fountain sat in the center of the hall, ten feet wide at its base, the marble of its upraised bowl cut so thin the water inside it splashed with a creamy half-light. A stone nymph poured water from an urn while another, an emaciated man twisted against the basin, reached up as if desperate to drink.

"*Tantalus at Juventas' Cup*," said a voice. Another man entered the hall. Savoy noted his resemblance to Kiria in his squared jaw and straight nose, but could not tell his age. One moment he seemed close to sixty; the next he carried himself much younger. "Sculpted by none other than William Carsbury," he continued, "right down to the mirrored floor. Do you see? A most remarkable piece." He considered the emaciated man's tortured face. "I am moved every time I look upon it."

"Mister Carlovec, I presume?" Savoy said.

"Do call me Wilhem, thank you," he said, "and this is not the first time we have met, professor. You may remember my attending your lecture on lycanthropy at Cambridge, a year ago last August? I even asked you a question, one you were unable to answer to my satisfaction."

"I regret I do not."

"Your findings were naïve. You accept the folklore more than it warrants, especially if you stoop to Baring-Gould as a reliable source. 'There are more things in heaven and earth,' as it's said, 'than are dreamt of in your philosophy.'"

"I believe in what I see," Savoy said.

"A curious philosophy for a man of the cloth."

"Where is Lasha LaCroix?"

Wilhem smiled. "Please...Mister Grant, is it?...enjoy some breakfast." He laughed at Grant's grim expression. "It's all right, my boy. All right. By the look of you it's been a difficult night. Crumpets and sausage and eggs and all the coffee you can stomach. Jeané..." He motioned to the butler. "...See to it. Have him wash up, if you please."

"Of course," Jeané said. "Your coat, sir."

Grant looked to Savoy, who nodded, and Grant followed the butler down the hall as he removed his overcoat. By the smell Savoy guessed the dining room was ahead and slightly to the right of where he stood. The scent of spicy meat and coffee was intoxicating. Wilhem led him to an open room on their immediate right—would they be taking their breakfast there?

They passed through double doors into a drawing room. It was designed, it seemed, for the sole purpose of exhibiting expensive *objects d'art*: decorative vases, rugs and framed mirrors, grim portraits, and statues of Greek and oriental design. The closed curtains bathed the room in diffused light, the air redolent with dust. Above the mantle hung a Remington shotgun, a single-loading Winchester, two German-made military pistols with handle clips, various knives of curious design, and a hundred-year-old Turkish Blunderbuss. A mounted boar's head, a water buffalo skull and three ape skulls leered from their trophy plaques on the opposite wall.

Savoy sat down on a padded sofa. There were no trays of sausage, no pot of coffee. Wilhem offered a cigar and, when Savoy refused, lit one for himself with a puff of pungent smoke. He sat in an ornate chair across from Savoy, puffing and crossing his legs as if the two might discuss the pleasantries of banking.

"So," Wilhem said. "Where is Reynard LaCroix?"

"He is dead," Savoy said. "He and your daughter lie crushed in the basement of Saint Dismas' chapel, thanks to those savages of yours."

"They are not mine."

"Does *she* command them?"

"Death is very subjective here," Wilhem said. "You would be surprised at its frailty in this *oubliette* of the world. The locals can be...excitable. A far greater work is made manifest, professor. There are prices to be paid."

"Including your daughter?"

Wilhem's took a breath of smoke. A flicker of emotion crossed his eyes, indiscernible. "She should have remained in America."

"We did not give her much of a choice," Savoy said, "seeing your...associate...forced our hand. Do you know the true nature of that abomination? Why unite yourself with such a murderous—?"

"Mind your manners," came a whisper.

Savoy's words caught in his throat. Long fingers brushed along the nape of his neck like a spider, soft and menacing. Had she been there all the time, lurking in the shadows? Why did he not see her? The woman was as Grant described—if not more fair and terrible—dressed in a red silk faille with velvet trim that contrasted against her pale skin. Her red hair, pulled back in a knot, hung like a horsetail off her shoulder. She moved with a deliberate, bird-like menace, tainted with the faint scent of vinegar and roses. He felt very cold.

"Lucinda," Wilhem said.

"You never told me our guests had arrived."

"I did not wish to disturb you."

"Posh." She walked around the sofa, focusing on Savoy. "You must give credit to my children outside. They consider me sacred, you know. I give them a certain sense of...a sense of purpose. More tangible then wafers and wine, don't you agree?"

"You are a fraud," Savoy said.

"You know nothing about me."

"Tell that to Mister Tukebote."

Blood blossomed in her cheeks but she continued to smile, nibbling at her sharp fingernail like a schoolgirl. She wandered to Wilhem's side. Master Carlovec stood, extended his arms, and she swept into his embrace. Savoy noted a strange look in Wilhem's eyes. Did he enjoy embracing that creature?

"So...how is it done?" Savoy asked with enthusiasm. "The mesmerism, the spine and head floating about, that sort of thing? Extraordinary. The nerves must fuse with the host organism to create a form of...biologic puppet? That requires instantaneous regeneration. I can see the need for a healthy supply of blood, but what of the acidic properties of your—?"

"My, but you *are* forward," Lucinda said.

"The stories say your kind feed on women," Savoy continued, "but there were plenty of dead men as well. What is unclear is why you emasculate them, as the—"

"Do what now?" Wilhem asked.

"Emasculate. The violent removal of a man's genitalia? Dreadful business, that. I surmised she prefers the femoral vein as the jugular is so damaged after she—"

"Is this true?"

"You are on the brink," she said quickly, "and this old man plays games."

"*Is this true?*"

Lucinda pulled from Wilhem's side. "He is a liar."

"Are you a liar?" Wilhem asked Savoy. "Is this what you are doing? Feed us lies, draw us apart, get us snapping at each other?" He laughed, wagging his finger. "You slippery rascal. Another such diversion and I'll become very cross, very cross indeed." He waved his hand at Lucinda and she sat in an adjoining chair. "Now then, professor. What is the composition of Monsieur LaCroix's remarkable bullet? Who made the thing?"

Savoy closed his mouth. *He does not know.*

"My grandfather studied silver in his earliest efforts," Wilhem continued, as if not expecting an answer, "but no combination served. I'd thought the idea of silver against lycanthropy was a myth. Yet there is silver and other metals in the bullet's remains dear Lucinda gave me—platinum, gold, iron. I noted herbs of unknown origin. This cocktail altered Monsieur LaCroix's cycle, yes? How was it done?"

"Where is Miss LaCroix?" Savoy asked.

"Tell me."

"Is she alive?"

Wilhem sighed. "We have much the same interests, professor. My daughter must have related my family's own particular problems, so I shall be frank. I will master my curse. I will do whatever it requires to see it done. Either Monsieur LaCroix will be persuaded to help me—or I will drain what remains I find at Saint Dismas. Either way, my grandfather's dream will immediately be realized."

"Soon?" Lucinda asked.

"This very evening, if I obtain the information I require."

Savoy felt as if his every emotion, every thought, radiated like waves of heat for Lucinda to see. He watched the way she looked at Wilhem, how she glanced at Savoy dismissively. *She barely notices I am here*, he considered, *Wilhem's presence is so dominant.* Indeed, Master Carlovec *was* dominant, despite his casual tone and shallow courtesy.

"Bring me Miss LaCroix," he said. "If you can see fit to release us all safely, then I am willing to assist you in your efforts. Perhaps we can—"

"When?" Wilhem asked. "A week? A month? After you have returned to America? After you've brought the government down upon us? No. I must have the answers now. I have waited long enough."

"Those are my terms," Savoy said.

"Ah, I see now." Wilhem's voice became measured, cold. "You thought these were negotiations. You are in no position to demand anything, sir. Nothing. I have not traveled so far, sacrificed so much, to be delayed by a man such as yourself."

"I do not presume otherwise," Savoy said.

"Then tell me what I want to know."

Savoy felt a tight knot in his chest and, to his surprise, thought of a game of Whist soon after leaving Rome. Grant and Miss Carlovec had beaten him and Reynard soundly; the round ended when Kiria slapped down an ace to take the winning trick.

It is time, he thought, *for my trump card.*

"I forged that bullet," he said.

Wilhem paused, considering him, then looked to Lucinda. She looked to Savoy, then Wilhem, with wide eyes. "Of course," he said. "I should have known; your relationship with Monsieur LaCroix makes a good deal more sense."

"Indeed. It is I who used it against him; it is I who helped him during his remission. It is I who can replicate the formula. You are correct—this is not a negotiation. This is a business arrangement. You wish my expertise, and I have my price. See Miss LaCroix safely home."

"Impossible. She cannot leave."

"So she *is* here?"

"He cannot have her," Lucinda hissed.

"Do not fret," Wilhem said. "She is yours."

Savoy frowned. "May I see her?"

"No."

"Then I cannot help you."

Wilhem drew a deep inhale on his cigar and snuffed it on a standing ashtray. "You choose to be stubborn," he said. "Very well. Those ancients who built the foundations of this house understood the pliability of the human animal. Birth and death and physical shape held no meaning for them. It is most unfortunate that for a man who claims an open mind..." He walked to the doors. "I am afraid you were right, my dear. I had so hoped otherwise."

"I told you," Lucinda said.

"So you did. Tell Jeané I will take tea in an hour." He made a slight nod toward Savoy. "I would offer you the usual comforts, but that would be inappropriate...considering."

"Where is Lasha?" Savoy said.

"If only we had met under, shall I say...less troublesome circumstances?"

"*Where is she?*"

Wilhem left, the sound of his footsteps fading. Lucinda settled to the sofa and placed a languid hand upon Savoy's shoulder. She gazed into his eyes. He tried to look away, caught in the attention of her black eyes. He thought she might kiss him, but then she began to speak, soft words that he felt more than heard. For a moment—just a moment—he wanted to declare he loved her, to share his fears, his dreams. He wanted to tell her how smart he was. Wouldn't she be proud? Wouldn't she hold close the man who had forged such a miracle as that silver bullet?

Am I the one opening the trapdoor now?

"...Pater noster, qui es in cælis, " he whispered, motioning the sign of the cross with his hand, clutching to the rites of exorcism, "sanctificetur nomen tuum. Adveniat regnum tuum—"

"Stop," she said.

"—Fiat voluntas tua, sicut in cælo et in terra—"

"I said *stop*," she said, slapping him across the face. "You can no longer harm me, shaman. Your God no longer holds any power against me."

"And Master Carlovec?"

"I do not fear him."

"So you say."

"I have seen *your* heart, old man." She stood. "You use your friends' tragedies to justify your own sins. You fail as a Jew. You fail as a Catholic. You fail as an academic. You think God would impart a portion of his grace to such a waste as you?"

"And what," he asked, "was your thirty pieces of silver?"

She slapped him across the face again, harder, the edge of her fingernail drawing a thin line of blood from his ear to his mouth. His trembling hands felt along his coat; he still had his glasses, a handkerchief, the letter from Ernst Stronheim—*should I ask her?* He wished they had given him breakfast. He removed the handkerchief and dabbed at the wound. His hands could not stop shaking. Would breakfast be coming? He wanted to leave, feeling a raw fear like a schoolboy.

Lucinda pulled a velvet cord along the wall; Jeané soon appeared in the doorway. "Fetch the other one," she said. "Master wants his service in an hour, and we still have those items to sort through..."

"Currently engaged," he said. "Shall I prepare rooms for our guests?"

"No. If what Master says is true, his labors will be completed this very evening. You know what you must do. This is an important night...for all of us."

"Yes. Thank you, Madame."

Jeané brought Grant in from breakfast, and then went to the front door and admitted four of the Eng Banka who had been waiting outside. Lucinda commanded the others with strange words and they were off, running as fast as they could down the slope toward the jungle. She started down an adjoining corridor into the west wing of the house. The natives followed, urging the men forward. Grant never once met Lucinda's gaze, preferring to focus on the floor.

At the hall's end they descended a long stair. At the bottom Lucinda turned a switch and electric bulbs illuminated from sconces, the dim, uneven light revealing a basement stacked with a dozen iron-banded glass coffins. At least half were filled with green liquid. Three contained nude, headless bodies, all female. There was an armoire and changing table heaped with towels and perfumes, a large sink with a pump, and a full-length mirror. The air stank of vinegar and blood and dead flowers.

Electric light, Savoy thought. *How?*

They continued into another basement filled with many shelves and racks of crates, bottled foodstuffs and bags of rice and beans and grains; shovels and picks and iron-riveted flues beside countless crates painted with Chinese letters; coils of rope and stacks of boots and lanterns and open-faced boxes filled with bracing pins and T-joints and many thick nails used in railroad ties. Savoy caught the words *active fusing* on barrels smelling of wet gunpowder. He could not guess why mining equipment would figure so prominently in Carlovec Manor's stores.

They passed through a larger basement dominated by six massive fire-tube boilers. Only two of the tanks were lit, the air hot and heavy with many pipes. Between two tanks the question was solved—there hissed a massive electric generator, its dials wiggling. Clusters of iridescent bulbs glimmered, their light dimming and surging as if the generator breathed. Savoy stared at the power-works in astonishment. He smelled no coal. As they started down another stairwell his next question was solved: the sound of rushing water roared beneath their feet and behind the walls.

An underground river. He had heard of such advances in America. Water-powered turbines provided electricity—a singular, extraordinary accomplishment.

The further they descended the quieter it became, but the air was more cool, the stone walls dripping. At the bottom of the stair Lucinda removed a lantern from a hook on the wall, lit it with a match, and guided them into a large, circular room. Carved from the rock itself, the chamber opened to three other entrances as black as pitch, the crossroads to a host of other rooms not made by modern hands.

A round, ten-foot-wide hole dominated the center of the floor. Rivulets of fetid water drained from the moist walls and poured over the edges, cascading down a deep, deep shaft into lightless space, only to splash onto a distant surface far below. It was a well, Savoy noted, an ancient forgotten well, and then a sick realization washed over him as he realized—

"Throw them in," Lucinda said.

Grant dashed for the exit. Natives leapt upon him like apes; he spun about with an angry cry, cracked one man across the head with his elbow, and shook the other man off. Grant moved backwards to slam another man against the wall. When another pummeled his bad arm, he cocked him under his chin and sent him to the floor. Another native stood between him and the exit; Grant buried his fist into his stomach, folding him over, and started for the exit.

Lucinda struck like a snake, sudden, violent—she caught Grant by the throat. Though nearly a third larger than her, he could not stop her from dragging him across the floor. He kicked and thrashed, writhing, hissing as her hand contracted, but she handled him as a rag doll.

She threw him into the hole. Grant dropped with a startled cry.

Two of the Eng Banka pulled Savoy's arms behind his back and forced him to the edge. "Killing me will not help!" he cried.

"I do not need to kill you," she said.

They shoved him, feet-first, into the hole.

The dark swallowed him up, rushed past him, the terrible falling and freezing air clutching his voice so he could not shout. He struck icy water, submerging. His feet touched something solid and he kicked up, finding air, and he thrashed to keep his mouth above the water, his brain threatening to black out at the shock and pain. Grant floundered in the water beside him, both men gasping and coughing and stinging with cold.

"I trust my hospitality will make you more pliable," came Lucinda's voice, high above. "Why did that bullet stave off the animal? How was it done?"

"What does it matter?" Savoy asked, coughing, the cold cramping his muscles and burning his skin. "You have everything you want!"

"Yes," her voice said. "You will tell me, Arté. You will." Her voice grew faint. "You cannot imagine what sleeps down here."

32

"Six months," Kiria said as she and Reynard sat before the ancient gate, the dead-filled grotto rising beyond, "before mother—before she died—father flew into one of his rages. This time she faced up to him."

"You do not have to tell me," Reynard said.

"I must," she cried. She wagged her head. "I have been here before. The screaming from the conservatory...I had forgotten. How could I have forgotten? I could hear them shouting. Mother commanded him to leave. He dragged her by her hair and she was screaming..."

She buried her face into her hands. Reynard placed his own hand on her shoulder, not sure what to say, what to do, but he felt her despair as keenly as his own. She did not protest.

"I followed them," she said. "Through a door that is not a door, down an endless stair, then orange light." She motioned to the sconces along the grotto wall, each with a shallow iron bowl snapping with oily flame. "I remember that pool and those stones and the bones, countless bones. Why build a house upon such a terrible place?"

"And your mother?"

"I thought she was dead, but..." She laughed an angry sound. "He caught her praying to her old gods. There must have been more...I...I found them—" Her body heaved with great, choking gasps, and she turned her face away. "He wanted to break her and he did, he *did*, because he was the animal...hurting her. The animal was my father and not my father—" She buried her face again in her hands. "Oh God!"

Reynard reeled, unable to comprehend such a dreadful scene. He examined his own life, those broken memories of past sins. Was he too capable of such depravity? *It is still you,* Savoy had said. *It is your hair, your blood, your bones. If it is of you, of that which makes you Reynard, then your reason and ethics must also remain.*

Kiria lost her battle, weeping. She leaned into him.

He wrapped his arm around her shoulders and drew her against his chest, saying nothing, knowing full well the poison of grief. With his other hand he took hers, her skin soft against his own. As he held her close and felt her relax, her breath slowing against his neck. He inhaled and drew in her scent, opened his entire heart to her, as deeply as anything he had ever known.

He did not know if he loved her—or wanted to tear out her throat. Sometimes he could not tell the difference.

"Thank God you are here," she whispered.

With a solid kick from Reynard, rusted hinges snapped from their bracings and the gate fell open with a dusty clatter. He led Kiria through, leaned the gate into place as best he could and tossed what bits of broken hinge he found back into the corridor. From their vantage upon the uppermost tier they saw two possible exits: a wooden door to their right, and an archway on the far side where a stair ascended into shadow. Reynard considered the closest corpse, the remains of broken bone and pagan jewelry, and his gaze fell upon the black pool.

Kiria clutched his arm. "Please."

They found the door unlocked; a stair led upwards. It was a long climb, hundreds of steps, ending at a short corridor with an oil lamp and a large iron ring bolted onto a bracket. Reynard pulled the ring and a portion of the wall slid open. As Kiria passed through, she brushed her hand along the exit as if to confirm it was real.

They emerged into a vast, neglected greenhouse. Assailed by the stink of rotten vegetation, they shielded their eyes against the afternoon light. The greenhouse bulged from the rear of Carlovec Manor with a dome of glass panels, the windows catching the light like the inverted, multifaceted eye of a giant insect. The assorted vines, flowers, potted plants, shrubs and trees were either long dead or had grown wild beyond their boundaries. Vines webbed the glass dome and fingered along tables and chairs. Discarded tools lay rusted or wreathed in cobweb. Then there was the mold: a carpet of green, leprous growths blotting out windows and dripping from tables.

Kiria went to one cluster of rotten husks. "Mother's *paphiopedilum* collection," she said, sliding a hand under one soggy leaf. "We left so quickly..."

She descended into memory, and Reynard looked outside. Behind the house, three acres of neglected gardens stopped against a sheer granite cliff that climbed a hundred feet or more. A waterfall cascaded off the cliff and into a lagoon, creating a slender river that wove around hillocks dotted with rusted lawn chairs, past a gazebo, and under a stone bridge through maze-like shrubs. The gardens held the shape and flavor of former decadence but, like the greenhouse, had long since been left fallow.

"Where does the river go?" Reynard asked.

"Beneath the house," she said. "The river continues underground to join the Kinabatangan. Grandfather built this house right upon it...can you hear?" Reynard listened, and he could indeed hear the faint, dull roar of falling water. "He tapped it for the boilers, fresh water from the tap. Father paid a large sum of money to bring in men from America. They installed a generator for electrics."

"Impressive."

Kiria led him out of the greenhouse and into a large kitchen. It was grimy and dusty and unused, the stoves rusted shut, cabinets and shelving draped in cobweb, the counters littered with animal droppings. They continued down a hall to a second kitchen and found it clean, its shelves filled with provisions. They found dried beef and saltine crackers and bottles of preserves, and Kiria twisted the faucet for all the fresh, cold water they could drink. They ate ravenously, trying to be quiet, trying to keep things as they left them.

"Tell me about this house," he said.

"Father's laboratory is here, on the ground floor," she said, "and where he spent most of his time. Drawing room, conservatory, servant's quarters and main dining room. There are four floors with East and West wings, and many cellars beneath. Second floor contains the guest dining room, master bedroom, smoking room, music room. Guest rooms on the second and third floors, along both wings. Higher up is the ballroom, billiards, more servant's quarters, observatory."

"Blazes."

"This is a big house."

It was an overwhelming prospect. There was no knowing what, or who, they might find. There could be five or fifty people to contend with while searching for Lasha—even if she was here, even if she was still alive. To the immediate right was another door with a tarnished brass knob. "Where does this lead?" he asked.

"Servants' stair," Kiria said, "to the guest dining room."

"We should avoid an unexpected encounter," he said, "and it seems this floor is the most likely place to have that happen, and the most unlikely place they would lodge a guest. If Lasha is here, I would deduce her upstairs."

"Mother told me not to use those stairs."

"Did you always do what your mother told you?"

"Yes."

Reynard tried the knob. It turned, soundlessly, and he opened the door to a dusty stairwell of steep, narrow steps. He meant to say something, then took Kiria by the arm and led her inside, closing the door as quickly and as quietly as he could.

"What—?" she started.

He pressed his hand against his mouth. The kitchen door opened. Two people entered, their heels clacking on the tiled flooring; they rummaged through the bottles and cans and containers along the cupboards. Reynard's muscles tightened at the fear they had left crumbs, a splash of water, something that revealed their presence.

"And this?" a woman asked in English.

"All of them," said a man with a subtle accent. "The water must be clean and infused with garlic, the rice mingled with thorns."

Kiria wagged her head. She did not recognize them.

"Does she lie to us?" the woman asked.

"Bite your tongue."

The man stood just on the other side of the door. Reynard held his breath waiting for the door to fly open, no idea what to do if that happened. He was more concerned with Kiria's immediate presence, her face so close, his hand having touched her face and lips. He wanted to hold her again.

"We have a right to know," the woman said.

"I trust the Mistress," the man said. "She will keep her promise."

There came the sound of dry goods being scooped from one container and poured into another, and soon both pairs of feet clicked away. A door shut heavily, and still the two in the servants' stairwell did not move. Reynard and Kiria expelled a nervous breath; he smiled like a cat, and she shook her head at his cozy indifference.

"Shall we?" he whispered.

ഇരൻ

Grant found a narrow ledge surrounding the well water and, with effort, heaved himself up. He pulled Savoy beside him, the two gasping and shivering. The walls were of black stone, slick with mold, the floor at least ten feet below the water's surface. Savoy praised God they did not break their necks; then he reconsidered it. Perhaps a quick death would have been better.

"If hypothermia does not kill us," he said, shivering, "then the unhealthy vapors in this terrible place certainly will."

"You could tell her," Grant said.

"I doubt she would believe anything I say. If she did, she will kill us just the same." He tightened his arms across his chest. "At least they gave you breakfast."

Grant laughed. Savoy looked at him with surprise, then found himself laughing in response. The two laughed deliriously until their voices echoed loudly up the darkness of the shaft. When their laughter finally died, once born of terror and pain, Savoy tried to think of fire and warm blankets.

"She is afraid of him," he said.

"What?"

"Lucinda. She is afraid of Master Carlovec, yet she loves him. I understand why she went through so much trouble." He paused. "I have known too many wives whose husbands treat them badly. One of those dirty little secrets: wives who suffer at the hands of so-called gentlemen. Yet these same women would defend their husbands to the death."

"Doesn't make any sense."

"It is a sad fact that passion will make us do all sorts of things," Savoy said. "Perhaps she is indeed determined to see her husband cured. Perhaps she does this out of love."

"You believe that?" Grant asked.

"No. Not really."

They sat a long time, hours perhaps, trying to ignore the fear that time was their enemy, that every minute shivering in the dark meant one minute closer to a dark and lonely death. High above, the lantern's light flickered and disappeared, filling the well with a deep, moist darkness. Neither said a word. For Savoy this was worse than a werewolf in a chapel, worse than wild men in the dark. Did the prophet Jonah feel such despair, he thought, trapped in impossible darkness, unsure if his Lord would save such a sinner as he?

"Look."

Grant pointed toward the water, to the bottom of the well. They could see the stone floor at the bottom of the well, illuminated by a vague, grey light. He slid into the icy water, submerged, and swam to the bottom with a splashy kick. He stayed below only a moment.

"A tunnel," he said, treading water. "I think this is connected to a drain, some kind of sewer. There is light at the other end."

"The house was built upon a much older site," Savoy said. "Who knows how far these ruins extend?" He could indeed see the tunnel entrance, the half-light revealing the outer edges grinning like broken teeth.

"I'll see where it leads," Grant said.

"The water is freezing," Savoy said. "You cannot—"

Grant sucked in a quick breath, dropped below the water's surface, and pushed himself into the hole.

Grant swam until his lungs clenched. Twenty feet further he decided he had made the stupidest, most rash decision in all his sorry life. Either he would swim to the light, or drown. His hands slithered along the walls, feet flailing as he strained to drag himself along. The tunnel was too small to turn around. With each yard he swirled up a cloud of grit and slime, joined by the last, trailing bubbles from his mouth.

The ceiling of the tunnel opened and, with a solid kick, he broke the waterline. He gasped and coughed and caught his breath. He bobbed in a black, shallow well, a metal grate just high enough to reach. He gripped it, twisting his body. It did not budge. Whatever lay beyond was dark as pitch and soundless, another abandoned chamber in a labyrinthine sprawl beneath the house.

He considered his options. *The light at the end of the tunnel*, he thought with no irony, *or back to our tomb*. He inhaled a deep breath, submerged, and continued down the tunnel.

I brought us to this.

The way seemed to go on forever, the light no closer, and with each frenzied pull forward his lungs began to burn. Memories emerged of swimming in hot summers, diving deep in the Great Salt Lake, the sting in his eyes, going deeper and deeper until sunlight fell away and he was tempted to open his mouth. He swam harder.

He shot out of the tunnel and into a much larger column of water. For a moment he hung there, suspended, unsure which way was up, but then he saw dull, flickering light above his head. Below him lay bones, pile upon pile of rotten, decomposing remains. Countless skulls stared up in frozen grins, their eyes filled with slime, the water saturated with chalky dust. When he kicked to ascend, a shape detached from the pile—the rotten husk of a man, his fleshy throat wriggling.

Grant scrambled up, horrified, bubbles streaming.

Something locked around his ankle.

He kicked and his leg pulled free. Foul water slipped down his throat. He shot up, crested the waterline into open air and snatched a quick, ragged breath—

Hands pulled him back under the water, clutching at his shoulders and shirt and belt and over his face. They dragged him down. Beneath him, a host of pale bodies ascended with reaching arms and slack faces. Some were mere bones, others scarecrows of rotten flesh and sinew. Their bony fingers pulled at his trousers. Cold, slippery skin brushed against his feet. One pair of hands covered his face, clawed at his eyes.

He yanked from their grasp, kicked hard and swam as hard as he could, clawing at the water, feeling like lead. He found a lip of stone, caught it, and launched from the waterline onto a stone floor—coughing, spitting, retching fluid. He rolled from the water's edge, scrambling to gain distance.

He lay beside a round pool surrounded by three tall, misshapen columns of stone, its broad surface now as still and black as ink. Around him rose a grotto, vast, rising like a ghastly amphitheatre with tier after tier of countless dead in all directions. Fresh bodies laid upon the closest slabs, native men and women with their throats and shoulders opened up like those back-alley drunks in Chalmette.

He had seen horrible things, but *this*—

The retching came so powerfully he groaned at the spasms, spewing until his lungs and stomach had nothing else to give. He sucked in a desperate breath. Two sets of stairs climbed up between the tiers to end at two exits, a closed door to his right and an open archway to his left. He got to his feet and started toward the arch.

The door to the right unlatched.

He fled to the top of the stairs and slipped through the arch, just as two people entered the grotto. He recognized the butler Jeané in his suit and polish, but now there was a woman in a black dress and white apron and cap. They each carried two wicker baskets down the steps, walking past the dead without a second glance. Grant prayed they did not notice the wet signs of his arrival—but they may not have noticed much of anything, focused on placing the baskets in a crescent along the far side of the pool.

Jeané opened the first basket, scooped in a bowl, and scattered grains of rice along the floor. The woman opened the second and cast flakes of dried herbs upon the rice. Jeané opened the third and, with a ladle, sprinkled arcs of water with a wide, sweeping gesture. They did not open the fourth.

"I'm hungry," the woman said.

"Quiet," Jeané said.

"She promised."

"Yes."

"Tell me," she said. "Tell me she will keep her promise."

"I cannot promise anything," he said.

Grant needed to move, now, to get as far as he could from that evil place. Another set of stairs, rising steeply into the dark, was his only option. He followed them quietly, not knowing, not caring where they took him.

33

Carlovec Manor was a fine example of craftsmanship: walls of mahogany and calcimine trim; knobs and hinges of brass; lamps in etched sconces of rose-tinted glass; multi-paned windows without bubbles. Along the walls hung many portraits, those austere ancestors whose eyes followed in passing.

Time had not been kind. Mildew dappled the wainscoting behind statues or dead plants, stinking, crawling where least observed by sunlight. Stubborn tuffs of mold spread from floor to ceiling, paint and wallpaper rotten with cancerous tuffs. Cobwebs lingered in corners and across chandeliers. The shadows were lengthening, and what sunlight managed through the windows began to die.

Upon their arrival into the guest dining room, Reynard and Kiria dared enter the hallway and cross to the other side, though they had not seen nor heard anyone since the kitchen. Wide corridors stretched into the east and west wings with many doors. To their left, the hallway stretched to a foyer where a central staircase led upstairs and downstairs. They kept a loose eye in that direction.

Reynard drew aside a curtain to glance over the front lawn, the windowpane streaked with frothy rain. A growing crowd of Eng Banka made rude camp all along the grassy hill. They came in twos and fives and more, clustering around campfires protected by rain breaks of stacked logs. Others erected wooden poles twice their height like giant matchsticks. At each pole there was a fire, and with each fire a caretaker, and each caretaker smeared dark fluids across each log. A man began to chant—a large, stout fellow splattered with swirling tattoos from his face to his feet—and his words were joined, man by man, until the entire crowd was singing. This was not a song of hunting or triumph. It may not have been a song at all but a demand, resonating until the glass of the window vibrated.

"This is the wrong time of year," Kiria said. "This looks like *katang*, but not like this. Not this big."

"What is it?"

"A sacred rite. Those *belawang* poles...anointed with eggs and animal blood. Raised up each year to drive away evil spirits, but this..." She shook her head. "The singing is much like *tiwah*," she continued, "a burial ceremony outsiders never see. You may be the first."

"Is that a good thing?"

"It requires blood sacrifice," she said, "but I see no bull, no goat."

Reynard fingered in his pockets. He felt the etched *petahu* stone given to him by Lingood, rolling it between his fingers, then rubbed his hands together and pressed his warm palms against his cheeks. "I wish Arté was here," he said. He would know what to do."

Kiria placed a hand on his shoulder. He turned and looked at her, really *looked*—then licked his thumb and wiped dirt from the end of her nose.

"You're dirty," he said.

She smiled. "You have smelled better yourself, *monsieur*."

He felt it again—a wave of tenderness for the same woman who had come to New Orleans and started this whole affair. Yet she had faced death and terror and still continued by his side, courageous when her memories threatened to break her, willing to risk everything to save another's life. She could have refused them. She could have abandoned them, yet here she stood. Since their shared intimacy beneath the house, the way she had relied upon him, all his doubts were cast aside. He meant to say something. An apology, perhaps.

Do I love her?

The sun was gone. Below, the Eng Banka's fires burned like so many wild stars. Reynard exhaled and his breath came like mist. He shivered. Kiria reached up and touched his cheek, her hand cold against his skin.

Light and heat dissipated like smoke, the same chill felt in that blackened cellar below Saint Dismas. He half-expected another skeletal shape standing in the foyer, staring, shouting at him. The thought stabbed a shiver down his spine.

"What is it?" she asked.

"Something," he said. "Something is *here*."

She opened her mouth but found no voice. As the dregs of sunset disappeared, the night thickened with a sickly-sweet odor. Darkness slithered through the corridors.

"It's so cold," she said.

"Do you feel—?"

...Renny...

"Yes?" he asked.

"What?"

"You said my name."

"Reynard," Kiria said, shivering. "I said nothing."

...See you...

Cold pulsed up Reynard's chest and prickled the hair on the back of his neck. A subtle tremor erupted from deep within his gut and pressed into his ribcage. *Stay away*, he commanded. *Stay away, stay away.*

...See you...

Laughter, distant.

...Always see you...

Stay away.

An arctic breeze fired up the stairwell. Dead plants leaned and scattered brown husks across the carpet, picture frames rattled, the chandelier pulled to one side and cobwebs dropped like old bandages. The air resounded with tinkling crystal as if the house inhaled a deep breath.

More laughter. Many voices.

...See you both...

Reynard felt anger like ants prickling at his flesh. Lasha was in that house. She had to be. If she endured such terrible nights in this place, then he would command the Beast to stay away. He would ignore the house as it tried to grind them under its boot.

He took Kiria's hand and together they walked down the west corridor. A tide of voices grew louder as they passed door after door. An invisible miasma smothered Reynard's senses as if the dark gained substance; he gripped Kiria's hand tighter. He did not know if she could hear them, but he smelled the palatable scent of her fear.

...*Toh joat*...

...*Toh joat sujan*...

When they reached the end of the hall, finding no trace that anyone had been that way in a long time, they doubled back to the foyer. The rain rattled against the windows. There came a distant *boom* and light flashed through the curtain. Another deep clap of thunder rattled the windows, the glass illuminated like a flashbulb. The chandelier shivered. Reynard tried to think; the moment the light died the house was alive, angry, filled to bursting. Outside, the tribal chanting grew louder.

Kiria shivered. "How can it be so cold?"

Reynard plunged his hand into his pocket and, without knowing why, removed the *petahu* stone. He held it up. The air around them coalesced into an ethereal crowd—men and women, transparent, emotion distorting their faces into terrible contortions. Their arms reached, dead mouths gaping. Where Reynard lifted the stone, the ghosts materialized and recoiled. He raised the stone higher; more ethereal bodies flittered back like an electric torch forcing the shadows away. When the stone moved, the nebulous spirits returned in force before disappearing from view.

...*Toh joat sujan!*...

"Evil spirits," Kiria said.

"Cursed," Reynard said. "This house..."

Above came a crack and a shower of plaster. The chandelier broke from the ceiling. Reynard clutched Kiria and threw her aside as the chandelier fell with a heavy crash. She shrieked. Wraiths poured over them like oily water; their graveyard stink filling Reynard's mouth. The *petahu* stone rolled from his fingers.

Kiria!

Thick, smothering darkness came. Reynard could not see the window, the chandelier, anything. Whispers drove into his ears.

Then came light, a pale yellow glow beneath a door at the end of the east corridor. He thought he saw movement—*Kiria?*—and he was on his feet, running for the light. When he arrived at the door he thought he smelled her, felt her wake.

He gripped the knob. Unlocked. He opened it.

Rain smeared the window. Mosquito netting draped a tall four-poster beside a bureau and nightstand. A single candle, melted to its base, struggled to breathe.

A shape huddled on the bed. Clad in a white nightdress, a young woman curled her legs against her chest.

"Lasha?"

"*No more!*" she shouted.

She had lost too much weight, too much light. She was gaunt and pale; clotted bandages wrapped both wrists and ankles. Her pale-gold hair fell in sweaty threads along her neck and shoulders. She reeked of vinegar and dried blood. Reynard felt such happiness and grief all at once that it took effort not to shout.

"Lasha," he said tenderly. "It is your brother."

She sat up. Fat, clean tears rolled off her cheeks. He walked toward her and touched her arm. She shook, eyes wild, as if to scream.

He offered a grin. "I am sorry I am so late."

She burst into sobbing. He drew her in and she wrapped her arms around his neck and wept. He held her tight, the way he did when she was little and only her big brother could make things better.

"Please be real," she whispered. "*Please.*"

"Blazes, girl, but you are filthy," he said, holding her at arm's length. "You would think they'd provide guests a hot bath and clean clothing?"

She rubbed an arm under her nose, sniffed, and managed a laugh. "It *is* you," she said. She removed a pair of slippers from beneath the bed, put them on, and slid on a woolen robe crumpled at her feet. "I am ready to go," she said. She pressed into him again as if expecting her hand to pass through. "I cannot believe it, Renny, but I knew you would—"

She stopped, looked past him.

She screamed.

Dull, heavy pain exploded in the back of Reynard's head. He buckled, his knees turning to water. As he collapsed, spinning to the floor, he turned to see—

—The world turned clockwise—

Kiria?

Lasha knelt to help her fallen brother and a harsh word came from the doorway; she stiffened and the word came again, louder. She recoiled to her bed. Kiria stood there. She looked at Reynard, to Lasha. A candlestick dropped from her fingers.

What?

Lucinda stood behind her. She entered the room and began to sing, an old Dayak song sung in younger days when Kiria was afraid to sleep. "*Stars winking,*" she sang, "*cast off clouds as spirits gather, rice from hand to baskets filling—*"

"Who are you?" Kiria said.

"*...Rivers run and cry to sleep...*"

Kiria stared at her hands, at Reynard, at the thin line of blood trickling from his head. Tears fell down her cheeks. She knew this song as well as that woman's black eyes full of rage and shame.

"So it is true," she said.

"This was the only way to love him," Lucinda said. "The only way he would love me. It was the only way to save you, my dear."

"Mother."

"Yes."

"I thought you were dead."

"I *am* dead, my dear. I am damned. The Virgin ignored my prayers. So I pleaded to Them who would listen. They did listen."

"What have you done?" Kiria asked.

"Tonight your father will be but a man," Lucinda said, "and we will be free. Already my Eng Banka chant for me, call upon Them, draw up favors I need to see things done. It will be done. Tonight."

"My mother is *dead!*"

Kiria strained against the whispering between her ears, the smooth, liquid voice commanding her to be silent, to understand those intimate longings born of fear and loneliness and hatred, made sacred by shared understanding. She wanted another song. She wanted to sleep. She knew this was no longer her mother but a foul thing, vomited up from beneath the house, but she could not help but feel such love. A memory came, a dream, of dry bones and dead faces beneath orange light, but the fear was all gone.

Daughters listen to their mothers.

"Mama." Kiria opened her arms.

Lucinda embraced her, swallowed her up.

"We will never be apart again," she said. "My little girl."

34

Savoy knew it was night. He felt it sink into his flesh, into his bones. He had lost all sense of time yet knew something had changed. He knew behind his eyes, deep under his ribs, a sense of knowing when the whisper of Spirit came calling.

He had waited with what hope he could salvage, praying whenever he felt terror, praying harder when he thought he could no longer breathe. When the well felt to smother him he looked at the water and the vague light—then he imagined Grant's bloated body, drowned, and he gasped and tried to think of sunlight. His rosary and cross and other implements were gone, lost or destroyed in the belltower, and he had neither mantle nor stole or any other trappings to prove he was anything more than a foolish, apostate old man.

Damn her to hell, but she was right!

She had unearthed his failures with all the skill of a surgeon. Even if he managed to escape, what then? She awaited him. There was also the matter of finding Miss Lasha, eluding the Eng Banka, finding a way back to civilization, *etcetera*. The impossibility gripped him with anguish.

I must not despair.

Was that not the measure of faith? To remain true in the darkest of hours? Did not Paul the Apostle stand before Caesar? Did not the Lord Himself stand before Pilate, knowing full well the outcome?

He had taken an oath to serve Christ and, just as Reynard said, he was indeed more concerned with the opinions of disbelieving colleagues than the truth. He had lied to himself; for as much as he sought to know the unknowable, he had first made an oath. All else should have been secondary. He sought signs and wonders through his discoveries and now, at the bottom of a well, he was as guilty as all those scholars of Cambridge whom he had condemned. He had always been looking for evidence, when in reality he should have trusted his faith.

Of course Lucinda no longer feared him. He was useless, faithless, a hypocrite of the first order. He was as cursed as Jonah, just as swallowed up by darkness. Lucinda knew any man who put his own interest before friends, before the Lord, had no power to confound her. The monks of Saint Dismas, he presumed, had given their lives against her. He expected to do better?

"Lord God," he prayed.

His voice echoed into the nothing above his head. He prayed for forgiveness, for power to confront such evil as could be found in this house. He prayed to be free from the belly of this dark place—spit out and given a second chance. He prayed until he no longer felt the cold.

The well water began to move. Savoy blinked and wiped at his face. Water sloshed against the rim. A shadow emerged beneath the water, tentative, groping at the edge of the slimy hole as if blind and grasping for purchase. First a head, than an arm.

Savoy strained to see, cursing his bad eyesight. The shape pulled from the hole like a newborn, grasping up, up, hands seeking the air. Savoy reached down and took a hand into his own.

Clammy and cold, the flesh melted away in Savoy's grip. A ruined face rose from the waterline, the eyeless sockets dripping slime, flesh oozing off pale bone. Savoy tore his hand free and flattened against the wall, horrified. The dead thing reached, gripped his legs, and jerked him into the water.

Savoy submerged. He thrashed, fought against cold fingers wrapping around his throat. Water poured between his lips and he opened his eyes to see a blank, dead face, terrible in its stillness. He tore free toward the air, but its hands gripped his shirt and pulled him down near the bottom of the well. Savoy kicked, thrashing.

Something heavy hit the water, something new. His hands reached and felt the prickly feel of hemp. He gripped it. The rope tugged and he held fast as he was pulled from the water. He kicked at the hands grabbing at his legs, his arms quivering, burning against the pain.

He could not let go. He would not.

Slowly, foot by foot, he was pulled upwards. He wrapped his hands around the rope. Where the hemp clutched his flesh the skin began to redden, purple. Blood seeped where friction tore him open. He refused to let go. With his feet he leaned against the wall of the shaft, steadying himself, expecting strength to give and he would fall back into that dead thing's embrace. He was an old man, a weak man, but the terror kept him clutched to that rope.

At the lip of the hole, the rope burned through his hands and Grant caught him at the shoulders. Both collapsed. Savoy coughed until water and bile fell from his lips and he retched, his body shivering with revulsion. He no longer felt his burning arms and fingers. Adrenaline, he guessed. Adrenaline saved an old man's life.

A hissing moan rolled from the well.

Grant helped him to his feet. "Time to leave."

They ascended to the upper basement. They warmed and dried themselves in the boiler room, opened bottled goods from the supply room to slurp down peaches and dried apples. Savoy fashioned a makeshift satchel from a leather bag and swath of rope and stuffed the bottom with rags. He filled it with a box of Lundstrom matches, a pair of leather gloves, a small oil lantern and other items he saw fit.

With a crowbar Grant cracked open a cabinet and discovered crates stamped with *caution* in both English and Chinese. Canvas sacks held coils of fusing. Barrels contained moist, browning bundles like clumps of old bedding. "Gun cotton," he said, "and there's enough gelignite here to punch a hole in a mountain." He opened another crate and slid free a paper-wrapped stick of dynamite. "Mining supplies. They'd still have a kick, I'd warrant, but it's awfully wet."

"In their basement?" Savoy asked.

"I've seen worse." Grant considered the lot, then motioned for Savoy to follow him. "I think you should see something."

Sliding the crowbar into his belt, Grant led Savoy back into the boiler room. He pushed at a section of wall and it moved inward, revealing a passage and a stone stair that dropped into the dark. Savoy lit the lantern and they descended a long time. Halfway down, they came upon a gaping head of stone, three times their height, and the stairs continued through its open mouth as if into the bowels of some fossilized god. His puffy cheeks, heavy lids, drooping earlobes, strong forehead, and intricate crown reminded Savoy of Siam and its exotic temples.

"If only I had my camera," he said.

They passed shallow alcoves gated with rusted iron and cobweb, most filled with piles of cracked bones heavy with dust—mostly skulls, many attached to their spines. When the stair ended, the grotto stretched high above their heads and down low. Savoy gaped in disbelief. Tier after tier of dead dropped before them to end at the black pool and its three standing stones.

"There," Grant said. "I came from there."

Savoy wished he held a cross or rosary, a scrap of silver, a portion of the Eucharist or any of his vials of holy water. In his life he had entered many places ripe with evil. Water and stone and old dead in and of themselves were of no consequence, but this place...

Whited sepulchers beautiful outward. Inside lie dead men's bones.

He started down toward the pool and focused on the twisted remains of a skeleton. A man's ribcage and spine blended into oversized limbs and bent claws like some bizarre mismatch at the Museum of Ancient History. Another nearby had a skull of grotesque shape and extension, its jaw bristling with four rows of jagged teeth. At least a half-dozen of the mutated corpses lay scattered throughout the crypt, each different in its size and peculiarity.

At first Savoy did not know what to think, then it struck him—lycanthropy was but a temporary transformation of a man's physical frame and, in theory, cells and membranes reverted to their original state upon death. These were failed attempts, he guessed, one man's obsession to master lycanthropy, bought with the currency of innocent lives.

What have you done, Wilhem?

He turned to look elsewhere and stopped, stricken.

"My God," he said.

The remains of an older man lay on one slab near the bottom, still dressed in ragged clothing befitting a gentleman of means. He had been dead for some time, perhaps a year or more, his face twisted by a rictus of decomposition. The flesh of his neck and shoulder hung off his collarbone like dried leather.

"Who is this?" Grant asked.

"My friend," Savoy said. "My friend Ernst."

35

Kiria?

Reynard tried to move, frozen, held fast at his wrists and ankles. He laid flat on his back on a gurney, strapped tight by leather belts. The fleshy crook of his right arm was exposed. He registered multiple stings along his veins; he had been pricked with a hypodermic.

He was in a makeshift laboratory, a mélange of lamps and mismatched sofas and side tables heaped with books. The air reeked of blood and carbolic and ether and sour vinegar. A table to his right held medical instruments and apparatus befitting a chemist, and there were racks of strange mechanical devices and instruments fed by pipes with many dials. He smelled propane and coal-fed steam. Across the room was a fireplace with a cluster of hearth-tools, its mantle capped with bottles of scotch and wine. A hot fire blazed despite the heat, heaped with the ashy remains of grey coke.

The harder he pulled, the tighter the straps squeezed. He tried to ignore his headache, to remember the last few moments before he was—

Lasha.

The doorknob turned with a creak. He closed his eyes and slackened his muscles. Two people entered. One slid a bottle from the mantle, poured liquid into a glass, and swallowed audibly. The other went to the table with fingers tinkling along metal instruments. By the gait and tramp of heavy boots this was not the same man whose voice he heard in the kitchen. He rustled of cotton and silk, smelling of musky cologne, the swish of a longcoat against his trousers.

The other lingered at the hearth, sipped, then clack-clacked in her boots across the floor to sit upon a sofa. The miasma of chemicals and smoke made her scent confusing, impossible to pinpoint. He recognized the cadence of her footsteps.

"Kiria," he said.

"He is awake," she said. She went to his side. "How do you feel?"

"Where is Lasha?"

"Our experience must have taken its toll," she said. "You fell to the floor with some violent seizure." She looked to the old, wiry man at the table. "The antidote should be ready any time...isn't that right?"

"Give him wine," Wilhem said, gruffly.

"I am not your servant."

"Give him wine and be quiet about it."

Wilhem slid on a pair of vulcanized gloves, opened a valve and lit a Bunsen burner. He set a beaker upon the flame, allowed it to boil, then poured the grey fluid into a vial filled with blood. The infusion created a dirty sludge. He placed a few drops onto a glass slide and examined them under a microscope; Reynard watched him work, enraged and intrigued at this turn of events. Was he indeed on the verge?

Kiria came with wine, but Reynard refused. "Take these straps off me," he said.

"Soon."

"Why are you doing this?"

"I trust him."

"I do hope our Old Father Basta is burning in some corner of hell, don't you agree?" Wilhem said, perched on his stool like a vulture. He poured more silver liquid into a vial filled with blood and started a fresh slide. "Ahhh," he said, examining it. "If only you had accepted my daughter's invitation at the first."

"Remove these," Reynard demanded, "and take me to my sister."

"No. Not yet."

"Get them off me!"

Wilhem turned on his seat. "Have you no concept of what this day means? My curse will no longer be a burden. Think of it!" He returned to his microscope. "Did you know the ancients who once lived here sought to transform themselves into beasts? On purpose? I do admire their courage. They delved into the deep mystery and drew up power, for here they could *sujan*, make their passions into animal form. Why not then, my grandfather reasoned, learn the secret of unmaking? He spared no expense."

Reynard wriggled against his bonds.

Not as tight–

"...With birth and death," Wilhem continued as he worked, "those fragile seconds of transition, there is potential to trap primal energies. Like all good practitioners of science I took what secrets my father uncovered and found the mechanics of their superstition. A pinch of blood, a pound of flesh, and we are baptized into new creatures. My father sought truth through spirit. I have sought it through science, and made it mine."

Wilhem went to the fireplace. With the tongs he lifted from the coals a dish with a blob of oozing metal. "Your bullet was either extraordinary skill or a miraculous blunder. In all my years I never thought such a thing–"

"And his blood?" Kiria asked.

Wilhem grinned. "Tonight, everything changes."

Reynard's anxiety became an itching until he wondered if they had infused the straps with wolfsbane. This was more than a chemical aversion–he needed to get free. Now. He had seen men escape from ropes and chains and straitjackets at the vaudeville, traps far more complex than straps on a medical table. He imagined the technique could not be too difficult with desperation and sweat at his disposal. He wriggled his ankles, moving them against, then away, from their metal clasps. He did the same with his wrists, moving them slow, allowing sweat to grease the insides of the straps. He worked carefully, relaxing when Kiria looked his way.

"You played me," he said.

"You heard what you wanted to hear," she said.

"You saw what happened on the *Kalabakang*."

"That was not his fault."

"Why serve a man who would abuse your moth–?"

Kiria pressed her hands over his mouth. Wilhem did not seem to hear, crouched over his microscope. His right hand jotted sloppy notes as enthusiasm overwhelmed his penmanship.

"You must forget what I told you," she whispered.

Her voice, her very manner, was ice. Everything she said, everything he felt for her dissolved in those indifferent eyes. It had taken him weeks to trust her. Only during the sharing of her memories below the earth did he truly believe in her. When he held her close and soothed away her grief he realized he needed her, felt strength knowing she needed him. No one had ever really needed him before. Not even Lasha, though she might have said otherwise, for he knew she could have lived quite happily without him.

As if he, Reynard LaCroix, could have ever considered a life of happiness!

"You lied to me," he said. "To serve your father."

"I love him."

"A monster who violated your mother?"

Wilhem's pencil fell to the floor. "What did he say?"

"As if you did not know," Kiria said.

"I've no memory of such a thing."

"You must remember."

"He may not," Reynard said. "Under the influence, one's memory is often—"

She slapped him across the face. "You are no better!" she cried. "Dragging me back to this awful place! How dare you!" She focused on her father. "Now she is dead. She is dead! She is dead because of you!"

"That was her choice," Wilhem said.

"She did it for you!"

"I claim no responsibility," he said, without emotion. "Lucinda knows what it means to remain at my side. If she is unhappy, she has no one to blame but herself."

He turned back to his microscope. Kiria bristled, the color leaving her face until she was white, bloodless. Her teeth clenched until the tension tightened the sinews of her neck, her fists constricting into quivering knots. She advanced on Wilhem. One moment he crouched over the microscope like a bird, oblivious, the next he spun with fluid grace and caught her hand before it could fall. When she tried to slap with her left hand he grabbed her wrist.

"What is wrong with you?" he asked.

"How dare you ignore me!" she screamed.

Reynard pulled his arms inward, twisted. The Beast forced itself into his arms, his legs. He commanded it to stay back as he felt the pressure in his body, felt as if he moved that pressure into his wrists and ankles. He strained until metal clasps began to squeal.

Now.

He lurched against the straps with all his strength. The buckles snapped. He pulled the straps off his ankles and rolled off the gurney. Wilhem released Kiria and slid from his chair. Reynard raced to the fireplace. He took the only weapon he could find—the iron poker. Wilhem slipped a hand under his coat and removed a black derringer—a four-barrel Sharps—and thumbed back the hammer.

Reynard yanked the door open. Wilhem fired.

The bullet splintered in the door's frame above Reynard's head. He ran into a receiving hall, past an obscene fountain toward a massive staircase. They were on the ground floor. He considered the front door, heard the collective voices of the Eng Banka outside, and aimed for the staircase. No exit there.

He ascended the staircase, three steps at a time. Wilhem burst from the laboratory door, took aim, and fired again. The bullet cracked above Reynard's left ear.

He continued to the second floor and raced down the east corridor. *They knew*, he thought, *knew I would come, they brought her here to lure me to this accursed house, to take my blood.* Both Kiria and Lucinda had played upon his emotions, his guilt, knew just how to manipulate him. They had played him in New Orleans, in Marseille, the stinging grief of his weakness filling him with rage.

It was still very dark, but he caught the faint glow creeping underneath the door of Lasha's room. He ignored the whispering, the fell traces of those collected spirits; his obsession overwhelmed any fear. He reached the door, found it locked.

"Lasha," he said. "Can you hear me?"

"You see what the unbridled animal makes us?" Wilhem shouted in the distance. "God has abandoned us. You, of all people, should see!"

Reynard leaned his shoulder into the door. It did not budge. He threw his weight against it and the door held. He slammed a third time and the door cracked inward, the jamb splitting open. He rushed inside. The curtains were parted to reveal the rain-splattered night, the candle on the nightstand nearly spent. He focused on the bed, confused at the disorganized covers and the heap of pillows. He would take his sister and fight his way downstairs, slip back into the underground, and he would kill anyone who tried to—

"Lasha?"

Reynard lifted the netting aside. He froze.

Wilhem entered the room. He started to speak, the pistol in hand, but his words caught short as he too approached the bed. In the candlelight he was a ghost, empty, life bleached from his pallid skin. His daughter said he was dying and, from his wretched look, he had been dead a long time. Both men stood dazed at the sight of the limp body stretched across the bed.

Kiria's head lay upon the pillow. Beside it, Lucinda's body lay like a discarded dress, shrunken and empty. Tissue and bones and flesh were all nearly dissolved, shapeless beneath the red silk faille, the sheets redolent with vinegar and sour blood.

Reynard's reeling mind registered the truth of it—it was not Kiria slapping him in that laboratory, not her, not her. The thing that now wore her face was the same that drank little girls' blood, she who killed Bill and Frederick and tore out his heart, she who slaughtered men with her bare hands, she who commanded wild men to burn monks alive.

"Damn you," Reynard whispered.

"My daughter," Wilhem said.

"*Damn you to hell!*"

Reynard raised the iron poker and charged—

Wilhem lifted his pistol—fired—

The bullet sunk into Reynard's belly. The poker fell and Wilhem kicked it away.

Kiria is dead.

Reynard fell to his face.

I am dead.

"This ends tonight," Wilhem said.

He clutched Reynard by the collar and dragged him out of the room. He pulled him down the hall and down every step of the staircase with a trail of wet crimson in his wake. Reynard could do nothing but suffer as he slid, limp, helpless. When his hands felt his stomach, warm fluid sluiced through his fingers.

At the bottom step Kiria—her shell, possessed by the penanggal that was Lucinda—stood waiting for them. She considered Reynard at the end of Wilhem's arm with a nonchalant expression.

"Whatever happened?"

Wilhem struck her across the face. "You filthy whore!"

"I did it for you!" she shrieked.

Wilhem struck her again and she dropped to her knees, cowering, screaming with wet sobs. He was not moved; he dragged Reynard through the front door and outside onto the lawn. Over a hundred Eng Banka chanted around bonfires strewn along the hill, many in groups, most wearing their snarling masks. Some had collapsed into a trance, twitching, while others opened their arms and begged the spirits of the house. Crude drums kept a rhythm. The natives focused their rites around the many belawang poles, makeshift idols smeared with raw flesh or eggs or blood.

Sacrifice.

Lasha is mine.

This ends tonight.

Sacrifice.

Something terrible to going to—

Wilhem dropped him in their midst. The chanting and drumming ceased. He spoke with a loud voice in a strange language, and though Reynard did not understand the words he understood the passion in it.

"*Maligang requires your voices,*" Wilhem cried, "*to cast off the River of Death. The evil spirit will leave tonight. We will complete the deed. The spirits of this house will be yours, thousands upon thousands into your nostrils.*"

Voices erupted in a triumphant shout.

"*You will drive the strangers from your rivers and mountains and cast them back upon the ocean. Your heads will know no equal. Your longhouses will be free from fear. You will rise before toh bulu and live forever at baway daha. Forever!*"

More shouting. Arms raised with spears and knives gripped beneath passionate fingers. They were a host of wolves, howling, a collective bestial cry.

"*This one is toh joat sujan,*" he said. "*He wants to hurt Maligang. He will tear your children from their mothers' breasts. He will drink their blood.*" He addressed the closest group of natives. "*Cut off his head and burn him with fire. Cast his bones upon the field for Maligang to see. She will know you love her. She rewards those whom she loves.*" With a loud voice he raised his arms, again addressing the crowd. "*Daa'tu Maligang!*" he shouted, and all joined him in unison, poised toward the house in common covenant. "*Daa'tu Maligang! Daa'tu Maligang!*"

Wilhem left them shouting, ascended the porch and back into the house. He closed the door and locked it with many latches, sealing it with a heavy iron bar. Voices followed him in a thunderous wake:

"*Daa'tu Maligang!*"

36

The rain stirred Reynard from encroaching blindness, scratching at his neck and hands and head, draining under his clothes. He inhaled and coughed up bile, and when he touched at his stomach his shirt was slippery with his own blood.

I've been shot.

His fingers edged against the wound, a hole the width of his thumb. His innards shrank into a painful fist and he groaned, sick, terrified to vomit for fear it would be blood. The pain clarified his senses, and his senses clarified his pain, and when he moved his stomach felt pierced with a knife. The pressure popped with a dull silence, and what seemed like the pounding of his heart became drums and voices. The Eng Banka had resumed their ceremony.

He rolled to his side and his gut provided fresh agony. It held the pain selfishly, refusing to let it reach his feet, arching into his ribs and lower back.

I've been gut-shot.

Hands clutched his arms and legs and lifted him. Pain threatened to sink him back into oblivion. Kiria spoke highly of Dayaks in general, finding them a resourceful people, but those misguided men under Lucinda's thrall were drunken with their own chanting, imbibed with blood-lust, hurtling the night along toward some dreadful end.

Kiria.

Faces leered down at him as they carried him into the frenzied crowd, bare-faced and snarling mask alike, their skin catching the firelight like gibbering demons. They dropped him beside the largest bonfire. He did not resist. The natives formed a wide circle. He opened his eyes to the rain and saw Carlovec Manor as it towered above them, its windows illuminated by another burst of lightening. It was impenetrable, a fortress. It had crushed him like an insect. He hated that house nearly as much as he hated himself.

Lasha.

In that second, he wished the Beast would come.

Boys have all sorts of inklings; doesn't mean we should follow them all.

Metamorphosis accelerates a man's metabolism...

Makes a man a raving animal...

You have been changed.

Everything was so clear now—no amount of alcohol or lust or anger or self-mutilation could dispel his lycanthropy, all because he had subconsciously encouraged the Beast with every indulgence, every raised fist to a silent god. True, both the existence and the removal of the silver bullet had altered his body forever, but there was more. He felt the change since Metairie, like grasping in the dark and knowing the Beast came because he had given it silent permission.

If it is of you, of that which makes you Reynard...

The Beast waited, as it had always waited. He imagined extending his arms with a silver bridle in his hands. He opened his arms wide to embrace it, tether its raving jaws with the bridle, hold it, fight against it, feel its strength bleed into his head. His skin flushed and his eyes dilated, He felt his muscles shift beneath his skin, that familiar edge of dying.

This is wrong!

—Raving animal—

I cannot do this!

—Who is the master?—

He had promised Lasha. Given his promise. She was all that mattered now, all that he cared to live for—to keep her safe. The Beast snapped and thrashed against that bridle in his thinking-hands and pushed it aside. He screamed at the awful, familiar pain that broke his body apart. Slippery agony stabbed at his knees and hips as joints slid from their sockets.

—That which makes you Reynard—

His claw-like nails brushed at his shirt and ripped it open. The natives surrounding him twitched collectively, backed off, and fell silent. He dipped into the wounds, plucked the lead slug from his stomach and dropped it like a pebble into the grass. He screamed again, more a howl than a voice. Blood pumped free, clotted, stopped. His body tensed and slackened until the spasm drew him forward into a grotesque fetal position.

The Eng Banka widened the circle even further, their faces wide-eyed with fear. From their midst came a tall, barrel-chested chieftain draped in necklaces of rattan and bone. He wore his wolf-like mask, its muzzle snarling with swirls of paint. Black tattoos ran from feet to belly and up his neck, and at his bare chest the markings shaped the hornbill, a bird of power. He gripped a naked mandau in his hand, the iron blade as long as his arm.

Reynard's muscles bunched and slid aside, his skin bathed in sweat.

—*Raving animal*—

Lasha!

—*Doesn't mean we should follow them all*—

He had not asked to inherit Basta's Legacy, but he had allowed it to become the doppelganger of his pride, his rage, his self-hatred. He had shifted accountability to everything and everyone but himself. When he realized this, really *knew*, the bones in his face cracked as the Beast shoved itself from beneath his skin.

Lasha.

Reynard leapt at the chieftain, snarling, his claws at the man's throat. The chieftain's mask tumbled free, revealing a face distorted by terror. He shouted a hoarse cry. Reynard bit down into his shoulder until a bone cracked between his teeth. He released his grip bit again, fast, jerking him hard. The salty flow of flavor ran over his tongue and down his throat and the thirst, the endless thirst—

—*Raving animal...*

—*What?*

The chieftain gurgled and spat blood.

—*What am I...*

...*Doing?*

Reynard thought of the most ordinary of things, a shipping manifest on his desk back in New Orleans: Thirty thousand seven hundred dollars of cotton from Macon, Georgia to West Virginia; his bedroom; how many steps between his door and the kitchen—sixty seven; what hour the post dropped by the office—ten o'clock and always late; the bitter taste of coffee before sugar; Lasha and Eleanor weeding in the garden with their knees brown with dirt; Gordon grooming the horses with his brush in fine, even strokes, smelling of oats and milk.

He dropped the chieftain from his mouth.

—*Doesn't mean we should follow them all*—

He snapped his maw above the chieftain's face, splashing saliva, and left the man writhing in his own urine. Movement surged around him. Eng Banka converged in a swirling wave, dozens strong, plunging at him with spears and blades and knives. Reynard stood on his hind legs, swiping at the spears with his paws, snapping with his jagged teeth, clutching one spear with his jaw and snapping it in half.

He broke through their line, dropped to all fours, and leapt up the driveway. Spears flew from all directions and thudded into the mud from both sides. From his back came a *whish whish* and two feathered darts thudded into his throat. He scraped them out and ran into another cluster of men, tearing them aside. One sinewy native confronted him outright, a spear fast in his hands.

Reynard did not slow. He leapt upon him, gripped the man's face in his claw and flung him to the ground like a doll. His nails sliced through his throat like butter.

—*What?*

The man twitched, blood seething in steady pumps upon the grass. Reynard's senses retreated from rain and voices and focused on the bellows of his breathing. He fought not to lick the blood from his fingers.

—*have I done?*

Lobis-homems queimadura no inferno.

He groaned the sound of the damned. His voice was both man and beast, howling above the rain. When Reynard convinced himself to move again, the Eng Banka did not follow. They kept their distance, crying oaths, while others fell to their knees and renewed their chanting in fell tongues. The dead man drained upon the driveway and they ignored him, adding wood to their fires, focusing their voices again upon the house.

Lasha.

Reynard ran, leaped onto the porch, hurled himself against the manor's front door. It held. He slashed with his claws, tearing gouges of wood. The door did not open. His panic became a fury as he raced along the edge of the house to the first window he could find. With a coiled leap he hurled himself up and crashed through in a shower of glass.

A metallic click echoed off to his left. He was on his feet, swiping out, and his paw connected with the cold shaft of a rifle's muzzle as it discharged in a flash of gunpowder and acrid smoke. He rubbed at his eyes, the spots swirling, but he smelled sweat, heard the ragged breathing. Reynard dropped to all fours and started for him.

—*Kill you—*

Another man darted between them.

"Reynard!"

He stopped.

"To me. Look to me!"

Reynard's attention focused on a bearded man, an old man, someone who held no gun. Reynard's rage melted into fear. He crawled up from the dark, inch by painful inch, hoping the man would leave, would get out of the way.

Move, Arté.

"Renny."

Move before I tear out your throat.

Grant edged to retrieve the rifle the creature slapped to the floor, a Remington pump-action stolen from above the mantle of the drawing room. He popped open the chamber, removed the smoldering cartridge, and slid in another. The creature regarded him, took a wet breath, and turned its focus back to Savoy. When it snapped its teeth, drops of blood flecked from its muzzle.

"Reynard," Savoy said.

Savoy reached out with one hand, trembling, and Grant pumped the rifle's lever with a resolute *snap*. Savoy thrust out his other hand, motioning for Grant to halt, but Grant lifted the rifle to his shoulder.

"Reynard," Savoy said.

"Move aside," Grant hissed.

"Put that rifle down," Savoy answered back, firm.

Grant's finger slid onto the trigger.

The creature lifted its claws, to the gore drying upon its fingers. It took a step back, coughed, as it considered the room and the two men, the paintings and statues and rugs, the shards of broken glass scattered across the carpet. Its claws brushed against its muzzle and hair began to fall from its face and arms; first like dandelion seeds, then in great clumps. The creature tore at the hair and pulled it away, slashing and cutting at its own scalp, peeling dead skin from its flesh. It collapsed to the floor as muscles shrank and lost their bulk. Its jaw slid into place with a wet pop, pelvis and shoulder blades cracked as they shifted, tendons stretched like ropes relaxed under strained flesh. Muscles slid into alignment. When his body stopped shivering, a sheath of dead skin encased him like a translucent cocoon, a newborn gasping his first breath of air.

Reynard touched at his own face and mouth with quivering fingers, his eyes adjusting, clearing. He saw Savoy standing over him.

"*Stay away from me!*" he cried.

"Reynard—"

"*I will kill you!*"

Reynard backed up in a panic, knocking over a pedestal and vase, retreating until he pressed himself against the wall. He was naked, filthy with dirt and blood. He clutched his head, his nails scratching at his face. He wanted to cut himself until he could deflate, vaporize into nothing. He did not care the wounds in his chest and stomach were knit closed, consumed by his grief.

"I am damned," he said.

Savoy took his hand. "Does the Beast claim you?"

"I...I don't..."

"Does it claim you?"

"They'll have heard my gunshot," Grant said.

"Another man is dead!" Reynard wailed.

"Does it claim you?"

"Are you listening to me? I *killed* him!"

"Those poor souls are as much under a thrall as you," Savoy said, his voice calm. "You cannot expect to conquer the animal in a day. Look at yourself! You were beast and now you are man. I ask again: Does it claim you?"

"I would have killed you both."

"You did not."

"I would have."

"Yet you did not."

Grant lowered his rifle. Removing his longcoat, regained from the kitchen, he tossed it to Reynard. He helped him to his feet and into the coat. Reynard started to speak, his mouth forming a word, but Grant clasped his shoulder and gave him a reassuring nod.

Nothing more needed to be said.

Savoy, however, showed no restraint. He swept Reynard into his arms and held him tight. A month ago, a week ago, Reynard might have resisted, but now he allowed Savoy to embrace him. Savoy knew his sins, the blood on his hands, and still he held him as tight as any father who regained his prodigal child.

"My sister is alive," Reynard said as they separated. "They mean to sacrifice her, I think. Kiria is dead. That woman...she killed her. I think she is her mother. That witch is wearing her daughter's body."

"Dear God," Savoy said. "So it has come to this." He walked to the broken window. Outside, the natives' voices fought to overwhelm the storm. "We found Wilhem's laboratory, found his notes. He has his solution."

"A cure?"

"He has created some kind of serum."

"Where is he?"

"I do not know." Savoy saw the anxious look in Reynard's eyes. "Whatever he has created, he is satisfied his search has come to an end. With her husband's lycanthropy no longer a threat, Lucinda can now end her own curse. She has summoned every Eng Banka under her command. Poor devils. If Lasha is indeed her sacrifice—"

"I know where they'd take her," Grant said. "Beneath the house—"

"I know it," Reynard said.

"There we make our stand," Savoy said. "Lucinda obeys the Father of Lies—we must not be fooled by her voice. Not again." He turned to face Grant. "She promises bread, Mister Grant, when there is only a stone. 'Man shall not live by bread alone, but by every word that proceedeth out of the mouth of God.'"

"I don't know if I—" Grant whispered.

"You can. We *must*." Savoy took two shards of slender wood from the broken window frame, wrapped them together with cord from the shredded curtains, and lifted up the makeshift cross. "We each have our tokens," he said. "This is mine."

He dipped his hand into his pocket to reveal something discovered in Wilhem's abandoned laboratory—the scant remains of the silver bullet, a thin slash of bright metal. He gave it to Reynard. "Faith against faith."

"I believe in nothing," Reynard said.

"You believe in Lasha."

37

Every sconce in the grotto beneath the house blazed with fire. Large, misshapen shadows danced against the walls, some cast by those standing beside the black pool, others with no visible source. The air was alive with whispering.

Lasha lay on her back, clad in a white dress, upon the floor beside the black pool. The servants Jeané and Claudette stood on either side, each beside a column of stone, silent. Lucinda knelt before a bowl smoldering with sour herbs, a long-handled mandau set before her knees. She too was clad in white—her old wedding gown, perhaps—her skin translucent against the firelight. Long, black hair hung in untidy strips over her colorless face—

—Kiria's face.

"*Doh Tenangan!*" she cried. "*Usun lasan urip ulun kam kelunan nini ketai natong tawang.*" Her voice grew loud. "*Doh Tenangan!*"

This she did four times, lifted the sword above her head, and the pungent smoke redoubled from the bowl. Lowering the sword she began to sing, the words akin to those natives upon the front lawn that both demanded and begged unseen forces. Light dimmed, flickered, and shadows fled their places to coalesce between the standing stones.

"Stop!"

From the upper tier stood Reynard—barefoot and wearing Grant's overcoat, a crowbar locked in his left hand and a pistol stolen from Wilhem's mantle in his right. Savoy and Grant stood beside him, each with a rifle. They did not hide their dismay as Kiria's face glared up at them.

Lucinda looked to Jeané, then to Claudette. Jeané ascended one set of stairs while Claudette took the other; Savoy and Grant each slid back the chambers of their rifles and confirmed—for the third time—they were loaded.

"Mistress demands that you leave," Jeané said.

"None of your business," Claudette added.

"Please join me in the conservatory." Jeané motioned toward the exit. "I am happy to provide tea or coffee or whatever else you might—"

"Move aside," Grant said.

"There is no reason to be rude."

Grant raised his rifle. Jeané transformed into a horror, all wide mouth and flashing teeth and eyes as if some fell creature writhed beneath his skin. Claudette too became hideous, her face corpse-like as the Lady of Chalmette, both creatures lesser than their mistress yet still burning flashes of gravelight. They lunged at the men with unearthly snarls. Jeané took Grant with an iron grip and tossed him to the floor. Claudette advanced on Reynard. He raised his pistol. She gripped his hand with long fingers and forced his arm down. The pistol fired with a *crack*. She grabbed his shoulder and gnashed at his throat, her mouth filled with sharp teeth.

"*Res sacræ, ritus, communio,*" Savoy cried. He lifted his cross, sweeping it forward. "In the name of God the All-powerful, Father, Son, and Holy Ghost!"

Savoy pressed the cross against Claudette's neck. She shrieked, rolled off Reynard and scuttled away like a wounded spider. When Jeané lunged, Savoy thrust the cross at him, pressing it against his face until the butler's expression became a Grecian mask of tragedy. The main shrieked an unearthly sound.

"Depart!" Savoy shouted. "In the name of—!"

"Not His name," Jeané cried.

"—Christ Almighty, who casts thee down!"

"*Not his name!*"

The servants fled, wailing, up the steps toward the greenhouse. Savoy helped Reynard to his feet and the three men started down toward the pool, the corpses on their slabs on either side gaining form and feature with every descending tier. Lucinda stopped her singing. Kiria's body and semblance of face hung off her like a badly-stitched costume, awkward, but the voice was all too familiar:

"*Stay away.*"

All three stopped. Her voice crowded their thoughts, plucked at their fears, their needs, those deep places. They fought to remember why they were there, who they were.

"*Mahonri,*" she said.

Grant imagined how the drunken monster slapped Emily down, ignored her screaming, forced his body upon her while his stinking breath smothered her face. He had imagined it a thousand times until his rage, the absolute rage, tightened his heart until he thought he might die. His hands squeezed on the rifle.

He looked at Reynard. A monster—he *was* a monster, a vicious, drunken, bestial monster. Did he not know she was with child? Did he not know she had made a promise to give herself only to her husband, only to him?

"*Do not let them hurt me.*"

Grant swung around and pressed the barrel of his rifle against Reynard's head. A bullet in the brain would not be enough to atone for such a miserable...

"*Please.*"

Who am I, Grant thought. *I should've seen justice done. But I shot him and watched him bleed.* He lowered the rifle.

"*You are supposed to protect me.*"

Grant lifted the rifle and took aim at Lucinda's—at Kiria's—heart. "I can't listen to you anymore," he said. "I'm sorry. I don't want to shoot you, but Lasha's coming with us. I figure we can work something out."

Lucinda frowned and rose to her feet. She opened the lid of the fourth basket and dipped the mandau's blade as far as it would go. Removing it, the blade dripping, she flecked blood and gore across the surface of the black pool. With another dip into the basket—filled with the slippery coils of human viscera—she flecked another curtain of blood over the water.

"*Manu bada, doh Tenangan,*" she said. "*Manu ba!*"

An invisible reek vomited from the water like mist, boiling up every tier until it filled the grotto. Reynard felt it sink into his flesh. He knew this feeling. He feared what would happen before—

"Grant!" he cried.

Two dead bodies shifted from their niches. One caught Grant's leg and pulled hard; he fell and his rifle discharged with an echoing boom. He clobbered the corpse with his boot, a slack-faced native with his throat open to the collarbone. The second clutched his other leg and pulled itself closer, fingers digging. With the butt of the rifle Grant cracked the corpse's head back with an audible *snap* and the thing loosened its grip.

Every corpse in the crypt began to move.

They rose from their slabs in all stages of decomposition, voiceless. Some rose with dry flesh and muscle, draped with rotting cloth, others mere bone and chalky dust, while others were fresher and stank and dripped fluids as they stood upon their ruined feet like ghastly mannequins. Their attention coalesced on the three men upon the steps.

"Lasha!" Reynard cried. She did not move. "Lasha!"

"In the name of God the all-powerful, Father, Son, and Holy Ghost," Savoy shouted, raising the cross. "*Ecce crucem domine, fúgite partes advérsae...!*"

Grant leaped to his feet as bodies stood from their slabs. He fired the rifle and disintegrated the closest, its spine blowing in half. The second swatted out with a bony hand at the barrel. Grant pulled the rifle free, pumped the lever, and fired again. The dead thing expelled its rotten entrails and folded in half. The next Grant struck across the face with the rifle's butt, dislocating its jaw. More corpses filled the gap with vacant eyes and reaching arms, their flesh sliding off exposed bones. Grant stepped back up the steps in a forced retreat.

"...May God cast out that evil spirit," Savoy cried as more bodies rose around him. "Impart a portion of His Spirit upon me, oh sinner that I am, that I may serve He who suffered..."

The dead kept coming.

"Depart! I declare you, Lucinda Carlovec, exorcised of the evil spirit that inhabits you! I condemn that diabolical dragon to eternal fire with—!"

Two corpses grasped Savoy's face, their fingers smothering his mouth, wrapping around his throat. He could not move, fixed upon the remains of his old friend Ernst Stronheim. His remains squeezed his throat with one hand, clutching Savoy's wrist with the other. It squeezed his wrist until Savoy's hand opened and the cross fell away and was lost. Reynard grabbed Stronheim's corpse and, with the crowbar, crushed in its skull like old pottery. Grant threw the second attacker off and fired into its ruined stomach, tearing it apart.

Dead gathered from all sides and surged toward them, pressing, reaching, slapping at their weapons, clawing at their faces.

Lucinda resumed her singing. A brackish glow materialized between the three standing-stones—faint at first, cancerous—then folded in on itself. The dark light folded again and again until it seemed the air might tear open and Hell itself would appear on the other side. Lucinda's voice grew louder. The atmosphere of the grotto, once stale and hot and heavy, began to move. Sconce fires snapped, the walls dancing with shadow. Smoke and dust rushed into the center of the stones.

One mummified skeleton knocked Savoy down and a host of dead rushed in to smother him. Grant caught him under his shoulders, lifted him to his feet and they raced for the archway leading to the boiler room; Reynard refused to leave, hacking with the crowbar, raging. Bodies piled upon him and, with a shove, he too made a stumbling retreat up the steps.

"Your tokens are worthless!" Reynard shouted.

"Do not blaspheme," Savoy snapped. "She is immune to it. I have no real artifact, no medal. She disregards my cross, and I could not get close enough to touch her. She has seen my heart, my damned foolish heart. She is *immune!*"

"How is this possible?" Grant asked.

"That black water, those stones," Savoy said. "The very weave and shape of this unholy place grants her necromancy. So many poor spirits are trapped in this house...she taps that energy to purge the penanggalen from her body—using Lasha, the host of her unclean sacrament."

Shambling dead broke through the gated doorways from burrows cached underground. Dozens upon dozens of bodies with any degree of shape and form added to the ranks, silent, relentless, drawing closer. Down below, the dark light between the stones solidified.

Savoy strained to think. *Then Simon Peter having a sword drew it …* *Then said Jesus unto Peter, Put up thy sword into the sheath: The Cup which my Father hath given me, shall I not drink it…*

Ordinary means would not serve. No rifles or fists or crowbars. They could destroy every glass coffin they found, kill the penanggalan's hosts, delay its work, but the entity itself was beyond their efforts. She had swung wide a door that needed to be shut. The unhappy spirits trapped in Carlovec Manor needed it shut.

That ye may put difference between unclean and clean.

The Cup.

Between unclean and clean.

Some doors need to be shut.

"I must get down to that pool," he said.

"That was the general idea," Reynard said.

"You must get me through!"

Reynard snatched Savoy's rifle and he and Grant advanced, confronting the first line of bodies. Their bullets spent, the men used the weapons like clubs. They hacked and pushed and plowed a slow path through the crowd, Savoy close behind. They broke through bone and desiccated flesh. For every dead body that fell aside, two or three took its place.

Lucinda's chanting grew to a fevered pitch, words from a time when ancient men toyed with deep mysteries—forbidden, unhealthy knowledge uncovered by Grandfather Carlovec in his quest to solve the unsolvable. She embraced it without restraint. Dark light swept off the stones and scattered rice and herbs at her feet. It filled into her nostrils until her lungs labored to inhale it.

She raised her face. The penanggalan strained beneath her skin. She opened her mouth to reveal rows of needle-like teeth. Hideous shades of others' faces rolled across her own: Lucinda, Kiria, Edward Tukebote, Frederick Burlington, whores and servants, policemen and ladies, rich and common, black and brown and white and more.

Take it from me, she cried in an ancient tongue. *Pluck the evil spirit into this girl. Let the spirits have it, feast upon it, suck its poison from her marrow and let it be gone forever.*

Then another voice, immensely loud, cried out:

"*Lucinda!*"

Dark light flittered away like smoke. The room rippled with a shifting of energy as the dead paused in their march, quivered, and dropped to the floor. Bones and sinews and tendon collapsed. Fresher shapes burst apart like rotten fruit. All fell like discarded puppets, the air thick with dust and noxious fumes.

Wilhem Carlovec had arrived.

He was gray and thin and haggard, his clothes rags upon his bones. His ashen skin hung like old paper, the veins in his neck dark and swollen. His eyes were large and moist, wild, and by his look it took every ounce of will to keep his sinews connected and moving. Yet he descended the steps, his eyes ever focused on Kiria's face. Man and wife and daughter locked gazes.

"Give her back to me," he demanded.

"What does it matter?" she said. "Your work is finished."

"It is."

"You have taken it?"

"I have." He touched against the flesh of his neck, the veins bulging. "But I would *stop* just where you are," he said to the three men as they descended the steps to the far side of the pool. "I may not agree with my wife's...methods...but she will complete the ritual." He glared at Lucinda. "That girl cannot be your sacrifice. She must be your shroud. Find someone else. I will not endure my daughter's face in my bed."

"You have done it," Lucinda said. "Your cure." Her voice deepened. She rose, the bloody mandau still gripped in her hand. "We are free, after all we have suffered."

He laughed. "You are a fool."

"I..."

"When did I *ever* say I wanted a cure?"

He clenched his hands. A faint tremor coursed from the muscles of his arms to his shoulders, tightening his neck. The veins of his neck and exposed chest darkened even further, like burnt silver. He closed his eyes and opened them again. Silver filled his eyes. His shoulders added bulk and width. Blood seeped from the ends of his fingers.

"What have you done?" Savoy asked.

"Dominion," Wilhem said. His muscles shifted. "You once claimed the curse was a matter of mind and body and—" He twitched, gasped. "When it was clear Monsieur LaCroix's cycle had been altered...I read everything you wrote, attended every lecture. Your friend Stronheim was more than happy to share what he knew once the right...persuasion...was applied."

"Damn you."

"A man's will can only..." More pain came, doubling him over. "...Can only do so much. It required a fundamental change of my body. When I watched Reynard on the front lawn, how he called the animal by will alone..." He seized, the tremor stiffening his back. Bloody foam spilled from his mouth. "...Magnificent."

"I was an animal," Reynard said.

"You were a god."

Wilhem fell to his knees. Bone cracked like iron knuckles snapping. His shoulders slid back and forced his head forward. He groaned, smiling too many teeth. Sharp, grey hair erupted from the back of his neck and hands as the stitching of his sleeves begin to fail. He smiled as if the pain brought him indescribable pleasure.

Lucinda watched, horrified. "You promised."

"You sold your soul to Satan," he said, "because you hate me. I never shared my true purpose, because I hate you." He doubled over, his jaw sliding from its socket. "We are both...monsters."

Lucinda raised her hands to her eyes, to the sky. She screamed as her husband transformed before her, her sound filling the grotto with the magnitude of her despair. The smooth surface of the black pool rippled. Older corpses, barely hanging together by fibrous threads, fell apart with gasps.

"I did this for you!" she shrieked.

Wilhem stood at his full height. The Beast inside him fought to shift every muscle, stretch every tendon to bursting. When he lifted his head he was no longer a man or an animal, but a madman's conception of a wolf. Lucinda watched her husband transform with horror.

Wilhem lurched at her, his claws extended. She swung the mandau—

—and Wilhem's head slid off his shoulders. His body dropped as his transformation halted, reversed, the beast dissolving from his skin.

The sword clattered to the floor. Lucinda gaped at her quivering hands, shuddering. She fell to her knees weeping, hysterical, clutching at her husband's body as his dark blood pumped across her gown. She cradled his corpse and plunged her teeth into the crook of his neck between shoulder and throat. With a spasm she heaved like a snake— once, twice, gurgling. His bleeding slowed and, in moments, ceased altogether.

"Take her," Savoy said. Grant ran to the side of the pool. He touched Lasha's neck and nodded. She was alive. He scooped her unconscious body into his arms. "You remember the explosives?" Savoy asked.

"Yes."

"Bring this cursed house down."

"You must be joking."

Savoy smiled. "You should know me better by now."

"What about you?"

"This place must be made clean."

Lucinda lifted her bloody mouth from Wilhem's neck and her head bobbed, loosening from her shoulders. The color in Kiria's dark hair bleached into white. The skin of her colorless head tightened against her skull, deepening the contours of teeth and jawline and eyesocket.

"We have no time," Savoy said. "She will consume her husband as she consumed her daughter. I daresay she cannot help herself." He knelt by the black pool. "I must purify this unholy place. Stronheim knew it was the only way. He knew I could do it."

"Mister LaCroix?" Grant asked.

Reynard imagined Lasha seven years old again, filled with the love of those ordinary moments of arguing and laughter and daily habits. He wanted to hear her laugh, yell, complain. He wanted to sip a warm sherry on the veranda while sunset blazed off the lake, to taste Eleanor's cooking, to smell the trees. He wanted so many things, so many things long gone.

Yet Lasha was alive. Alive. That was enough.

"Take care of her," he said to Grant.

Grant raced up the steps, Lasha cradled in his arms.

38

Lucinda heaved with a sound like drowning.

On the far side of the pool, Savoy motioned the cross with his right hand over the water. "I bless this water in the Name of Our Lord," he started, "Thy only Begotten Son—"

The flesh at Lucinda's neck split like old rags and her head slid from Kiria's shoulders. It lifted into the air, sliding from her neck its dripping, worm-like spine. It was not Lucinda or Kiria or any of the innumerable hosts she had taken—only the penanggalan. The creature rose higher into the air and flew, snaking around the standing stones, all shrieking head and scorpion spine. Its jaw snapped with a clack of sharp teeth.

It dove sharply as if to gnash at Savoy's impudence. He raised up the cross, confident, and the thing hissed and slid away. It coiled around the standing stones, circling once, and dropped toward Wilhem's body. Like a tentacle the spine slid into the stump of his neck with a gurgle of brackish liquid.

"We invoke upon this water," Savoy said, "the Name of Him Who suffered, Who was crucified, Who arose from the dead, Who sits at the right hand..."

The head upon Wilhem's shoulders knit flesh to flesh and tendons merged, nerves connected and muscles drew taut. The skin on Lucinda's face flushed from white to crimson with the onset of flowing blood. With a wide gasp she breathed again, choking and spitting as if tasting air after a deep swim, but soon her breathing calmed and grew strong. As she struggled to regain his feet her long hair, now iron gray, hung over

Wilhem's face as the body's hidden knowledge mimicked his contours. It was the black eyes that revealed the abomination: Man and woman, alive and dead.

"May all fevers," Savoy said, touching the water with his finger, "every evil spirit, and all maladies..." The water began to shift. Bare, chalk-white faces stared up from just beneath the surface. Reynard, standing behind him, could not help but look. "...Every evil spirit, all maladies be put to flight—"

"I warned you," Lucinda said with Wilhem's voice.

"...By him who is anointed with it..."

"Why do none of you listen?"

"...May that which is impure, be made whole..."

"Why must you hurt me?"

"...May that which is unclean, be made clean...."

"*Stop!*"

Lucinda started toward them, reaching down to take the mandau in his hand—then she gasped. She gazed at her husband's body, at his arms and stomach and legs, her expression filled with a new terror. The mandau fell to the floor. Reynard caught the familiar whiff of scent as the body began its inexorable movement to madness.

"Oh, my husband!" she cried.

A spasm sent her to his knees. Hair burst in beads of scarlet across Wilhem's cursed body, black and grey like coal-dust as limbs and joints shifted under his skin. When the spine shifted, Lucinda groaned and fell to her face. His shoulders and pelvis slid back and added height, muscles bunched and drew taut. The ragged remains of clothing tore apart like rotten cloth. When she lifted her head she was smiling, astonished at its magnitude, as if she knew not how to stop. It did not seem she wanted to.

"Arté," Reynard cried. "You must hurry!"

₧₧

Climbing the long stair was hard enough. Carrying Lasha's limp body was the kicker, Grant thought, as fat beads of sweat poured down his back and neck. So it was to his relief when she stirred. She opened her eyes, coughed. She squealed and hammered her fists into his chest until he set her upon her feet. She would have profaned his mother and the Lord Himself until she realized—

"Mister Grant," she said.

"That's right."

She hugged him around the neck. "Where is my brother?" she asked. "Is he hurt?"

"As well as can be expected."

"What does that mean?" He continued up the steps and she followed, passing through the hidden door into the hot, oily air of the boiler room. "What does that mean?"

They passed the fat boilers with its many rivets bleeding rust, the air resonating with pressure and hissing steam. They continued to the supply room with its heaps of barrels and crates of supplies. Grant removed as much dynamite as he could find, screwed on blasting caps, tied old fusing together, bundled the sticks into clusters and wired them into a single fuse. He worked without speaking, fluidly, until he noticed Lasha watching him with a strange expression.

"Santa Fe Railroad," he said.

"What exactly do you intend to do?' she asked.

He did not answer. It was familiar, if dangerous work, having been hired to blast tunnels during his time in the southwest and the Cascade Mountains. This was much different. There was no plunger, which meant he would have to trust old fusing, and that meant no real way of knowing how long it would take the charge to do its work. If it worked at all.

Packing five crates with gun cotton, he stuffed them with the clusters of explosives, trailing fusing behind each crate. He considered the boiler room's angle and shape, its foundations and retaining walls, the water that flowed beneath the house. It would have to do.

"Where is Reynard?" Lasha asked.

"Downstairs."

He placed all five crates against the boilers, the generator—anywhere he guessed would serve. The wall to the right was load bearing, and the main boiler carried enough—

"We must go get him," she said.

"Grab provisions," he said as he returned to the supply room, uncoiling rolls of fusing behind him. He tied the five fuses together and started another spool of fusing. He found a leather bag, emptied its contents of screws and wire and shoved it into Lasha's hands. "Dried fruit on that shelf. There. Matches...there...a bag of...grab that also."

"I have no shoes," she said. He tossed her a pair of old boots. She caught them with disgust. "We *must* get my brother."

He rubbed the gunpowder between his fingers. Moist. They clearly knew how to store such things, but did the moisture sap the spark from every stick and coil? Perhaps they were duds? Perhaps Mister LaCroix and Savoy were dead, and this was all that stood between them and that unholy place beneath their feet. He trailed fusing out the supply room door, through the chamber of glass coffins, and started up the steps. She followed with her white dress, a full leather bag and old boots on her feet.

"What are we doing?" she asked.

When one spool of fusing ran out he tied it to the next and continued up to the ground floor.

"Mister Grant, I am speaking to you!"

"I suggest you keep your voice down," he said.

He worked quickly, quietly, down the corridor until he reached the mahogany foyer and its absurd fountain. It was still dark. Outside, the Eng Banka continued their chanting. A steady rain slapped at the windows but, from a faint clarity creeping from the drawing room, the night began to soften. Grant tied the last of the fusing into a knot.

"Where do we go?" she asked with a heavy whisper.

"Match."

"There are a thousand headhunters on the front lawn."

"I need a match."

"What about my *brother?*"

Footsteps echoed and they froze. Jeané emerged with a lantern glowing in his hand. Claudette stood beside him. The two servants stood like wraiths, desiccated, their eyes empty. Jeané's slack mouth quivered as he looked at Lasha. The lamplight deepened the shadows until the servants seemed but skin and bones. A faint impression marked each of their faces, vague lines where Savoy's cross had touched their skin.

"What are you doing?" Jeané asked.

"A match," Grant whispered to Lasha.

"I thought you had them," Lasha whispered back.

"I asked *you* to get them."

"You said a lot of things."

"Mistress was lonely," Claudette said. "We kept her company. She wanted it that way, but it was not like she promised." She looked at the fuse trailing into the corridor. "We are damned. This old place is damned." A terrible need filled their faces, tightened the skin around their eyes and mouth.

Grant placed himself between them and Lasha, wishing he could do more than stand there and die. Jeané raised the lantern high and smashed it to the floor; fire caught the fuse and gunpowder burst into life, hissing and smoking toward the basement, racing down the hallway with splashing sparks.

"Go wherever it suits you," he said.

Claudette smiled sharp teeth. "We go to hell."

∞CR

The Thing that was both Wilhem and Lucinda Carlovec stood a head larger than Reynard, inflated with heaped muscle, bristling with fang and claw. It dropped to all fours, licking at the flecks of fluid on its hair. It sniffed deep like a bellows and coughed.

"May this be done..." Savoy toned.

The Thing barked a loud cry. Reynard ran around the pool to intercept it, protect Savoy, mentally commanding the Beast to emerge. He did not want it, not in his bones, but for all he knew it might give him the strength he needed. For all he knew, he would turn and tear Savoy's throat open. So he faced the creature naked save for an oversized overcoat, his crowbar and pistol lost, nothing but his will to defend himself.

You are a liar, he thought. *There can never be a cure. You wanted the very thing I cannot accept. To embrace this openly...*

The Thing came at him.

Never again.

It meant to leap for Savoy and Reynard ran into it, throwing himself into its chest, knocking them both against a standing-stone. The Thing caught him by his shoulders and forced him down, raking with its claws. Reynard fought back with fist and knee, covering his face against its beartrap jaw. He clutched at the creature's throat and pushed its head up as it snapped, snapped again, saliva splashing.

"And may this be done," Savoy shouted, "in the name of the Father...!" He paused, watching Reynard's distress.

"Finish it!" Reynard cried.

He raised his left arm to protect his face and the Thing bit down like a vise. Fangs pierced skin and cracked against bone. Reynard did not scream. He clenched his teeth and stared into those dead, black eyes, swallowing his pain, defying it with his silence. His right hand thrust into the pocket of the overcoat.

"...and of the Son..."

He removed his hand. Firelight gleamed off cloudy silver in his palm.

"...and of the Holy Ghost..."

Reynard shoved his right hand into the Thing's mouth.

You wanted it!

His fist slid past the Beast's tongue, his fingers released, and the remains of the silver bullet rolled down its throat.

It's yours now!

෨∞ඏ

Dawn approached, the clouds spent. The valley at the river crossroads was saturated with mud, the once green lawn of Carlovec Manor little more than brown fluid. The Eng Banka danced their dances and cried out their voices, hour after hour after hour, assured their efforts would lead to all of Maligang's promises.

She had been good to them, had she not?

She and *papa sujan* gathered them from many longhouses, discarded the weak, expanded their strength until village after village, white face and yellow face and black face were all driven away. They had reached the trail of the iron snake but vowed to keep moving, taking their enemies' heads. So she required blood from some of their women, some of their men, but she was Maligang, She of Countless Heads. What did it matter? They breathed in souls with every victory. They would consume the endless spirits in the Great Longhouse and live forever.

The front door opened. A white man and woman emerged, hand in hand, and sprinted down the driveway. The natives watched, dumbfounded, as the two continued straight down the center of their gathering as fast as they could, aiming for the front gate at the bottom of the hill. Men grabbed spears and slid blades from their belts, shouting a collective cry for fresh blood.

Then the house erupted.

Every window on the bottom floor burst open. Brick and wood and stone gave way to smoke and pressure, and flames leapt up as the boilers each popped *boom, boom, boom, thump*. The glass eyes of the greenhouse darkened and burst and a cough of glass scattered across the back lawn. The kitchens and conservatory and drawing room and Wilhem's laboratory—all his secrets—fell inward. The ceiling in the main hall gave way and an errant beam, tossed by the blast, beheaded poor Juventas from her perch upon the fountain.

Another massive *thump*, the generator, and the house exploded with a geyser of water and fire and smoke. The east wing sagged, leaned forward, and collapsed. Another blast and the remains of the house burst in half. Smoke rolled over the lawn like a living thing, growing upon itself. Fold after fold of dust and debris buried the natives with darkness. Where fire did not eat at the remains, the river behind the house flooded into its foundations and started down the grassy hill.

Those Eng Banka still on their feet scattered, the cloud of Carlovec Manor's death rolling at their backs.

හ⊙ශ

The Thing gagged.

It fell back onto its rump, scrambling, and when it retched nothing came up; it barked and scratched at its belly, thrashing, clutching at its throat. Reynard lay slashed and bleeding beside the pool, the light fading from the corners of his eyes. The head of the Thing twisted hard to the right. Flesh tore away like wet cloth. It rose off its shoulders, rising, trailing its bloody spine, and the Thing of Wilhem's transformation dissipated from his discarded body.

The floor moved. Dust and fragments of stone dropped with a massive *thump, thump* and a *pop* above their heads. Another powerful jolt set the floor to shaking and the black pool sloshed from its rim. Another roar came and the grotto vibrated, followed by a hissing, a rushing, growing louder and more violent. Stones fell from the ceiling.

Reynard's world went black.

Savoy was beside him, kneeling, pulling off his own coat, wrapping it around Reynard's arm, using his belt to tighten a tourniquet. From both entrances came water—first a stream, then a flood as water cascaded over the tiers. A strange sound like wet breathing, a fluid gasp, made Savoy look—a host of pale shapes wriggled beneath the surface of the black pool. Translucent, blubbery arms, clear as jellyfish and dripping with rotten flesh, scrabbled at the stone rim.

Savoy lifted up his makeshift cross, retrieved from the floor. He spoke loudly at the oncoming flood, his words as clear and clean as glass. They came with absolute assurance.

Water poured over the black pool. The well heaved and out came bones, countless bones, as the pool vomited up centuries of old dead. Above their heads came a cracking. Water poured from the ceiling like silver curtains. Bitter cold rushed over Reynard and he opened his eyes and realized he was underwater. All sound and pain vanished. He did not fear drowning. He felt light as the current swept him along, clean for the first time in his life. He wondered if this was Savoy's plot all along, to trick him—to baptize him.

Savoy pulled him up out of the water.

Lucinda sat upon a block of stone. She had taken Kiria's body up again, her white dress soaked with water and blood. She wrapped her arms around her chest and held herself close. When the water rose to her ankles she began to rock, whimpering, stroking her own cheek.

How did she ever fool me, Reynard wondered as Savoy led him up the steps. *She looks nothing like Kiria.*

She is dead.

"She is alive," Lucinda said, as if she heard his thoughts. "Alive. In me." The water reached her knees. She began to cry, shivering at the growing dark, and she soothed herself with a motherly voice. "*Shhh.* I am here, sweetheart. Mama's here. I will not leave you. Never leave you." She held herself tenderly. "*Stars winking,*" she began to sing, "*cast off clouds as spirits gather, rice from hand to baskets filling, rivers run and cry to sleep...*"

Savoy extended his hand. "Lucinda," he said.

She held herself tighter.

Another powerful wave rushed into the grotto and with it came great chunks of iron and wood and broken stone. Debris struck one of the standing stones and it leaned forward, cracked on its foundation, and fell into the pool. Water snuffed sconce after sconce until darkness swam in, erasing the last sight of that dreadful place.

Savoy and Reynard stumbled up the steps, tier by agonizing tier, fighting the current toward the entrance to the catacombs. At the top, Reynard snagged a bone from a nearby slab, swathed it in a scrap of burial shroud, and dipped its head into the oil of one of the remaining sconces. With a deadman's torch lighting the way, they passed through the broken gate.

Behind them followed a faint, rising sound, like a wounded bird above the roar of the water—

A girl's voice, crying in the dark.

39

From: Duncan Barnett,
Commandant, Sandakan Constublatory

To: Charles Vandelleur Creagh,
Governor, North Borneo Company

With personal grief I report the deaths of Sir Wilhem
L. Carlovec and his daughter, Miss Kiria M. Carlovec.
They perished in the destruction of their ancestral
home at the headwaters of the Jebata.

Early reports blame an explosion in the building's
boiler room. The resulting flooding dislocated the
house's foundation and led to total collapse. No
remains have been recovered.

The monastery of Saint Dismas has also been
destroyed, apparently by fire. The Archdiocese of
Sandakan has no information as to the monks'
whereabouts. It is suspected they may have moved
their missionary labors further upriver. I will
continue the investigation.

There is no evidence this is an act of insurrection,
though a local uprising seems to have voluntarily
disbanded and may have no bearing on this tragedy.
All those questioned confirm the explosion was an
accident.

Three men last associated with Miss Carlovec have
gone missing: M. LaCroix of New Orleans, Louisiana,
U.S.A.; M. Mahonri Grant, U.S.A.; M. Savoy of London.
No record within or departure from the country has
been confirmed. I have ordered their arrest for
questioning.

My long association with his family makes this a
difficult conclusion. At such a time I am reminded of
our frailty in this corner of the world.

Yours,

Duncan Barnett
C.I., C., Sandakan

40

Reynard leaned against the railing of the steamer *Nan Naong*, watching the eastern ocean as the sun dipped beneath the horizon. Moist, salty wind made him squint as Davao City and the Philippine coastline faded behind the horizon. Eastward, the Pacific Ocean stretched endless and grey.

He wished he felt happy, truly happy. He was, in the least, content—their steamer was bound for San Francisco. His wounds were dressed and healing, his sister had been returned in good health, Savoy had enough bizarre stories to write another book, Mister Grant had certainly proven his worth, and yet—

And yet.

The Eng Banka had disbanded, freed from Lucinda's influence. Carlovec Manor was a smoldering ruin. When Grant found him and Savoy shouting for help in the ruined basement of Saint Dismas' chapel, there had been happy reunions...and the wait in the belltower until a fishing ship saw the smoke and stopped to investigate. They chartered passage and bid a final farewell to that accursed valley.

The Lord saw fit to allow me one last blessing, Savoy said. *By the will of God, I purified both the source of Lucinda's evil and the rushing flood. Nothing evil will ever emerge from that place again.*

Reynard touched his chest where the silver bullet had been, wondering if it had ever been there at all. Through the thick fabric of his coat and waistcoat and shirt and undershirt and skin and muscle he sensed the emptiness like a hollow sphere caught above his heart. The void left him thinking. Had he become a new creature?

The Beast is mine, he thought. *It has to be.*

And yet.

He placed his hands at the small of his back, stiff, aching with too many recent wounds. He considered the task of restarting his business, reflecting on the grief that drove him to the ends of the earth. Perhaps it was time to change his life completely. Perhaps New Orleans no longer had any use for him.

"Renny?"

Lasha joined him beside the rail, a shawl close about her shoulders. The air was quick and warm, and gulls cried against the play of light. She smiled as if no fear had ever been her lot. She did not share much of her experience since her flight from New Orleans, and he did not press her, but he knew she had suffered. He smelled her dried tears at breakfast, saw the signs of nightmares and stolen sleep. He smelled the change in her scent when she lost her train of thought and began to remember.

What could he say?

"You are alone too much," she said. "Mister Grant is challenging Arté to a game of Texas poker, and there is real money involved. We should help him."

"Which one?"

"Arté will lose his shirt."

"He can fend for himself," he said. "You go."

"Is there something I can do?"

"You can breathe," he said, taking her by the shoulders, "and laugh, and dance, and behave yourself around our good Mister Grant. I wish I could bring more comfort." He considered the sea again, uneasy, his memories drifting to the granite vaults of Metairie Cemetery. "You shall never again see such terrible things. I promise you."

She embraced him, held him tight. She did so often since Carlovec Manor, and he did not discourage it. This time she pressed her head against his shoulder, and he was reminded when she was a baby and breathed in his ear and laughed for no other reason than she loved the sound of his voice. He wrapped his arms around her.

"I know," she whispered, "and I am not afraid."

His stomach tightened. She pulled away, brushing fluff and spray from the shoulder of his longcoat. "You will fuss over me worse than Eleanor," she said. "I will never be allowed out of doors again." She laughed and continued along the deck with a lightness—and a weariness— not expected from one so young. Perhaps she understood what she saw that terrible night in Metairie. Perhaps not. The day would come when he would tell her the truth.

But not today.

The moonless night combined sea and sky in equal measure until the path before the ship was a parade of stars. The air smelled of salt and smoke, and that brought the memory of a red cloak and black hair and lips, of a beautiful woman leaning against the rail of a ship. He thought of Kiria's soft hand on his own, the smell of her tears against his shoulder, the telling of childhood stories in the dark. He thought of a life that might have been, a fantasy really, one as insubstantial as the foam upon the water.

"Renny," Lasha's voice came. She beckoned from a doorway spilling with light. "They are serving ice cream."

"In a moment."

She smiled and left. The door closed behind her.

Reynard considered the sea. Perhaps he could dive into that endless dark and swim, deeper and deeper, leaving light and warmth and memory, just to see how deep he could go. Perhaps it could smother his heart, and make him forget.

AUTHOR'S NOTE

Though every effort has been made to remain true to the spirit of the era, timelines, locations, mythologies, languages and cultures herein, I claim creative license. Some characters are culled from actual persons in history or literature, but all specifics are fictionalized.

The indigenous peoples of Borneo and Malaysia enjoy a wide variety of dialects, and evidence of 19th-century native vocabulary, in all its diverse forms, is problematic at best. Chief sources include the Sabah State Library's *Kadazan Dusun Dictionary* (2003) and Charles Hose and William McDougall's curious *Pagan Tribes of Borneo* (1912). I also owe a great deal of thanks to Redmond O'Hanlon's evocative *Into the Heart of Borneo* (1987).

Additional thanks to the New Orleans Historical Society, the insight and encouragement of fellow writers, supportive friends and family, and to all those who helped provide a glimpse into dark places yet to be explored.

For information about the author, additional content, and a glimpse into the office of Artémius Savoy, visit www.ValourDesigns.com.

www.ingramcontent.com/pod-product-compliance
Lightning Source LLC
Chambersburg PA
CBHW030027180626
46810CB00001B/244